C000182263

The Salt Flats

Also by Rachelle Atalla:

The Pharmacist
Thirsty Animals

RACHELLE ATALLA

The Salt Flats

First published in Great Britain in 2024 by Hodder & Stoughton Limited
An Hachette UK company

1

A CIP catalogue record for this title is available from the British Library

Hardback ISBN 978 1 399 72729 7
ebook ISBN 978 1 399 72732 7

Typeset in Plantin by Manipal Technologies Limited

Printed and bound in Great Britain by Clays Ltd, Elcograf S.p.A.

Hodder & Stoughton policy is to use papers that are natural, renewable and recyclable products and made from wood grown in sustainable forests. The logging and manufacturing processes are expected to conform to the environmental regulations of the country of origin.

Hodder & Stoughton Limited
Carmelite House
50 Victoria Embankment
London EC4Y 0DZ

www.hodder.co.uk

For Fraser

'There is no truth. There is only perception.'

Gustave Flaubert

Tuesday

I

They've come to Bolivia for Martha's health, but it is Finn who is lying in the clinic's examination room. He is biting down on a rubber stopper, while a doctor forces a rod with a camera attached through a narrow hole down his neck. Finn grips the arms of the chair he's sitting in while the doctor tells him to *relax*. He's gagging, repeatedly. He can't help it – it's instinctual, his body repelling the procedure. He has such an acute awareness of what is happening to him, an invasive familiarity from the past which he cannot bear. It is taking everything he has within him not to pull on the rod like a rope and force its extraction.

The doctor looks at the image of Finn's oesophagus on display.

'Yes, you see?' the doctor says, pointing.

Finn widens his eyes in response, continues to gag.

On the screen, his oesophagus looks ulcerated, bloody and hostile.

The doctor, swiftly and without warning, pulls on the rod, bringing it up and out of Finn's mouth almost instantaneously. The relief is intense, and Finn presses forward, gulping for air, his eyes bloodshot and teary. When he swallows it is still agony but no worse than before the endoscopy.

The doctor is already washing his hands. There is something about his manner that strikes Finn as unusual, a casualness to his movements. He is tall, his tie appearing too long against his torso, his suit sharp and pristine. He runs a still-damp hand through a head of sleek dark hair and Finn, sitting feebly now, is aware of the contrast – his unkempt dirty-blond hair, his several-days-old stubble, his outdoor clothes suggesting he has just returned from a hike or a camping trip, whereas in fact he has done very little.

'You say you have been unable to swallow properly for days, is this correct?' the doctor says.

Finn nods, wincing from the pain. He is already preparing to be crushed by news that feels inevitable. Oddly, he wonders how his face will behave when he's told.

'You take medication?' the doctor asks.

'Only doxycycline now . . . for anti-malaria.'

The doctor straightens. 'You have been told to take doxycycline to prevent malaria . . . ?'

Finn nods again, wishes the doctor would stop deflecting. At thirty-nine years old, he still feels small and childlike when in the company of medical professionals.

Suddenly, the doctor begins to laugh. It's deep and chortling, rising out of his throat, just as the rod and camera had risen from within Finn. 'Who told you this?' the doctor says, his laughter finally subsiding.

Finn swallows, the jagged sensation ever present. 'The doctor from the travel clinic we attended before coming here,' he replies. 'In Scotland.'

The doctor shakes his head, a smirk still apparent on his lips. 'This will not help you with malaria,' he says.

Finn begins to fear that this man has no idea what he's doing, starts to accept that he'll have to go through the whole ordeal again with a different, more qualified doctor.

'Look, do you know what's happening to me?' Finn says, the words barely a whisper.

'You swallowed a doxycycline capsule and did not allow time for it to travel down to your stomach,' he says. 'You lie down, go to sleep maybe, and it dissolves in the wrong place. The acid, it burns and blisters the lining of your oesophagus.' The doctor pauses. 'This is why you feel the way you do.'

Finn closes his eyes for a moment, allows relief to settle in. He can visualise the incident happening – the bus journey from La Paz to Uyuni – before even setting foot on the coach they'd got scammed and were forced to pay a fee to put their own backpacks in the compartment below. The coach then travelled through the night, the toilet on board out of service, the road unpaved, making it unbearably noisy and bumpy, Finn awake for the entire duration. When, eventually, they arrived and settled into their guesthouse, he'd swallowed a capsule, brushed his teeth and immediately fallen asleep. That was two days ago.

The doctor walks to a tall metal cabinet and opens the door. Finn can see the shelves filled with different types of medicine, all bottles and boxes. The doctor begins to gather glass bottles in his hands, but as he steps back one slips from his grip and falls, almost in slow motion to the floor, smashing, shards everywhere, a white gloopy liquid spreading in all directions.

'Shit,' the doctor says, his English impeccable, never faltering.

There is a splatter of white on his leather shoes. He begins to shout in Spanish, his voice booming as he calls for someone to come and tidy up the mess he has made. He reaches for a replacement bottle and steps around the glass and liquid, returning to his desk. He places the medicine bottles down on the surface and settles into his chair, while an older woman shuffles into the room with cleaning supplies, unacknowledged by her superior. Finn wants to smile at her or nod his head in appreciation for what she's come to do – he feels responsible, having indirectly caused this inconvenience, and he needs her to know that he's sorry. But the woman isn't looking at him, too busy inspecting the mess that's been made, strategising a plan perhaps.

The doctor holds up one of the bottles in front of Finn and shakes it. 'I will write the instructions down for you. Okay?'

'Okay,' Finn repeats.

'You will be on a liquid diet for one week. Okay?'

'Yes.'

'Only liquid. And you take all this medicine until it is finished. Okay?'

Finn nods.

'After one week, your oesophagus will be healed. Then you can eat again.'

The cleaner is crouching, hunkered down in a way that looks uncomfortable, picking up shards of glass with her fingers. For some reason Finn can't stop staring at her. She's wearing flip-flops and he can see the backs of her feet, the skin of the heels cracked and sore-looking, little trenches within.

The doctor waves a finger in Finn's line of vision, needing to claim his attention once again. 'You understand? Only liquids . . . '

'I understand.'

The doctor begins to write instructions on the labels of the bottles, while the woman continues to clean behind them. Finn tilts his head and can see her wiping a cloth across the floor, her actions only seeming to spread the thick white liquid further. Finn visualises this same liquid working its way down his own throat, each swallow jagged with glass. He feels confused; doesn't think he should be here, believes it should be Martha. He can sense an irrational anger rising within him, knowing that she is sitting out in the waiting area, no doubt worrying about him, worrying about what all this means for their trip to the Salt Centre, her precious salt book balancing unopened on her knee.

He swallows again, the pain intensifying, and instinctively he is rubbing his neck, as if somehow this will soothe it from the outside in.

The doctor slides four 500ml amber bottles towards him. 'For you,' he says.

Finn bends and retrieves his backpack from under his chair, unzipping it and placing the glass bottles gently inside. When he straightens, the doctor is holding a piece of letter-headed paper, his handwriting scrawled across it, while the woman behind them is finally getting to her feet.

'The fee,' the doctor says. 'You pay in reception.'

Finn takes the piece of paper. He looks from the doctor to the women and back again. 'Thank you,' he says.

The doctor nods. 'Doxycycline . . . ' he says, letting another laugh circle his mouth.

2

In the empty waiting room of the doctor's clinic, Martha has been waiting a long time. Her book rests on her knee, unopened, a train ticket poking out from the top, behaving as a bookmark. She doesn't know where the ticket came from – never took the journey printed on it. But the book, old, its spine cracked with age and use, was gifted to her. On the cover is a picture of hands drawn together, a heap of salt balanced within, and she rubs at the image, a comfort of sorts.

Behind her, light streams in from a large window and she can hear people passing from the main street outside. The clinic sits one floor up and for some reason this feels particularly foreign, confirms to her that they are indeed in a place that does not resemble home. Is in fact not Aberdeen. The town, Uyuni, is small, built in a very basic grid formation, with a main street running through its heart. It has a quality that makes her think it's not real, that instead it has been built as a prop for a film or television programme, to be dismantled quickly in post-production, or picked up and placed elsewhere. All of it an illusion.

There is still no sign of Finn. She wishes he'd let her come into the examination room with him, focuses on the door, knows that this won't speed up the process and bring him back to her any sooner. She thinks then of the door to their room in the cheap guesthouse they're staying in. There is a strange wooden carving of a face on the outside of it, the texture unsettling, as if someone has taken a needle and pinpricked the wood thousands of times to create the image of a person. Inside, their guest room is damp and cold, with no television and intermittent wifi, so there is little for them to do while they wait to be collected for their trip. Martha spends most of her time trying to read her salt book and prepare, while Finn listens to downloaded podcasts or practises his basic Spanish – the reality that most people they've encountered don't speak English is something of a shock to her, and her ignorance is still flushing across her cheeks. In each shop or restaurant, she can't bring herself to speak, is embarrassed, words stalling, and she pulls at Finn, needing him to do her communicating for her.

All of this, of course, was before he started to experience the pain. She shifts in her seat, the book on her knee nearly falling to the floor. The wait is unbearable. It's the anticipation more than anything, of being teased, the imagined worst-case scenarios.

A strong smell of food is filtering into the room. She's had little appetite since arriving in Bolivia, the metallic smell of meat overwhelming when Finn sought out a KFC in La Paz. She's been blaming the altitude, had read this would likely happen, that her movements would slow too; even when she climbed the stairs to the clinic she was out of breath by the top. But now she is consumed by constant nausea, a peakiness that won't shift, and she knows it has nothing to do with the altitude and everything to do with anxiety.

Finally, Finn comes out of the examination room, looking shell-shocked and a little distressed. She recognises this look; has no desire to see it ever again, is annoyed at herself for not having foreseen the likelihood, of allowing her own health to become a distraction. The almost comedic timing of it all . . . She wants to laugh as she braces for the worst.

'What's wrong?' she manages.

'What's wrong?' he says, visibly in pain. 'Your man just gave me an endoscopy without any anaesthetic.' He starts to cough. 'Just rammed a tube down my throat as if it was nothing.'

He's struggling to stop the cough, the irritation catching, but Martha exhales and relaxes, getting to her feet, already able to tell by his aggrieved tone that the news won't be devastating. As she tucks her book back into her bag, she asks, 'And what did the doctor say?'

'A doxycycline capsule dissolved in my throat. I've to be on a liquid diet for a week.'

'But we're getting picked up tomorrow,' she says, trying to disguise any further anxiety in her voice.

'I'm aware,' he says, opening his bag and removing a glass bottle, opening it and swigging a mouthful of liquid, white and chalky.

She adjusts her expression back to one of concern. 'I'm sorry, are you okay?'

'I will be,' he replies.

Martha follows him to the receptionist's desk, where he hands over a piece of paper. The space is cluttered with fliers, but none is for health or medicine; instead they are all adverts for different tour operators promoting salt flat excursions across the Salar de Uyuni. Each flier is essentially a copy of the others, all promising the exact same experience. She takes one, folding it over and placing it in her back pocket. She likes to pretend for the briefest of moments that they are here only to play tourist. Wonders what it must feel like to be light of worry; to think that the world in its current state is something still worth exploring.

Suddenly she can't remember the name of the driver from the Salt Centre who is coming to pick them up, and this panics her, as if she will be left behind if she cannot recall the details.

When she looks up, she realises that Finn has paid the bill and is ready to go.

'How much was it?' she says.

'Five hundred and fifty bolivianos . . . '

'What's that in sterling?'

'Eh . . . I don't know, like £70 maybe . . . '

'Oh,' she says, nodding. 'That seems quite reasonable.'

She reaches up and kisses him on the mouth. He smells different, but again perhaps that's the altitude, or more likely the medicine he has just consumed.

He attempts a smile, doesn't particularly react to her kiss. He never does any more, which she supposes is fair.

'I'm so glad you're okay,' she says. 'But I'm sorry you can't eat anything proper.'

'The food here is shit anyway.'

Outside, they walk along the street and Martha tries to take Finn's hand, but he points to a pizza sign instead. 'This is meant to be the only decent place to eat around here,' he says. 'It gets good reviews on TripAdvisor. I read that an American guy started it with his wife. I think it's part of a hotel too.'

Martha inhales, a gentle breeze against her skin. It's a bright, moderately warm day in late November and they are 3,656 metres above sea level. She can't really grasp the scale of the number, accepts that it is high, tries to visualise the true vastness of their height, but it's still too abstract. Perception of space and distance has never been her strong suit. Even when using Google Maps at home, being instructed to turn right in one hundred, or three hundred yards, it means nothing to her.

She straightens, can see a small plane in the sky. They had flown from Amsterdam to La Paz through the night and she had been unable to settle for the flight's duration, every jump of turbulence a step closer to confirming her worst fears – that crossing a large stretch of ocean in the dark was bound to end in disaster. She had once read the black-box transcript of an Air France plane that crashed into the sea at night, caused by nothing more than human error, and is convinced that the plane wouldn't have crashed if the pilots had been flying in daylight, if they had been able to see without darkness. The guilt of flying anywhere now, as the climate collapses, her shame in needing to come here, by plane, is suffocating, and she is desperate to repent. She's already donated money to plant more trees in an attempt to offset the carbon emissions from their flights, but she knows it's not enough. She can't remember a time any more when she didn't worry, when anxiety wasn't constantly lodged into her chest.

'I think we should go to the pizza place for dinner,' Finn says, interrupting her thoughts.

'No. Not when you can't eat anything . . . I'm not that hungry anyway.'

'Who knows what they'll expect us to eat when we get to this salt place tomorrow,' he says. 'You should have the pizza,' he presses. 'If I can't, you should.'

3

It's evening, and the pizza restaurant is busy, busier than Finn would have thought possible for a place in Uyuni. They have to wait for a table, standing in the lobby of the boutique hotel it's attached to. Finn inspects the framed photographs hanging on the wall, each image taken on the salt flats, while Martha disappears off to the toilet. He turns and sees an older man and woman coming down the staircase, heading straight for the restaurant. They're laughing about something, and he can hear American accents. He smirks; they have the look of Americans too. He's envious, though, at the idea of them staying at this hotel, suspects their bed is comfortable and warm, that they have a television. He doesn't know why Martha booked them into the place they're staying, thinks about the weird wooden carvings on the doors, the insects that could so easily be living inside the tiny holes. It reminds him of the masonry bees that were living in the crumbling pointing of their granite stone house. He had someone come and repoint the house and seal the property, but it haunts him that there are no doubt still bees inside, stuck forever in a tomb they can no longer escape. He worries then if it's bad luck, if there are universal repercussions for carrying out house repairs defending against nature. They were small bees, solitary, not like those you would see in a conventional hive, so maybe that counts for something. He wonders if it's been sunny in Aberdeen today, if his solar panels have been capturing much light, if the lithium battery in his outhouse is full. He has the urge to check the app on his phone but reminds himself that there is little point, that it has only buffered since arriving in Uyuni.

Martha returns and he stops thinking about bees. She looks nice – he's told her this already but again he finds it to be true. He hasn't looked at her very much recently, not properly, but now he's really trying to remember her from when they first met, eighteen years ago. He'd been studying civil engineering in Glasgow and had gone out with some friends to the student union. It had been a Friday, late afternoon, fifty-pence pints followed by fifty-pence vodkas and an ageing and inappropriate DJ. In among it all was Martha, light brown hair and green eyes, dancing on a wooden stool, wearing a dress with purple tights and an old-lady cardigan. She'd given him her most obscure philosophical chat, which at the time he'd found interesting. And now he's looking at her as though he can't understand how they came to be: his leukaemia diagnosis at twenty-one, Martha never leaving his side, his unlikely recovery, going through the motions of a life he'd thought he wouldn't get to lead.

'You're staring at me funny,' she says, smiling, relaxed. He can't remember the last time he saw her like this.

'I don't mean to.'

The table is finally ready, and they take their seats. The place is nothing fancy – lots of stereotypical American memorabilia on the walls – but it is inviting, filled with relaxed chatter, and Finn believes they're in safe hands, suspects that even the soup will be nice. They might actually be capable of having a pleasant time, and suddenly it feels as though he could cry, and he doesn't really know why. He swallows and is once again acutely aware of the blistering pain in his throat. He reaches for his backpack, opens one of the medicine bottles and takes a mouthful, before clicking the cap back into place.

'There's minestrone soup,' Martha says, 'do you think you could manage that?'

He nods.

'I'll have that too,' she says, smiling as a waitress approaches.

'Don't be ridiculous,' he replies, more forcefully than he intended. 'Have a pizza. One of us needs to have a pizza if we're here.'

She's turning the menu over in her hand. 'Do you think they do vegan cheese?'

'Nothing about being here is vegan,' he says. 'No one is going to judge you for having dairy.'

'Fine,' she says, almost instantly. 'I'll have a margherita. As long as you don't mind.'

When the food arrives, it looks delicious. Finn stares at Martha's pizza, at the cheese bubbling on the surface. He hasn't seen decent-looking cheese since coming to Bolivia.

'Enjoy it,' he says, and he means it.

His soup is too hot, burning his tongue when he attempts to take his first spoonful. Usually he loves his food hot, hates anything being lukewarm, but he knows he won't be able to get this down him until it's cool. A milkshake – that's what he would like, but the milk isn't the same here. It's long-life, artificial stuff. He realises that they forgot to cancel their twice-weekly milk order and suspects bottles will be sitting on their front step, piling up. Surely the milkman will realise? He tallies up all the bottles over a three-week period, the time coinciding with his offshore rota. There is a familiarity and comfort to being on his North Sea platform that he misses already: the structure and order, of knowing what is expected of him. It's the weeks at home that he struggles with now, he and Martha skirting around one another, both with nowhere else to go.

He watches Martha cut her pizza into slices – she's very particular, the slices needing to be all identical in size. He wants to shout at her, tell her that it doesn't matter, that it'll all end up inside her stomach.

'Well?' he says. 'What's it like?'

'It's good,' she replies, her mouth full.

'You have your appetite back, then?'

She swallows. 'It would seem.'

He blows on another spoonful of soup, the restaurant around them abuzz with chatter and warmth. He can hear the American couple despite being several tables away – the man is asking the waitress what she'd recommend for dessert, his voice booming over everything else. Finn catches Martha's eye, and they smile, an unspoken understanding exchanged in their smirks. And for the briefest of moments he thinks that perhaps they could be happy again, but it passes quickly, the pain in his oesophagus taking hold. He attempts to swallow the soup, his hunched posture tight over his bowl. They've made plans to visit Tupiza, then cross the border into Salta and finally visit Buenos Aires. But they will visit the Salt Centre first, for Martha, and he's already apprehensive, worries that her expectations won't align with reality.

'How's the soup?' she asks.

He nods. Despite the pain, the soup is nice. Homemade. Something to be grateful for.

4

The guesthouse is deserted on their return, the place in near darkness. Martha leads the way, aware of Finn lagging a few steps behind, quiet. She fishes out the key from her bag. It's not hard to find; it's attached to an enormous piece of wood masquerading as a keyring. The room is freezing now that the sun has gone, and she plugs in a small electric heater, a yellow glow suddenly filling the room. Finn is rooting around for his toothbrush, entering the small en suite. He closes the door, and she starts to fold and pack her clothes away into her backpack, so keen is she to be ready for their trip in the morning. She's barely thought of home since leaving, barely thought of anything from their old life, nostalgic for nothing. Aberdeen already has the creeping sensation of a ghost town. The oil won't last much longer and nor does she want it to. She's riddled with guilt for how they've benefited from it all, how it was she who suggested they move up to Aberdeen after Finn went into remission, when he needed a job and a fresh start, her own family, and by extension herself, benefiting from the oil boom. She hadn't always cared but she cares so deeply, so painfully now that it cripples her.

When Finn emerges, he climbs straight into the double bed, his clothes still on. Martha begins to undress, a shiver passing through her body, the hairs on the back of her neck standing up. She thinks about instigating sex; she rarely initiates it now for fear of rejection, but she's feeling unusually optimistic this evening, hopeful even. There is something so liberating about finally, nearly, being where she thinks she needs to be, inching closer to the place that will heal her of her pain.

It had started small, an awakening of sorts. A trip to London and a chance visit to the Natural History Museum where an exhibition on plastic pollution and the environment had sparked something unsettling in her. Small changes in attitude and behaviour had followed, it all trickling, a need to engage, until there was a rush of despair. Then came the Just Stop Oil protests, the damage she is allegedly responsible for causing, her suspension from the oil company where she is still employed as a document controller, her court date. She doesn't want to be this person any more; it's too much.

Shivering, she climbs into bed and pulls the covers over her bare skin, shifting closer to Finn. His eyes are closed but she can tell that he's not yet asleep. She stares at his face, the skin over his eyelids. She adores him still; would do anything for him. Sometimes, as an exercise in endurance, she still imagines him dying; she is well-practised in never taking his existence for granted. Recently, she has become obsessed with reading the social media feeds of the recently bereaved. She is fascinated by their *before and after* timelines, constantly in awe of their vulnerability. She thinks she should be the type of person capable of endurance, but she feels nothing but weakness. She is of a generation that are now told to be more resilient. To be proud of resilience, to wear it as a badge of honour. But she is not resilient. Not at all. All her resilience has been eaten away.

She shuffles closer to Finn, can feel his breath. She kisses his earlobe.

He doesn't respond.

Her hand creeps across his body. 'Thank you for coming here with me.'

'You're welcome,' he whispers.

She climbs on top of him, their bodies pressed together, and she can feel him getting hard. 'It's going to work,' she says.

'Good,' he says, 'I'm glad.' But she can hear the sadness in his voice.

He shifts from under her, turning away.

She lies, wounded, before getting back up to brush her teeth.

Wednesday

5

It is after 8 a.m. and their backpacks are resting by their feet as they stand outside, having checked out from the guesthouse. Their driver is late. Martha wears a feather-and-down body-warmer, the zip pulled up to her chin, the fabric tag of the zipper in her mouth. She sucks on it, a repetitive motion that her tongue performs almost by instinct. She had been a thumb-sucker in childhood, both thumbs, and the habit has never really left her. She stares at her thumbs now, is convinced they are shorter than they should be, imagines the sucking to have caused the same result as foot-binding. She's still sucking the tag on her zipper, the fabric now moist and slimy. She wonders if thumb-sucking is an early indicator of anxiety, a clue to her future self, a constant need to be soothed.

There is the noise of a vehicle approaching, turning sharply at the corner and coming to a stop in front of them. It is a large, red Toyota Land Cruiser, as expected, but the promise of a modern four-by-four is, in reality, a battered and rusted old vehicle. The roof-rack is already crammed with possessions, a blue tarpaulin covering everything, clipped into place by several bungee cords. A local man is in the driver's seat, turning off the engine, and behind him, right at the back, practically in the boot, are two young women.

The man steps out of the vehicle and approaches Martha and Finn. He is short, wearing a knitted jumper with the word *lethal* randomly incorporated into the patterned design. A baseball cap is drawn down over his eyes and he's chewing on something, his right cheek protruding like that of a hamster. Martha assumes it to be coca leaves. He pulls a torn piece of paper from his pocket and looks at it for a moment, a hesitant expression on his face. 'Patterson?' he says, his tongue trying to make sense of the pronunciation. 'Finn . . . Martha?'

They nod, cautious, a little hostile in their posture.

He extends his hand out towards Finn, widens his smile. '*Hola*,' he says. '*Me llamo Elbert*.'

Finn takes Elbert's hand, shakes it, and Martha follows.

Elbert looks down at the backpacks by their feet, makes an apologetic face and laughs as if the luggage poses some sort of conundrum. From inside the vehicle the women stare out, one with blonde hair tied up in a bun and an angular face, the other with dark brown cropped hair and a hooped ring hanging from her septum.

'Thank you for collecting us,' Martha says. 'Where should we sit . . . ?'

Elbert continues to smile, and it is clear to her that he has no idea what she is saying.

He turns and steps up on to one of the back tyres, unclipping a bungee cord and pulling back the tarpaulin. Two large backpacks and several storage boxes are already up on the roof, as well as a raft of food and water supplies. He begins to adjust and push everything as far as he can reach, before heaving Martha's backpack up on top, followed by Finn's. After securing everything back into place, he steps down, smiles, the baseball cap hiding the expression in his eyes, and ushers them into the vehicle.

Martha climbs in, Finn following, and she settles in the middle seat, smiling at the women behind her, offering a polite hello. But Finn is already reaching over to shake their hands, introducing himself properly, sitting to Martha's left, forcing his small backpack down by his feet, his knees pressing into the driver's seat.

'I'm Zoe,' the blonde-haired woman says, her complexion an unhealthy, peaky grey colour.

The dark-haired one with the septum piercing has a wide smile. 'And I'm Hannah,' she says.

Both have English accents. They must be in their early to mid-twenties, Martha thinks, and she's confused by their presence, can't imagine either of them needing the Salt Centre, too casual in their approach. She thinks again of the tourist flyer she tucked into her pocket the day before, wonders if these women are somehow here by accident. She's aware that Finn is still talking to them, exchanging pleasantries, and she envies his ease in the company of strangers.

They set off, and with a newfound anxiousness lodged behind her ribs Martha reaches for her seatbelt, pulling it across her chest. But when she attempts to click it into the buckle it won't catch. She reaches over, tries the belt of the spare seat, and it doesn't catch either. 'The seatbelts don't work,' she says, interrupting Finn's conversation, alarm rising in her voice. 'They won't click into place.'

Finn looks down, shrugging. 'It'll be okay,' he says. 'No one cares here . . . '

'But—'

'We're here, Martha,' he says, his mouth practically touching her ear. 'We're on our way. We're exactly where you wanted us to be. It's going to be fine.'

She nods, knows he's right, tries to harness the hope she's been nurturing since they arrived, instead of imagining a fatal crash. She links her arm through the seatbelt strap, resting it over her shoulder, feeling somewhat more secure before she places her foot inside one of the shoulder straps of her small backpack, like a lasso. She likes to keep her essential items close, finds it difficult to explain, in the same manner that, as a child, she had to have yellow in a stack of colouring pencils. Other colours could be sacrificed but she needed to be moored by the presence of yellow.

Elbert is turning another corner and now they are on the main street running through Uyuni, and Martha feels as though she is being teased, that Elbert is drawing out their departure on purpose. The vehicle slows once again, stopping outside the boutique hotel attached to the pizza restaurant. An older couple are emerging from the entrance, dragging two large metallic suitcases behind them. Elbert is once again getting out of the vehicle, approaching them with his worn piece of paper.

Finn stares out at the couple. 'We saw them last night,' he says.

'Did we?'

'At dinner . . . ' He pauses. 'They're the Americans we heard in the restaurant.'

'Oh,' she says.

Elbert opens the door and the couple peer in. 'Hi, all,' the man says, his voice booming, an expensive looking camera dangling from around his neck. 'I'm Rick. And this,' he says, pointing to the woman beside him, 'is my wife, Barb.'

Everyone nods and smiles, murmurs of hello and a repeating of names.

'Scottish?' Rick asks, addressing Finn.

Finn nods, a smile spreading into a smirk that only Martha understands. 'Indeed,' he says, reaching across her to shake Rick's hand.

'Ah, I know Scotland well,' Rick says. 'St Andrews is my second home. So great to have some Scots on the trip with us, isn't it, honey?'

Barb nods, enthusiastic.

Rick turns then to Zoe and Hannah. 'And you guys?'

'London,' Zoe says, her voice clipped.

'We love London too,' he replies, 'don't we?' he adds, nudging his wife who nods and smiles again, diligently.

'We do,' she says.

Rick is broad, and Martha watches him make a clear assessment of the seating arrangements. 'Would one of you mind scooching over into the back row?' he asks, looking at Martha and Finn. 'I don't think either me or Barb will fit in there.'

Martha, as if waiting for permission, now jumps at the opportunity to move, sees it almost as a sign. 'I'll go in the back,' she says. 'I don't mind.'

'Thanks so much,' Rick says. 'Greatly appreciated.'

She climbs out and then over into the back row, next to Hannah, taking her small bag with her, keeping it close. Immediately she is clipping her lap seatbelt into place, reassured by the click as it takes to the latch. Outside, Elbert is struggling with Rick and Barb's two suitcases with nowhere to put them. He opens the front passenger door and begins to manoeuvre them inside, careful not to scratch the metal. He returns to the driver's seat, where he sits, removing a pouch from his pocket, forcing more coca leaves into his mouth.

Finally, they are leaving the roads and grid structure of Uyuni. The landscape is changing quickly, a sense of society being abandoned, yet the salt flats are still not in sight, only rock, rubble and unfinished infrastructure. As they move, Martha is aware of everything, hypersensitive to the way Elbert chews on his cheek, to the way Hannah constantly brings her fingers to her mouth, to Rick spreading out in his seat, his arm pressing into Finn. She will be spending four days with these strangers, and it feels real now, the Salt Centre's existence; others believe in it too.

They are passing an abandoned railway yard. From her window Martha can see tourists gathered like dots, some of them standing on the roof of an old, graffiti-covered train carriage, the metal corroded, eaten away by the elements. Rick raises his camera, snapping several pictures before the trains disappear from view, but to Martha it all feels desperately sad, a reminder that so much of life is corroding, destined never to reach its full potential. She watches as Hannah reaches, like a reflex, for Zoe's hand, their fingers linking together; Hannah's sleeve is pushed up, revealing a tattoo of a circle on her wrist. They look at one another, before Hannah nods, a sense of reassurance, and Zoe nods back. Hannah brings Zoe's hand up to her mouth, kissing it, and the exchange is so quiet and tender that it startles Martha, a wave of jealousy passing through her, a winding of sorts.

6

Finn is starving. Ravenous. He swallows and it's like glass; he is so conscious now of how often he swallows. So much of life is simply repeating the same action, again and again: walking, blinking, sniffing, breathing. Swallowing. He opens his hand luggage bag and lifts out his medicine, pressing down on the click-lock cap, taking a gulp of the chalky mixture, aware of eyes watching him. He places the bottle back in his bag and looks up, startled then to see the beginnings of the salt flats up ahead. This vastness of brilliant bright white, appearing as if from nowhere, contrasting with the blue of the sky. He straightens, captivated; he hadn't been prepared to be so startled by its appearance. A line seems to separate earth from sky, the simplicity of it reminding him of the pictures he used to draw as a child.

The gravel road ends abruptly but Elbert is continuing without hesitation, tyres changing their sound on this new, unfamiliar terrain. Finn's breath catches, a dip in his stomach, an irrational fear that the salt isn't capable of holding them. He thought he knew what to expect, had seen so many pictures, so why is he so taken aback?

Elbert keeps the Land Cruiser close to the salt's edge, running now parallel to the gravel road creating a thin barrier between two different worlds. They travel like this for another twenty minutes before the vehicle begins to slow once again. Finn turns in his seat, confused; he'd been under the assumption that they'd be travelling for most of the day, but they come to a stop in front of a structure made from rectangular breeze blocks, ugly and unfinished, as though part-way through construction, another floor soon to be added.

Elbert turns off his engine and gets out, gesturing for them to do the same.

Finn steps out on to the bone-dry, hexagonal-shaped slabs of salt, framed by thick crusts. Instinctively, he bends down and brushes his hand across its rough surface.

'Why have we stopped?' Martha asks, alarm already surfacing, his irritation at it close to matching.

'I know as much as you do,' he says.

The group follow Elbert, a sense of collective confusion growing as they pass hundreds of salt mounds, like molehills, drying in the sun. Ahead, the doors to the windowless breeze-block structure are open, and, inside, people are working, processing huge amounts of salt, a well-oiled machine in motion.

An older woman is crouched on the ground, hunkering over a flame, sealing bags of salt into small plastic pouches, working rapidly, moving on to the next bag within seconds. She looks up and offers a wide, toothy smile, before exchanging words in Spanish with Elbert. Finn is suddenly suspicious, suspects he is about to be sold something he did not ask for, wonders how many tourists are brought here each day, the same woman feigning enthusiasm with each new face. She's still hunkered low, almost statue-like, ready to turn into a pillar of salt, while others are busy around her, shovelling huge heaps of salt, adjusting, working in a methodical way that means nothing to Finn.

The woman finally pulls herself up to full height, bringing a sealed bag of salt with her. She hands it to Elbert, who tears at the plastic, re-opening it, handing it first to Rick. The woman gestures with her fingers for them to taste it, and everyone does, licking and dabbing their pinkies in as the bag is passed along. Finn is last to bring the salt to his mouth, and he sucks, lets it settle on his tongue, is reminded of a phase he went through in his teens, of constantly wanting to eat tomatoes, biting into the flesh and sprinkling salt into the wound.

He swallows, the pain in his oesophagus a constant presence, aware then of the woman looking at him, as if waiting for him to say something profound about the salt.

He steps forward and returns the opened bag to her. She widens her smile, points behind them, to where signs are taped up on the wall above their heads, each one written in a different language. And immediately, Finn is searching for the English translation, an American flag above it. The writing is small, and he squints to take in the bullet points of text.

- Ten days to get salt from ground to bag.
- Everything done manually.
- People work twelve-hour shifts, six days a week.
- The factory refines 25,000 tons of salt each year.
- This domestic salt is shipped all around the world.
- One small bag costs half a boliviano.
- Each worker makes 900–1,000 bolivianos per month.
- ALL DONATIONS WELCOME.

The woman lifts an empty plastic tub, extending it out towards the group, a dollar bill taped to its outside.

'What's the exchange rate again?' Martha asks, squinting up at the sign.

Finn pulls his phone from his pocket, works the exchange rate out on the calculator. 'So, each bag is maybe six pence . . . And then each of them makes like £100 a month—' He stops, catching himself. 'Wait, can that be right?'

'Fuck,' Martha says. 'That seems ludicrous. No, that can't be right.'

Compelled then, he places a few boliviano notes inside the tub, instead of US dollars, much to the disappointment of the woman holding it, but he refuses to feel any sense of guilt or embarrassment. He suspects that the tub is constantly being replenished, that the next batch of tourists will be along shortly, and that Elbert will no doubt be getting a cut. It's not so much the money he resents – it's pocket change in the grand scheme of things – but the sense of exploitation, of knowing it's happening, and how vulnerable he feels – of being made a fool of, in the same way he had been when they got scammed at the bus station in La Paz with their luggage.

Elbert leads them out of the makeshift factory and across the salt to where men wearing balaclavas over their faces are digging and shovelling piles of watery salt into new heaps, all similar in height and dimension, equal spacing between each. It's impressive, although the balaclavas are an alarming sight, but Finn would rather be visiting one of the lithium-producing mines. He'd read that the Bolivian government had paired up with a large Chinese consortium who had brought ingenuity and new technology to the land, when previously the lithium deposits, despite their vastness, had been thought to be too difficult to extract on any industrial scale. The engineering of it fascinates him: minds coming together to make the impossible possible; Bolivia soon to be the largest exporter of lithium, their extraction success welcomed by the enormous global demand. And despite the environmental challenges – the unpredictable rainy season often arriving earlier with each year, lasting longer – they seem to adapt, never slowing in production. On arriving in La Paz, and then Uyuni, Finn had expected to see this new-found wealth from the industry out on display, had imagined it would have been like Aberdeen in the heyday of oil; but looking around, watching these men shovel salt, he can see that the economic benefit has yet to trickle down, suspects that now, inevitably, it never will.

As they move back towards their vehicle, another Land Cruiser parks up, the whole show, no doubt, reset for new eyes, and Finn feels further vindicated in his thinking. They settle back into their former seats and depart, entering now the heart of the flats, the edges of life and domestic salt production fading away. Finn tries to comprehend the fact that the salt flats spread across an area of over eleven thousand kilometres, but he can't, the world suddenly seeming like an infinite place. They have left all roads and markings behind, and he wonders then, with curiosity, how Elbert knows where he's going. How does anyone keep their bearings when there appears to be no navigational device on board, or any signal for Google Maps? They are at the mercy of Elbert's sense of direction, unable to communicate with him in any meaningful way, but Finn reasons that Elbert has done this journey hundreds of times before, for a revolving door of guests. And it really is beautiful out here, perhaps one of the most beautiful sights he's ever seen. They are travelling across land that was for thousands of years submerged under the water of a prehistoric lake, and it feels as if they are defying the laws of gravity by simply being here.

He's aware then of Elbert rolling down his window, his hand flying through the air as he picks up speed, and Finn wishes to feel the same sensation, but there is no handle to roll down his own window. He's thinking of lithium again, of his solar panels and the battery in his electric car, of this land potentially being integral to its workings, helping him to negate his double standards and lower his carbon footprint.

He sees Elbert briefly tilt his face to the open window and spit out his mouthful of coca leaves, green mulch travelling through the air. And Finn smiles, is reminded that nothing is sacred, that they are all capable of forgetting to appreciate what they have in front of them.

7

Hours pass. There is the outline of the Andes mountain range in the far, far distance and in all this time Martha has seen only a handful of other vehicles, all Land Cruisers, everyone appearing to be heading in the opposite direction from them. It's disorientating, everything feeling as if it could tip over, the flatness cracking open, nothing but salt for thousands of miles. She doesn't like the way Elbert drives, finds it too haphazard and careless. When researching their trip here she had spent hours trawling the internet for information, had read several articles about fatalities on the salt flats, of head-on collisions, vehicles speeding, rolling, tyres blowing out and passengers being crushed inside, or, worse, thrust out on to the salt. There is this constant fear of her visit to the Salt Centre being taken away from her, hurdle after hurdle of endurance, the threat of not making it on to the last group before they close for the rainy season; waiting until the new year an unbearable idea. And then there is Finn's ulcerating oesophagus, another potential sabotage.

Her thoughts shift to the shaman awaiting them at the centre. Señor Oscar. She has read the most incredible testimonies about him and his practices, but she worries still that the reality of him won't live up to the image she has created in her mind. She thinks about the time she booked to see a female author. Martha had found the woman's work on the climate emergency to be insightful, hopeful even, but there was something about hearing her in the flesh that had been profoundly disappointing. The power of editing, she supposed: that on the page everything can be fine-tuned, but in person this woman seemed to constantly contradict herself, leaving Martha with a burrowing sense of further despair.

The weight of this trip suddenly seems immeasurable, everything hinging on its success. She closes her eyes, attempts to push her fears away, allows excitement to seed in her stomach. Yes, the fear is still there, but it's muted, bearable.

There is a jerk, like an unexpected speed bump, and Martha opens her eyes. Irrationally, she imagines it to be similar to the sensation of driving over a body, and she turns to check but of course there is nothing to see. Back home, there had been a fatal incident around the corner from their house not so long ago, a body found on the road. They only knew when they woke the next morning to discover heavy police presence, the road taped off and an appeal to those who might have witnessed something. The circumstances were unclear, suspicious, a person either hit at speed or thrown out of a moving vehicle. But Martha had developed an absurd fear that this person's death had had something to do with her. She'd had to constantly remind herself that she hadn't been driving at the time in question, that she had been at home, and yet she still couldn't shake off the feeling that she was guilty; that she was capable of such action and not willing to come clean; that, if it came to it, she would lie in an attempt to cover her tracks, like an animal desperate to escape. She'd even Googled the victim afterwards, read every news clipping that she could find. A twenty-three-year-old male with an infant son. They'd opened the road a week later. No one talks about it any more, the truth never discovered, the case gone cold.

The Land Cruiser starts to stutter, and it feels as though it is slowing but it's unclear whether this is Elbert's intention or not.

And then finally the vehicle comes to a complete stop, thrusting everyone forward slightly in their seats.

'*Pucha*,' Elbert says, muttering under his breath.

Everyone looks around, eyes darting.

'Is something the matter?' Rick says.

Elbert gets out of the car. He stands for a moment, staring at his vehicle, before circling it. As he comes to Martha's window, he nudges his cap on top of his head, and she can see his eyes now, a warmth to them that matches his smile. He's muttering to himself, reaching up then, on to the tyre closest to her, and she can feel the weight shifting as he pulls at something from the roof rack, stepping back down with a metal box in his hand.

He returns to the driver's door, opening it and removing a pouch, which Martha assumes to be more of his coca leaves. Then he comes to the back cabin doors and opens them, gesturing with his hand for everyone to get out. Martha reluctantly steps back on to the salt, the wind whipping through her hair, it all feeling harsher now with nothing to protect them from the elements. She grips her bodywarmer, zips it, hugs her arms around her torso. None of this, she thinks, bodes well, except no one is reacting, no one is questioning their standing out here, alone.

Elbert passes the small pouch he's been holding to Finn and Martha comes closer, her curiosity too great. Finn reaches in and, instead of coca leaves, he pulls out a small plastic toy dinosaur, displaying it in the palm of his hand.

Elbert nods, makes a clicking noise with his tongue, bringing his hand up to his eyeline, his fingers mimicking the press of a camera button. The group stare at him in confusion. He takes the dinosaur from Finn's hand, places it on the ground and says '*Vamos*,' gesturing for them to move further into the distance behind the toy, and again mimics the action of taking a photograph.

'Oh, I've seen this,' Hannah says, suddenly animated, her body stretching. 'It's like an optical illusion. All in the perspective. People take photos and it looks like the dinosaur is eating them . . . '

'Okay,' Finn says, seeming to take to the idea.

But Martha is confused – why are they being asked by Elbert to take photographs? She looks around the group; no one else seems to question why they are still not on their way to the Salt Centre.

'Finn . . . ' she says.

He looks at her, understands her concern. 'It'll be okay,' he replies. 'It's just a little bit of fun. You don't need to panic.'

She nods, slowly.

'Do you have your phone?' he asks, extending his hand out. 'Mine is back in my bag.'

Hesitating, Martha removes her phone from the pocket of her bodywarmer, unlocks it and hands it to him.

Finn takes charge of the situation, tells everyone to retreat backwards, holding the phone up to the image. Martha watches on. Hannah is the first to create some distance, Zoe in tow, Rick and Barb following too. But Martha wants to call them back, demand that they stop all this nonsense.

Behind her, Elbert has popped open the bonnet of the Land Cruiser and no one, except for her, appears to be concerned.

'You too, Martha,' Finn says. 'Get in the picture.'

And they're calling her name now, everyone else, these strangers. She doesn't like it, this whole charade reminding her of that game she used to play as a kid, What's the Time, Mr Wolf? The anticipation of stepping closer to the wolf, the fear and tension of someone getting ready to chase you. Reluctantly, she follows, and Finn continues to frame them. 'Look like you're scared,' he says. 'Look up to your right as if something is about to eat you.'

There is collective laughter, a self-consciousness, no one wanting to make a fool of themselves. Hannah again takes the lead, raising her arms up in mock despair, and the others follow, except of course for Martha.

'Martha,' Finn shouts. 'Don't ruin the picture.'

Half-heartedly she copies the others, but she's unable to relax enough to be swept up in the hilarity of the photograph and its absurdness. Afterwards, Finn tells them all to jump in the air and they do so. The jumping feels less ludicrous to Martha than the screaming at a toy dinosaur, and she smiles, begins to get swept up in the energy of others. There is a release, a moment of joy, and she clings to its sensation, squeezing the life out of it. The giddiness of letting herself go.

She pretends to herself, only briefly, that the bonnet to Elbert's Land Cruiser is not open. No one else has mentioned it, so perhaps in theory it is not happening.

The photos continue as Elbert works away, Rick coming now to take pictures of Finn and Martha together, so that it appears as if Martha is in the palm of Finn's hand. The illusion is startling. And finally they gather, looking at everyone's photographs. The images are exceptional, suggesting that these strangers are all in fact the best of friends, that they are having the time of their lives, nothing but tourists.

'We can exchange numbers later, when we get signal,' Finn says. 'Make a WhatsApp group.'

But the excitement is beginning to dissipate, the others acknowledging the open bonnet now, that it has been open for some time.

Hannah pulls on a curly strand of hair, making it straight. 'Should we be worried?' she says.

'It'll be okay,' Finn replies, seeming genuinely relaxed. 'Stuff like this must happen all the time. The vehicles are old, but they go on forever.'

As they draw closer to Elbert, they can see his tools spread out across the ground. Rick nods. 'He knows what he's doing.' But Elbert is searching, unable to retrieve whatever it is he appears to need. He clears his throat, begins to speak to them, frustration in knowing that they can't understand him. He pinches his thumb and index finger together, makes as if he is turning a key. He points at a screw inside the engine, further attempts to convey the problem. Defeated, he smiles, dutifully, the way he is meant to with guests.

'I have a Leatherman pocket tool kit,' Finn says. 'Would that be of any use?' He's already removing the device from his pocket.

Martha knows how much he loves that pocket-knife contraption. She often finds it in his trousers, discarded on the bedroom floor when he's at home. She begrudges having to remove it before throwing his trousers in the washing basket. One day she'll end up washing the device and no doubt ruin it. She doesn't know where he keeps it when he's offshore; maybe he takes it with him, unable to be parted from it.

Elbert inspects the Leatherman tool, obviously impressed. He opens it, pulls at one of the small screwdriver heads, his hand now lost to the belly of the engine. And then there is a jubilant noise from Elbert, one of relief. Finn's Leatherman has, in fact, been proven useful. Elbert smiles and nods, offering a quick thumbs-up as he hands the device back to Finn.

'Nifty piece of kit you've got there,' Rick says.

'Thanks,' Finn replies, returning it to his pocket.

'How much did it set you back?'

Finn shrugs. 'I can't remember, maybe like £100. I'm not sure what that currently is in dollars.'

Zoe snorts a laugh. 'You spent more on that than those people from the salt factory make in a month.'

Finn hesitates. 'I . . . I wasn't trying to be . . . '

'It helped,' Martha says, defence thick in her voice.

'True,' Zoe replies, shrugging. 'Of course.'

'Is that us, then?' Rick says. 'Is everything sorted?'

But Elbert isn't closing the bonnet over; he's not ushering them back into the vehicle. If anything, it is as if he's only getting started, rolling up his sleeves.

They hover around him, peering at one another with a collective sense of unease, yet Elbert appears unconcerned, a man with purpose, gathering the tools he needs.

'Do you think he knows what the problem is?' Barb says.

Martha reaches into the back row of the Land Cruiser and pulls out her small backpack, removing sunscreen. She fears that it is already too late, her cheeks flushed from the harshness of the sun; understands now why those men outside the salt factory covered their faces. Standing in the open, she slathers her face with the cream, particularly her nose, trying to ignore the prickling sensation already present.

She offers the cream to the others and they each take the bottle in turn, applying it to their faces, grateful.

'Thank you,' Barb says. 'All of ours is in our suitcases.'

'Help yourself,' Martha replies.

Afterwards, they sit in a circle on the salt, jumpers and jackets laid down to protect them from its rough texture. It has been nearly two hours since they came to a stop here and it occurs to Martha that no other vehicle has come into sight. She traces her fingers over the solid, compact salt, a familiar tension growing, her eyes constantly shifting to Elbert, who continues to work a few metres away. She tries to figure out when the sun is likely to set, suspects that it's not great to be out here in the dark;

the temperatures must drop to below zero. Her stomach churns. She's starving, but they all must be starving, having had no lunch. Finn rubs at the stubble on his face, and she is sure that his chin and face are thinner, even just from yesterday.

She places her hand on Finn's back. When he looks at her, she offers him her most confident smile and he smiles too, but she can see it is half-hearted.

'How's your throat?' she asks.

He shrugs, and shifts his stance, her hand falling away, and she wonders if he means to punish her in this way, if it's an active choice or if it's simply second nature now and he doesn't even realise any more. She thinks then about those Nest security cameras he had installed after there had been a few burglaries in the area, how the activity notifications go straight to his phone, and how after a while she completely forgot they existed. Yet the evidence of her guilt is there for him to see any time he wishes.

Hannah opens her small backpack, removes a Snickers bar and offers it to Zoe. In Bolivia the imported chocolate is extortionate, and Martha is amazed that they've chosen to spend their money this way – as if they've lost all concept of the value of things. Hannah pulls another Snickers from her bag and gets to her feet, tapping Elbert on the shoulder and offering it to him. Elbert reaches out to take it, a genuine smile of appreciation settling on his face, thanking her in Spanish. This act of generosity is fascinating to Martha – perhaps because she knows that if it had been her she wouldn't have shared expensive chocolate with strangers. She'd have rationed it for herself and Finn.

'Would anyone else like some?' Hannah says. 'I have one spare . . . '

There is only the polite shaking of heads, a collective mummer of *no thanks*. Martha watches Finn stare at the chocolate as Hannah takes a bite, appearing transfixed by each mouthful.

Barb has found some American-branded ready-salted crisps in her bag and is munching on them slowly, the crunch seeming especially loud to Martha, while Rick tears at an unidentifiable sandwich, the bread a strange shade of brown. Martha has nothing to eat except for a packet of mints and a bruised apple – she had assumed lunch would be provided, a pit-stop on their way to the Salt Centre, and anyway Finn can't eat, so really, carrying more would only have added to the weight.

Finn takes small, clearly painful sips from his water bottle, his eyes continuing to fix on everyone else's snacks.

'Aren't you hungry?' Barb asks, addressing Finn, conscious perhaps of his stare.

Finn nods. 'But I can't eat anything,' he says. 'I burnt the lining of my throat and am on a liquid diet for a week . . . '

'Oh, God,' Barb replies, her accent seeming to bounce off the salt. 'You poor soul.'

'That *is* shit,' Hannah says, her dark curls bobbing, her body rocking forward. 'That's awful, I'm so sorry.'

Finn shrugs. 'It is.'

'Did you let them know?' Barb says. 'When you filled in your health questionnaire . . . '

'What do you mean?' Martha asks, straightening.

'In the welcome pack . . . ' Barb replies. 'The forms they wanted us to fill out about ourselves before arriving.'

'Wait,' Martha says, with obvious alarm. 'You got forms to fill in? We didn't get forms, did we, Finn?'

'No, I don't think so . . . But I only got diagnosed yesterday, anyway—'

'What did they ask you?' Martha presses, interrupting Finn.

Barb shrugs. 'Mostly about our health. What type of diet we were used to, medication, our mental health history, that type of thing.'

Martha sucks in her breath. 'They won't know anything about us . . . What if the therapies don't work properly because they don't know our answers . . . ?' She has a lump in her throat, her panic so obvious. She has no desire to cry in front of these people but she's not sure if she can hold it back.

'Mar,' Finn whispers, 'it's okay, this isn't something you need to worry about. Everything will still be fine.'

His tone is soothing, loving, and she's overwhelmed. 'I just don't want to get off on the wrong foot.'

'I know, I know.'

Suddenly, Zoe places her head between her legs, abandoning her half-eaten Snickers bar on the salt.

'Zo, are you going to be sick?' Hannah asks, quickly coming to crouch in front of her.

'I thought the chocolate would help . . . '

'Altitude sickness?' Barb asks.

Hannah nods, while Zoe keeps her head tucked in between her legs. 'We've been to other places before,' Hannah says, 'and she's been fine. It's taken us completely by surprise.'

'Hopefully you'll feel better when we get there,' Martha says.

Her eyes dart over to Elbert, who's peering into the engine. He straightens, reaching into his trouser pocket to remove his bag of coca leaves. Martha watches on as he pinches a gathering of leaves in his fingers, placing them in his mouth almost ceremoniously, a slow chew taking hold. He looks completely calm, a peacefulness to his posture, and when he sees her staring he smiles and offers her another thumbs-up.

'We should get compensation for this,' Rick says, looking at his watch. 'I'm sure in the circumstances they'll want to make a gesture to us, considering the money that has been spent.'

Barb continues to crunch away on her crisps and Martha wonders if it would be rude to ask her for one. In the end she can't bring herself to do so, and reaches for her apple instead, taking a bite, avoiding the bruised section. Maybe Finn would manage some; perhaps he could mulch a few bites into a pulp.

Zoe straightens, her face white, and Martha questions if she'll finish her Snickers. What a waste otherwise.

'What happens if we're stuck here for much longer?' Martha asks.

No one says anything for a moment.

'I'm sure Elbert will have us moving in no time,' Rick says, but Martha isn't convinced by his tone.

She tries to remain calm, wants to rationalise their situation into something logical. 'I've read about people cycling across sections of the salt flats, camping even, despite the cold that comes with no sunlight,' she says, but she's not sure why she's saying this, isn't entirely convinced her comment is of comfort.

She glances up to the roof of the vehicle, remembers the food supplies and water containers strapped above, is reassured by the knowledge that at least no one will starve. But then she visualises having to sleep in the Land Cruiser overnight, and the idea is terrifying, creating knots in her empty stomach. Suddenly, Elbert closes the bonnet with a thud and climbs back into the driver's seat. As if by a miracle, the engine comes to life, and immediately Martha is scrambling, grabbing her possessions in haste, oblivious to the others, fearful of being left behind.

8

No one speaks for a long time, superstitious perhaps, Finn thinks, that the vehicle might break down at the mere sound of their voices. He hopes they arrive at the Salt Centre before darkness, has had enough of being surrounded by nothing. Bored, he looks over his shoulder, sees that colour has returned to Zoe's face. She's drinking from an aluminium water bottle with a prominent dent in the side. He imagines the dent is from throwing the bottle at something or someone, maybe Hannah; likes to visualise the reality that is hidden by the image of a happy couple. He thinks about the hole he punched into the kitchen wall, now plastered over, the paint not quite matching the way it should despite coming from the same tin. How long has it been since he caught Martha on the camera, bringing another man into their home? Eight months already?

In the distance, a huge rock formation appears as if from nowhere, positioned in the middle of the flats with nothing else around. Finn straightens in his seat, gazing out as Elbert curves closer towards it as if taking a left turn at a roundabout, shifting them into a slightly altered direction.

'What is that?' Zoe says, her voice travelling.

Finn presses his nose up against the window to keep the rock formation in his sight. It is bizarre, otherworldly, top-heavy, with nothing but a spindly, twig-like base holding the rest of it up. There is a hole in the centre, near the top, washed and grooved by the elements, no doubt, for thousands of years. It is an anomaly, something that he can't rationalise, but it is before them, and it is real.

'I've never seen anything like that,' Hannah says, taking a photograph on her phone. Rick is taking photographs too, snapping away on the camera around his neck.

'I think it's made of coral,' Martha says.

Finn tries to hold the rock formation in his line of vision for as long as possible, fearful of this being the loneliest place in the world without it. They are pinpricks in this flatness, insignificant, and he doesn't like it. He's not sure why he finds being here so unsettling now – normally he is happy to go offshore without hesitation, and the platforms are nothing compared to the vastness of the sea and its depths, yet he rarely thinks about it, carried away by the illusion of a city, its skyscrapers protecting him.

The rock formation is gone now, lost from view, as if it was never there, a mirage in this desert of salt. Finn is losing all sense of perspective. There's nothing around them except for the tyre marks they leave in their wake. And he wishes that Martha were sitting beside him now, instinctively wants her most when he himself feels ill at ease. He turns, wanting her attention, but she is engaged in a conversation with Hannah about Aberdeen, moving her hands a lot, her whole body part of the conversation.

'The city where we live I wouldn't say is great, but the countryside, westwards in particular, is lovely.'

'Why's that – what's wrong with the city?' Hannah asks.

'All the wealth, from the oil . . . it never got reinvested into Aberdeen as a place, and you notice it now: communities falling apart, the deprivation. People are beginning to flee; so many houses are up for sale.'

'So, what will you guys do?' Hannah asks.

'We're not sure yet,' Martha says, with what Finn feels is a tone of excitement. It's the most hopeful she's sounded in so long and he doesn't have the heart to break her fantasy.

He swallows, the jagged sensation worse than ever. There is pessimism in his heart, for this whole trip, because deep down he doesn't believe it capable of giving Martha what she wants. He's a man of logic, alive because of modern medicine, and yet he has allowed himself to be brought here based on so little information and evidence. The Salt Centre operates through word of mouth, secretive in its process, people reluctant to let anyone else experience the *enlightenment* they have acquired – some expert on YouTube extolling its healing powers and capabilities but unwilling to reveal its location publicly – Martha fixated, with no job to go to, all her effort and time consumed in pursuit of this – the networking with *like-minded* individuals, all for a promise that sounds too good to be true. They even drove down to Edinburgh to meet a climate activist she'd met online, a woman called Wilma who claimed that her life had been changed by the Centre.

Beside Finn, Rick is asleep, his head lolling slightly against his wife's shoulder. The weight of him is surely uncomfortable, yet Barb does not move, never attempts to shift or nudge him. And Finn thinks that perhaps this is what long-term relationships of any kind become: enduring pain to comfort the other. He thinks of his mother, always taking custody of apple cores or discarded tangerine skins, constantly just being there to make the lives of her children and husband easier.

'And you like London?' Martha is asking Hannah.

Finn looks over his left shoulder, can see Zoe's eyes are closed now. He rests his head against the back of his seat, closes his eyes too.

'I'm *from* London so I can't really imagine living anywhere else, and Zoe's from Oxfordshire, so not too far . . . I mean, it's hard to get on the property ladder, you know? Maybe if we wanted to have kids later then we'd move further out, but, for now, it works . . . '

'And what is it you both do?' Martha presses.

'I'm a script editor,' Hannah says. 'But I've just gone freelance, hence the freedom to come away. And Zoe is a dancer. Contemporary dance.'

'Oh, wow,' Martha says. 'That's incredible. Both of you.'

Hannah laughs. 'It's perhaps not as glamorous as you might think.'

'I wish I'd known there were more interesting jobs to do when I was younger . . . '

'What is it *you* do?'

Finn opens his eyes again, waits with interest for Martha's answer.

'I . . . I was a document controller, but I'm taking a break from work for a while. Need some time to figure things out.'

'Oh, yeah, for sure,' Hannah says. 'What's a document controller?'

Martha laughs. 'It's kind of like a librarian for corporate companies. Probably something that won't be a job forever, you know, with AI . . . '

'Sure,' Hannah says. 'AI is definitely something I worry about.'

Elbert has the heating blasting through the vehicle now and Finn is warm, his cheeks flushed. He closes his eyes again, feels himself going, a sinking sensation.

'Look!' Martha exclaims, and Finn startles, straightening in his seat.

Finally, ahead of them, a large piece of raised and rugged land with a building on top, and instinctively Finn knows this is their destination. Barb is waking Rick, forceful in her approach, needing him to see what the rest of them do. The Land Cruiser begins to slow, Elbert's foot on the brake, and everything is before them.

It is an island, rising from this ancient, evaporated bed of water, but the term feels wrong to Finn, doesn't quite fit in with what he is seeing. The white of the salt stops abruptly as the land inclines; its terrain is brown, composed of stone and dust, huge cacti growing everywhere. It feels as if they are approaching a place that should still be hidden, and the same reluctance as before is weighing heavy in his chest.

The vehicle comes to a stop, shunting Finn forward in his seat, and they are facing a narrow path, lacing its way towards the entrance to the Salt Centre. Elbert opens the doors for them and they gather their small bags, desperate to stretch their legs. When Finn looks back, Martha is still sitting, the only one left in the vehicle, while Elbert is already leading the way, the others following, all possessions and supplies still on the roof of the Land Cruiser, abandoned.

'You okay?' he asks Martha, his head peering in at her from the door.

She shrugs, nods.

'Are you nervous?'

'No,' she replies, defensive.

'Then get out of the car.'

She swallows. 'Finn . . . ' Her voice is nothing more than a whisper. 'What if it doesn't work?'

He stares at her, recognises the fear. There has been so much talk and preparation in coming, the idea of it almost enough to cure her in itself, but now they are here, and her theory will soon be tested.

'It's going to be okay,' he says. 'Please, get out of the car.'

Slowly, she climbs out. He holds his hand out for her, and she takes it, grateful, and together they walk towards the Salt Centre.

It is a single-storey building, the blocks of the structure constructed entirely from salt. Finn contemplates what it must take to build in this environment, the lack of infrastructure, constantly fighting against the harshness of the elements. The path is flanked by the biggest cacti he has ever seen, towering over all of them. He has this great desire to stand next to one of the tallest ones and gauge its height. The memory of the doorframe in his childhood home, against which his father would measure him and his sister, marking a line with their initials and the date into the wood. He imagines using his fingernail to score the smallest mark into the cactus, knowing no one will ever notice it or know what it means. Only him.

At the entrance, a man is waiting for them, beaming, his arms open wide in a gesture of welcome. Finn assumes this is Señor Oscar, as he's been referred to in emails, yet to Finn's astonishment Oscar is Caucasian.

'Welcome to the Salt Centre,' the man says.

He has shoulder-length, greying dark hair and a large, bushy beard. He spreads his hands out wide, ushering each of them to come forward. He is also younger than Finn was expecting, perhaps in his mid-forties, not that much older than Finn himself, and he's struggling to reconcile the man before him with the man he read and heard about in testimonials. Is it even possible to obtain the wisdom required of a shaman when you're still so young?

Elbert is speaking to Oscar, perhaps explaining the long delay, and Oscar is replying in quick and flawless Spanish. Finn can't keep up with their exchange, tries to grasp a word here and there, but feels disarmed and vulnerable by his ignorance.

The American couple, Rick and Barb, are the first to be properly greeted, Oscar embracing each of them in turn. He provides the kind of hug that friends give, and as he works his way down the line no one is resisting it, his arms capturing the next person in a scoop. Finn watches as Oscar places his hands on Martha's shoulders – he smiles and it is a smile that claims to know things, offers to make things better, and Martha is lapping it up.

'Oh, Martha,' he says, embracing her, pressing her body into his. 'We are so happy to have you here.'

Finn recognises something in Oscar's voice, a hint of an accent from long ago. Finally he places it: Australian. He is sure of it, wonders how long it would take for his Scottish accent to be tamped down, until it bore only a slight resemblance to who he used to be.

Martha and Oscar are still embracing, and Finn has an urge to pull them apart, but suspects it would be difficult, like opposing a magnetic force. Eventually Oscar retreats, holding Martha at arm's length once again. He seems to be lingering on her for longer than the others. 'You are finally here,' he declares. 'You are exactly where you need to be.'

Oscar reaches then for Finn, refusing to let him escape his embrace. Finn can only stand, feeling overpowered and weak, as this man pulls him closer. 'Welcome, Finlay,' he says. 'I'm so glad you're here.'

'It's Finn,' he replies.

'Oh, my apologies.'

They are led inside and down a hall. Finn inspects the walls, fascinated by the blocks of salt, the grain that runs through them. He wants to know how they are made, thinks about the rainy season, realises that perhaps the eye-watering fee they paid to come here is primarily spent on simply keeping this structure alive. On his offshore oil platform he spends his days trying to stop the salt in the sea from corroding the steel, but here it's all in reverse, a great fear of rainwater, eroding and melting the salt into nothing.

Oscar brings them into a large, circular-shaped room and Finn's eyes travel around the curve of the walls. He appreciates the complexity of building something that is not square, feels as though he's in an igloo, although he's never actually been inside one. On closer inspection, he realises that everything that can be is made from salt: the seats are carved from blocks of it, the tables, shelves too with books resting on them. A vase carved from salt holds dried flowers, and a salt-carved tube acts as a sort of umbrella stand, with two golf umbrellas pointing upwards mixed in with other random objects that serve no obvious purpose, including a short oar from a rowing boat, and a traditional-looking spear.

The ground has no carpet, just a thick covering of large salt grains, the consistency of bath crystals, compacting under the soles of Finn's walking boots. In the living area a cowskin rug is an attempt to tie the space together, and as he passes an armchair he runs a hand along a fur throw positioned on top, unable to tell if it's real animal fur or not.

Oscar gathers them into something of a huddle. 'We are so profoundly pleased to have you here,' he says, nodding then towards Elbert. 'You have already been introduced to our wonderful Elbert, a man of many talents. Not only is he our driver, he has also practised for many years in the holistic treatments we offer here, and will be providing me with his assistance.'

An older woman emerges from a side door carrying a tray with cups, a teapot, and a plate of savoury-looking snacks. She is wearing a circular bowler-like hat, beige-green in colour, trimmed in cord with a tassel hanging by its side. Its position on her head is striking to Finn, the circumference small, so that it balances on top like a book. The woman smiles at them without really meeting anyone's eye, bowing her head slightly, the hat remaining in place, seemingly capable of defying gravity. Finn has seen many women wearing these hats here, yet he does not know why, or what they signify. A woman at passport control when they landed in La Paz was wearing one, pleading with an officer before being abruptly removed from the queue, her hat the only thing he could see as she was pulled away, through the crowd.

Oscar nods the woman forward. 'And this,' he says, waving his hand up and down as if showcasing a display, 'is Ofelia, our cook, cleaner and general guardian angel. She looks after us all.'

Finn tries to gauge her age, and guesses her to be in her sixties, like Rick and Barb. She says something in Spanish as she places her tray down on a small table and Oscar bursts out laughing, leaving a strange energy in the room, the joke lost on everyone else. Ofelia departs the way she came, while Elbert disappears back in the direction of the front entrance.

'Let me apologise for your delay in arriving here,' Oscar says, 'but be rest assured that your treatments will not be compromised. We are working earnestly to make up the time,' he adds, nodding towards patio doors where a circle of plastic chairs have been arranged outside. He rubs his hands together. 'First, we thought you might like some coca tea, and a snack to tide you over until dinner.' He lifts the plate, offering it to everyone, and Finn watches as hands fly out, vultures, grabbing and forcing little pastry parcels into their mouths.

Oscar begins to strain and pour the tea, while Elbert goes back and forth, carrying their bags, taking them to where Finn assumes they must be sleeping.

'I'm not sure if any of you have had the opportunity to have coca tea yet,' Oscar says, 'but we find it to be a great cleanser before we begin.' He reaches forward, patting Zoe's arm. 'It's excellent for altitude sickness too, my dear.' He begins to distribute the cups, offering Zoe the first one. 'We use only the best loose leaves,' he says. 'We find it makes a huge difference.'

Elbert passes them once again with more bags.

Finn takes the cup that is offered to him, resting it against his chest, the warmth spreading across his torso. He takes a sip; it tastes of nothing particularly special, the same as any other herbal tea. The warmth travels down his oesophagus, painfully, and he imagines the blisters, the hot liquid not helping, the image of ulceration so clear on the screen in the doctor's examination room.

Elbert returns, this time carrying Finn and Martha's backpacks over his shoulders. Finn doesn't know what the etiquette is: whether he should take the bags off him or let him be. Do they work on the assumption that good service provides tips? He has no idea, but he looks on regardless, secretly grateful, because sometimes when he's lifting heavy things he's fine, but sometimes, still, the effects of his chemotherapy become so prominent, the ball-sockets of his arms weaker now than they used to be. The looks he and Martha get from strangers if she's the one lifting their heavy food shopping to the car, more than capable, while Finn walks beside her. Sometimes this role reversal in society amuses him; other times he wants to scream, tell anyone who will listen that he had cancer and it's a miracle that he is even alive.

'Our priority here is to offer you peace and uninterrupted contemplation so that you can get the most from your experience.' Oscar takes a sip of his own tea. 'We believe that by focusing on small groups, and giving you our guidance, each of you will come away from here feeling positively changed and fulfilled. We don't promise miracles, but we certainly find that if our guests give themselves fully to the experience, they leave feeling lighter and more enlightened. The more you give, the more reward you will reap.'

Finn looks around, his scepticism on high alert, but Martha is nodding, swallowing Oscar's every word. Zoe too, her eyes closed, blonde hair falling from its bun, a tear running down her face, relief in her expression, as if, finally, she is at peace.

'Love, devotion and surrender,' Oscar says. 'Think of these principles in everything you do here.'

There is more nodding.

'For the duration of your time with us, it will be just me, Elbert and Ofelia caring for you, in any way we can, regardless of the hour. Think of us as your family, and think of each other in this same manner also.'

He clasps his hands together in a gesture of prayer.

'You are here to take a break from society's social constructs.' He pauses, smiles. 'With this in mind, we ask that all watches and electronic devices be handed over to us for the duration of your stay.'

'Why?' Finn asks. 'There's no phone reception or internet signal here anyway.'

'We appreciate that, but the only marker of time we follow is that of the rising and setting of the sun. We do not wish to have our days dictated by minutes and hours, so we find it is best to remove any device that allows for that distraction. Also, we ask that no photographs be taken of your stay here. We want you to be present. We don't want you to miss out on an experience because you are trying to capture the image of it on a phone or camera.'

Ofelia returns, holds out a hessian bag, and Oscar takes it from her, waiting for possessions to be dropped inside. Finn watches as Martha unstraps her watch without hesitation, pulling her smartphone out from her pocket, ready to submit.

Oscar can see the alarm on Finn's face, the suspicion. 'I assure you, everything will be kept safely in our office. All of it will be returned to you on your departure.'

Finn nods, hesitant, aware of Martha's eyes on him, that pleading expression he sees too often, and finally he does as he's instructed.

'A few other ground rules . . . ' Oscar says. 'While you are here you will be eating a vegetarian diet. I know some of you are vegetarians already, so hopefully this isn't an issue. We also do not permit the use of any alcohol or recreational drugs. Of course, medication prescribed by a physician is acceptable—'

'Finn is on a liquid diet,' Martha says, blurting the words out, and he feels a sudden sense of shame, as though he has been exposed, despite having already told the others this exact same piece of information. 'Can that be accommodated?'

Oscar looks from Martha to Finn. 'Of course,' he says. 'This is not a problem. I did wonder about your dietary requirements, having not received your paperwork . . . '

'It's not a diet I've chosen; I hurt my oesophagus . . . ' Finn says, the speed of his words struggling to hide his embarrassment – an embarrassment driven by Martha's deep-seated need to care for him. He has a sudden desire to be cruel, knows that he could so easily belittle the reason they have come here. But he holds his tongue.

'Regardless, you will be well looked after, I assure you,' Oscar says.

'And we didn't not return the questionnaires,' Martha says. 'We didn't receive them.'

Oscar nods, appearing somewhat embarrassed himself now. 'I see. It is not a problem . . . I will capture all the information I need during our one-to-one sessions.' He pauses. 'We appreciate how hungry you must be, but the salt bucket treatment has to be completed before sunset. There really is no time to lose. And afterwards, as I mentioned, we will sit down to a delicious meal prepared by Ofelia.' He nods then, taking in each of them. 'Okay,' he says, 'let us begin.'

9

They sit outside on the patio area in a tight circle. Martha is uncomfortable on her plastic foldable chair, shivering, her feet bare and waiting, resting on a small towel. The sun is setting in the distance and Ofelia comes and goes, carrying buckets of water. One bucket is placed in front of Martha, and, when she peers in, she can see it's about two-thirds full.

There is a nervous camaraderie among the group, everyone half-smiling at each other in anticipation, a sense of bonding having begun. All except for Finn, who is hunched over, inspecting everything with his well-practised scepticism. It's obvious to Martha that he has decided to dismiss everything the Salt Centre has to offer. And silently she's devastated, because if he doesn't believe in it for himself, then he can't believe in it for her.

'Salt represents purity, preservation, incorruptibility,' Oscar says, clasping his hands together. 'These are all qualities that are deemed sacred here at the Salt Centre.' He glances around the circle. 'We begin your time with us by cleansing your auras in a salt bucket ceremony,' he says, his voice soothing. 'We will trap your negative black energy in the salt and your body will become free of its weight.' He pauses. 'This is a nice way of easing oneself into the therapies provided here. But first we will say a prayer to the gods of this land and thank them for the salt that surrounds us.'

Martha presses her palms together, tight and uncomfortable, before closing her eyes. She's never been fully invested in prayer before, considered it futile when clearly it did so little to diminish people's suffering, but perhaps she has been doing it wrong. She wonders if those who make a point of praying regularly experience a more peaceful existence.

Oscar begins to pray, and she tries to focus on his words as he asks the gods of salt to cleanse their souls but she's already overthinking, worrying that she's missed something, won't understand his meaning.

Afterwards, Oscar lifts a large, ornate bowl in his hands and begins to go around the group, measuring two tablespoons of salt and tipping them into each bucket of water. When he gets to Martha's bucket he's less careful, and some of the second tablespoon of salt spills on to the ground. He moves on, oblivious, but Martha, alarmed, doesn't know if she should bend down and attempt to gather the lost particles. What if less dark energy is taken from her because of the slightly altered salt-to-water ratio?

'Now place your feet inside the buckets,' Oscar says with a commanding tone.

Martha plunges her feet into the bucket; the water is freezing, and feels as if something is piercing her skin, everywhere, all at once.

'Keep your feet two to three centimetres apart,' Oscar says.

She's not sure if her feet are that distance apart but she's too scared to move them, worries that she's overcompensating – she has never been great at following instructions, always the person in an exercise class that needs to be corrected.

'Never forget what Mother Earth has provided us,' Oscar whispers. 'Silently, thank her again and again.' He pauses, circling behind the group, and Martha feels his presence as he approaches her. 'When I tell you all to remove your feet from the bucket, do so immediately. To delay is to allow the dark energy to be reabsorbed into your body.'

Martha realises then that everyone else's eyes are closed, even Finn's. She tries to centre herself, thank Mother Earth for bringing her here, but she's so aware of the others, of Oscar continually moving behind them. A familiar sense of despair returns, a weight in her stomach. Why won't her anxiety allow her this moment? Is she wired wrong? How can she thank Mother Earth with any conviction when she sees every day what they have done, what they continue to do to her? Her feet grow numb; she has no idea how long they have been resting in this bucket, has no grasp on how long they are expected to sit here, like this. It's torturous. And then she remembers that she should be thanking Mother Earth still, asking to have her dark energy removed from within.

In the silence, Oscar clears his throat, and it makes Martha think of exam invigilators getting ready to tell students to put their pencils down, before walking slowly down aisles gathering up papers. She knows that she has not passed this test. She feels nothing – there is no change, no lightness, only a knot of anguish, a sense of futility.

'Now gently,' Oscar says, 'remove your feet from the bucket and place them on to the towels.'

Martha does as she has been instructed, a stinging sensation travelling up her feet. She peers into the bucket as if expecting the colour of the water to have changed. Others are inspecting their buckets too, and she has this fear that someone is about to declare a miracle.

Oscar smiles at each of them, knowingly. He rests his right hand on his chest as if to cup his heart. 'I can feel it,' he declares. 'I can feel the darkness lifting from each of you already.'

But Martha still feels nothing, except for panic, which climbs up her throat. Is it because she had less salt in her bucket? Is it because she couldn't give Oscar her personal history beforehand? Is it because she does most things in life wrong?

Ofelia removes Martha's bucket of water, careful not to come into direct contact with it as she tips it over the side of the rocky terrain and down towards the salt flats. And Martha wants to tell her that she doesn't need to worry, that the blackness of her soul is still within her, and not hovering at the bottom of the bucket like a sediment. What a waste of water, when they probably don't have much in the first place. No, Martha's blackness is still within, she's sure of it, solid as a rock.

Finn is beside Martha now, standing awkwardly over her as she continues to towel her feet, meticulous with her actions, never once looking up at him. The other couples in the group are embracing, whispering words of love and encouragement, but not Finn and Martha. Finally, she begins to put her socks back on, reach for her shoes, aware of him watching her.

'So,' he says. 'That was new . . . '

She bites down on her lip and looks up. She goes to say something but changes her mind. She nods instead, tries to remain calm, gets to her feet.

'Martha, it's okay, you know . . . if you didn't . . . '

'Did you feel anything?'

He shrugs, nonchalant. 'I mean . . . it was relaxing enough,' he says. 'But you know I don't buy into all the *negative energy* stuff.' He stops, really seems to take her in – perhaps he suspects that she needs more from him right now, a reassurance of sorts, but she knows better than to expect it. Except then, to her astonishment, Finn reaches forward and pulls her closer to him, wrapping his arms around her. It is so rare for him to show her any form of affection like this, especially in public, that she stands stock-still within his grip, conflicted in her emotions.

They follow the others back into the circular room, where the large salt dining table has been set. Behind them, darkness is descending quickly. They sit down at the table next to each other in chairs also made from salt, Oscar at the head. The lighting is dull, as though an energy-saving bulb has just been turned on, but it doesn't appear to adjust in brightness as the minutes pass, and it is difficult to see what is on all the various plates and bowls Ofelia is placing down in front of them.

Without asking, Barb is making up a plate of food for Rick, everything in separate little dollops for his consumption. She ladles some tofu stew into a bowl, which must be hot in her hands because she plonks it down in front of Rick with a bump, some of the liquid spilling over on to the plastic-textured tablecloth that covers the surface. And Martha thinks that if it were not for the tablecloth, surely the broth-like stew would erode the salt-carved table, bore holes into its surface.

When Ofelia finally finishes bringing out the food, she bows her head slightly, hat remaining in place, and both she and Elbert retreat into the kitchen.

'Are they not joining us?' Barb asks.

Oscar shakes his head. 'They like to eat afterwards.'

Martha fills her bowl with stew, steam rising from the surface, aware of Finn waiting and watching. Light conversation is happening around her but she's struggling to engage. She takes a sip of water from a glass that doesn't look especially clean before taking a spoonful of stew. It's tasty, the broth holding more substance than she was expecting – chunks of tofu, silken and soft, practically disintegrate in her mouth, and she's grateful, knows Finn will manage this. She takes another spoonful, finally tuning in to the conversation across the table, an agreement about how delicious the food is, and she nods, really meaning it.

'How did everyone find the salt bucket experience?' Oscar asks.

She casts a glance around the table, sees collective nodding, works hard to join in, to hide any seeds of doubt, needing, more than anything, to convince herself.

'Well, I, for one, feel better prepared,' Barb says. 'For the journey ahead, I mean.'

Oscar nods. 'We find it really does help to elevate participants in the direction of the light – readies them for what will be an intense few days.'

'Does it always work?' Finn asks, reaching forward to ladle some broth and a few pieces of tofu into his bowl.

Martha's breath catches in her mouth.

Oscar observes Finn. 'I find that if a person fully gives themselves to the process, really allows their mind to relax, then yes, there are always benefits.'

A silence hangs in the air and Martha feels at risk of crying.

'How long have you been here, Oscar?' Rick asks, his American accent seeming particularly strong in this moment.

Oscar appears to think about this, dipping a piece of bread into something that resembles hummus. 'I came to Bolivia on a pilgrimage over eighteen years ago and never left. It is my home now.'

'But this . . . ' Finn asks, nodding at their surroundings. 'How did you come to acquire this?'

'I've been lucky,' Oscar replies, clipped. 'Blessed.'

There is silence.

Martha glances across the table and catches Hannah whispering something to Zoe that only they can hear.

'I don't think I've ever visited a landlocked country before,' Barb says.

'Yes, you have,' Rick replies.

'Have I?'

Rick shrugs. 'I'm sure you have.'

Oscar nods, a dribble of stew on his beard, a sombre expression settling on his face. 'We in Bolivia have not had good luck with those we place in positions of power.' He pauses. 'It is said that in 1869

Bolivia's dictator Mariano Melgarejo gave Brazil a huge chunk of the country's land in return for a majestic white horse.'

'What, really?' Hannah says, pulling on a dark curl of hair that hangs over her eye.

He nods. 'He drew the shape of a horseshoe on a map to illustrate what land he was willing to hand over.'

'That must have been some horse,' Rick says.

'And then in 1884 Bolivia lost nearly 120,000 square kilometres of land to Chile because of conflict, including its coastline. This is why we are now landlocked.'

'Am I right in thinking that Bolivia still has its navy, though?' Rick says.

Oscar nods again, growing animated, scooping more hummus with bread. 'Many continue to exploit this land. We are losing more, every day, inch by inch. Now it is the lithium mines, large foreign companies coming in and taking everything, at real threat of ruining our sacred land.'

Silence fills the room again, nothing but the noise of people swallowing. Martha looks at Finn. She waits for a reaction but he's refusing to engage.

'We *both* work in oil and gas,' she says, spluttering the words, confessional.

A chuckle escapes from Rick's mouth. 'And how's that working out for you these days?'

Finn shrugs. 'It is what it is.'

'What is it you do?' Rick presses.

'I pilot remote operating vehicles,' Finn says, 'for integrity inspections . . .'

'Oh,' Rick says. 'Well, you're not directly linked to drilling, then.'

'But,' Zoe says, leaning forward, 'your job is to help prolong the lifespan of an oil rig, right?'

Finn straightens, defensive. 'If it makes you feel better, we're in the end-days on my platform. It'll be decommissioned soon . . .'

'What's that like, then?' Zoe asks. 'Feeling like it's the end of days . . . ?'

'It's what you'd imagine,' he replies.

'And afterwards?' Hannah presses. 'What comes afterwards?'

'Renewables, of course . . . ' Finn replies, almost smiling. 'But we can't have renewables without lithium.'

Oscar snorts, placing his cutlery down on the table. 'Elbert,' he says, pointing towards the kitchen. 'His son is working at the big lithium mine because the money is so good. It is breaking Elbert's heart. Already, our land, our water, our resources, everything is compromised. And you say it is in the name of renewables . . . In the end, it is all for greed.'

Finn shrugs, swallowing his first mouthful of stew. Martha takes another sip of her water, feels the need to busy her hands.

'And what is it you do?' Finn asks, addressing Rick.

'Oh, I'm long retired now.'

'Well, what did you do before?'

Rick nods, seems to smile to himself. Martha is already trying to guess. He has the look of a doctor, but she doubts a doctor of modern medicine would come here.

'Investment,' he says. 'But it's not a career that ages you well,' he adds, laughing, as though making a joke.

'So, where are you all planning on going after being here?' Barb says, her voice attempting to lighten the mood.

'We're going to cross the border into Chile,' Hannah says.

'Argentina . . . ' Martha says, her voice barely a whisper.

Rick pats his wife's arm, as if needing reassurance. 'We'll be heading home to San Diego. But we've come from Argentina. Can't recommend it enough. Glorious place. We saw so much:

Iguazu Falls, BA, El Calafate, Puerto Madryn. The flights are so cheap.'

'We won't be taking any domestic flights,' Martha says. 'We're polluting enough as it is . . . '

Rick laughs. 'You'll spend your life on buses, then.'

Oscar clears his throat. 'We suggest that you focus on the present while you're here and not contemplate the future too much.'

'Of course,' Barb says. 'I apologise for asking.'

'Not at all,' Oscar replies, offering his widest smile. 'Not at all.'

10

They are led along a corridor to the sleeping quarters, Finn running his fingers along the salt of the walls as he moves, little bumps under his clipped fingernails, the thumbnail catching on a jagged edge. He brings his thumb to his mouth and tears off the strip of nail, letting it fall to the ground and mix in with the salt under his feet, unsettled now by the idea that something of him will be here forever. The conversation at dinner is playing over in his mind: his agitation, the judgement of others, all of it bubbling away under the surface. He's never been very good at letting things pass over him, at moving on easily, at not holding grudges, but he can feel Martha's eyes on him, can see the knots in her body, the tightness of her posture, the panic in her mind. He attempts to let go, vows to try harder, doesn't think he can bear the guilt of not allowing her this one opportunity to thrive.

Oscar forces open the door to a large salt-built dormitory with eight single-sized beds, their luggage heaped together on the floor. The space is a perfect square, the height of the ceiling seeming to match the width of the walls, one large window splitting the room in half. It makes Finn think of sugar cubes, another substance to be dissolved.

In the absence of sunlight, the space is freezing.

'You can choose a bed and make yourselves comfortable—' Oscar says.

'Sorry . . . ' Rick interrupts. 'I was under the assumption that we would have our own private rooms.'

Oscar smiles. 'We believe in a shared environment. This, as you can see, is a small facility. Rustic but nurturing, and we find that each person gets more from the experience of being together.' He spreads his arms out, as if taking in his disciples. 'Considering our location within the salt flats, naturally our infrastructure is basic and with limited space, but soon you will begin to see the benefits of living a simpler life, the conveniences of the modern world stripped away.'

The expression on Rick's face is one of alarm. 'What about snoring?' he says, the words practically falling from his mouth. 'I'm known to snore.'

And Finn understands this, imagines falling into a half-baked stupor and these strangers being disturbed by him. The idea of being laughed at, behind his back, his body deceiving him and he having no control over any of it.

'We take each of us as we are,' Oscar replies. 'And I'm not sure if you're aware, but salt therapy is known to help with snoring.'

'There are no other rooms?' Barb presses. 'We are much older than everyone else.'

Oscar shakes his head, offers a smile that is wrapped in an apology. 'As I said, our facilities are limited and the staff, including myself, need a separate place to sleep.' He clears his throat, a line being drawn. 'Each bed is the same,' he says, pointing to them. 'No bed is better than another. Just like people.'

'There's no curtain on the window . . . ' Martha says.

Oscar nods. 'The sun will guide you.'

Finn is too slow, glancing around as others begin to claim beds, flopping on to mattresses positioned on top of solid salt-blocked bedframes. Zoe and Hannah are quick to snatch the two beds on the left, furthest away from the door, with Rick and Barb now taking the same two on the right, leaving Martha and Finn with either of the sets of beds closest to the door. Martha makes for the free bed on the left side next to Zoe and Hannah, launching herself at the mattress as if she were at risk of losing it to someone else. Finn takes the bed next to her, saying nothing, exasperated further by the mattress's sogginess. It makes him think of biting into a sponge. There is only one pillow, and it is flat like a pancake. He can't believe how much he paid for them to come here.

'One more rule . . . ' Oscar says. 'We also ask you to abstain from sexual activity while you are here.' He lets a laugh escape from somewhere down in his throat. 'Hopefully that won't be a problem, considering the shared environment.' He nods to himself, as if working through a checklist of information. 'Oh, also, don't be alarmed if the power goes out abruptly. Because of our location the power supply can be erratic, particularly at night. We have provided each of you with a handheld battery-operated torch.' He points to one resting on the ground next to Finn's feet.

'How is this place powered?' Finn asks.

'A mixture of generators, and solar and hydraulic pumps,' Oscar says, shrugging. 'It is never easy, attempting to exist somewhere so remote.'

And Finn understands this, accepts that people are constantly trying to survive in places that don't want them.

'Okay, I shall let you all get some rest now,' Oscar says, before departing.

Finn presses his palms further into his mattress, straightening his back. There is nothing appealing about this room; it will be used as a space for the necessity of sleep and nothing more. He reaches for his medicine in his small backpack, is aware of the noise of the click-lock cap, of Zoe watching as he takes another dose. She is gripping her torch, clicking the button on and off again, repeatedly, a warning signal directed to the ceiling.

He gets up and stands awkwardly, feet too far apart in the salt, staring at the heap of bags, reluctant for some reason to bend and retrieve his luggage. He's not usually overwhelmed by groups, loves being around people, much more than Martha, but he feels caught off guard here, judged.

Hannah manoeuvres round him to get to her backpack. A bright orange compact tent and sleeping bag are strapped to the top. As she pulls at the weight of it, she narrows her eyes, really seeming to take him in. He had done life modelling in his first few years of university, before Martha, and he feels as though he's posing once again and being studied. He wonders where all the drawings of his body are now, whether they've been discarded or are in some loft, to be discovered years from now. A small part of him hopes that one is framed somewhere, hanging on a wall.

He finally lifts his backpack to his bed and unzips it. He's not even sure what he wants out of it. He's aware that there's no lock to the dorm and if someone were to come in he would be the closest point of contact. He thinks of a holiday to Mallorca they took years ago, of this strange noise that he heard through the night while Martha slept soundly, of being convinced that someone had entered through the patio of their ground floor apartment, his heart beating, time slowing, his eyes on the handle of the door, fully expecting it to be opened. He had spent so long deciding on a strategy: whether to look for a weapon, wake Martha, or pretend to be completely asleep. He'd reasoned that perhaps the intruder was simply there to take possessions and nothing more, and to disturb them was to provoke. But really it was because he was scared, too cowardly to act in a moment of fight or flight. No one did enter in the end, and in the morning their living space was as they had left it the night before, everything untouched.

He takes everyone in, these strangers with whom he is now sharing a room. Martha is reaching into her backpack, removing an extra pair of socks and a jumper. Barb is already getting under the covers, pulling an eye mask down, wishing them all a good night. Hannah clears her bed of possessions and in the process drops her toothbrush on to the salty floor, swearing under her breath, attempting to wipe the bristles. The thought of her putting that toothbrush in her mouth now makes Finn wince.

He grabs his washbag, making for the toilet, but the bathroom outside the dorm is occupied. Finn carries on back to the circular room, where Ofelia is clearing the dinner plates away. She appears startled by his presence, a knife falling to the floor.

'*Baño?*' he asks, and she nods, pointing. '*Gracias*.'

The bathroom is basic: a toilet without a seat, a shower cubicle in a frame that is barely holding together and a small sink. He takes a piss, willing his bladder to empty completely; he has no desire to get up in the night. The toilet barely flushes, nothing but a half-hearted attempt. By the sink there is a holder with a bar of soap resting in it, ridges running along the soap, threatening to split, and as he stares at it he has a strong suspicion that everything here has the potential to split open. He runs the tap, but the pressure is weak, the water discoloured. He brushes his teeth, spitting toothpaste on to the porcelain, wiping his mouth with his hand, untrusting of the towel that hangs on a hook. He looks up. There is no mirror.

He walks with urgency, looping the circular room, poking his head into the other bathroom that was occupied only moments before – no mirror in there either – before finally returning to the dorm room. He sits on his bed, takes his shoes off, hesitant, pulls back his duvet, mouths, 'Goodnight,' to Martha. The lights go out then, plunging the space into total darkness. Finn can still hear Rick rooting about for something in his suitcase, shuffling, salt crunching underfoot.

Finn settles, clutching the duvet to himself, his back to the door, but decides that that might be a bad idea. He turns the other way, aware that he is now facing the door but unable to make out its shape, the darkness feeling complete. And it is so chillingly cold that the duvet is up at his nose. Time passes and he becomes aware of someone's relaxed breath, a gentle thrum of rhythm. He's not slept in a room like this since he was in hospital; six beds to a ward, everyone dying. The nurses would pull the curtains around each bed, and despite the noise of others Finn found it to be cocoon-like, an odd comfort of sorts. He remembers Martha coming to visit him, recalls being aware of her approach as she spoke to the nurses at their station, and his instinct to hide, to allow the curtain to work its magic and protect him from her visit.

Rick is snoring, a deep gurgle from his throat, and Finn knows this will continue all night, that this is the way of things. He rubs at his face, the stubble rough, his cheeks feeling gaunt. He thinks about the fact that there are no mirrors, anywhere, and he lets an irrational worry consume him – that he will forget who he is.

Thursday

11

Martha stares at the eggs on her plate that she did not ask for, fried with runny yolks. There is a slice of toast too, and some chopped-up avocado on the side. The table around her is full, everyone from the dorm present, the sun shining into the circular salt room, Oscar once again at the head of the table. Yet a fog fills her mind, everything blurry; she is not sure if she has slept, is unnerved by how quickly the concept of time has been taken from her. It must be early, she thinks, but she has no way of gauging specifics, only that she was awake when the sun began to creep into their room.

While others snored around her, she spent most of the night thinking about the salt bucket ceremony, going over each detail of her failure in depth, as if by dissecting it she could alter the outcome. This morning she envies the well-rested, believes this too is a failing within her – what a skill it must be to fall asleep so quickly – to be able to compartmentalise your worries and abandon them for the time being.

Oscar sips on his tea, while Elbert appears busy outside on the patio, and Ofelia continues to come and go from the kitchen, the same hat with tassel on her head from the previous day, unmoving. Even as she bends to place a smoothie down in front of Finn, it does not shift, and Martha wants to know what the trick is – how *does* she keep it in position?

She takes a sip of her orange juice, freshly squeezed, delicious. She pops one of her egg's runny yolks with her fork and it feels cathartic, a sense of release.

Next to her, Finn unscrews the click-lock cap of his medicine. He takes a gulp, and she stares at his throat, the bulge of his Adam's apple as it all goes down.

She looks down at her plate to see the split egg yolk is already congealing.

'We will begin our one-to-one sessions once everyone has finished their breakfast,' Oscar says. 'In no particular order . . . I thought I'd start with Barb, if that's okay?'

Barb looks up at him, startled.

'Then Martha . . . '

'How long do they take?' Barb asks.

Oscar offers her his warmest smile. 'It will last for as long or as short a time as you need it to. This is an opportunity for me to begin to truly understand each of you before we commence our first salt ceremony at dusk tonight.' He takes another sip of his tea. 'A time for you to be honest with me about your expectations, and what you hope to gain from being here.'

There is nodding, murmuring of yes.

'And then, after Martha's session, I'm thinking Hannah, Finn, Zoe and finally Rick. Does that work for everyone?'

Martha nods, her whole body moving with it, a spill of orange juice landing on her jumper. 'How will we know when it's our time to come?' she asks.

'Well, when each of you is finished, I will ask that you inform the next person in turn. It's quite simple really.'

'Okay,' Martha says, feeling chastised, an anxiousness settling on her face for somehow getting it wrong again. 'Of course.'

'Martha, none of this is a test. There are no wrong answers here.' Oscar wipes at his mouth, missing a string of something in his beard. 'Great, well, Barb, I'm ready when you are.'

Barb is crunching on a piece of toast, but she stands, almost instantly.

'Follow me to my office,' he says, getting to his feet too. 'The rest of you are free to enjoy your time until you are called. The hot springs are particularly lovely in the morning.'

Martha watches Oscar and Barb depart, is grateful not to be going first, thinks of all those corporate awaydays where she had to stand in a circle and tell the group something random about herself, the first person always the guinea pig for gauging what was appropriate to share.

'Are you okay?' Finn asks.

'Just tired,' she whispers, barely holding herself together.

He reaches under the table and squeezes her knee. Usually she is desperate for his touch, but today it offers her little comfort. She picks at some avocado on her plate, mashing it with her fork.

'You could go back to bed if you wanted . . . ' he says.

She shakes her head. 'No, I don't know how long he'll be with Barb. I'll not be able to relax. I'll just wait here,' she says.

But she's aware of the others departing the table, of Ofelia attempting to tidy up after them all, stacking dirty plates in her arms.

'Come outside with me,' Finn says. 'Let's get our bearings.'

'But what if they're looking for me?'

'We won't be long,' he says, 'I promise.'

She stares at him, suspicious of his behaviour, of his kindness.

Finn opens the patio door and waits for Martha to go first, stepping on to the same broken slabs from the night before, the plastic chairs folded away, no trace of the salt buckets. The patio space feels vast now that it is empty of people and to their right is a hammock strung up between two poles, the fabric turned in on itself. Martha doesn't remember seeing it last night. Ahead, the salt spans endlessly in all directions, and as she comes closer to the edge of the patio she sees that there is a rough trodden path making its way steeply down on to the flats below.

Finn starts down the path, stopping halfway to inspect a huge cactus, glancing up towards Martha. Very carefully, he reaches out and touches the cactus, instantly retreating, letting out a yelp.

'Obviously that was going to happen,' Martha says, looking down at him from the patio area, one hand now on her hip, the other shielding her eyes from the sun.

He shrugs, a muted laugh escaping. 'I just wanted to know.'

'And?' she says.

'It's fucking sharp. Feel it for yourself.'

'You're okay.'

Finn begins to make his way back up, stopping beside her to take in the salt's expanse once again.

'It's achingly beautiful . . . ' she says. 'It's almost too much.'

'Sometimes I think the most beautiful things in the world shouldn't be seen. Like, there's a reason so many people die climbing Everest.'

She's still shielding her eyes from the sun. 'Finn . . . '

'Yeah?'

'What if I can't get better? What if . . . '

He hesitates, turns to look at her. 'You're going to be okay,' he says.

'But you don't believe in this place. So how can you be so sure?'

'I'm trying, Martha, but it's not me who needs to be convinced.' He pulls her in for a hug, his arms hanging loosely around her. 'Anything can happen,' he whispers. 'You know that as much as me.'

She bites down on her lip, trying her best not to cry.

'You've always carried more worries than everyone else,' he says, 'the weight of the world. And it's too heavy for just you.'

'But I felt nothing. Last night, during the salt buckets.'

'Put the salt bucket behind you,' he says. 'Draw a line under it.'

He pulls away from her and continues his tour of the property. Martha follows. They turn a sharp corner to find a stretch of yard space. Ahead sits a large dome-like structure made of wooden branches, resembling a den, with a fire pit facing its entrance, and to their left a washing line is strung up, empty except for pegs. Martha imagines clothes drying out on this line, salt embedding itself into the fabric, an irritation waiting to happen on her bare skin. And then, tucked away in the shadiest of spots, they see it – a llama, with beautifully coloured pink ribbons tied around its ears and neck, hunkered down, a rope tethering it to a hook.

The llama appears not to be distressed by their presence and Martha comes closer, hesitating before putting her hand on the llama's mane.

'How did it get here?' she asks.

Finn shrugs. 'I don't know . . . '

'But why?'

The animal barely moves. Its coat is coarse, cream and grey in colour.

'She has kind eyes,' Martha says.

'How do you know it's a she?' Finn asks.

Ofelia comes out of a back door and jumps in surprise, startled to see them crouched down beside the llama. She nods at them, offers a smile, and bends to tip a plate of scraps and vegetable peelings into a bowl for the animal.

Feeling a sense of intrusion, Martha makes to leave, offering Ofelia her most generous smile. They carry on, taking another turn, finding another slope, a more favourable gradient than the path towards the salt flats. And at the bottom they can see the thermal salt spring Oscar has mentioned, steam rising from its surface. In keeping with the rest of the centre, it is basic – a makeshift pool with half-formed edges, an attempt to formalise its natural existence. And it's all so bizarre, Martha thinks, that this is here, as if waiting for them. She doesn't understand how natural thermal pools work but she accepts them, as any tourist accepts an attraction. It is not for her to work out the natural wonders of this world.

She walks towards it, slowly, the ground uneven under her feet.

'Do you want to go in?' Finn asks.

She shakes her head, bending now to feel the temperature of the water with her fingers; its colour is murky and grey. 'Finn . . . if I get better . . . we can start again, can't we?'

He's standing close behind her. 'We don't need to talk about starting again,' he says. 'I hate when people say that, as if it's healthy to wipe everything away.'

She takes a breath, the warmth of the water alluring. 'I just mean, we could move forward, properly . . . Maybe then we could start a family, you know . . . I am turning forty next year.'

He stops. 'You said you didn't want one. You said the idea of bringing a child into this world terrifies you.'

'Isn't that why I'm here, to worry less?' She pauses. 'And you want one, so . . . '

Finn bites down on his thumb, and she waits. She wants to please him, but still wonders if it is selfish to bring a child into this world, simply because the person you love wants it? She had once been desperate to have a child too, soon after they married, before her climate anxiety eclipsed everything else, but it had been he who'd been reluctant, he who had told her he wasn't ready.

'What is it Oscar says?' Finn finally says. 'That it's best to focus only on the present for now.'

She laughs. It's sad and defeated, and she brings her hand out of the water, shaking the drops away. 'You listen to everything, don't you? Even if you don't buy into the words.'

'Martha, one step at a time, okay . . . ? That's all I'm saying.'

She nods, is thinking now of the holiday they took to Majorca years ago, checking into their suite to find a baby's cot made up next to their king-size bed. A sheet had been carefully, almost lovingly tucked into the small mattress, a little blanket with a panda on it resting over the edge of the frame. And it had felt as though she was being taunted, a horrible, sadistic prank being played on her, reflecting the greatest debate of their marriage. She had cried suddenly, a real, ugly release of emotion that had shocked her. Finn had phoned reception and they had apologised for the mix-up, reassuring him that they'd come and collect the cot. But no one ever did come and then they just began to move around it, eventually discarding their dirty laundry into it like a basket, a constant reminder of the unspoken.

'Will you try embracing this experience, for me?' she says.

'I'll try.'

Behind her she can hear other voices, Zoe and Hannah approaching. They are wearing bikinis and making their way down towards the pool. They're so young and beautiful, and Martha longs to be in her twenties again, rose-tinted nostalgia for when her worries were so irrelevant in the grand scheme of things. She wants to ask these women how they cope in the face of the climate emergency, how they plan for the future, but she doesn't. Instead, she makes room for them as they approach the water.

'Are you not going in?' Hannah asks.

Martha shakes her head. 'No, I'll head back and wait for my session with Oscar.'

'I'll wait for you,' Finn says.

'No, don't,' she replies. 'Who knows how long this will all take. Go in. It's lovely and warm.'

12

Finn returns to the dorm room and finds his swimming shorts in his backpack. He sits on his bed and covers himself with the duvet, doing his best to remove his trousers and boxers without exposing any part of himself, despite the room being empty of other people. Afterwards, he places his bare feet on the ground, the salt sharp and uncomfortable underfoot, and wishes he had brought flip-flops.

The room is a mess, people's possessions spread across the space, and he feels a lack of control. He likes things to be in their place. He makes his bed, the cheap synthetic duvet in his hands repulsive. He realises he's shivering, goosebumps travelling up his arms, hair standing on end. He looks over his shoulder, checking that he can hear no one coming, before approaching Hannah's bed, peering down to inspect the objects she has left out: a scarf, some glasses, dental floss, a typed-out manuscript with the title *Invasive Species,* someone else's name on the cover sheet. He flicks open the first page, glancing at the words without actually reading them, closing it over again. Zoe's bed is neater – a tube of moisturiser, a hooded sweater with some sort of dance motif sprawled across the front. He lifts the tube of cream and opens it, squirting a little on to his hands, rubbing it gently into his palms. When he brings his hand to his nose, the scent is nice, eucalyptus perhaps.

There is a clatter behind him, out in the corridor, and he drops the cream on to the bed, the scent still strong on his hands as he darts away.

He departs, making his way out through the patio doors, sloping his way back down towards the makeshift edge built around the thermal spring's shape, amazed by its mere existence. He dips his toe into the water, tests its temperature; steam is floating from its surface and it's odd to him that humans are so trusting of this – what's to stop the temperature from rising, what's really keeping them from boiling? He thinks of the crude oil he helps bring up from beneath the seabed, about the climate and the changing temperatures, everything continually rising.

Hannah and Zoe are in the middle of the pool, crouched, only their heads and necks exposed, and they watch as Finn sits on the edge, his legs dangling down in the water. He finds that he's once again uncomfortable under their gaze, wonders what it is about them that he's struggling with when he's usually so at ease in other people's company. And as if they can read his mind, sense his awkwardness, a sniggering laugh is exchanged between them.

They straighten, move through the water with ease, coming to rest on a ledge on the opposite side. Finally, Finn pushes himself off the edge, the murky water coming mid-way up his chest. He wades cautiously, untrusting of its depth, of what is even under his feet. He's buoyant, practically floating from the salt content. He stretches out, his body horizontal, and thinks about how as a kid his favourite thing to do in a pool was to pretend to be dead, suspended by the water, face down, arms sprawled, holding his breath for as long as possible. But now, here, he can't bear to put his face in this water, worries the salt will ruin his eyes.

He straightens, aware of Zoe and Hannah watching him again. He moves further across the water, towards them, settling near one end where it is shallower and possible to sit. A few metres away, the women are speaking in whispered tones, and he has the strong suspicion that they are talking about him. Do they continue to judge him? He assumes so, feels old in their presence, worries about saying something flippant that they might take offence at. When he casts a look one way there is the incline of the path back up towards the Salt Centre, a few large cacti, and the other way, nothing but the salt flats. He closes one eye, opens it and closes the other. He wonders if this is where the flat-Earth movement started. It isn't possible to see any curvature of the Earth here, and this is alarming, untethering, everything he has always believed feeling as though it is in jeopardy. He glances upwards then to the sky, sees only blue. He's been looking at the sky ever since arriving in Uyuni, paranoid that the rain will arrive earlier than predicted, that it will catch him off guard.

'Is something wrong?' Hannah asks, the ring of her septum piercing glinting in the sun.

He looks at them. 'I don't think so.'

They sit in silence, Finn frantically thinking of something appropriate to say to them, something that will get them on side. He remembers Martha, buoyant as they drove towards the Salt Centre, talking to Hannah about their jobs, about living in London.

'How long are you guys away for?' he asks.

Zoe's head is tipped back, blonde hair soaking in the murky water.

'We're not sure yet,' Hannah says.

'Did I hear you say that you're an editor?'

'Script editor. For film and television. I basically interrogate scripts with writers . . . help them get the best story they can, you know?'

'That's really interesting,' he replies.

'Yeah, it can be.'

'And how did you get into that?'

'I went to film school.'

He laughs, a ripple of water moving in front of his mouth. 'Of course,' he says. 'It would never have occurred to me to do something so creative when I was at school or uni.'

'No?'

He shakes his head. 'Where I grew up, people don't do things like that . . . '

'What do they do?' Hannah asks, almost teasing.

'Conventional stuff, I guess.' He shrugs.

'Well, no job needs to be for life,' Hannah replies, smirking.

Finn laughs. 'I wish it was as easy as that.'

Zoe straightens, her hair no longer submerged, a grey complexion present once again.

'And you dance . . . ' Finn says.

She nods. 'Well, not at the moment.'

'She will again,' Hannah says, as if almost forcing the role on to her.

'Taking some time out,' Zoe replies with little emotion to her voice.

'Injury?' Finn says.

She stops, looks at Hannah, as though needing reassurance. 'Something like that.'

He nods and the women look at each other again, an unspoken language being transferred between them.

'How is your throat today?' Hannah asks.

'Shit,' he replies. 'How's your altitude sickness?' he adds, addressing Zoe.

She tries to laugh. 'Shit,' she says.

They can see Elbert coming down the path towards the pool, carrying a broom. He comes to a stop at the edge, inspecting them and the water, before bending and dipping his hand into the water, nodding, satisfied. When he straightens, he gives them a thumbs-up and they all collectively return the gesture. Elbert reaches into his pocket then, removing his little pouch of coca leaves, forcing some of the leaves into his cheek.

'I don't think I've ever seen him not chewing on those leaves,' Hannah says.

'Do you want to try it?' Finn asks. 'See if it's any better than the tea they served us.'

Hannah looks from Finn to Zoe. 'It is meant to help, Zo . . . '

Zoe nods. 'If he'll let us.'

Finn wades towards Elbert, wonders then if the leaves might also soothe his oesophagus and stave off his unbearable hunger. 'Señor Elbert . . . ' he says, looking up at him and offering a wide smile. '*Coca, por favor*,' he asks, pointing to his own cheek.

Elbert understands. He pulls the bag out once again, offering some to Finn, Hannah and Zoe following. He instructs them in Spanish, encouragingly, and they put some of the leaves into their mouths. Finn experiences an instant buzz, perhaps more so because of his empty stomach – an earthy taste, a gathering of saliva, like the strangest flavour of chewing gum.

'*Gracias*,' Finn says, and Hannah and Zoe copy him. Elbert nods, smiling obligingly before beginning to sweep the path.

They return to their previous positions, and settle in, Finn mulching away on the coca leaves, grateful to Ebert for his generosity as a mild but pleasant numbing sensation takes over. 'What do you think?' he says, turning to Hannah and Zoe.

Zoe shrugs. 'Time will tell, I suppose.'

'How did you find the salt bucket exercise last night?' Hannah asks.

He exhales, can't seem to stop looking at the ring dangling from her septum, wonders if she's ever tugged on it, like a farmer with his bull. 'I'm not sure . . . ' he says, feeling the need to hold his tongue despite beginning to relax in their company.

'You don't believe . . . ' Hannah presses.

Finn goes to speak but a little of the salty water enters his mouth. He spits it out, flustered, the sting of its taste mixing in with the coca leaves. 'I came for my wife,' he finally says.

'You have nothing to be healed from?' Zoe asks.

He hesitates. 'Not that I'm aware of.'

The women look at each other, and a sensation of being mocked returns to him.

'What about you both?' he asks, still trying to remove the salty taste from his mouth. 'What do you need healing from?'

They appear taken aback by his question, shifting in the water, and he understands that he's crossed a line, that he's lost the thread of what's appropriate.

'I'm sorry,' he says, shaking his head, feeling adrift. He can usually morph like a chameleon into the shape others want him to be, is skilled in finding a common ground, but right now he's drowning. 'Being here, it's overwhelming . . . ' he says. 'Clearly I'm struggling a bit.'

'It's okay,' Hannah says, moving her hands through the water, rubbing her arms then as she inspects her skin. 'Salt is a healer . . . It can heal so many things, even the smallest of ailments, did you know that?'

He shrugs.

'Bad skin, respiratory problems, allergies . . . Arthritis, mental health, long Covid.' She pauses. 'So, it can't hurt, being here, can it?'

He dips his chin back into the water. 'I suppose not,' he says.

Zoe places a kiss on Hannah's shoulder. The gesture is so unprompted and loving that he finds himself startled by it. They behave as though showing emotion were an easy thing to do.

'How long have you been together?' he asks, his tone gentle, friendly.

They smile at each other before Hannah says, 'Two years.'

'How'd you meet?'

'Online,' Zoe says.

He smiles. 'Cool.' He's never done online dating, meeting Martha too early for it to be the norm. But it intrigues him, the experiment and thrill of it. He can't really remember what it must be like to date, imagines it could be exhausting, like learning to read and write again, the energy it must deplete.

'What about you and Martha?'

He's lost track of the conversation, and it shows on his face.

'How long have you been together?' Hannah presses.

Finn tries to tally up the years in his head. 'I think we've been together for seventeen, no, eighteen years, married for eleven.' He pauses. 'We met when we were twenty-one, at university.'

'Wow,' Hannah says. 'That is . . . impressive.'

'What's it like to be with the same person for so long?' Zoe asks.

He exhales through his nostrils, the force causing little ripples across the water. 'Hm, well—' he begins, almost laughing. But the conversation is interrupted by Rick, stepping precariously down towards the pool, asking them if it's too hot.

'It's nice,' Finn replies.

They watch Rick as he slides in and wades towards them. He stops next to Finn, a tense smile settling on his face. 'Rustic, isn't it?' he says.

'Not what you were expecting?' Finn asks.

Rick shrugs. 'Well, I suppose I thought, for the price, there would be a touch more luxury, you know?' He laughs, his large shoulders disturbing the water. 'We did this safari in South Africa last year,' he says, 'and it was also in the middle of nowhere, but those people know how to make you feel special, you know?'

Hannah catches Finn's eye, smiles. 'We're just exchanging relationship longevities,' she says.

'Is that so?' Rick replies, coughing through his words.

'Finn here is beating us by a long shot with eighteen years, but I reckon you can do better than that,' she says.

'Oh, no, me and Barb – we're practically newlyweds. We were married to other people before we got together.'

'Divorce?' Hannah says.

Rick shakes his head once again. 'Death, unfortunately. Our spouses died within a year of each other. Robert, Barb's first husband, and I, we worked together. We all used to be friends.'

13

Martha sits, looking around Oscar's office: a desk littered with paper, crooked shelves with folders threatening to overflow, generic faded pictures of the salt flats hanging on the walls. The cluttered space is completely at odds with the sparseness of the rest of the Salt Centre, and she has a sense of walking into another time, another place, far from where she physically is. There is a large chair behind the desk and another smaller chair facing it, and when Oscar asks her to sit she feels that she is being spoken to by a teacher, is about to be told off for inappropriate behaviour.

Oscar eases himself down into his chair and, once settled, grips a strand of his beard with his fingers, pulling the wiry hair straight. 'So,' he says, smiling at her. 'How have you been settling in?'

Martha nods. 'Good.'

He tilts his head to one side, really seems to ponder her. 'My dear,' he says, 'I understand. Truly I do.'

Martha swallows, a swell of emotion surfacing, and rubs away a tear that moments ago wasn't there. He must be able to sense that she needs this more than everyone else, that her life depends on it.

'How did you find the salt bucket exercise?' he asks, a warmth to his voice.

The tears are still coming, and she rubs at them with her sleeve, embarrassed. She shakes her head, defeated.

'It's okay,' he says. 'It's important to be honest with me so I can fully understand your needs.' He pauses, leans back. 'I think I'm starting to understand but do you want to tell me a little, in your own words, about why you felt compelled to come here.'

She gathers her breath in a deep inhalation, and raises her hands, sweeping the space around her. 'It's hard to explain . . . It's everything. The world is burning, and no one really cares. And it feels like it's too late to reverse it, that we're unable to change. Our own worst enemy.' She straightens. 'I feel this hopelessness in the face of it. It's overbearing, crushing; everything feels unsurmountable.'

'What worries you most?'

She shrugs, overwhelmed by the question. 'There are tribes in the Amazon, communities completely disconnected from the modern world, and they have no idea that the rest of us have ruined everything. How will they ever understand the emergency that is unfolding?'

Oscar tilts his head, a knowing expression settling on his lips. 'I suspect that the natural world they respect and listen to *is* telling them.'

She nods, a flush spreading across her cheek at the sense of her own stupidity.

'Martha, you have no control over how Amazon tribes will adapt to climate change.'

'I think . . . I meant, in a way, I'm jealous that they're not bombarded by the world in the same way that so many of us are.' She shrugs. 'I don't know what I'm saying . . . I'm just scared. We're a civilisation ready to fall.'

'When did these concerns, in their extreme sense, begin? Have you always been worried about the climate?'

She shakes her head. 'It was gradual and then a tipping point . . . like everything.'

'And no previous trauma in your life to compound these feelings of despair?'

She shakes her head. 'Nothing terrible has ever happened to me personally. I've seen others suffer, in my periphery – I can imagine very vividly the potential for suffering – but it's not a lived experience.'

Oscar is quiet for a moment. 'Do you ever consider that what you are feeling is grief?'

She shrugs. 'I'm not sure I've ever experienced proper grief. There has been the terrifying fear of losing someone, but I've never had to really live through it. Grandparents have died, of course, but that's the natural order of things, isn't it?'

'Grieving is not simply about the loss of people . . . I wonder if you are beginning to grieve for our planet, for the loss that has already taken place, the loss of its future.'

'So you understand?'

'The climate we have today is better than the climate we will have tomorrow, and so forth . . . ' he replies. 'I think most people agree with that.'

'So, what, we just accept it?'

'I think it's about control. About accepting that so much of this is outside of our control . . . '

'But it's the injustice . . . All the billionaires, all the greed . . . They could do something if they wanted to.'

'It doesn't matter about them,' he says. 'You can't control their actions.'

She nods, rubbing another tear away. 'What I want is to not feel like this any more. I'm tired of this sick sensation that I carry. It robs me of joy in every moment, everything tainted by this feeling of existential fear. It's as though I'm waiting for my own death.'

'What other coping strategies have you tried, before coming here?'

She exhales, almost frustrated by the question. 'Antidepressants, exercise, counselling. This technique where you time yourself for thirty minutes and that's your worry window, and after that you're not allowed to let your worries enter your thoughts. But it doesn't work.'

'And those who love you, how do they treat you?'

She tries to laugh. 'The people who are still willing to keep my company don't want to talk about the environment. They want fun, and lightness, and the assumption that everything is and will be fine. They want the person I used to be, the old carefree me.' She pauses. 'And I get it. Negativity spreads like a bad smell; it seeps in, and my loved ones don't want to be dragged down by me.'

'How do you know this is how they feel?' he asks. 'Have they said this to you?'

'I can see it in their eyes, in the exchanged glances. I'm the one they talk about when they think I'm out of earshot. I'm sure my friends have a separate WhatsApp group too, that I'm not included in.'

'Perhaps people who treat you like that aren't friends . . . '

'You speak as though things are black and white. It's not that easy.' She glances around the room, exasperated. 'Why is no one else panicking about the future?' She shakes her head, filled with despair once again. 'I can't understand why there isn't fear in *everyone's* eyes. My friends who have children – I cannot contemplate how they continue to go about their day-to-day routine, school pick-ups, food shopping, swimming lessons, as if nothing is wrong.'

'You're angry, that they don't worry too . . . ?'

'I'm jealous,' she replies. 'I wish I could be that way.'

'And Finn?' Oscar asks. 'Does he understand?'

'He accepts that there's a climate emergency. He doesn't deny it. But it's complicated for him, what with his job, our jobs . . . He doesn't feel the urgency I do. He thinks that things can be salvaged, that good people and actions eventually defeat bad ones. That there is still time.'

'And clearly this is affecting your marriage . . .' Oscar says.

Martha snorts. 'That would be an understatement. As it stands, Finn tolerates me, but only because he has to, because he feels he owes it to me.'

'What do you mean, *owes*?'

'When we met, we were young, both twenty-one. I adored him, but I don't think he meant for things to get serious between us. If I'm honest, I think I enjoyed the challenge of that.'

'What happened?'

Martha is quiet for a moment. 'He got leukaemia, and we thought he was going to die.'

'So, you stayed?'

'I wanted to stay. And he never asked me to leave.'

'And now you feel he is doing the same for you?'

Martha shifts, defensiveness pricking through her bones. 'We're loyal to one another.'

'And what about the relationship you have with your parents?' Oscar presses.

'I have *a* relationship with each of them. Individually. They're no longer together.'

She thinks about her childhood briefly, always only briefly: thinks of how she would sense the mood of the room, understand instantly if something was amiss between her parents. A sinking feeling, of knowing that the air had changed. Of absorbing that feeling and carrying it with her in everything she did.

'So up until somewhat recently you feel that your life has been otherwise a success?'

Martha pauses, runs a finger over her lips, tapping them. 'I think I've been lucky, materialistically. But I . . . what is success? I don't think I've ever been particularly good at anything. I think I've just made reasonable, pragmatic, strategic choices.'

He nods, tilting his chin, seeming to contemplate her answers. 'Have you ever attempted suicide?'

She shakes her head, too quickly, too erratically. 'I've thought about it, in my biggest moments of despair. In a way that it would be more dignified than waiting to see the world crumble around me. But I can't . . . '

'What stops you, do you think?'

She narrows her eyes, feels suddenly confused, as though she has answered a question incorrectly. 'I want to live.' She pauses. 'There would be no room to change my mind or go back. And what if we do . . . ?'

'Do what?'

'What if humanity does find a way to make things okay? What if I've acted too soon?'

He smiles. 'Well, clearly you still have hope in your heart. That's a good sign.'

She looks down, her fingernails dirty, would like to feel clean.

'What is it you hope to achieve by coming here?' he asks. 'What is it you want?'

Martha sits back, feeling that surely it should be obvious to him.

'Is it peace, and acceptance of this broken world?'

She hesitates.

'Or do you simply want to care less?' he asks. 'Be oblivious once again to the world's problems?'

'I . . . '

'It's good to be specific about these things,' he says.

'I want to be told it's going to be okay,' she replies.

He nods. 'And if you can't be assured of that, then what?'

She closes her eyes, her heart feeling heavy in her chest. 'If I'm mourning then I want to get past the darkest stage. I want to move on and find – yes, peace and acceptance. More than that. I want to know that I can find moments of joy again.'

Martha opens her eyes and Oscar is smiling, as though finally she has given him a correct answer.

'We are not going to cure the world's problems here,' he says, 'but we can help build resilience in a way that allows you to still find joy in your life, in the world that surrounds you.'

Martha smiles, a tear running down her cheek.

'Martha, I believe that if you submit your whole self to this process, you will find a way to see a world that you still want to be part of. But you must believe in every stage of the journey.'

She nods.

'Try to relax and stay in each moment. I can work with you more on your breathing, too, which I think will really help. Remember, no feeling is ever constant.' He claps his hands together, rising from his seat to signal the end of their session. 'Do you think that's something you can try?'

'Yes,' she says, practically panting. 'Yes.'

14

Finn's face is flushed, his whole body overwhelmingly warm as he sits down in the chair opposite Oscar. His skin is prickling, the sensation intensifying with every second that he remains stationary. He wants to scratch and claw at his arms, thinks back to the eczema of his childhood and the weeping creases of his elbows. But he remains perfectly still, his eyes darting around the chaotic space, wondering where his phone and watch are, in what hidden drawer they sit.

He had expected to see personal artefacts from Oscar's life, pictures perhaps of family members, ornaments of symbolism, but there is nothing. And Finn acknowledges this with a strange curiosity – he knows nothing about the man that sits opposite him. He thinks then about the emails that were exchanged in the process of booking this trip, never directly with Oscar, always with a third party. Oscar was spoken of as a messiah of sorts.

'How are you feeling?' Oscar asks.

'I'm fine.' Finn nods, swallows, the jaggedness of his throat refusing to recede.

'Did you enjoy the thermal pool?'

Finn can feel his fingers digging into the crook of his arm, an attempt to simply stroke the skin and not scratch it. 'Yes,' he says.

Oscar clasps his hands together, placing them on a stack of paper, appearing peaceful and at ease in front of Finn. 'Is the Salt Centre what you expected?'

Finn looks around, as if taking it all in for the first time. 'I wasn't sure what to expect if I'm being honest,' he says, a defensiveness slipping into his voice.

'Honesty is exactly what we want,' Oscar says. 'And with this in mind, why don't you tell me more about yourself so I can build a picture of your needs and goals while here . . . '

'It is my wife who wishes to be here,' Finn says.

Oscar stares at him. 'So, you are simply supporting your wife, offering moral support?'

'I want Martha to get better.'

'This must be a huge sacrifice for you . . . ' Oscar says.

Finn swallows, the pain again jagged, and he winces in his seat, shifting his shoulders, everything uncomfortable.

'There is a darkness about you, in your aura, did you know that?' Oscar says.

Finn doesn't reply.

'Maybe,' Oscar says, 'the darkness is an imbalance in your ego.'

'My ego . . . ?'

Oscar nods. 'Freud's theory of id, ego and superego. It's what makes up our personalities. The id is our inherited instincts and traits, the ego our reality and sense of self, and the superego is guided by our societal and moral compass. Only if our id and superego are in balance with one another can our ego be grounded.'

'So, what are you saying?' Finn asks.

'Your ego is out of balance. Your id is tipping you too far to the left, is desperate for self-gratification, blinding you to new possibilities.'

'Okay . . . ' Finn says.

Oscar stares at him. 'Am I correct in thinking that you battled cancer in the past?'

Finn prickles, wonders why Martha felt the need to mention this when it has nothing to do with them being here. 'I dislike that term, *battle*,' he says, without meeting Oscar's eye. 'That's not how I would describe it.'

'I apologise,' Oscar says. 'How would you describe it?'

Finn looks down at his itchy arms, thinks about his bones, his blood cells. 'It's all luck, who lives and who dies. I can think of no other logic as to why I get to continue on when so many others around me died.' He pauses. 'My mother would say that her love and prayers, and the love and prayers of those who cared so deeply for me, kept me in this world, but everyone around me who died was loved too, deeply and desperately.'

'That must have been very traumatic, for everyone involved.'

Finn stares at Oscar. 'It was a long time ago.'

'Well, thank you for sharing that with me.'

Finn doesn't say anything, lets his eyes dart around the room again.

'This is a safe space,' Oscar says. 'You can say anything here.'

'Why are *you* here?' Finn asks.

'I'm where I need to be.'

Finn laughs. 'But you're Australian, right?'

This seems to catch Oscar off-guard.

'Where in Australia?' Finn asks.

'Does it matter?'

'You want me to answer all your questions, but you won't answer mine? If I'm sceptical of your methods and intentions here, perhaps it's because I know nothing about you.'

'Okay,' Oscar says. 'I take your point. What would you like to know?'

'Where in Australia?'

'Melbourne. Have you been?'

Finn nods. 'Why did you leave?'

Oscar seems to really consider the question. 'Do you remember the 1994 Indian Ocean tsunami, or were you too young?'

'I remember it . . . ' Finn says. 'On the news.'

'My parents were scuba-diving instructors, and we were in Bali on a trip when it happened. I was sixteen.' He pauses. 'We were staying high up, in the hills . . . But they'd got up early that morning to do a dive and I'd stayed behind, wanted to sleep instead.' He pauses. 'I never saw them again.'

Finn stalls, taken aback by what he's hearing. 'I'm sorry,' is all he manages.

'In the aftermath, all I could think about was what the sensation must have been like to be under the water when something like that was unfolding. What happens to a body in those circumstances?' He stops. 'Afterwards, I had no desire to return to Australia. It took me a while to find my way here, to the salt and its ancestors, but I was taken in and saved. And now I spend every day trying to help people who are hurting and lost. Because I know what it feels like to want the world to end.'

Finn feels numb, doesn't have the words to match the magnitude of what Oscar is telling him. 'I'm sorry,' he repeats.

Oscar smiles. 'It is okay. Truly.' He nods, almost as if he admires Finn. 'Often our guests don't have the capacity to ask questions about others, so this is refreshing. I thank you for the opportunity.'

Finn nods. 'Thank you.'

'Do you want to ask me anything else?'

Finn shrugs. 'How do you feel about the climate emergency?'

Oscar narrows his eyes. 'Why do you ask that?'

Finn shrugs. 'I guess it's on my mind.'

'Because of Martha? Or because you worry about it on your own terms?'

'I worry, of course, but I don't believe every waking moment needs to be consumed by misery.' Finn pauses. 'As you've demonstrated by what you've shared, anything can happen to any of us at any moment, so what's the point in living in constant fear of what might or might not transpire.'

'And Martha?'

Finn shifts, claws at his skin. 'Martha struggles to see that we're all stuck in a societal system that can't just be changed overnight. New infrastructure and technology, new ways of thinking – it all takes time. Whether we like it or not, we revolve around capitalism, and that isn't going away any time soon. There isn't time to find an alternative. And anyway, Martha's whole life has benefited from capitalism. The fact that she doesn't acknowledge that is . . . infuriating.'

Oscar taps his finger off the desk. 'Is money important to you?'

'No one wants their life to revolve around money – but our mortgage still needs to be paid; our day-to-day existence, our lifestyle – it still costs money.' Finn pauses, takes a breath. 'Martha behaves as though the rules we've all been playing by no longer apply to her.'

'In what way?'

'Did she mention that she got arrested? Defaced a building in a Just Stop Oil protest. Has been suspended from her job, soon to be let go.'

'Some might say that it's for a noble cause . . . ' Oscar says.

Finn scoffs. 'Martha comes from a privileged background and a family with money, so she's never had to worry, not in the way that I have. Sometimes I think she's reacting to the climate emergency in this way because she's never truly had to worry or fear for anything in her life until now.'

'How would you say you value physical health over mental health?' Oscar asks.

Finn closes his eyes. 'I value them both equally,' he says. But he knows this isn't true. Sometimes he wants to grip Martha and really shake her because she has no idea – she has no real idea about death, of one's own body fighting against you, eating you up, a game of divide and conquer. She has no real concept of wanting so desperately to live, of making deals with gods and devils that you're not sure exist, in pursuit of living.

'Do you treat Martha's behaviour as a choice, something she has control over?'

'I . . . I only want her to find a healthier perspective on the life she leads.' He can feel a new agitation growing in his mouth. 'We don't live in a war zone. There are people dying all around the world from actual conflict and violence.' He pauses. 'We live in *Aberdeen*. Can't she see how lucky she is?'

'How would you describe your marriage?'

'Complicated.'

'Can you elaborate?'

'She was unfaithful, so it's not been great . . . '

'When did this happen?'

'About eight months ago. I was working offshore, and she went on a climate march in the city and met some eco-warrior dude.' Finn swallows, shakes his head, refuses to let any further emotion surface. 'Maybe it's a relief, to be with someone who despairs as much as you do.' He pauses. 'I caught them coming into the house on the home security camera. I don't know what she was thinking – she knows we have cameras. Maybe, subconsciously, she wanted me to see. Finally react.'

'Were you actively keeping tabs on her?'

Finn shakes his head. 'Of course not. There had been a few robberies in our street. Folk coming into people's houses in the middle of the night, stealing their things as they slept. It was unnerving, especially when I wasn't there half the time. Anyway, she confessed as soon as I asked. A one-night thing. Nothing more.'

'Have you forgiven her?'

Finn pinches his nose. 'We have a sense of loyalty to one another. An unspoken agreement of sorts.' He takes a breath. He's struggling to understand how this stranger has managed to extract so much information from him.

'Why did you come here?' Oscar asks.

'I've told you: for Martha. She believes this is the only place left that can help—'

'That is why *Martha* came,' Oscar replies. 'But it's not why you came.'

Finn hesitates. 'I'm not sure what you want me to say . . . She didn't want to come alone.'

Oscar smiles. 'Will you do something for me?'

'What?'

'Don't focus on your wife while you are here. Focus on yourself. I think if you allow yourself to contemplate the traumas of your past you will find great reward and harmony.'

'I'm fine,' Finn says. 'Really I am—'

Oscar holds up a hand to stop him. 'All I ask is that you try. This experience doesn't have to be life-changing only for Martha.'

'We'll see,' Finn replies, already getting to his feet.

15

They are in the main circular room, which Oscar is now referring to as the *opening* room, and the space is aglow with candles. Outside, dusk has arrived, and Martha glances around as if expecting to find a clock, but of course there is none. Anything that can be removed from the circular room has been, and six thin mattresses have been laid down. Next to each mattress sits an empty plastic bucket and a roll of toilet paper.

Oscar gathers them around a small salt-carved table, everyone crouched down, a cushion underneath to stop their knees from coming into direct contact with the salt particles of the floor. Oscar is sandwiched between Elbert and Ofelia, his shoulders sitting slightly higher than theirs, as if he is the peak of the mountain and they are the paths guiding the others to him. In front of him sits a large glass jug, its contents a murky brown liquid, while small glass tumblers are stacked in threes. There is the anticipation of what's to come, a low murmur between the group and Martha feels her chest flutter – a nervous excitement.

'Before we begin,' Oscar says, 'I want to thank each of you for being so open and honest in our one-to-ones earlier. I see it as a tremendous privilege to be here to witness your words and I thank you all for putting your trust in me and this process.' He closes his eyes and slowly opens them. 'And in return, I want to be honest with you about my life before coming here, about my own salt healing journey.'

Martha nods. It's instinctual. Oscar has a voice that could say anything, and she'd likely listen.

'I shouldn't be here,' he says, looking around the group. 'I am someone who has been despicable and done despicable things. I have faced most demons and addictions. I have treated people appallingly and done things that bring only shame, including several stints in prison, the last stretch taking almost four years of my life. For various reasons which I will not bore you with, the odds were always stacked against me.' He pauses. 'But then a miracle happened. I came to South America with a one-way ticket, and I met a man, a shaman who is no longer with us in this world. But it was he who encouraged me to come here, and it was he who saved me with these very same salt practices you are about to experience for yourselves.' He looks as though he might cry. 'I came to this land a sceptical person, believing there was nothing in this world for me any more, but with help I found reason to live again. And for nearly eighteen years now I have been learning from the ancestors of this land, following their teachings and using these practices to help others.'

Martha holds her breath as Oscar's gaze lands upon her, and it is as if he can read her mind and anxieties.

'You are all here because something ails you. You may not even know yet what it is, but if you trust me, you will come to understand truly what has brought you here, and if you let me, I will help you to release whatever trauma anchors you down. You will become unburdened by your sorrow and leave here the person you so desperately want to be. But only if you open up your mind and body to the possibility.'

Martha nods again, swallowing his words whole.

'Now we pray,' he says, closing his eyes and lowering his head, directing his words to the ancient ancestors of the land. Afterwards, he opens his eyes and looks right at Martha again.

The silence he holds is almost too long, the wait and anticipation unbearable. And she immediately chastises herself, knows her own miracle won't happen if she doesn't focus, if she doesn't give herself up fully to this experience.

Oscar nods, a silent command, and Elbert lights a pipe stuffed with something that resembles tobacco. He gets to his feet and begins to work his way around the group, starting with Rick. Elbert puffs on the pipe, pulling it away and, through hand gestures, instructs Rick to copy. It's a damp smell, as if bark and moss have been gathered and burned. The pipe is then passed on to Barb, who is generous with her inhalation, her nostrils quivering.

'This will clear your passageways,' Oscar whispers. 'It is preparing your body to receive our specially prepared salt brew.'

It comes to Martha, and she's worried she's going to cough; she remembers smoking a cigarette for the first time in high school and being unable to inhale properly. But this smoke passes through her, circling down her mouth, her throat. She's survived this. She is ready.

It's Finn's turn and she smiles at him, encouraging, pleading almost, worried that the smoke will only irritate his oesophagus further. Finally, Elbert offers the pipe to Oscar and then Ofelia, before tamping it down, extinguishing the smoke.

'As each of you is new to salt ceremonies, the brew we will be drinking now is not at full strength. It should allow you to experience the beginnings of enlightenment without being overwhelmed. I should point out that, at the beginning of this process, you are likely to witness things about yourself you do not like, but this is an essential part of the process. We must strip ourselves down to build ourselves up.' He clasps his hands together. 'Ninety-nine per cent of life is suffering,' he says. 'Learning to embrace our suffering is the first step to overcoming it.'

Ofelia begins to unstack the cups, sliding them along to Oscar, who pours the brown liquid, one third of the way full into each one. The cups are then distributed around the coffee table, nine in total. And it occurs to Martha then that Oscar, Elbert and Ofelia will be partaking too, when she had assumed they were simply there to supervise.

Zoe is staring into her cup. 'What's in this?'

Oscar smiles. 'It is an ancient recipe that has been passed down for thousands of years,' he says. 'It contains many things, including salt and our special plant and vine blend. It is important that we all respect each ingredient and the gift it continues to offer. Each brew is slightly different; no two salt ceremonies are ever the same.' He pauses. 'Everyone will drink and then you are free to move around this space or outside as you please; however the thermal spring is off limits, for your own safety.'

Martha can feel the energy of the room, an eagerness.

'Hallucinations are common but occasionally some people also feel as though they can see into another person's mind, see their thoughts. I should warn you that the process often involves purging, so follow your body's needs and instincts. If you need to, you can lie down on one of these mattresses and we will tend to you. When it's time for another cup . . . ' He holds up a small brass bell, demonstrates its ring. 'I will ring this bell, and, if you can acknowledge the sound of it, then you return to this table and drink another cup. We'll do this with those who can tolerate it, up to three cups in total. Remember we are here to help you and guide you. You will not be alone. Does everyone understand?'

Martha is nodding but she's not sure she does understand. A sense of panic rises inside her at the amount of information provided, the overload. What if she misses one of the steps? She's never been good at taking in instructions, is thinking of the time they did white-water rafting, how, once in the raft, she felt ill-equipped, grew terrified that she'd fall out as they dropped down a waterfall, that she'd be unable to retain any of the information they had provided for dealing with this specific outcome, began to imagine she'd get trapped, drown.

Oscar turns to Elbert, whispering something in Spanish, and Elbert nods in return.

'I can tell already that we have a good group here,' Oscar says. 'A wonderful group with which to end our season.' He focuses once again on Martha. 'Use this evening's ceremony to ask yourself *who am I*? And tomorrow, we will begin our day with a listening circle.'

There is only silence, Martha's eyes flicking from the glass in front of her to Oscar.

He lifts his glass.

'Drink,' he says.

The concoction is disgusting, tasting of earth and dirt, and it takes everything in Martha to consume it. She's never had her face pressed into a puddle before, but she suspects that, if she had, this is exactly what it would taste of. The texture is odd – not smooth, but not lumpy either. Gritty. Perhaps if hair had been chopped up and blended then this would be the texture created. It works its way down her throat. She swallows, tries to clear the taste with her own saliva, wants to gag but manages not to. She slides the empty glass along the table towards Oscar, and it clinks against another. Finn is slower with his cup, unable to gulp it back. She can see him wincing, struggling. His eyes are closed, his cheeks tight with discomfort.

She sits in one of the salt-carved armchairs, feels no immediate effect. She fears she's at risk of failure already, can feel it. *Please*, she begs, a voice only in her head. She thinks about the holiday she went on with her friends, the summer before she got together with Finn – there was a visit to a cheap bar where a hypnotist was working his techniques on members of the audience. Martha was somehow called up on to the stage with another six or seven people, and the hypnotist instructed them to focus on rubbing their hands together, quickly and constantly, as if sparking embers in a fire, a concentrated friction. But Martha felt nothing as she repeated the action. She assumed everyone else was in the same position, but to her disbelief she was the only one not to be cast under this hypnotist's spell, and he'd had to ask her to leave the stage. She had proceeded to watch the other participants make complete fools of themselves; for example, the woman next to her in the line-up was instructed to demonstrate the noise of her orgasm. It was humiliating, and the unassuming woman was told that she wouldn't remember any of the details until she was sitting on the plane journey home. And Martha often wonders still about that woman and how she felt afterwards, whether she shrugged the whole experience off, or whether it troubled her for years to come. The indecency and violation. But also, why hadn't the hypnotherapy worked on Martha? What if her mind is wired differently from everyone else's? What if all of this means nothing?

She shakes her head, tries to remove negative thoughts, focuses on her one-to-one with Oscar. Remembers: no feeling is constant.

16

Finn sways, enveloped within the folds of the large canvas hammock strung up outside on the patio. He looks up at the night sky and tries to take in the stars. He's read somewhere that the southern hemisphere sky is one of the best places to stargaze, but he has no idea what he's meant to be searching for. He's someone who has never been able to make out constellations, even when they are drawn out for him. He's thinking that it's amazing that he's looking at a completely different sky from what he would see at home. Yet, suddenly he is overwhelmed, conscious that there is nothing here to anchor him to his family and friends. Right now, everyone he knows will be going about their lives, their jobs, basking in daylight.

He shifts, the hammock moving with him; there is nothing to grab on to and it's unnatural after years of holding on to handrails, a habit drilled into him through work protocol. He swallows, with difficulty, some residue from the cup of brown liquid that feels stuck. He coughs, attempts to clear his throat but it is blisteringly painful.

Maybe twenty minutes have passed since he sipped his first cup, but he has no real way of knowing, simply relying on some natural rhythm in his body. Zoe and Hannah come out on to the patio, walking hand in hand, whispering something that he cannot hear. To Finn, Zoe looks like someone who could be easily swayed, susceptible to manipulation, and he finds himself worrying about her, can't imagine what troubles her but fears that it cuts deep. Her altitude sickness seems to have subsided but there is a sadness she struggles to shift.

Martha arrives, attempting to climb into the hammock. He watches her, takes in the challenge she is having, seeming to enjoy it, before finally, in a somewhat undignified manner, she settles next to him, positioned head to toe.

Hannah and Zoe are still in his line of vision, peering out into the darkness, heads tilted to the sky, and he wonders if they know anything about stars, if they could tell him what any of it means.

'They think they know what love is . . . ' Martha whispers, her words slurring slightly. 'But they don't, not yet.'

'What?'

She nods towards Zoe and Hannah. 'They don't understand the monotony, the routine and domestic existence. They're still too young.'

'Are you jealous?'

She hesitates, her thoughts seeming to come slowly, her articulation questionable. 'Maybe . . . ' She nods. 'Maybe I am.'

'Do you feel anything yet?' he asks.

'Honestly . . . I feel like there is something slowly working its way through me.'

He nods. 'That's a good thing, is it not?'

'And how do you feel?' she asks.

He hesitates. 'Honestly . . . I don't think I feel any differently.'

She places her hand on his shoe, presses her fingers into his toes.

He closes his eyes, his thoughts landing on his one-to-one with Oscar, on how their conversation spiralled far from where Finn was willing to let it go. Now, shifting, he's remembering, so clearly, the day in the hospital when he nearly did break up with Martha. There was the humiliation of her witnessing his decline, her constant need to comfort, the fact that she seemed to come into her own when nursing him. None of it was what he had imagined for himself. The times he'd wake to find her still sitting by his bedside and he'd wanted to say, *Martha, go. Don't stay here, with me.* But he never did. It was selfish of him, but he'd kept her tethered, an insurance policy. It was easier to continue as they were, wondering how far she was willing to take her commitment, so sure he was of his impending death. And then they both kept enduring, forging love through shared experience, and now they are here, and he still has love for her, but he can't tell any more if it's a healthy love or something akin to Stockholm syndrome, to being too scared to give up what you have for fear of there being nothing better.

'How much do you love me?' Martha asks.

He opens his eyes. 'This much,' he says, spreading his arms out as wide as they will go.

'Finn . . .'

'Yeah?'

'I think it's working. There's this sense that nothing really matters, but not in a despairing way . . .'

'That's good, Martha. I'm so pleased, really.'

The bell rings in the opening room and Finn sits up, startled, meeting Martha's eye.

'Already?' she says, attempting to climb out of the hammock, and all Finn can think is, *After all that effort, to get inside the hammock. Why bother*?

He forces himself to the edge and swivels, placing his feet on the ground. He can still taste the muck of the first cup and has no desire to swallow any more.

'Why do you think they call it the opening room?' he asks, but Martha doesn't appear to be listening, too busy making for the next cup.

He follows her inside, can see that Barb is lying down on one of the worn mattresses. Her body is rocking ever so slightly, her hands clasped to her chest, eyes closed, a bucket positioned in line with her face, while Rick sits in a salt-carved armchair, watching her from a few metres away. When he looks back, Zoe and Hannah are by the patio doors. Zoe is pressing her hand up against one of the glass panes, rubbing furiously at something that isn't there.

Finn nudges Martha, wanting her to acknowledge what he sees, but Martha is too focused on returning to Oscar.

Hannah pulls Zoe's hand away from the glass, guiding her back.

Everyone, except for Barb, suddenly appears to be around Finn, and he feels a kind of claustrophobia, the others having no sense of personal space. He glances at their faces, including Martha's, and they look hungry, ravenous even for this brown concoction, and yet he still feels nothing. Oscar begins to pour, but this time there are only eight glasses, Barb forfeiting hers. A cup is slid towards him, a murky brown line of liquid working its way down the outside of his cup. He wipes it away, inspecting his finger, sniffing it as if this will hold clues to what is in the mixture. Oscar raises his glass, and they follow. Finn chokes it back, painfully, particles spluttering out of his mouth. It is exactly the sensation of when he's trying to stop himself from being sick – two different parts of his body working as opposing forces, his mouth muscles doing their best to keep everything in, his throat and stomach doing what they can to expel this foreign substance.

Rick has returned to his salt-carved armchair and Finn sits next to him.

'How are you feeling?' Finn asks.

Rick looks at him with a wide grin. 'Marvellous,' he says, sweating from his temples. 'Poor Joni isn't faring so well though,' he adds, pointing at Barb. 'I should probably take her home. It's embarrassing at this point.'

'Barb?' Finn says.

Rick pauses, shakes his head. 'Yes, Barb. Of course, Barb.'

Finn watches Martha make her way back towards the hammock they had been occupying not so long ago, but he has no desire to join her. He sees the salt brew working its way through everyone else, the effects obvious, and he's suddenly sad, wondering if it's his cynicism and narrow-mindedness that stops him from feeling it too. And he wants to weep, because what is the harm, really, of buying into something ludicrous, if it offers you hope or happiness? He sits with his sadness and the possibility that things don't need to be the way they are. But then he remembers that he feels nothing, truly nothing, and he worries he'll never feel anything ever again.

17

Martha sways in the hammock, looking up at the sky. The stars feel alarmingly close, as if she could reach up and touch them. She imagines they would burn like a firework, singe her hands, dissolve her fingers. Instinctively she shields her face with her arm, one elbow jutting out. She breathes, counts to three then peeks out from behind her arm. The stars have retreated, are less likely to stab her, but they are different colours. All the colours of the rainbow. She blinks and looks up, but the array of colours remains. The sky starts to spin, and she thinks she's going to throw up. Everything is moving too fast. She falls out of the hammock, meeting the ground, but she feels no pain. She stumbles back inside and grips the walls to keep herself upright. She's aware of others, but she can't differentiate one face from another; for some reason this does not cause her alarm.

Someone is guiding her now to an empty mattress. She begins to yell but doesn't know what she's trying to say. She curls her body up on the mattress and furiously licks her lips. The bucket, beside her, begins to morph into hexagons, and other similar shapes, but she's not quick enough to count the sides before it changes again. She can see through the bucket now, to the salt below. She sticks her tongue out and attempts to lick it, convinced that she can reach the salt through it, believes she can taste it. When she looks up, she can see Finn watching her, crouched by the wall, his hands hugging his knees, but he will not come to her. She thinks she's calling out to him, but his name sounds strange in her mouth. She sits bolt upright and begins to heave. There is someone beside her, an angel, and they offer her the bucket into which she begins to vomit. There is so much to purge, and it feels endless and painful. She worries that she'll fill the bucket, that she'll need to borrow her neighbour's one. She looks around, sees Rick, talking incessantly to Oscar, his voice always too loud. Someone is patting her lip with toilet paper, then her brow. She grips their arm, tries to be gentle, grateful. But she's suddenly scared too, something opening within her that she has no desire to see – the worst of the world and the worst of herself. Her unfaithfulness. Her neediness. Her mistakes and jealousy. Her calculated pursuit of Finn, his illness and her perseverance even when she could see it wasn't really what he wanted. She looks at him now, so thin and gaunt – she wants to bring her mouth to his, inflate him. She's thinking of Finn's hospital bed, all the hours, endless, the smell of sickness so close to her, the odour of decay. But she stayed, knew this was her way of keeping Finn tethered to her.

She straightens, nothing left to purge, and is struck by a sudden urge to fully and inescapably contemplate the practicalities of disposing of Finn's body. Crematorium backlogs, remains sieved to remove metal and jewellery, ash mostly just bone that has been crushed, everything else burnt away. Or burying him, gravediggers having to displace so much earth, hiding him in the darkness of the ground and leaving him to rot, a premium price for the land despite no one ever visiting. Before, if Finn had died, his parents would have made all the decisions. They would have chosen his clothes, his shoes, his casket. But now it's different. Now she would be the one to decide.

Everything is moving quickly around her. Memories and imaginings are becoming muddled, and she can't tell any more what is real and what is not. She sees, so vividly, the climate and societal collapse that she anticipates, all her worst predictions projecting out before her. And she hates the version of herself she sees – a person only interested in self-preservation, in stockpiling and denying others shelter in their hour of need. She is the woman who refuses to let Finn get a dog because they are not conducive to fighting climate change; instead she is forcing chickens and bees upon him as pets, an attempt to stave off their dependence on the collapsing food chain. And none of it helps, none of it makes her feel better.

She slumps back down on to the mattress but she's too scared to close her eyes for fear of what else she might see. She looks up at the curve of the ceiling, the strangeness of a circular room, as if they are all at risk of rolling around, a constant motion, of finding no natural point in which to stop. Finally, another bell rings out, more persistent. An ending, of sorts.

Friday

18

Finn wakes up alone in the dorm, disorientated, the sun beaming in. He gets to his feet and stumbles out towards the opening room, where everyone else from the dorm is lying out on mattresses, while Ofelia moves around the bodies, attempting to return what she can of the room to its original form. He keeps moving, heading for one of the bathrooms only to find it out of service, a yellow plastic hazard sign blocking his path. He pushes the door open and from where he stands he can see that the toilet is blocked, the stench unbearable.

He returns to the circular room, sitting down at the dining table. There is no food laid out and he ponders whether Ofelia is waiting for everyone else to stir before serving breakfast. It all feels too quiet, and this deep sense of loneliness sets in, at the reality of his experience, or lack of it, being so at odds with everyone else's. He thinks of the rock formation they passed on the way to here, how it felt like a totem, and his distress at losing sight of it.

Ofelia emerges now from the kitchen, sees him sitting at the table. Like a fool, he brings his hand up to his mouth and mimics sucking something from a straw, 'Smoothie,' he says. '*Por favor.*' He can't think of any other way to articulate his request, all Spanish lost from his mind, except for the phrase: *trae la cuenta por favor*, but he has no reason to ask for the bill; his Duolingo attempts are completely useless.

Ofelia hesitates, appearing to understand what he means. '*No*,' she says, shaking her head. '*Señor Oscar, no*.'

She moves on, shuffling past the table towards the out-of-order toilet. Finn isn't sure what he is meant to do now. There is the sensation of being in someone else's home and trying to interpret the rules, of wanting to seamlessly fit in, and not be judged for doing things differently. Even in their own house, having people come to stay only reminds him that his routine is perhaps obscure, unhealthy, not conducive to normal life.

Zoe stirs from her mattress on the floor, sitting up, appearing a little shellshocked.

'Hey,' Finn says, his voice travelling across the room.

Slowly, she comes and sits down next to him at the table.

'How are you doing?' he asks.

She shrugs, meekly, struggling to form her words. She glances at Finn only briefly before casting her gaze downwards. 'Where did you go?' she asks. 'Last night . . . '

Finn hesitates. 'I went to my bed. I thought I'd sleep better in the dorm.'

Zoe nods.

'Did I miss something?'

She picks at her fingernail, brings it to her mouth and tears at it. 'Is there anything to eat?' she says.

'Ofelia says no.'

'No?'

'That's all she said,' he replies, shrugging. 'Oscar says no.'

The others begin to wake, slow in their movements, and he looks at each of them – tired, nauseous but not particularly enlightened, no rolling wave of euphoria.

Martha comes and sits opposite him, a strange, unsettling expression spreading across her face, almost trancelike.

Oscar appears soon after, looking fresh and revitalised, as if he's had a full night's sleep; somehow he looks younger. 'Good morning,' he says, a wide smile spreading across his face. 'What a beautiful day we have before us.'

'Oscar . . . is there any breakfast?' Rick asks, unusually tentative, as though asking for a favour.

Oscar narrows his eyes. 'Today is our salt trek and day of fasting.'

'Sorry?' Rick says, eyes widening. 'No . . . I don't . . . '

Oscar smiles at him. 'As I've said before, there will be challenges to face, and fasting is one of them.'

Finn looks around the table, everyone mute, unquestioning, the air shifting in Oscar's presence.

'It is a short fast, only until dusk,' Oscar says. 'Nothing whatsoever should pass your lips until sunset, no food or water.'

'Why no water?' Finn asks, swallowing, the pain in his throat unbearable.

'We fast to honour those who came before us, who sacrificed so much while walking this land.'

Behind them Ofelia is rolling up mattresses, attempting to tie rope round them.

'If we are all present, we will begin our listening circle,' Oscar says, pulling his chair back to sit down at the head of the table. 'Has anyone done a listening circle before?'

Finn watches everyone shake their heads.

'It's simple really,' Oscar says. 'We'll go around the group, and everyone has the opportunity to talk. Most people tend to share their experiences of the salt ceremony, but equally this is a space to say anything that you wish.' He pauses. 'We're not here to offer advice; this is simply an opportunity for everyone to be listened to without judgement.'

Again, Finn is aware of nodding, collective, compliant.

Oscar smiles. 'Okay,' he says. 'Who would like to go first?'

No one speaks.

Oscar's smile widens. 'You do not need to be afraid,' he says. 'We are among friends. You are on this journey together.'

Martha raises her hand. 'I can go first, if that works . . . '

'Of course,' Oscar says, nodding.

Martha straightens, pushing back her shoulders, and Finn can visualise the curve in her back, the bones protruding. 'Well . . . ' she says, a nervousness to her voice. 'There was a lot of purging . . . And things felt off-kilter, blurry . . . as if everything was simply a dream, a nightmare too – but it's difficult for me now to decipher what is real and what was imagined.' She rubs her eyes, the skin of her eyelids looking sore. 'I was on this huge piece of ice, an ice sheet, there were thousands of people on it, and we were all huddled together. But pieces kept falling off, and we kept pushing closer and closer. There just wasn't enough space for us all. Crushing.' She stops and sits back, lowering her gaze.

Finn feels a tightness in his chest; he wants to reach for her but she's too far away.

Oscar nods. 'Great, thank you, Martha. Who's next?'

Rick glances around the group, exhales loudly. 'I thought it was an incredible experience,' he says. 'I really tried to let myself go and what I saw made no sense, except that it did, in a way. All these shapes and colours, and shadows, the silhouettes of animals. Some threatening, others lovely. I don't know what it means but I think that's okay.' He pauses. 'I . . . I feel as though I'm still holding back. I think I'm scared to see the worst of myself.' He stops, shrugging, suddenly melancholy. 'I don't feel like I really know who I am any more . . . '

Oscar nods, before pivoting his attention to Hannah. 'Hannah . . . ' he says, elongating her name in his pronunciation. 'How about you?'

Hannah's eyes are fixed on Zoe. 'I don't remember much but I don't like what I do remember,' she finally says. She looks down, crinkles her nose in concentration. 'It felt like something was coming for me. Not people but shadows. A darkness. I don't think . . . What if . . . ?' She stops, bites on her cheek. 'I have this addictive personality; I've always known this about myself.' She pauses. 'I take things too far, always the last one to want to leave the party, always the first to spend my money, to drink and take drugs. And last night, it showed me all of this, but . . . it was worse, and I worry that one day it will ruin everything.'

Oscar presses forward, looking as though he is about to slip off his chair.

Hannah crosses her arms over her chest, hugging herself.

'Barb?' Oscar says. 'What about you?'

Barb nods, almost as if she is replying to a specific question. 'I feel it too,' she says, pointing towards Hannah. 'A darkness, as though my mind isn't mine any more, and I can't shift it. It won't let go.' She pauses. 'It feels painful, or it did at the time. Physically painful.' She pauses. 'I only drank one cup. I know that probably makes me weak. But I didn't like the feeling. It scared me.'

Oscar nods, clasps his hands together. 'Zoe . . . ' he says, altering his voice, a more cautious tone. 'Tell us how you feel . . . '

Zoe blinks. The words seem difficult. 'Something happened to me last night . . . ' She shakes her head. Finn can see that she's fighting back tears. 'Something bad. That feeling . . . familiar, of knowing something's wrong.' A tear dribbles down her cheek, her breathing erratic as she tries to control herself.

Finn straightens; he doesn't understand the source of her fear, but he sees it so clearly, almost feels it.

Zoe wipes her face and takes a gulp of air, doing everything she can to stop the tears.

They sit for a moment in silence before Oscar nods to Finn. But it feels wrong and disrespectful to start speaking when Zoe is clearly struggling, her suffering raw and on display. He's so thirsty too, swallowing hard and wincing from the jagged sensation that travels down his throat.

'Please . . . ' Oscar says, encouraging Finn to speak.

Finn hesitates, looking at Martha for encouragement, but her gaze is elsewhere. 'I don't feel any different. Maybe apart from feeling a bit woozy.' He exhales, clamps his eyes shut, but it doesn't block out the noise of Zoe struggling to maintain her breathing. 'I'm sorry . . . I'm not sure what else you want me to say.' His eyes remain shut, tight and sore, but he won't open them yet. Zoe is still whimpering, the rhythm erratic, like a failing heart. He fears that her pain will spread, take hold of him and he wants no part of it.

'Okay, good,' Oscar says, a hint perhaps of condescension. 'This is not easy. But I thank each of you for your honesty.'

Abruptly, Zoe gets to her feet, struggling to push her chair back in the salt.

'Zoe, please . . . stay,' Hannah says, pleading. 'We just want to make it better for you.'

But Zoe doesn't reply, simply retreats towards the dorm room.

Oscar offers another reassuring smile. 'It's okay; the first ceremony can take a lot out of people,' he says. 'This is normal.' He stands now too. 'I think you all deserve some rest before we begin our salt trek. When it is time to go, I shall ring the bell and we will meet out on the patio.'

'How long do we have?' Barb asks. 'How will we know?'

Oscar smiles at her. 'It will be time when you are rested. We have the whole day ahead of us,' he says. 'Accept the hunger that is now working its way through your bodies, embrace it.' Finally, he departs towards his office, everyone else remaining in their seats, only the noise of Ofelia tidying up behind them.

19

There is an anxiousness rooted in Martha's stomach as she walks back to the dorm room – caused by Oscar's vagueness, the feeling of not ever being able to fully relax despite his telling them to do so. If she knew she had several hours she'd make a conscious effort to sleep, but the idea of finally falling into a deep slumber only to be woken up, abruptly, is too much – is almost a form of torture. She follows the others to the dorm, where nearly everyone is climbing back under their covers, desperate for sleep, the silhouette of Zoe's curled-up body visible under her duvet.

Martha begins to rummage in her backpack for her swimming suit, crouching down in the salt, and she can feel someone brushing their hand up against her back. She turns to see Finn, extending his hand out from his duvet, not applying any pressure, simply wanting to be acknowledged.

'Are you okay . . . ?' he says.

She nods, offers a smile. 'Are *you* okay?' she whispers.

He nods back, yawning.

She has found her swimsuit, her fingers gripping the Lycra fabric. 'Get some sleep,' she says, rising to her full height, allowing his hand to fall away.

As she makes to leave the room, grabbing her travel towel, Barb calls out to her. 'Are you going to the thermal spring?'

Martha nods.

'Can I join you? I want to try it, but I don't want to go in alone.' She laughs, shrugging. 'Fear of the unknown and all that.'

Martha waits for her, but Barb is slow in her movements, tiptoeing around, careful not to disturb Rick. Zoe turns, a harshness in her movements that suggest she's annoyed by their continued presence, by their delay in leaving the dorm. Barb shrugs at Martha, finally holding her bathing suit in her hand, twirling it with her finger, and they leave.

As they walk along the corridor, a piece of salt wedges itself in between one of Martha's bare toes in her flip-flops. It's uncomfortable but she is hesitant to stop. Maybe this small sense of continued suffering will help, keep her focused. Perhaps the salt will rub its healing properties in between her toes, a cure in the most unlikely of places. She thinks about the energy this place must carry, the aura it creates, and then she's thinking about her own negative energy, about it being purged out of her until there was nothing left but bile.

She can't take the discomfort any more and bends to retrieve the piece of salt from between her toes, inspecting it. She cups the little chunk of salt tightly in her hand, wanting to believe that this exact piece is special, the sharpness against her skin offering further validation.

Outside, the sun glows over everything, but a wind travels across the salt flats, meeting them with a shock at their slightly elevated position. They walk around the property, passing the kitchen's back door and the llama, who remains in the same spot, sitting in among its own shit. They carry on, Barb needing Martha's hand for support, and make their way down to the hot spring.

Martha changes awkwardly, wrapping her travel towel around herself, the fabric strange against her skin. She pulls down her pants and leggings, hidden under the towel, and struggles to balance as she slips her swimming costume on. She's aware of Barb beside her, stripping off, naked, baring everything to the wind and salt and sun. Martha trying not to look but she can't help it, marvels at Barb's ageing body, thinks she'd be lucky to look like Barb when she's in her sixties.

Barb is quick to get her costume on and Martha watches as she enters the water without hesitation, wading through the water, a ripple disturbing the surface.

'Aren't you getting in?' Barb says, looking back, her body slipping further into the cloudy water until it laps around her shoulders.

Martha nods, following her, registering the immediate warmth of the water against her skin. She continues forward, her toes touching the bottom, rubble and sludge underfoot, as though she is walking across a loch. She's nervous she'll get some water in her mouth, and she realises that every liquid she's seen since arriving here has this similar tinge of murkiness. Even the water in the taps isn't running clear; only the barrels of water Elbert brought are fit for consumption. She's staring down, can't see her outstretched hands that are submerged. She lifts them out of the water and touches her face, feels the roughness of salt. She moves further through the swamp-like water and thinks about those stories of people bathing in lakes only to be eaten by crocodiles. The horror that you can disappear so easily, so quickly, leave no trace . . . What is in with them now? Maybe nothing. Maybe everything.

She comes to a stop next to Barb, a ledge acting as a make-shift seating area.

Barb smiles. 'If I close my eyes, I can almost imagine that we're at a spa. Almost,' she says, smiling.

Martha nods, smiles back.

'You don't have kids, do you?' Barb asks.

The question catches Martha off guard. 'No.'

'I have a grandson,' Barb says, 'I don't know if I mentioned him already . . . '

Martha shakes her head.

Barb's face fills with affection at the mere thought of her grandson. 'Carson,' she says. 'He's six.' She pauses. 'No one tells you what a joy having grandchildren will be. I guess it must be something to do with being able to hand them back.' She shrugs. 'The weight of responsibility doesn't fall on you the way it does when you're raising your own kids.' Her smile deepens. 'I'd spend all the time in the world with Carson if I could, but Rick . . . Well, he doesn't have any grandchildren of his own, doesn't have the same attachment, I don't think, being a step-grandpa and all.'

'Sorry . . . ' Martha says. 'I'd assumed you and Rick had been together for a long time.'

'That's not to say he isn't great with him.' She pauses. 'Last summer we took Carson to Disneyland, and he had the most wonderful time. But this summer Rick wanted us to go to Europe, on our own.' She laughs, flicking water with her hands. 'Carson is the son of my son, Marcus, and boy, did he put me and his dad through the wringer with his antics back in the day.'

'I don't think any of us are easy to raise,' Martha says. 'It's a miracle really that so many continue to have children.'

'Is it not for you, dear?'

Martha stares at Barb, amazed that this woman thinks asking her such a question is appropriate. 'I . . . Maybe one day. I wouldn't rule anything out yet . . . '

'How old are you, dear?'

Martha hesitates, slightly affronted. 'Thirty-nine.'

Barb nods, knowing. 'It's nice to have the freedom to get up and go,' she says. 'That's the first thing that changes when you decide to have kids. And then that's it, eighteen years of worry and stress . . . What is it they say: you're only as happy as your least happy child.'

Martha nods. 'I guess so . . . '

'Do you know why I really wanted to have children?' Barb says, not waiting for Martha to respond. 'I got to a certain age and was overcome by this real, tangible fear of loneliness. The idea of no one really knowing, in real time, if I was okay, no one worrying about me.' She pauses. 'I don't think I have it in me to ever be completely alone. I'll always need people. I'll always want to tether others to me.'

'But you wouldn't be alone,' Martha says. 'You have Rick.'

Barb settles her gaze on the salt flats. 'Well, you see, Rick has recently been diagnosed with Alzheimer's disease,' she says. 'I don't think you would know to look at him yet . . . Although I'm starting to see it.' She pauses, exhales. 'We only got married two years ago, so it feels especially cruel.' She shrugs. 'We've investigated all sorts of therapies, which is why we've ended up here. We heard that something like this could have a profound effect in stunting the symptoms, delaying the decline. Anything to give us more time together as we are.'

Martha nods. 'I'm sorry,' she says. 'It's a horrible disease.'

They sit in silence, a flock of birds passing over them in the sky.

'I don't think I'll make a very good carer,' Barb says. 'I'm probably a little too selfish, will resent him for making me look after him.'

'I don't think we really know what we're capable of until we find ourselves in that position,' Martha replies.

Barb gazes upwards again, tracking the birds. 'I'm reliably informed that he wasn't always a nice man. I worry that he'll become that person again, revert to the old version of himself . . . I'm not sure I could cope with that.'

'I understand,' Martha says.

Barb looks at her. 'Do you, though?'

'I don't think I'm a very good person either,' Martha replies. 'Like, outwardly, I'm doing and saying all the right things, but I'm not sure I believe them. More going through the motions because I want to appear to be an upstanding and principled person.' She pauses. 'My worries, these worries about the world that cripple me . . . I think they only worry me now because they might actually affect me . . . When, all the time, everywhere, terrible things are happening to others.'

But Barb isn't listening to Martha; she is dipping her mouth into the pool and gathering water, swallowing it. She begins to cough and splutter. 'I don't know why I did that,' she says. 'I think I thought it would be like the mixture from last night. But it's just salt. All salt.'

'Are you okay?' Martha asks.

Barb nods. 'I'm glad we're fasting today,' she says. 'It feels like it's what we deserve.' And she gets up then, wading back towards her discarded clothes, leaving Martha behind.

20

Elbert leads the way, guiding them from the patio, down the steep path towards the salt flats. The ground feels loose under Finn's feet, others close behind, and he worries that if one of them trips they'll take out everyone else with them. Oscar, he acknowledges, is tactically at the back, Ofelia remaining at the centre.

Standing on the salt flats, they spread out, as if needing physical distance from one another. Elbert is carrying a large backpack on his shoulders, and he opens it, removing what looks like black woolly hats. Without speaking, he begins to distribute one to each of them. Finn stretches the item in his hands, sees that it is a balaclava, the same as the ones the men wore at the salt factory. He can't remember when that was, or how many days have passed, everything blurring into one.

'Are these really necessary?' Rick asks, holding up his balaclava.

'You don't want to burn, do you, from the sun's reflection on the salt?' Oscar says. 'Because we will be on the salt for hours.'

Finn hesitates, his fingers rubbing the fabric of his balaclava. He watches Oscar and Elbert put on their ones before he brings his own up and pulls it down over his head, covering his face. It's uncomfortable and itchy. The eye holes feel a little too small and he wants to take his fingers to them, pull them further open. When Finn looks up, Rick and Barb have theirs on too and it's disconcerting, an unlikely image of villains. Martha comes to his side, her balaclava pulled down, her lips jutting out from the hole in the fabric for a mouth.

'This is a little unsettling, don't you think?' he says.

Her mouth morphs behind the balaclava into what Finn suspects is a smile.

Oscar inspects each of them, everyone now standing much closer together, faces hidden, a desire to be part of the pack. 'Okay, we go now, yes?'

'Where are we going?' asks Barb.

'To the Lagoon of Promise.'

'How long will the trek take?' Rick asks.

'That depends on us and our speed,' Oscar replies. 'But please do not worry, we have had eighty-year-olds manage this pilgrimage, under the same conditions.'

Finn looks out at the blinding white. 'Can we get lost?'

Oscar shakes his head, letting a small laugh escape him. 'No, no. It is a loop. We've done it many, many times.'

'And there's no risk of rain?' Finn presses.

'Finn, relax,' Oscar says. 'You are in safe hands. Please don't worry.'

Oscar turns and speaks to Elbert, his Spanish second-nature, pointing out towards the salt. Finally they set off, Oscar leading the way now, with everyone else following in various formations, Elbert stationed this time at the back. Finn's breathing feels heavy – he becomes so conscious of it, worries that there's something wrong. He despises the fact that he feels so weak most of the time. When they do a hill walk, it is always he who needs to stop and catch his breath. He swallows, the pain a frustration. Before leaving the dorm, he took double the dose of his liquid medicine, so hungry and dehydrated was he, and now he's worrying that he won't have enough to complete the course. He looks ahead, attempts to distract himself, focuses on Zoe and Hannah a few steps ahead, holding hands. Hannah's head is slightly turned and she's saying something to Zoe, encouraging her maybe. Looking over his shoulder, he sees Barb and Rick keeping a good stride in front of Elbert.

Finn has an urge to ask Oscar how far *exactly* they're meant to be trekking for, but the answer scares him. Perhaps it is best not to predict, to know it will be more than he thinks he's capable of achieving, especially when dehydrated and on an empty stomach. The lack of knowledge feels like a form of punishment. Oscar keeps so much from them, and he can't decide if this is something to start embracing, if in fact it is easier to accept the workings of the world with limited knowledge and a narrower vision. He tries to harness the memory of exercising, of the first ten minutes being torturous but then finally your body adjusting, your mind allowing you to focus on other things. He tries to forget that he is thirsty and hungry, that he had to force a new hole into his belt, and focuses instead on his movements.

He glances over his shoulder again, sees Rick deviating slightly from their path, undoing his trousers. Finn is too far away to see any piss landing on the salt, but it doesn't stop him from thinking about it. He's amazed that Rick has any fluid to give, imagines it being the darkest shade of yellow.

'Do you know what direction we're headed in?' Finn asks.

Martha shakes her head.

'So,' he says, a nervousness to his voice, his memories of the ceremony circling, Martha so unfamiliar, sitting on a mattress on the floor. 'Your experience last night . . . it sounded pretty intense?'

She nods. 'It was, but . . . I think that means it's working.'

Finn exhales, closes his eyes for the briefest of moments before opening them again. His face feels clammy and slick with sweat, the balaclava itchy, and he rubs at it, but it brings no relief. Ahead, Oscar is turning to check on them, offering a thumbs-up which Finn instinctively returns.

'There's a cruelty to this behaviour, don't you think?' Finn says. 'Pushing us under these conditions . . . It can't be healthy.'

'Maybe some circumstances require a cruelty to be kind,' Martha replies. And he realises that she's fully invested now, that questioning Oscar and his methods is off-limits as far as she's concerned.

He licks his dry lips, a thread of fabric from the balaclava sticking, getting inside his mouth. The sensation makes him gag and he comes to a stop.

Martha stops too. 'What is it?'

His fingers are struggling to locate it, his tongue pulling on it. 'A thread is stuck . . . ' he says, his fingers finally landing on it, removing it from his mouth.

He starts walking again, can feel Martha's hand on his back, rubbing it tenderly. When he swallows, he thinks for the first time that perhaps his throat is starting to feel less like glass; maybe doubling the dose is the cure. But his mouth is still unbearably dry.

'I'd give anything for some water,' he says.

Martha doesn't respond.

'What are you thinking about?' he asks.

'Oh, it's random,' she says. 'Weird.'

'What is it?'

She shakes her head, shrugging, everything about her appearing so unnatural with the balaclava hiding her face. 'I read this thing once about John F. Kennedy's younger sister. Rosemary. She'd supposedly been slower to walk and talk compared to her other siblings. Anyway, she didn't seem to comply with her father's expectations, became quite opinionated and angry in her early twenties . . . This was the 1940s.'

'Okay . . . ' Finn says, wishing she would get to the point.

'Like maybe she had some mild mental health issues, not that people talked about stuff like that back then, but anyway her father . . . her own father, he authorised for doctors to give her a lobotomy. And I just can't . . . I can't imagine a parent doing that to their child.'

'What happened after?' Finn asks, now interested.

'She was left incapacitated, unable to care for herself. Someone who had functioned reasonably well as an adult suddenly had the capabilities of a two-year-old. Can you even begin to imagine what that must have been like? To have no say, your life altered like that . . . '

'But people did do it,' he says.

'She was shipped off to some school where nuns cared for her. The father, according to the article, never once went to visit Rosemary. And it took her mother over twenty years to eventually visit.' She pauses. 'The loneliness of that . . . of being removed like that.'

'It's awful,' Finn says.

'The irony is that she still lived to be eighty-six years old, outliving JFK – isn't that mad?'

'What made you think about that?' Finn asks.

She shrugs. 'Barb was talking to me about kids in the thermal pool earlier.' She stops. 'I don't know, it got me thinking. Sometimes it's easy to imagine that you might not make a good parent but really, you don't get much worse than Joseph Kennedy authorising his daughter's lobotomy and still being a respected member of society. The whole thing, it just makes me so sad.'

'I don't doubt that you would make a good mother, Martha,' he says. 'You don't need to think that about yourself.'

'Okay,' she replies, reaching for his hand, and he lets her take it.

He imagines them after the Salt Centre, imagines finally telling her what he should have told her all those years ago in his hospital bed. *Martha, go. Don't stay here, with me.*

21

Martha doesn't know how long they have been walking. Her stomach is cramping, desperate for nourishment, her mouth bone-dry. Her memories of the salt ceremony are hazy, and she has the fear, like with a hangover, is nervous about what she gave away of herself, feels vulnerable to the gaze of others. She's consumed now by the thought of children. But there is still the constant worry that she'd be creating a person destined to have a miserable existence, committing them to a life of pain in a world that is crumbling. She doesn't know what to do with the uncertainty of it all. But she would like a child; would like to have Finn's child. And they're lucky because the doctors had had the foresight to suggest Finn have his sperm frozen before commencing his chemotherapy and radiotherapy, the only conceivable way for him to have children, his samples kept for a fee in a special storage facility for up to fifty-five years. And she marvels at the science of it – the idea that a baby could be made in this way, their hypothetical child already displaced, a person from the past, hoping to exist in the future, of legal voting age in another universe.

Everything feels too much. She doesn't think she's slept since arriving, not properly, and suddenly she wants to fall to her knees, can't breathe with this balaclava on, believes that she won't make it any further, her hand struggling with the simple action of removing the fabric from her face.

Ahead, Oscar is now turning, waving his hands in the air. 'Nearly there,' he shouts. 'I promise.' And he begins to point at something, excitedly, and she can almost sense the smile behind Oscar's balaclava.

And there it is: a lagoon, appearing like a mirage, majestic and shimmering in the sun, positioned before them as though it is the most natural thing in the world. Martha attempts to run, but her movements are muted, as if wading through water, her clothing tugging at her. She kicks her walking shoes off, as if they are the problem, weighted, and moves more quickly now, her socks hitting the rough surface of the salt. And Finn is shouting, the only word she can hear being *shoes*.

Flamingos are everywhere. There is an acidic, pungent smell and Martha can't decide if it is coming from the birds or the water. She regards the flamingos with cautious amazement, as if they are a newly discovered species that she is seeing for the first time. Around the edges of the water the colour changes, a pink of sorts, some chemical reaction taking place that Martha doesn't understand. She sits down on a large boulder near the edge of the water, and Elbert brings her walking boots to her. Embarrassed and foolish, she thanks him before forcing the boots back on.

'This lagoon,' Oscar says, addressing the group, casting his hand across the water, 'is usually home to thousands of these beautiful Andean flamingos, more so during the rainy season. However, as I'm sure you're all aware, because of the climate, it's getting harder and harder to predict the changing seasons.'

Finn comes to stand beside her, looking upwards to the sky.

'Are the flamingos at risk? Because of the climate . . . ' Martha asks.

Oscar nods. 'They mate for life,' he says, 'and lay only one egg per year. So, you can imagine . . . Their numbers continue to dwindle, particularly now that lithium mining is so intensive. The water quality, our ecosystem – it is constantly threatened.' He pauses. 'My greatest fear is that one day all of this will be gone.'

'Devastating,' Martha replies, still sitting in her crouched position.

'Can you swim in the water?' Hannah asks.

Oscar laughs, her question appearing ludicrous to him. 'No,' he says, 'the shallows and shore are encrusted with arsenic and sulphur. Naturally forming; that's what makes it the colour it is. It would be very bad for you. Fine for the flamingos, but not for you.'

This whole time Zoe stares at the water.

'As I'm sure you are also probably all aware, these salt flats used to be a prehistoric lake called Lago Minchin, which began to shrink and evaporate about fifteen thousand years ago. Difficult to comprehend if you think about it too long. But the terrain of the Salt Centre dates from the same period, so we are touching a part of the world that has seen so much of life.'

Oscar ushers everyone towards a small stone circle. There is some ash present, perhaps from the last group that Oscar brought here. This is a prickly thought for Martha, the idea of others before her diluting the significance of her experience. She looks around, expecting to see people now, remembering the tourists arriving at the salt factory, a conveyer belt, the route well-trodden. But here, there really is no one else, and she acknowledges, is grateful, that they will continue to be completely alone.

Beside the stone circle Elbert is already unwrapping a parcel made of fabric, opening it up carefully. Resting within the material, Martha can now see, a wooden flute, various gemstones and incense sticks that remind her of sparklers. There are leaves and twigs too, bits of cactus arms, ripped from their bodies, and an old-looking flask with a blue plastic cup for a lid. It all appears completely random to Martha, and she struggles to make any meaningful connection between the objects.

'Everyone, please,' Oscar says, 'sit down.'

Barb looks down at the uneven stony ground and then around at the group as if she's needing further instruction. 'Are there cushions?' she asks.

Oscar offers her one of his knowing smiles. 'Remember, when we suffer, we learn.'

Barb goes to say something, her mouth open, but Rick touches her elbow, stopping her, before helping her to the ground, where she settles with her legs cast to the side. Martha sits down next to Barb, and the ground is indeed hard and cold, something digging into her leg. Finn sits beside her, unprompted, and she's grateful, marks this as another sign of the trip's potential success.

Elbert comes now to stand behind Oscar, and Martha senses a shift in power, that perhaps Elbert holds more sway than Oscar likes to give him credit for. Oscar hands the wooden flute to Elbert, who brings the instrument to his mouth. Martha suspects that the music is meant to be soothing, but she finds it jarring, its tone off, and she wants him to stop, wants to reach up and pull the instrument from his mouth. This is such a peaceful place, and the music is creating too much noise, disorientating, tainting it all, and there is incense burning too, the smell strong and overpowering. It's more stimulation than she can bear.

Oscar brushes his hand over all the random objects lying on the mat, before unscrewing the lid of the flask, pouring a liquid now into its lid. 'This is a special recipe, taken from the land, taken from our own cacti,' he says. 'Drink as much as you feel comfortable with. The effects are likely to come quickly but they should be pleasant, less intimidating than the salt brew.'

He passes the cup clockwise, Rick taking it, quizzical and hesitant before taking a large gulp. Martha can see the repulsion on his face.

Barb closes her eyes as she swallows, forcing the cup towards Martha as if she can't physically bear to hold it any longer.

Martha peers in at the cup. The liquid is green and gelatinous, but regardless, she forces herself to fill her mouth, before passing it on to Finn. The liquid chokes her, her cheeks filled to the brim. She imagines it is similar to eating aloe vera gel and houseplants, chewing the leaves up with her back molars. She swallows, but it's too much gloop for one gulp. She wants to scream in panic, feels a momentary sensation of drowning, the cactus juice clogging her throat. Her eyes are watering, and she takes a final gulp, relaxing with the sensation of her mouth emptying.

She watches Finn bring the cup to his lips, but he takes very little, if any.

Zoe is next, taking a mouthful, almost robotic, before passing it on to Hannah.

Oscar nods, pours more into the cup before taking a large gulp, reaching up then to offer the cup to Elbert who finally, finally stops playing his flute.

'Let us begin with a meditation,' Oscar says.

Martha nods, rolls her shoulders as if preparing for a race. She closes her eyes, the sun shining on her eyelids.

'Take a breath,' Oscar whispers, his voice a soothing hum. 'I want you all to focus on that breath, on the simple act of breathing. In and out through the nostrils. Focus only on the breath. In and out.'

Martha inhales deeply, holding it before exhaling. She's aware of a tightness in her back and she shifts, forcing herself to relax.

'If your mind is being drawn away,' Oscar says, practically purring, 'bring it back to your breath.'

Martha nods, eyes still closed, and thinks about her breath again.

'Now,' Oscar says, 'take your mind to a place of pure happiness. Something that fills you with joy.'

Martha's mind begins to dart, worried she'll land on the wrong memory. She tells herself to relax – there are no wrong answers. She settles on a holiday to France with Finn, attempts to focus on her perfect day – the warm evening sun, the beach, she and Finn sitting on large chair beanbags, drinking beer. It's the most beautiful place and everything feels well in the world. He's healthy; they're about to get engaged but she doesn't know it yet. It's just them, and they're happy and grateful. She's looking at the water, at the waves lapping, and she's thinking that Finn could so easily be dead, yet he's here, and he's breathing and drinking, and it's everything to her.

'Now harness that joy,' Oscar whispers. 'Remove the circumstances and just focus on the sensation of joy, of gratefulness.'

But Martha doesn't know how to separate the two from each other, the whole sensation, and the smile that has appeared spontaneously on her face is at risk of being lost in her confusion. She catches the noise of the waves in her ears, the feel of Finn's touch when he used to touch her all the time. Who cares if she can't let go of the environment in which she felt most happy? Who is ever going to know?

'Now open your eyes,' Oscar says.

Martha blinks several times, the sun now blinding her. She looks over to Finn, smiles at him with affection. He smiles back but he's distracted, and she wonders only then what his moment of joy was, suspects that it didn't include her. Regardless, she feels oddly calm, the cactus juice working its way through her. She swallows, thinks that she's beginning to feel lighter, has the sensation of her body floating upwards, capable of seeing the world from an elevated position. The tightness in her chest that she's so used to carrying around, the burden in every moment of the day, is absent. And she can't believe it, didn't think it was possible to not have that crippling pressure resting against her ribcage.

Near her, she sees Barb and Rick touching each other's faces, gentle strokes up and down their cheeks, eyes closed. Rick is whispering something to Barb, and she is still, expressionless, completely vacant.

Martha turns her face away from them, could so easily sleep, close her eyes and fall into a blissful state of rest. She spends most of her life struggling to sleep and now suddenly she can barely keep her eyes open. She is aware of Elbert playing his wooden flute again, but it's not bothering her any more; if anything it is serenading, and she smiles, filled with joy as she stretches out, lying flat on the ground, the sun warm on her face. She thinks she could stay like this forever, everything simply washing over her like a wave in the ocean. Everything passes. Everything is just thoughts. Fleeting. Nothing more. Her eyes are so heavy and there's no point in fighting it. Finally, she lets sleep come to her.

22

Finn surveys the landscape. A group of flamingos are staring out into the distance, their heads all pointing in the same direction, yet there doesn't seem to be anything to hold their attention. Martha is lying out on the ground next to the stone circle, asleep, face upwards towards the sky. He thinks again about last night's ceremony, about Martha vomiting into a bucket, aided by Ofelia, he remaining completely hands off, feeling the guilt of not caring for her when she is always willing to care for him.

Next to Martha, Hannah sits on the ground, legs crossed, eyes closed, and she's swaying backwards and forwards, a smile on her face. He shifts, aware of Zoe further along, standing too close to the water, the toes of her boots touching it. Finn moves towards her, suddenly fearful and anxious although he can't explain exactly why. He hovers, practically touching her, but Zoe seems unaware.

The colours of the lagoon unsettle him, the flamingos standing perfectly still within its shallower shores.

'Zoe, are you okay?' he says.

She turns briefly to look at him before returning her attention to the water.

'Is there something . . . Can I help?'

Still, she does not respond.

When Finn focuses once again on the water, he sees a flamingo lying horizontal, its head fully submerged. He understands now that it is this that has been holding her attention – this limp body, floating on the surface, its legs so long and bendy, its feet webbed. The rest of the flamingos, further in the water, seem oblivious. Perhaps they had shunned this one, pushed him out, perhaps there was a fight. Or had he died independently, taking himself away to spare the group? Had he been sacrificed?

Hannah comes to stand beside them, linking her arm into Finn's.

'She's beautiful, isn't she?' Hannah says, nodding towards Zoe.

He nods, smiles back at her, her eyes wide to the world.

'You should see her dance,' Hannah says. 'There's nothing like it. Your breath catches. It's my favourite thing in the world to watch.' She rubs at her nose, the ring through her septum moving up. 'But she won't dance any more . . . I was hoping, by coming here, that she would . . . ' Hannah still has this strange smile on her face as she speaks, despite the sadness of her words. They stand for a moment, still linked together, watching Zoe continue to stare at the dead flamingo. 'This feels nice,' Hannah says. 'This cactus juice, it's definitely better than the salt brew.' She glances up towards Finn. 'It's a shame you didn't try it.'

He lets a small laugh filter out through his nose. 'I just . . . I don't think this place is for me.'

'But Martha . . . ' she says.

'Martha seems to be getting what she needs from it,' he replies, glancing behind to see her still sleeping on the ground.

'It really is nice, you know,' Hannah says, unlinking her arm now and going to Zoe, gathering her into a hug, smiling, whispering words of love. And a pang of jealousy surfaces within him. He needs them to stop behaving as though all they need in the world is each other, when clearly that isn't true.

Finn goes to Martha, a selfish desire to be soothed by her, despite everything. He bends down, attempts to shake her awake. 'Martha . . . '

She's resistant.

'Martha,' he says again. 'Please, wake up!'

She opens her eyes, startled by him standing over her.

'You'll get cold lying there,' he says.

'I don't feel cold.'

He pulls at her, and she is reluctant. But her hand does feel cold, and, when he looks down, the tips of her middle fingers have already turned a strange shade of grey.

'Did you see this?' he asks, pointing to the water and the dead flamingo.

She looks. Nods. Her smile spreads.

He narrows his eyes. 'Martha, what is it you see?'

'A beautiful fish. I don't think I've ever seen a fish that bright pink before.'

Finn stares at her, an expression of alarm on his face. 'You see a fish?'

Martha walks with purpose, bends to touch it in the water.

'No,' Finn shouts, pulling her back from the water's edge. 'Don't touch it.'

She shrugs, indifferent to his warning.

'How do you feel?' he asks.

'I feel amazing,' she says. 'Everything is so beautiful.' Spontaneously, she reaches forward and plants a kiss on his lips. He smiles.

'It's nice to see you happy,' he replies.

He brings his hand to Martha's cheek. Her skin is hot to the touch. He finds her balaclava, pulling it over her face, fears that the damage has already been done.

Suddenly there is shouting, circling them, and he looks around, bringing his hand up to shield his eyes from the blinding sun. The shouting persists, grows louder. He can see Rick, sees his mouth open wide, feels the energy of his voice, but the words coming from him make no sense.

Martha is moving back towards the water, and he grips her by the arm, his fingers digging into her jacket. She looks down to where he's holding her and begins to giggle, the noise of her laughter intensifying.

'Martha,' he shouts, shaking her a little. 'Stop.'

'Quick,' Oscar shouts. 'Where is she . . . ?'

'Who?' Finn asks.

'Barb,' Oscar replies, casting his arms out wide.

'Have you tried the water?' Martha says.

Finn is aware then of Elbert running, tracks him as he moves around one side of the lagoon, his silhouette getting smaller and smaller. For a moment Finn thinks to follow Elbert, attempt to help, but he worries then that the rest of the group will scatter, that they'll never get them all back together.

'What happened?' Finn asks, confused as to how Barb managed to get so far without anyone noticing.

Oscar shakes his head. 'She was right by the water . . . and then she was gone.' He pauses, watching on as Elbert runs. 'Sometimes I think people move quicker when they're not being watched.'

Elbert is a distant creature now, so small he could be a dot. He could be nothing.

Rick is still sitting on the ground, distraught, making no sense. Finn goes to him, grips his shoulders. 'What happened?' he asked. But Rick won't answer, is crying too deeply.

Finn watches as Elbert slowly drags Barb back towards them.

Oscar is packing up the objects that rest on the colourful fabric, wrapping everything up into a neat parcel, while Rick sits on the ground with his head in his hands, muttering to himself. Finn glances around, feeling the need to account for everyone else – Hannah and Zoe are still standing by the shoreline, unmoving, and he looks at Martha again, her balaclava covering her face, a manic smile exposed through the hole cut out for the mouth.

The closer Elbert and Barb get to them, the more Finn can see that she's putting up a fight, desperate to be free. Elbert manages to get her back to the group but she's hysterical, screaming, begging to be left alone. And there is blood on Elbert's hand, skin broken, and Finn can see now that Barb has bitten him. Oscar reaches into the backpack, fraught words being exchanged between him and Elbert in Spanish, and Finn thinks that neither of them gets paid enough for this type of shit. He's glad that he made the decision not to swallow any of the cactus juice – that he's able to document all of this, a fly on the wall. He thinks fleetingly of his friend who doesn't drink, who doesn't mean to rub his sobriety in their faces yet remembers each of them at their worst.

As Elbert continues to restrain Barb, Oscar cleans the bite mark on Elbert's hand with an antiseptic wipe, before placing a plaster over it.

'It is time to begin the journey back,' Oscar says, trying to retain his composure, taking Barb from Elbert's grip. 'Let us go.'

Elbert takes the backpack and slings it up over his shoulder, surveying the land, ensuring that nothing has been left behind.

Finn swallows, his throat feeling like glass again, any benefit from his double dose now long gone. 'Oscar . . . ' he says. 'I think I need some water before we go . . . My throat . . . '

Oscar looks at Elbert, conversing with him again in Spanish, and Finn can only make out the work *agua*, knows it means water.

'Elbert has some in the bag which we bring only for emergencies.'

'Okay . . . ' Finn says.

'Is this an emergency?' Oscar asks, doing his best to keep his tone even and calm.

'I wouldn't say it's an emergency . . . ' Finn replies.

'Then I urge you to refrain.' He pauses. 'This trek is about sacrifice and suffering. And travelling in the sun without water is what thousands of people are forced to endure every single day.'

Finn bites down on his lip. 'Okay . . . ' he says.

They carry on in silence, Oscar never letting go of Barb, the lagoon now completely out of view. Finn misses it, thinks it's unsettling to be able to see only salt and sky again. He's exhausted too, desperate to collapse on to a bed. He's aware that his pace is slowing, while the others, perhaps revitalised by the cactus juice, appear to be faring okay. Oscar is up ahead and he's marching, his arm linked tightly to Barb's in anticipation of her bolting again. Rick is behind them, weeping still, whispering words of repentance, offering them like a scattering to the sky. Elbert is staying close to him. Zoe is focused on nothing more than the salt ahead, while Martha walks with Hannah, both similar in height, their steps in sync, their balaclavas making them appear eerily like twins and difficult to tell apart.

Finn swallows, the broken-glass sensation travelling down his oesophagus unbearable. From somewhere within him, he finds the strength to call out to Oscar in the distance.

Oscar comes to a sudden stop, half-turning to acknowledge the call.

Finn tries to pick up his pace, feels as though he's dragging his feet across the salt. As he approaches Oscar, he pulls up his balaclava, bunching it over his forehead.

'Oscar, I'm sorry but I really need some water . . . ' he says.

'No, you don't,' Oscar replies, his usual soothing tone gone. 'You only think you do, but your body is more resilient than you give it credit for.'

Finn shakes his head. 'No,' he replies. 'My body is telling me what it wants, and it needs water. I'm ill.'

'You've been ill your whole life,' Oscar says. He shifts then, pulling Barb's arm closer to him. 'Only now are you giving yourself the opportunity to become well.'

Barb's head hangs low, but she's staring up at Finn.

'The whole idea of this trek is to sacrifice our own needs to Mother Nature. Submit ourselves to this environment. Become acutely aware that it is hostile to us. That nature is in control here, and only by submitting to it and sacrificing our perceived needs can we come to truly accept what this landscape has to offer us.'

Finn stares at him. 'I don't think Mother Nature is going to feel angry if I have a sip of water.'

'You will come to regret it,' Oscar says.

'I think I'll be fine.'

Oscar stares at him.

'Just give me some fucking water,' Finn shouts. 'Please.'

Everyone is waiting.

'Finn, my friend, speak to your mind, find your inner strength. Look around you. No one else is demanding water. Everyone else here understands the sacrifice they set out to make.'

But Finn is unflinching.

Slowly, Oscar shakes his head. Still linked to Barb, he asks Elbert for the *agua*, and Finn knows he's won.

Elbert unzips his backpack and removes a small plastic bottle of spring water. He gives the bottle first to Oscar, who then jolts it back in his hand when Finn reaches for it.

'Are you sure?' Oscar asks.

Finn swipes the bottle from his grip and begins to unscrew the lid.

'Take note,' Oscar says, addressing the others, his voice booming. 'This is what weakness looks like. Occasionally, we all need to be reminded of weakness, so use this as an example to strengthen your own minds.'

Finn snorts with laughter, before bringing the bottle to his lips. He can't gulp it; it's too painful. Instead, he takes small, measured sips, aware that all eyes are still on him. When he's finished, he goes to hand the bottle back, but Oscar won't take it.

'We don't need it,' Oscar says. 'Please, finish it. Come dusk there will be a banquet of food and refreshments, a reward, and everyone else will feel the benefits of their restraint.'

Finn nods, letting a wide, angry grin settle on his face. 'I can't fucking eat anyway.'

Oscar shakes his head, and he begins to move again, the rest of the group following, controlled in their steps. Martha doesn't even look back, oblivious to his pain, and he's furious, because she's always acknowledged his pain, has always been the one to deal with it, to care for it.

'I'm dying to know,' Finn shouts after them. 'What were your convictions for, Oscar? What deplorable things put you in jail?'

But Oscar does not reply, and no one else registers his words. It is as if he has not spoken. He stands, watching them all retreat further, and he unscrews the lid of the water again, taking another sip.

He crouches down, deciding to sit on one specific slab of salt, running his fingers along the edge of a crust. Despite the sun bearing down, the salt surface is cool to the touch. He brings his mouth to the surface and licks it. It's rough and tastes nothing like salt. He can feel a sting on his tongue, taps it against the roof of his mouth. He sips more water, looks around and realises that they are so far ahead of him now that he could easily get lost. What would happen if he just continued to sit here? When would they finally look round and check? He finishes the last of the water, scrunches the plastic bottle up and screws the cap back on. He stares at its deformed shape, thinks it resembles a sculpture, placing the bottle down on the hexagonal-shaped slab that he's been sitting on. Perhaps it can serve as a marker for his being here, a guide to return to if need be. He doesn't see it as littering. If there is no one to see him perform an action, does the action even exist?

He gets to his feet, seeing only the faintest glimpse of the group now. He closes his eyes and turns himself around in a circle a few times. When he looks out, every direction looks the same. He glances down at the plastic bottle and the direction in which its lid is pointing. He smiles and sets off, the empty bottle his compass. As he walks further away from the bottle, he turns to look at it. He feels so overwhelmingly lonely, has an urge to return and retrieve the bottle. But he carries on instead, one foot in front of the other, the balaclava warm against his skin, the sun in his eyes. The beauty of the salt flats is no longer awe-inspiring; he can only be grateful for something for so long.

23

In front of Martha there is a banquet of food, more plates than she thinks she's ever seen, Ofelia continually returning with more. But the basket of hard-boiled eggs sitting closest is what holds her attention. She can't get enough of them. There is eggshell on her plate, her mouth full of egg, the yolk solid and dry. Her gaze is off in the distance, to the darkness outside, the circular room shadowed by dim lighting. Her hand reaches for another egg. She bashes it down on her plate and begins to roll it from side to side, pieces of shell coming away. She brings the egg up towards her, cupping it in both hands as she works more of the shell off, tiny jagged fragments falling away, landing everywhere.

'Where is Oscar?' Martha says, glancing at his empty seat at the head of the table.

'Maybe he's had enough of us for one day,' Hannah replies.

'Pass the eggs,' Rick says.

Martha's eyes dart around the room, in the hope that Oscar will appear at the simple mention of his name. She thought everything had been going well, the healing process commencing as it should. But then Finn's outburst, and Barb now sitting here, pretending that she hadn't attempted to run away.

'Martha, the eggs!' Finn is saying, already reaching for the basket, handing it to Rick.

She looks up, sees Hannah take a handful of carrot sticks from a bowl, scooping a huge dollop of hummus on to her plate. There is hardly any hummus left now. Hannah crunches the carrot, her chewing loud.

Zoe has nothing on her plate.

'Aren't you eating?' Martha asks, biting into her new egg.

Zoe looks up at her, a glazed expression behind the eyes.

'Zoe,' Hannah presses. 'Please speak . . . This isn't healthy.'

But Zoe doesn't respond, and no one says anything.

Martha gulps down her glass of water – a thirst she cannot slake, a coating on the tongue.

'I'd kill for a steak,' Barb says.

Finn reaches for a tomato, breaking the skin with his teeth, juice squirting in his eye. 'Jesus fucking Christ,' he shouts.

Martha prickles, forcing another bite of egg into her mouth, feeling as though everything is at risk of collapsing. She closes her eyes, opens them again. 'I don't feel right . . . ' she says.

'Stop eating eggs, then,' Finn replies harshly.

'I've lost all sense of time, completely,' Barb says. 'I don't like it any more.'

Rick reaches for more bread. His plate is littered with unfinished food.

'There isn't an infinite amount of food,' Martha says, pointing at his plate. 'You do know that they had to bring all of this with them?'

Rick holds her eye as he rips a chunk of bread with his teeth. 'My money paid for this bread.'

'So did mine,' she replies. 'It's just consume, consume, consume, is it?'

Rick stuffs more bread into his mouth, at risk of choking.

Finn picks up the jug of water and pours himself a glass, before unscrewing one of his medicine bottles. 'Well, aren't we one big happy family this evening,' he says.

There is silence as everyone watches Finn take his medicine. To Martha, it feels as though they've been watching him do this for a lifetime.

She pours herself more water. She gulps it, can't seem to get it down her throat quick enough, yet it makes little difference to her dry mouth and constant thirst.

'Barb . . . ' Finn says. 'I can't stop thinking about it . . . Where were you going earlier?'

Barb stops, looking up at Finn. 'Sorry?'

'I'm wondering where you thought you were going when you ran away?'

'I . . . '

Rick places his hand on Barb's arm. 'We're not talking about this,' he says.

'You were on a real mission . . . ' Finn says.

Barb looks as if she is on the verge of tears, but Martha can tell that Finn won't stop, that something has changed in him, a familiar cruelty that he's capable of imposing, prepared to take things too far. He can fixate on the smallest detail, convince himself that it all means something when perhaps it does not.

'Were you trying to get away from here?' he presses. 'Had you just had enough?' He picks up his tomato before placing it back down again. 'Because I get that,' he says. 'Really, I do. I've had enough too.'

'Finn . . . ' Martha says. 'Don't.'

'Why?'

'Because some of us actually fucking *need* this. Okay? So, please, just shut the fuck up.'

Rick slams his fist down on the table. 'I've been having an affair, okay? That's the reason Barb ran. It's because of me. I have a compulsion. I need to change. I know that. I'm not a good person.'

Barb is crying now, and Hannah reaches over, handing her a napkin.

'We were all friends,' Barb whispers. 'Rick and I, we were cheating on our spouses, with each other, for years – that's how all this started,' she says. 'So, it's not as if I didn't know what you were capable of . . . '

Rick pushes his plate full of food away from him. 'There you have it,' he says. 'And it's not even a listening circle.'

'Martha has experience in that department too,' Finn says, tilting his head, prodding his finger at the tomato on his plate.

Martha's breath catches in her mouth. She sits forward, ears ringing, blood coursing loudly through her body. 'Finn . . . ' she pleads. She can feel the tears, surfacing, the wet sensation on her cheeks, her humiliation cast out across the table along with the food.

'Is that why you came here?' Rick says.

Martha shakes her head, struggles to find the words. 'It's a symptom . . . '

Oscar arrives, gripping the back of his chair and Martha wishes he would sit, anchor them back to where they need to be.

He smiles. 'Have you all enjoyed this feast Ofelia has prepared?'

Martha nods, wiping her tears away, feeling exposed.

'I told you your sacrifices would be worth it,' he says. 'I hope you see that now.'

From the way he looks around the table, Martha suspects that he's been listening to their conversation the entire time, standing just out of sight.

'I suggest rest,' he says. 'It has been a long and challenging day, and our final full day is ahead of us tomorrow.' He pauses. 'There is no right or wrong way to approach your time here, just the knowledge that you are always learning and evolving, facing your fears and traumas head on.' He nods. 'A certain level of anger and confrontation is to be expected. Do not linger on it; do not punish each other for the past.'

Finn gets to his feet.

'You only gain what you put into this experience,' Oscar presses.

Finn grabs a torch and walks out towards the patio. Martha sits, a heaviness in her chest, while Ofelia begins to tidy up around them, gathering and stacking dirty dishes in her hands. As she comes to Martha's side, Martha reaches out and touches her green suede bowler-like hat. Ofelia, startled by Martha's touch, straightens, nearly dropping a plate.

'I'm sorry,' Martha says. 'I just . . . I think it's beautiful.'

Ofelia speaks to Oscar, her words low. Oscar turns to Martha. 'She asks that you do not touch it.'

Martha nods, closing her eyes for a moment. 'Of course, I'm so sorry.'

The others depart for the dorm and Martha makes to follow, but hesitates, deciding to peer through the windows of the patio doors, the darkness total. She grabs another torch from a coffee table and heads outside.

'Finn . . . ' she calls.

He's nowhere to be seen.

She shines the light around the patio area, checks the hammock. She has this fear then that he's left, inspired by Barb's exploits earlier. She casts the torch out, shining its light across the salt flats, but she can see nothing. She begins to work her way around the side of the property, turning a corner into the small courtyard in front of the kitchen and where, opposite, the strange dome structure sits, made entirely from branches, bent into shape. She sees him then, crouched down beside the llama, stroking its coat.

'I'm sorry,' Finn says. 'I shouldn't have said that in there. I just . . . Being here, it's all too much, Martha.'

She steps closer. 'Why didn't you drink the cactus juice today? You said you'd try.'

He turns to look at her, shielding his eyes from the glare of her torch. 'I am trying, Martha. I'm trying really, really, hard.'

She shakes her head. 'You're making a mockery of why we've come here.'

He stands, tall and thin, so thin. 'You've made a mockery of our life. You've become this self-righteous person . . . constantly angry, desperate to find the unjust in everything you see. It's unbearable.'

'I just want the world to be habitable – is that too much to ask? I just want things to be fairer for everyone . . . '

He shakes his head. 'We are only here, right here, because we are privileged. That's why we're allowed this opportunity. It's all corruption and geography; some people get more, some people get less. That's the system we're operating in. You think you want to be a socialist but are you willing to give up everything you already have to become one?'

'Like what?' she counters, defensive.

'The house . . . Our way of life, our middle-class existence.'

'I would give the house up,' she says. 'I would give it all up tomorrow. It makes me feel dirty.'

'Leave me too, then, if I make you feel so dirty.'

She stares at him, taken aback. Even when she confessed to her affair, he never asked her to leave. 'Do you mean that?' she asks.

'We can't keep going round in circles like this . . . '

'Today, asleep out by the lagoon, I had this dream, this image of a child—'

'Martha—' He holds his hand up, as if needing her to stop.

'I'm feeling so much better already,' she says, her words flowing quickly. 'This place is making me better.' She falters, the cold of the night seeping into her bones. 'I don't want to live my life being scared any more.' She pauses. 'It's okay for you, you have all the time in the world to father a baby . . . '

'It's okay for me? It's okay that if I want to have a kid I've got to have my sperm defrosted in a facility that I pay an annual £365 storage fee for? That's fair?'

'That's not what I meant,' she says, shaking her head. 'Please . . . you're putting words into my mouth.'

He exhales, rubs at his face. 'Martha, I want you to get better,' he says. 'I'm desperate for you to get better, because then . . . '

'Then what?' she says, a hopefulness seeping into her voice.

'Honestly . . . because I don't think this marriage *is* working any more.' He shrugs. 'Maybe if you're better, then . . . then finally we'll be able to go our separate ways.'

Martha sucks in her breath, everything feeling tight, a winded sensation in her chest. She shakes her head, the idea of his words difficult to comprehend. 'Okay . . . ' She sits down now on the ground, slowly, as though at risk of falling, the torch resting on the ground beside them.

'I just think . . . it might be for the best, for everyone,' he says.

'Finn, have you ever actually liked me?'

'What? Of course. I love you.'

'Your way of showing love . . . It's not fair.' She clicks the button of the torch, on and off, on and off, the feel of the rubber satisfying. 'Is this because of what happened with Jacob?'

Finn doesn't say anything.

The memory is so clear in her mind – this stranger coming home with her at 2 a.m., the camera catching their faces as she fumbled, drunkenly, for her keys. There had been footage of a fox the week before, eating the early buds of their freshly planted apple trees, its eyes shining bright as it looked up at the lens. She hadn't meant to sleep with Jacob, not the first time. But she'd liked his company, felt understood, instead of feeling shunned by those around her. And she was lonely, Finn's distancing already in full swing.

'I think you wanted me to fuck things up, so that you had a real excuse to hold a grudge against me,' she says. 'Sometimes, I think you're a coward who can't bear the idea of being in the wrong when it comes to our relationship, so you wait, and press, and prod me into making the mistakes so you can play the victim.'

He's shaking his head. 'That's not true . . . ' is all he manages.

'It wasn't a one-off,' she says. 'I was just more careful after the first time. And I did feel terrible, mostly because I do really fucking love you. I've always loved you. But it kind of felt like it didn't matter. That you didn't really care either way.'

He says nothing.

'Finn, say something.'

'Let's just get through this last full day tomorrow,' he says, before walking away.

The llama looks up into the torchlight, hunkered down for the night, oblivious.

Saturday

24

Finn stands outside in the morning light, wearing a vest and his boxer shorts. He is watching Elbert, in a loose-fitting white garment, strengthening the large wooden dome-like structure that is positioned near where the llama rests. Elbert is weaving long branches into the curved shape, delicate in his actions, working around an obvious entrance, adding to the intricacy of it. When the dome is finally to his liking, he begins to heave a huge canvas over its frame, anchoring it down before layering it up with large blankets and animal skins.

This, Finn has been informed, is the *sweat lodge*. Layer after layer is piled on, each positioned in a particular way, the dome somehow looking smaller for it, solid and compact, and Finn can't imagine any of them fitting inside.

Opposite the dome sits the fire pit, black ash within. Ofelia, wearing a white floor-length gown, is carrying an armful of logs, coming towards him, dropping one by accident near his bare foot. He watches as she builds the fire, quick in her actions: kindling, one match, the flames taking hold before him. He thinks about the multipurpose Leatherman penknife in his bag, knows it wouldn't help him start a fire, decides he should buy a fire flint and starter when he gets home. But he'll never be as capable as either Elbert or Ofelia, accepts this in a way most defeatists accept everything.

Peering closer into the fire, he can see that she's stacked the wood in a specific way, pyramidal in fashion, adding more kindling, muttering words in a prayer-like fashion. Finn is transfixed by her actions and the glow of the flames. Finally, she steps back and circles the fire. Elbert now has large stones scooped up on a spade, the weight heavy in his hands. The stones are smooth, appearing carefully chosen, and Elbert tips them into the fire. One stone hisses and Elbert and Ofelia peer into the flames, attempting to identify the stone; Elbert forces it out with his spade and on to the ground.

The others arrive, led by Oscar, who is wearing a similar garment to Elbert. Martha, like all the women, is wearing a long nightdress, which Finn is sure she would never normally wear. Rick is last, having also stripped down, vest and Y-fronts.

Finn has a sudden desire to run, as Barb had the day before, but he suspects that he wouldn't get very far, simply returned to be further shamed. Instinctively, he looks to Martha for reassurance, but of course she won't meet his eye.

Oscar clasps his hands together. 'I will carry out a brief *smudging* ceremony,' he says, 'an offering, usually tobacco,' he adds, pulling a pouch from his pocket, 'then we will begin to bring the stones into the centre of the sweat lodge. We are praying to heat the *grandfathers* – the rocks. The greater we pray, the hotter the grandfathers become. We will experience all elements through this ceremony, earth from the ground, air from around us, the sacred fire before us and water from its steam.'

Oscar takes the spade from Elbert and lifts one large stone from its centre, balancing the weight of the spade in both hands. Elbert holds layers of blankets and animal skins up from the dome's makeshift entrance and Oscar stoops to get inside. Almost immediately, steam is escaping from the sweat lodge and Oscar returns with the empty spade, walking with purpose to retrieve the next stone.

When Oscar is finished, he turns to address the group. 'There are four stages to a sweat lodge. I encourage and urge you,' he says, focusing on Finn, 'all to remain until the end.' He pauses. 'This will not be easy, nor is it meant to be, but this experience will prepare and cleanse your body for our final salt ceremony tonight.'

The others are nodding, even Zoe, and Finn feels helpless, yet he'll not allow himself to be beaten by this – won't allow Oscar the satisfaction of claiming Finn's next failure.

'I will enter first,' Oscar says, 'and then the other men, oldest to youngest, and finally the women, again oldest to youngest.' He inhales deeply, closing his eyes for a moment as he exhales. 'May I remind each of you that this experience is about purification, and connecting with the spirits who protect us. You must show the sweat lodge your utmost respect. No distracting others, no expulsion of bodily fluids that are not perspiration.'

Everyone is still nodding, and Finn carries the sensation of simply being an observer.

'There will be a short break between each part, where you will be allowed to leave the lodge, get a drink of water or go to the toilet.' Again, his attention lands on Finn. 'This first part is about enduring, acknowledging your discomfort and believing in your ability to overcome it.' He pauses. 'This first round represents air and the birth of life. A time for mindful reflection and thought. Prayer is often useful, so feel free to pray aloud or to yourself. Are there any questions?'

No one says anything.

'Okay, let us begin.'

Oscar enters, followed by Rick, then Elbert, and Finn hesitates, looking at the women; he has a sense of them banding together, turning on him. And then he enters, having to hunker down, his back bent at an awkward angle. He can barely make anything out in the darkness, aside from the silhouette of the other men sitting on the ground, huddled close in the limited space, while steam rises from the stones gathered in the centre. He sits down, next to Elbert, and Barb is now entering, shuffling in, almost stumbling until she is settled beside her husband, followed by Ofelia. Martha enters next and sits beside Finn; whether she means to or not, he doesn't know. Next is Zoe, and Finn is surprised to realise that she is older than Hannah; he'd had it in his mind that she was the younger of the couple. When Hannah settles, the layers of fabric are pulled down over the entrance, plunging the small enclosure into almost complete darkness.

The heat of the lodge settles on Finn quickly, a swallowing, overwhelming his body, his bones, his thoughts. It's suffocating and he stretches his chest out, attempts to take a deep breath but the air is empty. There is nothing to suck on.

There is the familiar noise of hissing, Finn thinking he can make out the shape of Oscar adding water to the heated stones, before the steam begins to blur his vision further.

He realises that he hasn't drunk nearly enough water for this experience. Everyone's breathing is so heavy and caustic. Oscar is whispering words, but Finn has already lost the thread of their meaning – something about self-belief, about a baby's desires being so simple and pure.

'It's easy to feel lost,' Oscar whispers soothingly, 'especially in the current world we inhabit. As a child our souls are pure, but as we enter society, enter adulthood, we quickly lose our childlike love for the world.' He pauses. 'By being here and partaking in this sweat lodge you are opening yourself up to finding that love once again.'

Finn straightens, his legs crossed, uncomfortable, the steam making his eyes sting, clamping them shut now, the tension of it all spreading across his face. How are they meant to endure this for hours? He shifts, thinks of a strategy for coping, tries to imagine that he's listening to one of his podcasts, words being able to hold his attention for prolonged periods of time, or that he is driving on autopilot to the heliport for work, with no memory of the journey. How hours disappear when you don't want them to, but minutes feel endless when you're desperate for something to be over. He thinks of the BOSIET survival training he must endure every four years to ensure he can work offshore – of being strapped into the body of a helicopter, his survival suit on, the mouthpiece and small bag he has for blowing oxygen into, the body of the helicopter being submerged into a pool, of them being rotated until they are upside down. And only then are they allowed to attempt to leave, unbuckling their seatbelts, climbing out of the open windows, offering the hand gesture of *okay* to the supervising pool divers. All of it extreme, yet he's made to feel as though it is all perfectly reasonable. He's paid well for his time and effort, but mostly because, despite no one wanting to talk about it, there is significant risk to his life. And he knows that the training is pointless – knows that if his helicopter did ditch in the North Sea it would be nothing like the simulations they practise. He knows he wouldn't be coming back.

He can hear someone crying now, the whimpering coming from what he thinks is the other side of the circle. He moves his hand, as if blind and needing to feel his surroundings, bumping up against Martha's hand. Reflexively she pulls away and he doesn't blame her – they have not exchanged a single word since the night before.

He tries to imagine his life after this, them no longer being together. There is a sense of excitement but there is also the flutter of nerves, of the unknown. He shifts his mind to the practicalities of their separation, of everything being divided in half. It occurs to him that they'll have to sell the house; he wonders how easy it is to change their joint membership at the gym. There is so much to unpick between them, a life built from his sickness that has endured nearly twenty years. Suddenly a sadness fills him, a mourning he wasn't expecting. Despite their differences and troubles, there have been good times: private jokes, celebrations, an understanding of one another's likes and dislikes that takes time. He imagines seeing her with another man, maybe Jacob, walking down the street together holding hands, and he doesn't picture himself getting jealous, more fascinated – he'll think, *that used to be the hand I held, the mouth I kissed.* He'll still know her body and mind better than most who come after him.

He swallows, the pain in his oesophagus still jagged and sore. He knows this environment isn't helping – the thirst, the perspiration. He thought he was coping with it but he's not. It's unbearable.

Finally, there is a shaft of light. And Finn is struggling, moving slowly on his hands and knees, and then the light is everywhere and far too bright. The coolness of the air hits him, a winding to the chest as he struggles to his feet. Ofelia appears composed, handing him a glass of water that he brings to his lips, gulping on it, choking on it.

25

Steam is stinging Martha's eyes but there is nothing for her to rub them with. The new stones that have been placed in the centre feel unbearable. She can't imagine enduring two further rounds of this. There is a familiar sensation of panic, the heat overwhelming, no room to stretch out, a negative energy seeping in that feels all too familiar. She could mop parts of herself up, tip cups of her perspiration back on to the stones in the centre, revel in the noise of the hiss. There is a strange, almost metallic smell and she becomes consumed by thoughts of what its potential source could be. The sweat is still stinging her eyes and she clamps them shut, wants to claw at her sockets, everything once again itchy and excruciating. She has a sensation that the sweat is morphing her into an entirely different person, that parts of her have come away. Her hands have puffed up in the heat, her wedding ring cutting into her skin. She thinks of the metal rails next to a footpath by their house, and how the branches of a large tree have grown in between the rails, contorting and stretching, the tree and the rusting metal now entwined. She questions what will happen in the end, if the tree will be cut away from the metal or if someone will take an angle-grinder, free an intact tree from the metal's embrace. She suspects that the intact metal will be valued more. She thinks again about her swelling fingers, wonders how she will ever get her wedding ring off. She wishes then that her hands were smaller. All her relatives before her had small hands.

Every ring she has inherited had to be significantly resized to accommodate her knuckles. How delicate people before her were.

She shifts, wants so desperately to stretch her legs. It's unbearable. She feels as if she could die in here, but she will not leave. She quit most things in her youth, stuck at nothing, but she will not do that here, not when she feels so close to something that until now has seemed unattainable. She is aware of someone's breathing, short and rapid, a panic attack in motion, and all she can think is, *oh, God, what if it's Finn*? She tries to swallow but there is no saliva. She wants to lick something, thinks about her grandmother dying in hospital, the nurse dripping droplets of water on to her wafer-thin lips.

Her own breath is quickening. She's thinking of a trip to Thailand with university friends, of attempting to learn to scuba-dive, of being weighted down at the bottom of a pool, breathing frantically and erratically through a mouthpiece. The diving instructor had signalled to the group to ask if they were okay, index finger and thumb together in a circle. But she could only shake her head, the gauge on her oxygen tank low, she in her panic inhaling everything.

Someone opposite her is coughing now. It's hacking and harsh, but it must be hard to clear. The sweat is pouring off her and she runs her hand through her hair; it feels wet and sticky against her skin. She brings a strand of hair to her mouth and begins to suck on it, tries to use its moisture to hydrate herself. It's salty. Everything is salty. She speculates how much water she has lost to perspiration. She brushes her arm up against Finn and immediately she shifts. All these years she has been imagining a life where he's finally taken from her, against their will, but now he's promised to simply walk away of his own accord. And she can't visualise it, not at all. She thinks about her bank card of all things, wonders if you keep your married name after a divorce or if you revert back to your maiden name. She tries to imagine living in her own place, making decisions about every piece of furniture, when they have always made decisions like that together. She went to visit an old schoolfriend not so long ago in Glasgow. This friend had no long-term partner or children – her flat was beautiful, and when Martha was left alone in it she had spent so long wandering from room to room, marvelling at the idea of someone being so self-sufficient, having everything exactly as they, personally, would like, without compromise, when from the age of twenty-one she has done nothing but compromise.

Martha has no idea how long they have been sitting here for now. Maybe this is what hell is – never being able to leave an uncomfortable situation. She thinks about her last trip to the hairdresser's, how a junior had been tasked with washing the dye out of her hair, but the girl must have been struggling, because she kept rinsing, again and again, while Martha remained stuck in one of those basin chairs, for forty minutes, her head tilted backwards in an awkward position. She had begun to lose all sense of reality, too polite to say anything, but holding an irrational fear that she'd never be allowed to leave this basin. That she should cancel everything in her life because she lived in that basin now, existing with her head always positioned at this uncomfortable angle.

Somewhere in the distance, Oscar is chanting, but the person's cough is drowning him out. Martha can tell from the breathing that the person is desperate for it to stop, would do anything to make their cough stop. She thinks it is Hannah, but really it could be anyone. She can't remember what she was meant to be thinking, what she was meant to be focusing her mind on. She licks her lips. Nothing but salt. *Fire and ripening*, that was the theme of round two, she remembers, but is unclear as to what it means.

Finally, they are allowed to leave again, and Martha is not polite in her exit, shoving past others on her hands and knees to emerge behind Ofelia. She worries about a stampede, of bodies in a bottleneck, all fighting to get outside, desperate for air, for water, for life. When she turns, Zoe and Hannah are beside her, Barb slowly crawling out behind them. Finn is after Barb, and he looks as though he's surviving, and she can't help but feel grateful that he's okay.

As Rick emerges, attempting to pull himself up to full height, something gives way. It's a noise of suffering, animalistic and uncontainable, and it shocks Martha. He collapses, flat on to his stomach, with Oscar stuck behind him.

'What's wrong?' Barb shouts. 'Rick, what is it?'

Rick lets the pain seep through his body, grunting as he attempts to turn on to his side, into the foetal position.

Oscar manages to squeeze past him and rises quickly to his feet, standing over Rick, bewildered and perhaps a little distressed. 'Rick, do you have a heart condition you did not inform me about?'

Rick closes his eyes, breathing out the pain. He shakes his head. 'No, I don't have a heart condition . . . I'm not having a fucking heart attack. I've pulled my fucking back coming out of this fucking hole.'

'Oh, God,' Barb says, peering down at him. 'You're in spasm.' She looks up at the group, pleading. 'He's not had trouble with his back in so long.' She pauses. 'Does anyone have any diazepam?' she says. 'Anyone? Please . . . '

But everyone is shaking their heads.

All attention turns to Oscar. 'We of course don't keep Western medicine on the premises,' he says, gesturing now for Ofelia. He stands over Rick, as though contemplating a puzzle. 'We have other traditional means of treating neurological pain. Salt rubs, herbal options too.' He's oddly detached as he speaks, as if reading from a manual for the first time. 'I'm sure we'll be able to alleviate your pain.'

Elbert is instructed to lift Rick and he does so obediently, but it's difficult, Rick wailing out in agony as Elbert attempts to heave him upwards, Finn now hovering around the edges, hesitant to help but clearly feeling as though he needs to get involved. He's always been like this, and Martha finds it irritating. If Finn were to find himself witnessing an emergency – a car accident or someone collapsing on the street – he'd stop, but not because he wanted to, more because there would be an expectation, an obligation to do so.

They eventually manage to get Rick into a vertical position, but he's turning an unhealthy shade of grey. His vomit comes, filling his cheeks, spluttering out on to the ground, too close to the sacred fire for Oscar's liking. Some of the vomit lands on Elbert but he remains composed, guiding Rick slowly away from the entrance of the sweat lodge, while Barb flutters around them in panic, and Martha decides that Elbert is definitely not getting paid enough for this job. If anything, he should be the one getting the biggest tip at the end of their stay. She wants to laugh at the absurdity of it all, and it seems to her only then that she's been thinking about this whole experience as if it were a test, as if the couples were in competition with each other. Everyone appearing to fail.

Rick and Elbert are out of sight, yet she can still hear Rick's cries of pain; they all can. Oscar attempts to take new hot *grandfather* rocks into the sweat lodge, Ofelia tending further to the fire, and Martha braces herself to be called back in, to submit herself to the third round of sweating, its theme *water and ageing.* If anything, at least there will now be more room without Rick; she might even enjoy the darkness, try and relax into an almost meditative sleep, stretch out a little and let her head touch the earth.

But Ofelia is pointing to something and calling Oscar, saying his name repeatedly. When Martha looks, she can see that Ofelia's attention and distress is directed towards Hannah, her pointing finger ridged. Hannah looks alarmed, shuffling backwards, terrified to be under anyone's scrutiny, but Ofelia keeps saying the same word, *la sangre*, again and again.

Oscar marches over to Hannah, gripping her wrist, forcing her to turn while Zoe watches on, mute and lifeless.

'*La sangre*,' Ofelia is still saying, almost shouting.

And then Martha sees it: the blood. A perfect shade of red, delicious against the off-white of her nightdress, a stain that will be unlikely to come out.

Oscar shakes his head, but it looks as though it is taking everything in him not to smack Hannah. 'I told you . . . ' he says, his voice tight. 'A sweat lodge is a place of purity. I explained in very specific details earlier that the only bodily fluid allowed in a sweat lodge is perspiration . . . I made that abundantly clear. I don't think I could have been any clearer.'

Hannah's mouth is open and she's struggling to find the words, her throat perhaps stuffed with shame. 'I didn't know . . . ' she says. 'I didn't know it was coming . . . My body is confused.'

Oscar is still shaking his head. 'It's ruined now,' he says. 'Do you understand? We will not finish the sweat because the space is now contaminated. It is no longer pure and therefore our own purification cannot be achieved.'

Hannah looks at the group, as if needing to be rescued, and this vulnerability is new. 'I'm sorry,' she says, her eyes wide and watery. 'I'm so sorry. I didn't mean to ruin anything for anyone.' She shifts her posture, crossing her feet at the ankles, pressing her legs together to no doubt stop any more blood from seeping through the fabric or down her legs. Zoe slowly reaches for Hannah's hand – it's the only gesture she seems capable of making.

'I suggest,' Oscar says, really trying to contain his fury, 'that everyone retreat to the dorm and take some time to rest while we deconstruct the sweat lodge and extinguish the sacred fire.'

'But what about tonight?' Martha says, a pleading sense of desperation present. She's come too far not to experience their final salt ceremony.

Oscar is quiet for a moment, sizing something up in his mind. 'The final ceremony will still go ahead.' He pauses. 'Menstruation does not alter the ritual of a salt ceremony.'

Martha can feel herself exhaling, a long breath she didn't realise she was holding in. 'Thank you,' she says. 'Thank you.'

Hannah's voice is quivering. 'I'm sorry. I really am . . . '

Martha comes to Hannah, taking her other hand. 'It's okay,' she whispers. 'Honestly, it's okay.'

Hannah crumples, titling her chin to her chest, and she cries, so deeply.

'Do you need a pad or a tampon?' Martha whispers.

Hannah nods.

'Don't worry, I have some,' she says. 'It's okay, it's happened to us all. Come on, let's get you cleaned up.' She begins to rub Hannah's back, gentle the way she might soothe a child if she had one. It seems to be working, Hannah catching her breath, while Zoe stands awkwardly behind them, everyone still watching. And Martha can feel the humiliation, has witnessed a cruelty that didn't need to be exhibited. It brings back the shame of her own first period, when she too was caught off guard. She'd been one of the last to get her period in school, many of her friends getting theirs two to three years before, their bodies ready for the harsh future that lay ahead. But finally, at fifteen, after pretending that she was already menstruating, it arrived with such ferocity, and despite the supplies she kept in her school bag she could not keep up with the blood. She would fill a sanitary pad while simply sitting in one lesson, and by the time she'd get to break-time the pad would be fully saturated, the blood soaking into her pants and black trousers. She wasn't sure how she was meant to get through each day like this, naively unprepared for what lay ahead. She still remembers tying her jumper around her waist to hide the blotch and streak stains, her arms freezing in the cold, the hairs standing up, riding the bus home, desperate to remove the bloodstained clothes, grateful that no one had noticed. The shame if it all – the shame that was still being imposed.

But for Martha, there is such relief too, because most importantly the salt ceremony will still go ahead and she is ready to be healed, is willing to be a citizen of the world again. With or without Finn, she is ready to live.

26

The circular opening room is aglow with candles. Everyone but Rick is crouched on cushions around the salt-carved coffee table, the same large glass jug with a familiar-looking brown liquid inside, small glass tumblers stacked in rows, nine in total. Rick has been permitted to sit on one of the armchairs, wincing with even the most minor movement of his lower body, unable to find a restful, pain-free position. Around them, mattresses, buckets and toilet rolls have been laid out once again. Behind Finn, the dining table has been completely cleared of plates and cutlery, leaving no trace of their last, awkward dinner together.

'As I'm sure some of you have experienced,' Oscar says, 'these ceremonies can activate repressed memories, and of course this is difficult, but try not to shy away from this tonight. This is your final opportunity to work through personal blocks and expand your mind. Some of you have already relived your worst fears through this process, but tonight you will hopefully also experience some of the most joyful and euphoric moments too.' He pauses. 'Are there any questions so far?'

Finn raises his hand.

'Finn?' Oscar says, his voice tight.

'Is this brew stronger than before?'

Oscar nods. 'But you are all ready, and we will be with you, to help you through this journey.'

Others are nodding and Finn looks around the space. He's nervous, an awareness that everything has been building to this, but he's ready to leave, grateful that the experience is nearly over.

Oscar clears his throat. 'We spend our whole lives pretending and ignoring the fact that we are all going to die. This ceremony is about learning to become comfortable with uncertainty, remaining present and active in the midst of fear and grief. Because that is life, in all its beauty and gore.'

Finn finds himself nodding, agreeing for once with what Oscar has to say.

'This is an opportunity to abandon anxieties about self-preservation, allowing you to open your hearts to one another, to connect better.' He pauses. 'Before we begin, let us go around the group and express our hopes for this evening . . . What is it each of you ultimately wants to see from your final night here?'

No one speaks.

'Why don't we start with you, Barb? What answer are you hoping to see?'

Barb shifts her gaze around the group, swallows. 'I just want to know if I'm a good person,' she says, somewhat feebly. 'If I'm up to whatever challenges lie ahead.'

Oscar nods, whispers a 'Thank you,' to Barb. 'Rick?' he says, turning to look at him propped up in the chair. 'Would you like to go next?'

'It's guilt,' Rick says, struggling as he speaks to hide his discomfort. 'It's always guilt. We'll do anything to rid ourselves of a guilty conscience.'

'Hannah, how about you?' As Oscar says her name, he tilts his head to one side, in what perhaps is meant to be a comforting manner. It suggests, to Finn, that he wants to undo the anger he expressed at the sweat lodge, reframe himself, remind

Hannah that he is a healer. 'What question are you hoping will be answered?'

Hannah bites down on her lip. It looks sore, as if she has been gnawing on it for some time. 'I don't have the love and support of my parents any more and I want to be sure that I don't need them.'

Oscar shifts his gaze. 'And Zoe, what about you?'

She shakes her head.

'Zoe, it can be anything . . . Whatever you wish . . . Truly, this is your night. All of you.'

Zoe is quiet, really staring at Oscar. 'Okay,' she says. 'I want to know if I'm capable of overcoming real trauma . . . If I will ever again feel the way I used to, before I was raped.'

Finn closes his eyes, Zoe's sadness settling over him, so much beginning to make sense. And he's so sorry, can't imagine what she has endured, and he knows there's nothing he can do.

Oscar too seems to be momentarily thrown by her response. Finally, he nods. 'We cannot change our pasts, but we can alter how we carry them with us. Tonight, face your trauma head-on, and you will discover the life that is afforded to you after.'

'But I was fine,' Zoe says. 'I'd dealt with it. And then we came here and now I can't unsee—'

Oscar cuts her off. 'Allow yourself to trust the process, and you will find what it is you are looking for.'

Before Zoe has the chance to say anything else, Oscar points to Finn. 'Okay, Finn,' he says, 'are you ready? Have you thought of your question?'

Finn drags his tongue across his teeth, finds it soothing in a sort of destructive way. He doesn't know what question he wishes to ask himself. Too busy focusing on what he thinks he doesn't want, rather than thinking about what he does.

'I suppose,' he says, 'it would be nice to know the secret to a happy life.' He pauses. 'Sorry,' he adds, shrugging. 'Maybe that's too generic.'

'That's okay,' Oscar says. 'Let the spirit of Mother Nature inside you and I am confident you will receive your answer.' He swivels then from his kneeling position. 'Martha?' he prompts.

'I . . . I want to know if we're going to be okay.' She takes a breath. 'I don't think we're capable of the change that is needed to save ourselves, but I want to know if there's hope . . . If there's a way to find hope in the chaos.'

Finn looks at Martha, a sudden wave of affection washing over him.

'Okay,' Oscar says, 'thank you for being so honest.' He places his hands, palms down, on the surface of the table. 'Now, there is one last part of this salt ceremony that you will not be familiar with, and it will happen towards the end. It can feel alarming and has the potential to cause some distress, which is why we are explaining it to you now.' He pauses, looks around the group. 'We take so much from Mother Earth that, in order to feel worthy of her wisdom and love, we have to offer a sacrifice to the land and to her. Blood means life, and gods don't bleed, so we must give them some. At sunrise, to show her our appreciation, we slaughter the llama outside and offer the land its blood as a *sulla*, a sacrifice.'

A noise catches in Finn's mouth, something physical.

Hannah slowly raises her hand. 'But you don't eat meat here . . . '

'I thought I was clear,' Oscar says. 'I'm not killing it for its meat. We owe the land, and we must repay our debt.'

Everyone is quiet for a moment.

'Will it be painless for the animal?' Barb asks.

Oscar nods. 'Of course, quick and painless. The llama will feel no distress whatsoever.'

'Do we have to watch?' Rick asks.

Oscar inhales, his eyes narrowing ever so slightly before answering. 'Participants are usually present but, if you need to, you can close your eyes.'

Finn clears his throat. 'Who does it?' he asks. 'Who kills it?'

'Me,' Oscar says. 'It is always me.'

No one speaks.

Oscar claps his hands together. 'Okay, if we are ready, let us begin.'

Finn is offered his first cup of salt brew, and he brings it to his lips. It is thicker than the last time, more twig-like, and smells distinctly of mud. He works himself up to it, silently counting to three, worried by the thicker consistency. Martha has already finished. He empties his glass into his mouth, lets the liquid sit there, the taste absorbing, grit behind his molars. His body shakes with its repulsion, is telling him to spit it out, but he won't – he has decided to commit to this final act, has nothing to lose by being present, still sceptical but quietly curious. Finally, the liquid makes its way down his throat, and he pushes his cup back with such a force that he knocks it over, the dregs of the brew spilling out. He knows Ofelia will clean up the mess, is accepting of this, and decides to go outside, where candles and torches illuminate the space for their last night.

He walks with purpose, feeling no effect yet but on high alert, vigilant to his surroundings and to himself. He reaches the llama, tied up behind the kitchen, and stands, staring at it, taking in the pink ribbons dangling from its ears and collar. He wonders who put the ribbons on. Ofelia? Why bother? he thinks. He offers his hand, calm and steady, but the llama retreats, inspecting him with newfound suspicion. 'It's okay,' he says, 'it's me.' And slowly it begins to lick his hand, this small, pink tongue. 'See, I'm not going to hurt you.'

'Do you think it believes you?' Martha asks, startling him.

'What?'

'That you won't hurt it.'

He keeps his eyes on the llama. 'Well, *I* won't.'

'In there, is that really the question you wanted to ask? The secret to a happy life . . . '

He looks at her, hesitant.

'You can tell me,' she says, 'I'm still your wife.'

'I don't know what I want. I don't think I've ever known what I wanted . . . Except, maybe I know I don't want cancer again.' Suddenly he feels as though he could cry, a swell of emotion he isn't expecting. 'I couldn't survive going through that again.'

She brings her hand to his face. 'Finn . . . I'm so sorry about everything that's happened.'

'I'm sorry too,' he says, closing his eyes. Her touch feels nice.

'Please . . . ' she says. 'Don't leave me.'

He opens his eyes. 'There's the start of a tingle coming through now. Do you feel it too?'

She wraps her arms around his thinning waist. 'What can you feel of me?' she says.

He lowers his head, resting it against her shoulder, and she runs a hand through his hair. 'I feel like you are made up of all these little parts,' he says. 'That you can be rearranged in a different order and then be an entirely different person. That you are a different person from the one I thought I knew.'

'I love you so deeply,' she says. 'You've always known that. I've never been one to hide that from you.'

He steps back, a little unsteady. 'I think I need to lie down on one of the mattresses,' he says. 'Things are beginning to spin.'

He doesn't wait to see if she follows him, only quickens his pace, his desire to lie down now overwhelming. He stumbles into the circular room and sees Barb lying down on a mattress, and already she's crying, endlessly crying. Finn brings himself down quickly and lies perfectly still. This, he acknowledges, is entirely different from his first salt ceremony experience, and he fleetingly questions if he's imagining this change, if he's capable of simply sitting up and shrugging everything off, as though drunk and talking his mind out of needing to be sick, of swallowing saliva away and holding his breath until it all passes.

He feels suddenly adrift, floating in the abyss. What does he want? What does he think will make him happy? He's done everything that was expected of him in society, he did all the things people told him would lead to a successful life. But really, what has it all come to? He's a tiny cog in a machine, as disposable as everyone else. Part of him wishes he could have been born earlier, been working in his industry in the seventies maybe, when they'd first discovered oil in the North Sea, when the narrative was different, when the environment wasn't on the agenda. Now he's embarrassed, often avoids socialising with people who don't work with him, for fear of being judged. He's locked into Aberdeen, too invested in his own self-preservation. He's thinking now about the Just Stop Oil protests, their increase in frequency, his horror at discovering Martha had been taking part. And he understands now, doesn't grudge these people, is secretly impressed by their conviction. But it's his job. And he likes his job; is good at it. It's how he's spent his life for nearly twenty years, and he can't bear to think of it all as a waste. Yet, he's willing to sacrifice his marriage. If he can let go of one, can he let go of the other?

He clamps his eyes shut, wanting nothing but darkness, but instead there is a blinding brightness, as though the sun is glaring directly into his eyes. It's pressing down on him, heavy against his chest. He pulls at it and then tries to throw it away, as if it is a picture that can be torn down from a wall. He opens his eyes, but the blinding brightness remains. All the colours of the rainbow begin to explode around him, balls of colour dropping on him, but they don't hurt, even though they are falling from a great, expansive height. He tries to sit up, grab at the balls of colour but they keep slipping through him, physically seeping through his skin. He turns his hands around in front of him. When he looks out, he sees one of his friends from the hospital, a year younger than him; they are sitting in fake leather reclining chairs, PICC lines – hours of chemotherapy. Finn glances from himself to his friend and back again. He begins to shake his head, distressed to be back in this place, but the friend smiles, nods in an encouraging way. And Finn is howling, his whole body shaking. 'I'm sorry,' he whispers. 'I'm sorry.' But his friend is oblivious, is pulling his PICC line from his arm and climbing out of the chair. When Finn looks down for his own PICC line site there is nothing but a jumper and sleeves, no hands, or arms within them. He's body-less. He has no idea how much time has passed but a bell is ringing, he is being summoned, and he knows he must go.

27

Martha forces the second cup of salt brew down her throat. She's on her hands and knees and she's not sure why. She shuffles back out to the patio area, where she somehow manages to climb into the hammock. The sky is behaving oddly, jumping and folding and straightening in front of her. She closes her eyes and opens them again. She looks back up at the sky where not only space, but now time seems to be folding. Everything is moving fast, a rush behind the ears, but then it is also slow, as though she can reach out with her finger, freeze-frame whatever she chooses. She clambers out of the hammock and back on to her feet, feels a great urge to tell Finn what she is seeing. As she stumbles into the room, she falls forward, towards the armchair where Rick is sitting, but he's frozen like a statue, stretched forward in his seat, a hand extended towards something she cannot see. She touches his arm, senses something through him, momentarily becomes him. She feels American. She laughs, spittle on her face, realises she's in a peach bathroom with a bidet. She, or Rick, is drunk, can barely walk but they're pulling harshly on the ankle of a woman, dragging her, repeating the name *Joni*, speaking to her as though she were a child. Joni is screaming out to them to stop but they won't. Finally, they have Joni where they want her, dropping her leg, pulling on her hair and slapping her across the face. 'No,' Martha shouts. 'No hitting,' she demands. They let go of Joni's hair, the woman crumpling to the floor, and they kneel before her, crying and begging. But now Joni's face is Finn's, and they're simultaneously in her Aberdeen home, and Finn's asking them, *Why? Why did she sleep with him? Why?*

Martha releases her grip from Rick, and they look at each other. 'Why did you sleep with him?' Rick repeats. 'Why, Martha?'

She shakes her head, desperate and confused. 'Who is Joni?' she asks.

Rick begins to cry, huge sobs, and she walks away, finally finding the real Finn.

She curls up next to him on his mattress, wrapping an arm over him. She can feel the pain of Finn's oesophagus now as he swallows. It's agony. She wants to cry from the pain, clutches at their throat. It's too much to bear. She asks him for forgiveness, but he won't look at her. They are back in Aberdeen, and she is on her hands and knees begging him to forgive her. Promising that it meant nothing, that he is all she has ever wanted. And Finn does say he forgives her but it's not enough. She wants him to punish her, and he says he won't, but he has been, in the smallest yet sustained and painful ways – in the lack of physical contact, in his further withdrawal and unwillingness to talk about it – and she sees it all, feels everything that he feels: the shame and anger, but also the comfort and love and affection he buries deep. She is breathing in their conflicted emotions. Their cruelties and judgements. Their doubt for one another, from the very beginning. But there is joy too, appearing again simultaneously. Laughter and lust, admiration and pride. They have benefited from one another and manipulated one another in a thousand different ways.

He's falling away from her now and she is on the floor. She thinks she can see Hannah. There is blood coming out of her mouth, her tongue gaping. Martha feels around her pockets, removes another sanitary pad. When she finally reaches Hannah, she tries to unwrap the sanitary towel and place it on Hannah's bleeding tongue, but someone is pulling her away before she can help, saying *no gracias, no gracias.* It is Ofelia, basking in a warm glow, the softest colours of yellow and orange, the love she has for her son, the strength and pain of it. It is a type of love that feels unconditional, a love that Martha has never felt for another human – she can't contemplate its strength. Martha needs to kiss Ofelia on the cheek, needs to be close to this woman, absorb the full love she has for her child.

28

Finn is three cups in and floating in an all-consuming, vibrating liquid. He is one thing but also a thousand things – it's beautiful and he never wants to leave. He can't breathe but that doesn't seem to be a problem. He can hear an echoing noise in the distance, and he tries to block it out, but it won't go away. He's being forced closer to the noise, a pressure that momentarily relaxes before returning. He can hear the cries of his mother and the pain she is enduring. He doesn't want to leave; everything feels overwhelming. His mother is in agony, but she won't stop, there is a determination to what she is enduring. The liquid washes away and he gasps, can't catch his breath, his mother and father gazing down at him, adoring him. He is calm and tranquil in his mother's arms, but now she is older and weeping in a hospital corridor, and he is nowhere to be seen yet somehow still present. His father is sitting on a chair, and he is praying, muttering words to God, begging, making a trade, offering himself up if only his son might be spared. This emotion, when usually his father is emotionless, is too much for Finn; he can feel the physical weight of it.

Finn turns on his mattress, sees someone facing him, back slumped against the wall, knees drawn up. He shuffles towards them, wants to feel the safety of another person. It's Zoe. Her head is flopping from side to side. She has been sick, a little puddle of liquid separating them. There is dribble on her chin and she smiles at him. Instinctively he wipes her dribble away, his finger making contact with her face. He can see her pain so acutely now. They are in a dance studio, on the floor. Finn can feel the weight of a body pressing on to them, them trying to push this torso away, an immediate sense of familiarity. Their hand is on a face, pressing it, but they are weak, have no control over their body. They thought this person wasn't capable of inflicting such pain, were completely wrong in their judgement of character. There is a flicker, their eyes rolling in their head, something inevitable happening, something uninvited. There is no fight left in them, so they are still, resigned. Their eyes lock with this person. It's Oscar's face peering down on them, forcing himself further on to them. Finally, Zoe shifts away and Finn is himself again, looking at her and she is staring back, bringing her finger to her lips and gesturing for him to be quiet. He goes to reach out to her again, to comfort, but she darts away, leaving the circular room.

He crawls along the floor but it's soft and spongey and he worries he'll disappear through the salt, be swallowed whole. He has this sudden desire to find Martha, needs her, but he has this crushing sense that she no longer exists. She has been removed, vanished, and she will not return. Maybe she was never here; maybe she has always been a figment of his imagination. But now they're having sex, and it feels so real – a showreel of their bodies and movements, of the pleasure then calmness. And he loves her so deeply in these moments, wants no one else. He can feel her gently running her fingers through his hair, but when he runs his own hands over his head it confirms that indeed she does not exist. And now he will never be able to say sorry for all his failings, for his selfishness. He sees every time now that she tried to talk to him or asked for his affection – all the grudges he held as leverage, so that she could never relax, never be sure that they could move on from the past. He was too cold and he's sorry, so very, very sorry. He undermined her, did little to encourage her. He's terrified, is shaking, because it's too late, and he can see so clearly how much love he really has for her, has always had. Images and snapshots of their life are rolling quickly before him, but they're not just in his mind, they are in front of him. All those times she put her hand out for him to take it, all the times she embraced him, and he gave her little back in return. The financial burden he begrudged her. It all amounted to keeping her on eggshells. And now she is gone.

But there she is, he can see her now, in cat form, licking her coat; it's definitely her. She is sitting on a cactus arm above his head and she's looking down at him, purring at him when he'd expected her to show him her teeth. Her coat is black and white, as it always has been. A fear takes hold then: how long do cats live for? How will he catch her? How does he get her home? He reaches for her, the needles of the cactus piercing his hand, but there is someone reaching for him. When he looks up it is Elbert. And he can see through Elbert's eyes, the chaos that is unfolding behind them in the circular room. When Elbert nods politely at Finn, Finn nods too. When he scratches his nose, Finn does too. Finn can feel the coca leaves in the pouch of his cheek, is swallowing back the taste that mixes in with his saliva. But he can feel Elbert's calmness ebbing away behind the exterior. He can sense Elbert's distaste for them all, his frustration, the little, if any, satisfaction he gets in shepherding these tourists through this experience. It's a violation; them being here is a violation and Finn can feel that now.

There is screaming coming from somewhere outside and Finn looks around, turning himself in a circle. Out across the salt he can see nothing. But Elbert is following the noise, moving with speed around the property, Finn following, waving to the llama as he passes, the sweat lodge in view, and now he's making his way down towards the thermal pool behind Elbert, the noise intensifying yet Finn still has no idea what it is, feels no alarm, only curiosity. Hannah is standing at the edge of the pool, her mouth an 'O' shape. The noise is coming from her. Elbert is running, barely any light to guide him, and he is entering the water with his clothes and shoes on, and Finn wants to laugh. But Finn sees now the shadow of something in the water, sprawling, beautiful. It reminds him of the dead flamingo suspended, up-ended in the lagoon. There are emotions surfacing that feel familiar, a sense of fear, but he's still too detached for them to form into any tangible sense. Hannah crouches down, her knees pressing into the hard ground, arms extended out. And Finn understands now that she's getting ready to embrace a loved one, while Elbert, trudging through the water, has a heavy weight in his hands, blonde hair wet and covering a face. Of course, Finn thinks, calmly and methodically: Zoe. It is Zoe. Elbert attempts to heave her over the edge of the makeshift pool, struggling, and she's screaming at him, furious at being removed from the water. And she scares Finn – he remembers what he saw when he was with her last, can only stand as Elbert struggles to calm her down. Finn takes a step closer, watches as Zoe rolls from side to side, desperate to be free of Elbert's grip, her outdoor down-feather jacket sodden, the pockets bulging, weighted. Finn presses at the pockets, needs to know what is within the fabric. Rocks. Or maybe coral. Really, who can tell.

29

The moon is full, and Martha is howling at it, asking for it to come back to her. It changes colour, an emerald shade but the moon suits it. She can see through the emerald and far beyond. It's an eye to the past, present and future, and it pulls her backwards and forwards, stopping at different periods of time. She sees the first ancestors of her lineage, her parents never having offered her much insight into their pasts. And now she sees her own old hands. She's looking into a mirror, but she has no concept of her appearance, can't remember what qualities her face used to hold. She's being shown her own failures now, a critical eye over the past that she'd prefer stayed at the recesses of her mind. There's the accident on a ski slope where she hurt a child and although she didn't do anything with intention – it was a genuine accident – the event fills her with shame. The look on the child's face, the fear that she was going to be hurt by Martha losing control on her snowboard. There is the affair, a one-night stand that turned into something more through relief in collective despair. And finally, buried deep down in a place that could almost be forgotten, are the other indiscretions, doubts and lusting that Finn has never been privy to – thoughts she only goes near when she's alone and knows no one can read her mind and judge her. All of these thoughts from the mundane to the extreme are coming with her now as she moves through time, moving fast, up through the sky. She keeps going, leaves this earth and atmosphere. But her worries and fears are coming too. Nothing of her, good and bad, will be left behind. The anxiousness she carries every day is with her too, the anticipation of the world collapsing in on itself, jealous that it can't be something instant like a meteorite; instead she sees heat and the prolonged suffering and hunger, a slow-burn misery all around her until there is nothing left for anyone. She has laid every fear and failing out before her. She opens her mouth and a language she does not understand is coming from her, except, she does seem to understand it, despite having never spoken it before. Is her mouth even open? Can she communicate telepathically? There is a shift, everything lifting from her, no more suffocation. This is a new existence, a new universe, and it's glorious. This must be what heaven is, she's sure of it now, can feel it in her bones. She's never really believed in an afterlife before but she's basking in bliss, a feeling of complete contentedness that she didn't know was possible. Everything is moving fast, light-years of travel passing in seconds, a constant rushing in her body that she does not fear. There is nothing to fear any more. There are too many universes to count; it's all endless. Whether in this life or in another, it is all one. And there is nothing to fear. There is beauty still to be found in the world, beauty in life and beauty in death. Perhaps it is a terminal beauty that is left to appreciate – being able to see the world at its best because of the knowledge that it won't last forever. So much is already disappearing before her, but she can adjust, adapt; she can still find ways to love. Her grief will not consume her; there is a time to accept, and that time is now. And yet there is still this creeping sense of hope, of clinging to what was – if Finn can survive against all odds, then why not her? Occasionally, miracles do happen.

But someone is trying to pull her back to the old earth. She shakes her head, high up in the sky, over thousands of kilometres of salt. But the pulling won't stop and she's coming back, floating down gradually. And she wants to weep, can't bear to leave the place she's discovered, the feeling she's been longing for all her life. And the people, if they are people – they have been waiting for her; they are smiling and telling her she is loved, that there is nothing to fear. She opens her eyes and finds herself back outside the Salt Centre. When she looks up, Barb is standing on the edge of the patio, tilting forward, with bright strappy pink tango shoes on. Barb is shouting out to the universe, telling everyone who will listen that she is loved, that she is not a bad person. She raises her arms out wide, showcasing the land that belongs to them all. 'What have we created?' she shouts. 'Can you believe it?' Martha sees now that Barb is wearing a long black evening dress, camouflaging with the night, and Martha thinks she looks like a bat. Maybe she is a bat. But she's not upside down. Martha bends and tries to look at Barb through her legs, see her as a bat is meant to be seen.

Someone is beside them, shouting at them, but the tone is aggressive and harsh. It is Ofelia but she is tiny, barely a few inches tall. Martha blinks at her, keeps looking. Ofelia is trying to get to Barb, to pull her back, demanding something in Spanish.

Martha focuses on Ofelia's mouth, thinks she can understand her by lip-reading.

'I will take her away,' Martha says to Barb, simultaneously attempting to lift a tiny Ofelia gently in her hands. She can see Ofelia's world again, but it is now one of monotony and work, the worry of money, and the endless faces of the people who keep coming here. The privilege and wealth of them. The neediness of them all. And now Oscar is here, but his face is odd, morphed somehow. And he's trying to release Ofelia from Martha's grip, pulling Ofelia towards him. Martha demands that he lets go, that

Ofelia's going to be kept safe in her pocket. It's a game of push and pull, Martha bumping into Barb.

There is a thud, Barb having disappeared over the edge of the patio area, a thrum of activity, a solid cry of pain that doesn't feel right. Martha peers over the edge, sees Barb, far away down the hill, lying in among the rocky terrain and cacti. There is blood splattered across the ground and Barb is releasing an elongated noise, but it bounces off Martha, refusing to penetrate. Oscar and Ofelia are climbing down the hill, assessing, rescuing Barb, trying to lift her between them, this odd noise still present but slowing. And now it is muted, Barb closing her eyes, and Martha thinks that a nap would be nice. As they slowly make their way back up, she watches, can see bone protruding from an ankle, her eyes widening, completely fascinated. Martha reaches out and touches Barb's hair, feels the pain Barb is experiencing through the fog. It winds Martha and she steps back, buckling from the sensation in her right ankle. Martha peers over the edge once again and begins to weep for the exposed bone, for the fluid that has left Barb's body, that is now feeding the gravel below. She can still sense Barb, can feel not only the physical pain she is enduring but the pain she brought with her – a twitching eye, the scar that hurts after a mole was removed, the crippling shame of mistakes and injustices. And there is still so much anger. For everything. Does it belong to Martha or Barb? Why can't they let go of their anger, any of them? She can feel it in the universe. She can feel it in all of them.

30

Back in the circular room, Finn is vomiting into a bucket. He hurls the contents of his stomach up into it, the vomit appearing to him then as one solid mass, like play-putty. There is a lot of noise around him, but he can't untangle it all. On his hands and knees, and with his bucket, he pulls himself along the ground, desperate for some fresh air. He passes Zoe now lying out flat on a mattress, having been dragged in by Elbert. She's awake, stripped of her clothes and covered in a blanket, drops of water from her hair falling on to the salty floor. She blinks, smiles at Finn, seems to be filled with genuine elation. Close by her, Hannah is vomiting into a yellow bucket, a blanket wrapped around her shoulders. It's cocoon-like, and Finn wants to be huddled and held in a similar way. He looks back but his blanket feels as if it's light years away, in another time and universe, one of noise and fear, and one he wants to stay away from. He pulls himself along, not entirely convinced his legs still work. He's not sure if he needs legs in this new world, the one he is desperate to reach. He barks at Hannah, like a dog, but she appears to understand him, and makes room under the cape of her blanket for him. Their arms touch, their faces fixed on Zoe, and their thoughts become aligned.

There is the fear of loss, of standing at the edge of the thermal pool and accepting that Zoe is gone, of recognising fragments of her in the dark water, of wanting to touch her but not knowing how to any more. They close their eyes in sync, block the darkness out. They share a vision now of purple in the sky despite the sun not yet ready to rise. They are children together. It's Hannah's earliest memory, of sitting on a swing, of a sudden and overwhelming pain that she's never experienced before. A wasp sting. They're screaming at each other, childish wails that are blocking out all other noises, locked in eye contact. *Make it go away*, Hannah begs. And Finn can now feel Hannah's mother cradling them on her knee, while someone else rubs vinegar on the sting, dampening the pain but not removing it fully. The smell of vinegar is overpowering and Finn's nostrils flare as he inhales deeply. Hannah turns to him then, grips him by the arm, the blanket momentarily falling away, before they struggle to gather it back up and wrap it round their shoulders again. Hannah brings a corner of the fabric up to her mouth and begins to suck on it. He does the same. Through her childish glance she smiles, hesitates. 'Don't worry,' she whispers. 'It won't come back again.' He blinks, a tear falling down his face that he rubs away. Her voice is that of a child, the voice that's recovering from her wasp sting. 'Whatever made you ill,' she says, 'it won't hurt you again. It won't come back.' And Finn nods, grateful. Hannah puts her arm around Finn, rests her head against his shoulder. He can feel her shame then, but it's his shame too – Hannah exploring another woman's body, her first girlfriend, experiencing pleasure, all in secret, but Hannah's mum has returned home when she's meant to be at work. And there is disgust on her face, a jolt of horror. Hannah is paralysed by the look and Finn can feel it too. It takes his breath from him. All affection and love swept away by that gaze, and the mouth is telling them that what they're doing is wrong. They want to claw at the mother, bite her face until that look of disgust is removed, but they don't.

'You don't need her,' Finn says. 'You have love all around you.'

She smiles, her eyes darting from Finn to Zoe and back again.

'And she will come to change her thinking,' he says. 'Eventually . . . '

Hannah pulls away from him, nodding and crying, taking the blanket with her.

He stretches on to his back, sees the world as he should, upside down. Rick is having an argument with Oscar, something to do with Barb, but each word is spoken with elasticity, making no sense. Finn starts laughing, hysterically; he can't control it. What a joy it is to be alive. He is here and not here – he is in a million different places all at once: he is stones at the bottom of a stream, a crust of salt in the middle of the salt flats, a speck in the sky, a tiny fraction of all life on Earth. He seeks Martha – she is there in everything he does. He waves his hands, calling out her name. With a knock, he tips over his bucket of vomit, a solid blob beginning to slide along the floor, now jumping little globules, talking to each other. He thinks he can understand why dogs eat their vomit now, attempts to crawl after the cheeky little blobs, vibrating to a tune. Someone stops him, Elbert, gripping the back of Finn's shirt, shouting at him in Spanish. Finn pulls himself up to a sitting position, looks up at him, touches him, sees a man struggling to make enough money to survive, a man who is tempted to follow in his son's footsteps and take a job at the lithium plant and betray the land he has spent his life adoring.

Ofelia mops Finn's vomit and he thinks about telling her to stop but he doesn't want to get in trouble again. Martha is next to him now, sitting down and crossing her legs, and he wants to weep at her physicality, that she is before him in the flesh. It fills him with terror because it's all precious: unspoken looks of understanding, the discussions, the hugs, the sex, the smiles, the debating what route to take in traffic because she really cares and hates the idea of time being wasted even by only a few minutes. He attempts to sit opposite her and wants to cross his legs in the same way, but he can't do it, rolls on to his side. Ofelia and Elbert are shouting at Oscar, their hands gesturing around the room, to each of them, and Oscar raises his voice too; it penetrates through the bliss, and it feels as though something is coming, something they won't like, an ominous invasion that will destroy what's been created here. Elbert keeps trying to interrupt, '*Médico,*' he insists, pointing at Zoe, pointing at Barb, but Oscar is shaking his head. Finn cups his ears, watches an argument take place that he'll never understand, watches as Elbert and Ofelia depart from the opening room with purpose. Then Oscar is the only one standing, surveying his work, looking at each of them as they purge their impurities, purge the blackness within, and Finn feels elated again, a glow that isn't sunlight. And he wants to embrace Oscar, is so immensely grateful to him, but Oscar won't let Finn touch him, is ordering him to back away. Martha embraces Finn instead, her head on his chest but it feels as though it could be inside his chest, that they are one again, fused together.

'Did you see it?' he whispers.

She nods, joyful. 'I've seen everything. The whole universe.'

Oscar passes them, keeping a wide berth, making his way outside, and Finn remembers the llama.

Hannah has Zoe up on her feet, supporting her, and they approach Finn and Martha, know exactly where they're going, can communicate without words. The sun is beginning to rise in the distance, making the world once again appear flat. It's so beautiful and they're grateful. The most grateful they've ever been for anything in their entire lives. It's joyous. The elation of finding this emotion in life is almost too much to bear. It's otherworldly. Finn looks down at his body, the one that could easily have stopped working. What a marvel it is. The randomness of it all. But it's not luck, he realises; he's special. They're all special. And they're here, worshipping this land, this air, this salt. They're ready to sacrifice whatever it is the spirits command, and the llama is now in their sights.

Sunday

31

Martha wakes in the circular room, the sun blinding, the space empty except for her, Barb and Rick, who are still, despite the light, sleeping. She doesn't feel hungover, but she does feel odd, happy, fog-like and disorientated. Like a lamb getting to its feet for the first time, she struggles to walk to the bathroom barefoot. When she finally makes it to the toilet, the one closest to the dorm, she pulls her trousers down and sits on the seat, everything seeming to fall out of her before she wipes. There is a strange metallic taste in her mouth, and she tries to swallow it away. Her skin is clammy and feels rough to the touch. She blinks, realises that she's about to faint. Her vision is narrowing; there is a darkness coming from somewhere near the base of her skull. Slowly, she brings herself down on to the salt-grained floor and lies flat, before curling herself into the foetal position, its coolness soothing against her skin. She breathes in and out, controlling her breaths as best she can. She's not sure if she locked the door, or if the door has a lock. But she doesn't care. In this moment, everything is about focusing on her breathing, about bringing her back from the brink of losing consciousness. She closes her eyes, opens them again. She feels better, but small chunks of salt are digging into her skin, along her bare thigh, her left bum cheek. Around her, the small bathroom is grubby and unkempt. She wonders who would have installed this bathroom. What an odd job to be asked to do, all the way out here. She thinks of her bathrooms at home, of the tiles and chrome fixtures, of the pan-head shower, and she's grateful, is reminded that soon she'll return to civilisation.

Slowly, she tries to stand, gripping the edge of the shower tray. She balances up on to her knees, but the salt is piercing and more painful against her kneecaps. Finally, she is on her feet again. She reaches for the flush of the toilet, but it does nothing, a small trickle of brown liquid dripping out from the underside of the rim. There is a plastic measuring jug sitting next to the sink. She grabs it and turns on the tap, but the pressure is too poor to fill it. With the little volume that she gathers, she tips it into the toilet, but that too has little effect in flushing anything away. She puts the lid of the toilet seat down and walks away.

Unsteady still on her feet, she makes her way to the dorm room, where the door has been left ajar. She sees Finn lying face down under the covers of his bed. He's completely alone, unmoving, his body positioned awkwardly across the mattress, as if capable of tipping over at any moment. His stillness is alarming and suddenly she has this immediate fear that he's dead – that inevitably the time she has always feared has arrived. In that moment, she doesn't know what to do because as soon as she acts there will be no going back; as soon as she has confirmation, then he will forever be dead. She takes a step closer, watches him, is sure she can't see any rise of breath in his body. She reaches for him, everything seeming to clog inside her. The anticipation is the cruellest part.

She places her hand on his back, is still convinced that there is no movement from his body. She coughs, chokes, panic flooding every aspect of her body as she begins to shake his shoulders, pressing his torso into the bedframe.

He stirs, turning to look at her, and she stumbles back. 'What?' he says, squinting, the light from outside causing him discomfort. He keeps one eye closed, the right one, and looks at her, confusion growing. He has something painted on his face, stripes and dots of red set out in a smudged pattern.

'What is that?' she asks, pointing to his face.

'What?'

She rubs the bridge of skin between her eyebrows. When she brings her hand away, something reddish has left a mark on her fingers.

'Your face is painted,' Finn says, his voice hoarse and painful.

'Yours is too,' she replies.

He struggles to sit up, everything he does seeming to take effort. And she straightens too, something distant and unfamiliar forcing its way forward in her mind. She starts to rub at her cheeks, her actions becoming frantic. Her hands stain red and she spreads them across Finn's covers, desperate to wipe them clean.

'Don't,' Finn says. 'Stop doing that.'

'Wipe it off your face,' she says, reaching for him, attempting to rub at his face.

He pulls away from her. 'Piss off,' he says, almost laughing. 'I've just woken up. Will you let me be . . . '

'It's blood, Finn. It's llama blood that's on our faces.'

He stops, his mind doing something similar to what Martha's was doing moments before. He starts rubbing, grabbing a discarded T-shirt from the floor and lifting it to his face.

'Oh, God,' she says. 'Why did we put llama blood on our faces?'

He looks at the red stain rubbed on to his T-shirt, finally something seeming to click in his mind. 'It was a sacrifice,' he says. 'It's okay.' He pauses, looks around the chaos of the dorm. 'A good thing.' He's smiling at Martha, and she remembers now, that he loves her, that he won't leave her. That all is well.

She brings her hand to his bloodstained face, and she begins to laugh, is joyful. She reaches forward and places a kiss on his mouth. He kisses her back. There's an energy between them that she can't help but adore. She could make love to him right now but she's filthy and he's filthy. Does that matter? Tonight, she thinks. When we're clean, when we're lying in a hotel room in Tupiza with fresh white sheets. It's as if he can read her mind, is nodding as he gets to his feet, eager to complete their final listening circle, eager to leave.

'How is your throat?' she asks.

He swallows, nods, making now for the door. 'It's getting better.'

'Where are you going?'

'The toilet.'

She pauses, flattens her palms down on the duvet. 'Don't use that one in the hall there,' she says. 'It's blocked from last night.'

She hears him walk away, the salt moving under his feet. She smiles as she stands, deciding to follow him, feels euphoric with an overwhelming sense of peace, anything and everything now possible.

She waits in the circular room. Rick is snoring, sprawled out on a mattress, and when she takes a step towards him she can see that he too has blood streaks painted across his face. She tiptoes to Barb, remembering then in the vaguest of terms that something happened to Barb's leg the night before. She lifts her blanket a little and sees a puddle of soaked-in blood on the mattress. Something is clearly wrong with her ankle, which is mangled, bandaged up awkwardly. Startled, she drops the blanket and steps back. She comes to the top of the bed where Barb is lying and peels back the duvet to see red streaks and dots across her face too. Barb's breath is foul, her lips pressing into the fabric below her, a wet patch of drool. On the floor beside her are a pair of high-heeled tango shoes, dirt-stains covering the bright pink satin fabric.

Finn walks out of the toilet moaning about not being able to wash his hands properly. But she's not really listening; the space feeling odd to her now. Too quiet. She points to Barb. 'Can you remember what happened to Barb's ankle?'

Finn is still rubbing his hands down his jeans. 'Did she trip?'

Martha tilts her head, really studying Barb, doing her best to bring logic to the situation, a creeping recollection rolling in. Finn nudges her, pointing then to the doors on to the patio. From where they stand, they can see Hannah and Zoe huddled together in the hammock, blankets loaded up on top of them. They are awake, their heads pressed together, moving, their faces pointing out towards the salt.

Finn opens the patio doors, and they make their way out to the hammock.

Becoming aware of Martha and Finn, Zoe stops talking, her lips parted. There is something in her gaze that unnerves Martha. The way they're huddled together should be a warm, comforting scene, a sense of togetherness after sharing a profound experience, but something is off. She can feel it. It's within the walls of the centre, it's in the land. It's in the energy of the salt and its ions.

Hannah and Zoe turn in unison, their faces also painted with llama blood.

'Where is everyone?' Finn says, glancing around. 'Where is Oscar?'

Zoe points towards the path that will take them round to the back courtyard. She is alarmingly pale, her lips turning blue. She is shivering, her teeth making a clattering sound that she can't seem to control.

'You shouldn't have slept outside,' Martha says. 'You'll catch pneumonia or something . . . '

Zoe begins to climb out of the hammock, Hannah following her.

'We've been waiting . . . ' Zoe says, a passive expression on her face. 'We don't know what to do.'

Martha steps back, suddenly cautious. 'About what?'

'We thought that maybe it's just a hallucination . . . ' Hannah says. 'But we need you to check . . . Check that we're not imagining it.'

'Check what?' Martha presses, although she thinks she already knows the answer, has this familiar sense of déjà vu. Somewhere in her mind, none of this is new. She's lived this experience already. She can foresee what she's about to learn, but she's reluctant to let it happen, is happier staying in this current limbo. She has an intense desire to be cast under the salt brew's spell again; needs to be taken back to that other place, a different dimension where pain and suffering no longer exist, where only love and acceptance remain.

They follow Hannah and Zoe around the side of the property, but Martha grips at Finn, her feet slow and dragging across the gravel, her body resisting the act of moving forward. Before they turn on to the courtyard, Martha stops, practically digging her feet into the ground, her toes curling up on the gravel.

'Wait,' she says. 'I don't want to . . . '

'We have to know,' Hannah says. 'If it's a miracle . . . '

Martha feels the weight of it all so acutely now, the pain of her toes in the gravel, the weight of their suffering, the sacrifice that was made.

There is a noise that she does not understand or recognise. Finn looks at her, equally confused. A sniffing, grunting sound, a shifting across the ground. It's enough to force her round the corner and into the bright light of the courtyard. And that's when she sees the llama scratching its nose on the ground, blowing air through its nostrils, the beautiful pink braids of fabric majestic in the sun. And Martha releases a squeal of delight to see the creature standing, to see it moving and nuzzling. It's not a hallucination; it really is a miracle. She goes over to offer the llama her hand, which it sniffs before licking, its tongue out, washing away the red streaks from her palm. It removes all traces of blood from Martha's hands and Finn approaches, kneeling beside her, offering himself to the llama too, and now the animal is also licking the streaks and dots from his face, a cleansing of sorts.

But slowly, there is a change in Martha, an understanding of something. She stands. It is not the llama's blood that covers her. It is not the llama's blood that they offered as a sacrifice to the land.

32

Finn's eyes move around the perimeter of the courtyard, reluctant but searching. Finally, his eyes fix on the rich droplets of blood soaked into the ground by the sweat lodge, the flaps of the fabric to the entrance blowing slightly in a mild breeze. He comes closer, is mesmerised by the colour, almost wants to stroke it. There is nothing but silence, echoing through his ears, and he pulls the flap of fabric back, already knowing, already understanding because there is nothing left in the universe to understand.

Oscar is lying on the floor, eyes open, looking directly up at Finn. Behind Oscar's beard, blood gathers all around him. Oddly, for a moment, Finn finds this quite beautiful, before the realisation slowly dawns on him that it is Oscar's blood on his face, on all their faces. He lifts Oscar's beard, gripping the wiry hairs in his fist, and sees now the open slit across his throat. He gags, saliva behind his molars but there is nothing to bring up. His breathing is rapid, and he tries to think back but his mind won't allow it. Everything is moving slowly, pictures being snapped and placed together to make a flip-book. Nothing is clear; nothing means anything any more. Everything stunted.

The space is dark, but he can see the bloodstained knife resting nearby, placed in the centre, on top of the sacred godfather stones. A selfishness takes over, and he is grateful to be alone with him, even if only briefly. But there is the noise of weeping, close by, and he realises then that he is not alone – in the darkness they are here too, Elbert and Ofelia, sitting as far back from Oscar's body as possible. Finn's eyes adjust to them, huddled together, hands pressed in gestures of prayer, Elbert muttering words of sorrow, or grief or maybe even repentance. Finn will never know.

They stare at him; he sees the terror in their eyes, the blinding loss. He attempts to come towards them but Ofelia shrieks, waving her hands desperately in a bid to keep him away, reaching then for the knife, which Finn instinctively grabs first. Everything is confusing and he closes his eyes for a moment, naively anticipating a reset of sorts, but when he opens them Oscar remains, the bloodied knife still in Finn's hand. The flap over the entrance is lifted once again; Martha is on the other side and she can see everything. She stares, paralysed, her attention focused on the blood, and Finn realises that he's kneeling in it, the fabric of his jeans cold and heavy. She begins to scream, bloodcurdling, the sound of it too much to bear, everything off. Finn scrambles out of the sweat lodge, falling on to the ground.

Hannah and Zoe stand before them, staring at him and the knife in his hand. He shakes his head; it's involuntary, tick-like in manner. 'Oscar . . . ' It's all he can manage. He points to the sweat lodge, as though expecting Elbert and Ofelia to confirm what he's trying to say.

He calls their names, demands that they emerge from the sweat lodge, all the while aware of Hannah backing off a little, pulling Zoe to retreat with her. Elbert and Ofelia finally emerge, their eyes blinking and adjusting to the brightness. Ofelia looks terrified, speaking frantically to Elbert, gripping his arm as though her life depended on it.

'I didn't do this,' Finn shouts, waving the knife. 'I grabbed it before she could,' he adds, gesturing towards Ofelia.

Elbert shouts at Finn, words tripping, a fury being purged, as he points to the knife.

And Finn shakes his head, holding his hands up in protest. '*Nada, nada*,' he says.

A tension builds around them that confuses Finn; he doesn't understand how they have arrived here, but the knife feels familiar in his hands, capable of causing further harm. There is so much noise – a thrum in his ears, a constant beat.

'Finn, put the knife down,' Martha pleads.

And suddenly, as if he were allergic to it, as if it were now capable of branding him, where only moments ago he felt its comfort, he drops the knife with a clatter, flecks of blood landing on the gravel between them all.

Finn falls to his knees and begins to cry – the loss of Oscar a grief too great to carry. He can't quite make logical sense of why his grief is so painful. It feels as if he's been waiting to grieve like this his whole life. He wants to be held; he wants to sob until there is nothing left. Yet his emotions and their attachment to Oscar feel strangely disjointed.

Martha grips Finn, forces him to get back up on to his feet.

'We should go inside,' Zoe says, a confidence to her that feels new. 'We should all be together while we . . . While we try to remember what happened.'

He remembers then the thermal pool, her being pulled out by Elbert. Was that only hours ago? His memories are hazy, but he is sure that this happened, that it was not an illusion. She appears reborn, stronger now and he does not understand how.

Zoe bends then and retrieves the knife, holding it out at arm's length, the blade pointing downwards to the ground. She leads the way with certainty as she opens the door, holding it with her free hand, ushering everyone inside. Finn follows her instructions, stepping into the circular room, where Rick and

Barb are now awake. When Finn looks back, he sees Ofelia and Elbert still standing outside. Zoe gestures once again with her hand, telling them to come, guiding them back with the knife as a pointer.

Finn follows Martha to one of the empty mattresses, needing to be close to her, while Rick and Barb continue to lie on theirs. Elbert and Ofelia remain standing, together, their backs pressed up against the wall closest to the kitchen. Zoe and Hannah sit on the two-seater salt-carved sofa. A circle of sorts being formed within the group, everyone loyal to their pairing. Everything eerily calm, a sense of waiting for reality to hit.

Barb attempts to sit upright but the movement causes her to scream out in agony, the colour draining instantly from her face; she is at risk of fainting. It takes everything in her to speak. 'What's wrong with me?' she pants.

'I . . . we think you broke your ankle,' Martha replies.

Barb's eyes are wide, landing on Finn, a pleading expression. 'Why haven't I been taken to a doctor?' she asks, panic lacing her voice.

'I don't know . . . ' Finn says.

'Where is Oscar?' Rick asks, demanding now as he searches the room. 'How has he allowed this to happen?'

No one speaks.

Finn's mind is erratic and flighty, and he is unable to hold on to or grasp any one coherent thought. He scratches his eyebrow, feels something crusty and picks at it, flakes of red powder coming away, more traces of Oscar. He chokes at the knowledge, struggles for breath.

'Why is no one answering me?' Rick presses, panic now also in his voice.

'Oscar is dead,' Zoe says, matter-of-fact.

'What?' Rick says.

Hannah nods, sombre, a tear running down her cheek. 'It's true.'

'How. Did. This. Happen?' Barb gasps, and even through the pain it sounds, to Finn, as though they are being reprimanded.

Hannah hesitates, her eyes shifting momentarily from Finn to Elbert and Ofelia. 'We don't know . . . '

Rick shakes his head, refusing to accept. 'Are you sure he's dead?'

'He's dead,' Martha says. 'His throat has been slit.'

Barb cups her hand to her mouth, tilts sideways and begins to vomit on to the floor.

Martha shakes her head, biting down on her lip, shaking. Yet Zoe appears to remain oddly calm, still clutching the knife.

'We need to take a minute to think,' Zoe says. 'We need to figure out a way to make sense of this . . . '

'The way they looked at me . . . ' Finn says, addressing Ofelia and Elbert. 'But I . . . I didn't do this. Why would I?'

'No one is saying that,' Zoe says, a droplet of blood from the knife landing on the salt by her feet. She stares at it, before seeming to realise what she's holding and slowly placing it down on the coffee table. 'What *do* you remember from last night, Finn?'

He starts to shake his head, frantically, a sense of already being judged. And he feels the shame of guilt, simply by association. 'I . . . I remember the euphoria,' he replies. 'I thought I'd seen the whole world.' He closes his eyes, really tries to remember. His heart is racing: the image of Oscar's face, the blood pooling out from under his chin. It's as if someone has placed a memory in his mind, with him in it, but it doesn't feel like him or something he would ever think or do. It feels like an idea. The idea of something but the idea does not belong to him.

'What else do you remember?' Zoe presses. And it is odd to Finn, this sudden change in her. He can't decide if it is down to some enlightenment from the salt ceremony or Oscar's absence that brings her confidence.

'What else do *I* remember? I remember thinking that my vomit was dancing, literally dancing. I remember being high up in the sky until I could touch the stars, that they didn't burn when I pricked them.' He pauses, holds Zoe's eye. 'I remember your pain,' he adds. 'I remember that clearly. I also remember Elbert having to fish you out of the pool.'

Zoe shifts, uncomfortable now in his gaze.

'What about you?' he says.

'What about me?'

'Well, you seem quick to judge me, yet you're the one who seems the least affected by the fact that we have a fucking dead body out there, especially when you tried to kill yourself only hours ago.'

'I . . . ' She stops, seems to search the room for something, a fear circulating. 'It wasn't Oscar that harmed me. I know that, okay?' She takes a breath. 'Whatever you saw of my mind, Finn, and I of yours, parts of them are still hallucinations. They are not all fact. I have no reason to harm Oscar.'

'Please . . . ' Hannah says, begging now. 'We're grieving. Let's not do this.'

'Do what?' Finn demands.

'Tear each other apart.'

'We're in shock,' Rick says. 'But, look here, Barb and I haven't moved since we were placed here, by Oscar and Elbert,' he adds, defensiveness creeping into his voice. 'That would be the last time we saw him . . . '

'Yet you have his blood on your face,' Zoe says, a hostility surfacing to meet Rick's defensiveness.

'What are you implying?' Rick warns. 'Look around you. We've all got his blood on our faces, all of us except for . . . '

Finn follows Rick's gaze, his eyes once again landing on Ofelia and Elbert.

They're standing so still. Ofelia's hat is sitting perfectly straight atop her head, despite the stray strands of hair that fall from it, making her appear much taller than Elbert. She is still gripping Elbert's arm, a tight hold, and Finn wonders for the first time whether in fact they are a couple, if they are husband and wife.

Elbert says something in Spanish, under his breath, refusing to look at the group.

Finn brings his knees up to his chin, hugs them, and Martha wraps her arms around him. 'We were together,' Martha says, suddenly sure of herself. 'When the sun began to rise, we were together. I could see everything Finn was seeing, and it was beautiful. We had nothing to fear.'

'We were together too, Zoe and I,' Hannah says, her words quick in her mouth. 'We wouldn't have done this. None of us. It's not something any of us are capable of.'

33

Martha sits, her arms still wrapped around Finn. She is not yet ready to fully accept that Oscar is gone in any true sense, her mind floating the idea of other prospects, delusional. She has dreams where she sees herself do terrible things but then wakes, relieved, needing sanctuary from the vividness of her own imagination. She tries to harness that same feeling now, the wash of gratitude when a dream is confirmed not to be reality. Yet, there is a sense of guilt and shame pitted in her stomach – a feeling she would do anything to be rid of. She thinks about Rick before the last ceremony, telling them that it's guilt that eats at people, that guilt makes you sick, and she agrees. It's the most sickening feeling in the world. Her hallucinations from the night before are a blend of fact and fiction and she's still struggling to separate them with any clarity. She looks at Rick again, the memory now surfacing of him beating his first wife. But can this vision be trusted? Just because something feels plausible and looks plausible doesn't necessarily mean that it is true. Perhaps any moment now Oscar will walk into the room and ask them to begin their final listening circle.

The conversation is still moving quickly around her, snide accusations being spat, rebuffed, and she cannot allow their experience of being here be reduced to this. The positive must be extracted from the negative.

She stares at Elbert and Ofelia, finds it suspicious now that they don't even appear to be attempting to follow the thread of everyone's thoughts, aren't grasping at words. There is no effort from them to explain what they know even if they can't be understood. She tilts her head, an idea occurring to her that cannot be tamped down. She speculates, with more certainty now, if they can in fact understand English. What if they've been able to understand every word that's been spoken this whole time? She thinks about Elbert and Ofelia witnessing their uninhibited actions during the ceremonies, and suddenly she feels violated, because they've seen everything of her, of them all, yet have given very little of themselves up in return. A leverage being held over Martha that she hadn't necessarily agreed to. Her emotional vulnerability traded for their physical labour. How foolish of her to think she could come to another country, not speak the language and still retain some level of power. The ignorance of it, the sheer desperation in her desire to come here.

Martha leans into Finn, attempts to whisper. 'I think they understand us . . . ' she says.

Finn looks at her, narrowing his eyes, and she bobs her head in the direction of Elbert and Ofelia.

'No . . . ' he says, shaking his head.

'How do you know?' she presses.

'Know what?' Hannah asks.

Finn sniffs, wipes his face. 'Martha thinks Elbert and Ofelia can understand us . . . '

Everyone's eyes pivot once again.

'How would you prove it?' Rick asks.

'She shrugs. 'After years of ferrying tourists backwards and forwards, of course you'd learn, wouldn't you? You'd want to know what they were saying about you.'

No one speaks for a moment, a new narrative building.

'And they were already inside the sweat lodge when you arrived, Finn . . . ?' Rick asks.

'They were mourning,' Finn says. 'I don't think . . . '

'We don't know these people,' Martha says. 'Not really.'

'They must know what happened to him,' Rick says. 'They know everything that happens during these salt ceremonies.'

Ofelia begins to shake her head, proving to Martha even more that they understand every word that's being said. She is aware of Elbert shifting then, a hesitation, his eyes fixing on the knife, as though calculating a strategy. There is this sense that he could turn on them at any moment, a belief in her mind that if he were to get hold of the knife there would be nothing left of any of them. And she's so sure; has never been surer of anything in her life.

Martha shouts at him to stop moving while simultaneously she grabs at the knife, its handle damp in her hands, almost slipping from her grip. Her breathing is rapid, her footing unsteady, and she jabs the blade of the knife towards Elbert, a warning he seems to understand, retreating, both he and Ofelia now standing perfectly still.

She looks to the others, manic. 'I think they did this . . . '

Finn stares at her, something akin to horror appearing on his face. 'We don't know that, Martha, we don't know anything . . . '

'Then why did you grab the knife before, in the sweat lodge?' she asks.

He hesitates. 'I was scared. But so were they.' He looks at her, his eyes wide. 'They've had plenty of opportunities, if they had wanted to hurt anyone . . . '

'If you know a better version, then tell me,' she says.

In this moment she can see that he's unsettled by her – her ability to alter her train of thought, to find solutions so quickly, a means of self-preservation.

Rick struggles to get to his feet, a sciatic pain seeming to pulse through him as he grips his hip, shuffling forward. 'Oscar is dead, and they were with the body . . . ' he says. 'That's fact, isn't it?'

Finn shakes his head, refusing to play along.

'Why are you so reluctant to believe it was them?' Martha says.

'Why would they do that to him?' he says. 'They loved Oscar.'

'We all loved him,' Martha replies, her voice at risk of breaking. 'And now he's dead.'

'The land, maybe . . . ' Zoe says. 'Perhaps they don't think he has the right to be here, to be healing people, *here* . . . '

Martha nods. 'I saw their distaste for us being here, last night, when I touched them. You saw it too, Finn, don't pretend you don't remember.'

'Maybe he was exploiting them,' Rick says. 'How would we know . . . '

Finn continues to shake his head. 'You can't just say stuff like that without having any real proof . . . ' He looks around the room, a pleading expression in his eyes. 'You can't just make something up because . . . because it's the easiest way to rationalise things.'

But Martha isn't really listening to him any more. 'Think of all the money we've each paid to be here,' she says. 'No way are they seeing a fraction of what must be coming in.' She jabs the knife like a pointing finger once again at Elbert and Ofelia. 'I wouldn't be surprised if this had all been planned,' she says. 'Last group of the season . . . '

'And to think that we let these *people* take care of us in the ceremonies,' Rick says, pained. 'It makes me feel a bit sick.'

Finn cups his head in his hands. 'We're turning on the only people who can get us out of here,' he says. 'How are we even meant to get Barb to a hospital without their help?'

Martha grips the knife tighter, in fear of having to rely on their captors. 'We should check Oscar's office,' she says. 'Maybe there's a radio or a walkie-talkie for emergencies, you know? Something that sends a mayday signal.'

Others are nodding at her suggestion, a group working together as a collective, and she is already handing the knife back to Zoe. 'You keep an eye on them and we'll search, okay?'

Zoe nods, gripping the knife, the blade pointed directly at Elbert and Ofelia, Rick shuffling closer as though capable of offering support.

Martha moves through the circular room, Finn and Hannah in tow. When they get to Oscar's office, she tries the handle, but it is locked. 'Fuck,' she says, turning abruptly to Finn. 'What's the word for key in Spanish?'

'How the fuck should I know . . . '

Martha runs back to the circular room, stopping to face Elbert and Ofelia. 'Key?' she says, frantic, pretending to turn a key in her hand.

Elbert shakes his head, fearful. '*No tengo*,' he says, pointing outside.

And Martha understands with a deep sinking sensation.

She returns to Finn and Hannah, ashen-faced.

'Well?' Hannah says.

'I . . . I think the keys to Oscar's office are with Oscar.'

Everything feels as if it has come to a stop around Martha, unmoving, statue-like.

'I'll do it,' Hannah says.

'No,' Martha replies, yet she has no desire to volunteer herself.

'It's okay,' Hannah says. 'Honestly, I don't mind. I feel I should see him.'

And they watch her leave, neither of them stopping her.

'Martha . . .' Finn says. 'It doesn't need to be like this.'

She ignores him, her head bowed down to the salt. She tries to visualise the process: Hannah entering the sweat lodge, the darkness, doing her best not to touch Oscar's blood, reaching into one pocket to find nothing and having to try the next – Martha wonders if she'll look at him, really look – in a way that Martha has not yet had the opportunity to do.

Hannah finally returns, her face expressionless, a set of keys in the palm of her hand. She passes them to Martha, but it feels forbidden now, entering the private space of a person no longer with them, a person no longer able to object to his privacy being invaded.

She is struggling to find the right key and it takes everything in her to remain calm. Finally it opens, and she is back inside this cluttered and unremarkable space. Everything is as she remembers it from her one-to-one, and she looks around as Finn and Hannah file in around her. The desk is littered with paper, and she picks up a pen, branded with a red and white logo that she doesn't recognise, reminding her for some reason of a trombone. The top of the pen has been chewed, small grazes from Oscar's teeth, and she brings it to her own mouth, feeling the little dents with her tongue.

Finn and Hannah are frantic around her, their hands rifling, opening drawers and cupboards. Finn finds an old laptop, attempts to bring the device to life with no avail, while Hannah discovers a stack of patient questionnaires in a drawer, spreading them out on the table.

'There isn't one for either of you . . . ' she says, gripping her own.

'There won't be,' Martha replies, a calmness to her voice. 'We never got them sent to us in advance, remember?'

Finn opens a cupboard, and suddenly he has the hessian bag their possessions were placed into. He empties out the bag's contents across the desk, cupping his own phone and watch to his chest. They're turning on their phones, waiting and watching for bars of reception to appear, but nothing comes. They rifle further through the room, Martha too, leaving nothing untouched, searching for anything that might help them communicate with the outside world, but again there is nothing.

Martha sits in Oscar's chair, feeling momentarily defeated.

'How can they have no means of communicating with the outside world?' Hannah says with real despair. 'I mean . . . accidents must happen all the time out on the salt flats . . .'

Martha opens the drawers of Oscar's desk that have already been explored. It's all sheets of paper, off-white and long discoloured. She finds herself staring at the corners, wants to touch them, ponders how long it takes for paper to change colour, a natural progression, reminding her that nothing ever stays the same. All her former worries and concerns, all her grievances, it all seems like such wasted energy now. She continues to flick through the papers, more for something to do than anything else. It's mostly all Spanish, the occasional document written in English. Near the bottom of the pile, she finds a birthday card, a generic cake with candles on the front. Inside, it says: *To Mark, I hope this card finds you well. We love you. Happy birthday. Mum and Dad x.*

Martha turns it over in her hands as if there might be a clue on the back. She assumes Mark must be Oscar, acknowledges that his mum and dad, wherever they are, won't see their son ever again. Except, for now, with mercy, they don't know he's dead. Maybe he can live on in their lives through ignorance – they'll imagine what he's doing each day, make up a version of him for themselves.

She offers the card to Finn, isn't sure why she wants to show it to him. 'This must be Oscar,' she says. 'He looks like a Mark, actually, don't you think?'

Finn reads the card, stares at it, confusion on his face. 'Oscar told me his parents were dead.'

'Well, maybe this is from years ago.'

He shakes his head. 'No,' Finn says, 'he told me his parents died in a natural disaster when he was only sixteen, long before he came to Bolivia.'

Martha stands and pulls down a folder from a shelf, flicking randomly through more pieces of paper. She stops, goes back, reads a document written in English – the recent dates, the negative bank balance, the large repayment fees, the threat of bankruptcy. Underneath, more final notice statements. 'These are bills, aren't they?' she says, forcing the first letter into Finn's hands. 'From an Australian bank . . . I'm not hallucinating, am I?'

Another one. Government letter-headed paper, written in Spanish yet despite her lack of understanding she is convinced it is an order for compulsory land purchase, a red and white circular logo embossed next to the government's emblem, the same logo that is printed on the chewed pen she had in her mouth minutes before.

'What's taking so long?' Zoe shouts from the circular room, her voice shaking slightly.

Finn peers at the letters Martha keeps handing him. 'This logo,' he says, pointing to the official-looking document. 'It's the logo for that Chinese consortium that the Bolivian government signed a contract with to extract lithium from the salt.'

Hannah is staring at the bank statements. 'The lack of upgrades . . . the poor water and power supply. I guess that makes sense now.'

Martha stops, her eyes darting around the office. 'He wouldn't let me touch him . . . ' she says. 'I don't even know why that seems important . . . But during the ceremonies, he went out of his way to not have to touch me.'

'He didn't want us to see any of this, did he?' Hannah says. 'He was hiding his worries from us right until the end.'

Martha is nodding. 'Everything was going to shit, and he couldn't stop it.' Her mind is moving quickly now, aligning her thoughts. 'He must have done this to himself . . . '

And Finn isn't disagreeing, this narrative version clearly more favourable than the last.

'How could he put us in this position?' Hannah says. 'Did he not care about us at all?'

Martha shakes her head, attempts to comfort Hannah. 'No,' she says. 'I think he did care, deeply. Perhaps too much.'

Martha decides then, definitively, that it had to be suicide. She tries to understand the courage it must have taken, for Oscar to open their eyes to what they didn't know before he chose to depart. His last group.

And it occurs to her that Zoe is still pointing a knife in Elbert and Ofelia's faces.

34

Finn sprints into the circular room, Martha and Hannah following. On seeing them, Zoe's shoulders visibly relax, the knife dipping slightly in her grip. She looks exhausted, ready to crumple on to the ground, and it reminds him of the night before – he can't undo seeing her blonde hair floating in the murky salt water, Elbert dragging her out.

He comes to Zoe, taking the knife from her, placing it down on the table.

'What are you doing?' she says, her eyes darting from him to Elbert and Ofelia.

He's shaking his head, a little out of breath. 'We've been picking each other apart, trying to make sense of how any of us could do something like this to Oscar . . . But we didn't. He did it to himself.'

Zoe stares at him. 'You think he cut his own throat?'

Finn nods, his confidence dipping slightly in the face of her doubt.

'He was in trouble,' Martha says. 'When there was no way back for him . . . he gave himself up fully to the land.'

'Are you sure?' Rick says. 'I mean, I agree with Zoe . . . the idea of someone doing that to themselves seems a little . . . '

But Finn is already handing over the documents, forcing Rick and Zoe to look at the only tangible proof they have. 'Oscar should never have brought us here,' Finn says. 'Especially so close to the rainy season. But it seems he felt that he had no other choice.'

Rick inspects the paperwork, slowly nodding, passing pieces of paper to Zoe. She looks down, gripping the letters in her hands, shaking her head. 'But I just can't imagine someone doing that, in that way, to themselves . . . '

'What's the alternative?' Martha asks, a sternness to her voice, a warning.

Zoe falls silent.

Finn approaches Elbert and Ofelia, cautious, his hands raised in a gesture of peace. He stoops down directly in front of Elbert and attempts a sympathetic smile, something that he hopes resembles a soothing expression. He thinks about an article he read somewhere that said most communication is understood through body language rather than verbally. He wants to convey that he never believed them to be a threat, but also, he needs to explain that he is no one to fear either. People are good, inherently they are good, he believes that.

'*Lo siento*,' Finn says, 'I'm sorry.' He places his hands on his heart, thinks that will further highlight his message.

But Elbert does not react.

'Oscar . . . ' Finn says, and his eyes begin to water, his heart genuinely breaking. Slowly, he reaches forward, and Elbert allows him to take one of his hands. He squeezes it, the coarseness of Elbert's skin, the dirt and salt under his fingernails, the grazes and cuts. He wants to offer Elbert something, but he has nothing left to give. The weight of it all is too much, his body shaking.

Slowly, Elbert reaches forward and hugs Finn. The smell of him is comforting, like leather, like oil, tools. How do you learn this sort of kindness? Finn wonders. His whole life, when Finn has needed saving, he has been met with kindness, which he knows isn't always the case for everybody.

Hannah is approaching Ofelia, crouching to embrace her. Ofelia remains motionless, but she's not resisting Hannah either. And it feels as though there is a universal acceptance for what has happened here, for what they've lost, united by a trauma that no one asked for. This is love, Finn thinks; regardless, there is love here, for each other and for what they've lost in Oscar.

He wipes his eyes, his head still resting on Elbert's shoulder. There is the shame now for needing this man's comfort but never having thought to learn anything personal about him, having taken no interest, assumed that it wasn't worthwhile asking questions when he had to wait for responses through translation.

Elbert finally pulls away from him. '*Auto* . . . ' he whispers.

'*Auto?*' Finn replies.

Elbert brings his hands up and pretends to drive a steering wheel. '*Médico*,' he says, pointing to Barb on the mattress.

'*Sí*,' Finn says, nodding his head frantically. '*Sí*. *Auto*. Doctor.' He turns to look at the others. 'Elbert will drive us, take Barb to the hospital,' he says. 'I think that's what he's saying . . . *Auto*,' he repeats, mimicking Elbert's impression of gripping a steering wheel. 'We can get help . . . '

The group grow feverish and disorientated in their actions. Barb is just saying the word *hospital*, again and again, as if she does not understand its meaning, while Hannah attempts to help her. Finn tries to tune it all out, has an overwhelming desire to shout at them all, order hush and a moment's silence out of respect for the land, for Oscar, for the gift they have all been given.

Those around him who can do so are moving with purpose, collecting their things, gathering anything deemed useful for the journey back. Finn watches it all in slow motion, the way they scurry around like ants, attempting to carry things that look too big for their bodies. He walks away, outside to where the hammock is strung up. He peers inside the fabric and sees a hairpin tucked into a fold; he has no idea whose it is, but he takes it anyway and forces it into his pocket, he doesn't know why. He walks around and sees the llama again, careful not to go near the sweat lodge, won't even look at it for fear of seeing Oscar's blood. If he can't see it, it's not happening. He pats the llama on the head, strokes its soft coat.

'Finn . . . ' Martha says, standing behind him. 'We need to remove any trace of us being here. Make sure you leave nothing behind.'

'But we didn't do anything.'

She pauses. 'There is still a dead body. None of this looks great.'

He nods, understands. She's always been great like this, so calm and assured, even in a crisis. She brings a comfort that no one else can, and he is listening to her now, grateful that she is always there to guide him.

'What about the llama?' he says.

Martha looks around their environment, frustrated, as if he has brought a problem to her door that she does not want. 'I don't know what you want me to do . . . ' she says, her voice close to breaking. 'We have to forget about the llama. We have to forget about a lot of things.' She grips him now. 'But we'll take the good stuff with us, okay? All the beautiful things . . . All the possibilities.'

He hesitates, chancing a glance in the sweat lodge's direction. 'Do you think Oscar will be okay on his own?'

She nods. 'He'll be okay. I think he's exactly where he wants to be.'

Finn follows her back towards the circular room, crossing the threshold, but as Martha returns to Oscar's office he makes for the kitchen, seeking out Ofelia. He realises that he's never stepped into the kitchen before, never thought to do so. He looks around; the term *kitchen* could be used loosely – it is a space with worn cupboards and doors, a peeling Formica work surface. It is a room unfinished, yet functional enough for Ofelia to prepare food. The fridge creates a constant hum, louder than any fridge he thinks he's heard before. How does she work in here? How does it not send her mad?

She is busy packing up food, quickly placing it into plastic containers and carrier bags. When she turns, she is startled to see him, nearly dropping a bowl of browning slices of avocado.

'*Señor . . .?*' she says, her voice trembling slightly.

'Llama,' Finn says, pointing to the back door.

She stares at him, her eyes wide.

'Llama,' he says again, louder. He gestures with his hands, as if bringing an imaginary sandwich to his lips, puckering his mouth. 'We need to leave it some food,' he says, dropping his hands, feeling helpless, knowing his words are pointless. Yet he can't bear the idea of the llama being left to starve to death.

Ofelia looks from the door and back to him. '*Sí, señor, sí.*' She nods her head as though he can have anything he wants, as if she is merely there to serve him.

He retreats then, making his way to the dorm. Rick is standing straight up against one salt-carved wall, his hands bracing his hips, while he directs Hannah around his bed, as she packs up his and Barb's possessions.

Finn begins to gather the last of his things, zipping up his backpack. It's heavier than he remembers as he struggles to pull it on to his shoulders.

'Did you get everything?' Rick says.

'I think so,' Hannah replies.

When Finn returns to the circular room, Ofelia is attempting to return the space to its normal order, as if she is simply preparing for the next cohort to arrive. He can see that someone has managed to perch Barb on one of the solid salt chairs, her leg elevated on the salt-carved coffee table, a cushion underneath. The bandage appears haphazard around her ankle, the blood soaked through, her toes exposed. She looks as though she has been dragged from a desert, her face and body mottled with bruises, her hair poking up in every direction, a beautiful black evening dress ripped and ruined.

'Are you ready to go?' he asks.

'Yes,' Barb says, struggling to speak. 'Please.'

35

As Martha heaves Rick and Barb's suitcases down the path towards the Land Cruiser she believes with every fibre of her being that things will be okay now, that everything can be understood and explained so long as they get away from here and back to civilisation. She watches as Elbert secures her backpack to the roof of the vehicle, along with the others, passing him one expensive suitcase, and another, heavy in her hands, and of course there is room for it all now, their food supplies and water depleted in time for their departure. Rick appears, unaided, but barely managing. He's bent over, his hand gripping his back, his left hip swinging his body forward, overcompensating for the rest of him. Finn and Hannah are behind, helping Barb down the path, her arms around each of their shoulders, and she's chewing furiously on something, perhaps coca leaves. Martha recognises the pain despite never having broken a bone in her body before; she can almost feel the sensation, it's so familiar. It confuses her.

She tries to focus on the task at hand, of getting off the salt and getting Barb to a hospital. What to do about Oscar is something that she is pushing to the recesses of her mind. She reasons that things like this must happen all the time, equates it to people dying in hotels or cruise ships, and the staff being left to deal with the fallout.

Finn is attempting to help settle Barb and Rick into the back row of the Land Cruiser and Martha decides that she's not sitting next to them. Instead, she hovers around, making herself look busy, and finally Hannah climbs in beside them. Ofelia is the last to return from inside the Salt Centre, carrying the final haul of bags. Her hat atop her head is completely unmoving and Martha, despite everything, is still in awe.

Martha takes her seat, goes to clip her seatbelt in, and remembers that it doesn't work. But she doesn't care, because the worst has already happened; there is no room left for anything else. She looks back at the Salt Centre. Tries to hold its image in her mind before they depart; now is not the time to unpick everything, she reminds herself – she just needs to focus on leaving, on moving further away from here. She has such a desperate driving desire to live now, and she refuses to let anything get in the way of that.

Finn climbs in next to her, his hand touching her knee, squeezing it. Zoe is beside him, calm and almost at peace; the pain and trauma which crippled her before is gone. There is the comfort of Zoe slamming her door shut, of them all being contained within this back compartment, of being so close to one another. Elbert opens the door for Ofelia, and she climbs into the front, where there are two spaces, one meant for Oscar. His absence is suddenly all-consuming. Elbert walks around the front of the vehicle, his cheek full and protruding with coca leaves, chewing on them, and Martha's jealous, remembers the comfort of her thumb, thinks about slipping it into her mouth. Elbert settles into the driver's seat and closes his door. Martha looks down at her hands, sees traces of Oscar's blood embedded around her nails. She pulls her hands into her sleeves, hugs her torso, reassures herself that before long this will be a distant memory.

Elbert turns the key in the ignition. The Land Cruiser makes an unhealthy sound, coughing and spluttering, refusing to come to life. He stops, sitting forward. No one says anything. He tries to start the engine again. Everything has slowed down, a static ringing in Martha's ears. *Please*, she whispers, and she's not even aware of herself saying it, except that it is coming from her mouth. Zoe reaches forward in her seat, hands wrapping around the thin metal poles of Ofelia's headrest, and Martha focuses on Zoe's knuckles, of the colour being drained from them, the severity of her hold.

Elbert tries a third time. Nothing. The vehicle refuses to start.

He lets go of the key in the ignition and sits back in his seat, his hands resting on the steering wheel. Martha, when she leans forward, can see a keyring swinging from his bunch of keys, a plastic llama.

There is total silence.

Suddenly, Elbert flings open his door and climbs out, going to the front of the vehicle and opening the bonnet. The change in light is startling, a darkness descending directly upon them. Ofelia shifts in her seat, pulling rosary beads out of a pocket in the folds of her skirt. She begins to rub them forcefully, muttering words under her breath. This startles Martha; she is struck by the contradiction. Can you be a Catholic and also worship Mother Earth?

Finn reaches past Martha and opens her door, climbing around her, a gust of wind travelling through the vehicle like a portal as he departs. She watches him move towards the bonnet and then he is gone from view, just like that, an illusion of sorts.

'This cannot be fucking happening,' Rick says. 'Jesus fucking Christ, this cannot be happening to us now.' Beside him, Martha can hear Barb weeping, but she doesn't dare turn around and look – to look is to legitimise the severity of their situation.

'He's fixed the car before,' Hannah says, trying to inject confidence into her voice. 'He'll know what to do.'

Martha begins to turn her wedding ring around her finger; the sensation must be helping, she decides, in the same way that Ofelia must get comfort from running her fingers up and down those rosary beads. Martha can see that Ofelia's grip is tight, as tight as Zoe's hold on the thin metal poles of the headrest, and it feels as if at any moment everything will break, the headrest coming away from its sockets, the beads bursting across Ofelia's skirt, Martha's wedding band sliding off. She thinks about her diamond engagement ring back home, nestled in its box; they'd heard rumours of things being stolen in Bolivia, of criminals just looking for a reason to rob you, of fingers being chopped off in a bid to take your gemstones. The ring came with a certificate confirming the diamond had been sourced ethically, but really, what did that mean? She misses the sharpness of the claws in which her diamond sits, thinks it would cause someone harm, wishes she could force the harshness of it into the palm of her right hand; maybe then it would stop her from wanting to scream.

Elbert comes into view, placing a cigarette in his mouth, lighting it. He steps up on to the tyre, reaching for something on the roof rack, rummaging, the body of the car moving slightly from his weight. He brings down his old, battered toolbox, everything so familiar. Martha can see a spanner in his hand now, as he returns once again to the bonnet and out of view. She waits. They all wait, in silence. Martha looks at her recently returned watch, the minutes seeming to go slowly, seconds elongated, time now nothing but a frustration, an unbearable reminder. Irrelevant.

Elbert slams the bonnet of the vehicle down, and Martha's breath catches in her throat. All is still. Suddenly, he starts to beat the body of the Land Cruiser with the spanner, first on top of the bonnet and then, as they flinch, terrified, he comes around to the side, and starts hitting the driver's door, again and again. There is nothing for the rest of them to do except sit and take it. Finn stands in the distance gazing at the spectacle.

Finally, Elbert drops the spanner to the ground and takes a step back, drawing deeply on the cigarette that still dangles between his lips, the embers glowing bright. He hands the cigarette to Finn, who takes it and, like a reflex, brings it to his lips and inhales. He opens his mouth and lets the smoke out, the inhalation deep, and Martha watches on, nothing making any sense any more. Elbert walks to the back of the Land Cruiser. Martha turns to follow his movements. He jumps up on to one of the back tyres, a bungee cord cast to the ground as he begins to haul their backpacks off the roof.

Martha gets out of the vehicle, sees Elbert now lifting all the storage boxes and supplies. Everything is coming down, stacked into messy piles on the salt, while Finn continues to stand, smoking this cigarette as if it's the most natural thing in the world.

'What are you doing?' Zoe says, climbing out of the vehicle, Hannah behind her.

Elbert does not reply.

Only when everything has been brought down from the roof does Elbert go to the front passenger door and open it, holding out his hand to help Ofelia down.

Elbert and Ofelia begin to walk back together, expressionless, each lifting what they can in their hands. Hannah runs to Elbert, pulling at his jumper, commanding him to stop. 'Please . . . ' she says, begging. 'We can't stay here. Please, let's try again.' She won't let go of his jumper, its zigzagging pattern elongated in her grip.

For the briefest of seconds Martha is sure that Elbert is about to finally lose his temper, react, push Hannah away from him. But he doesn't. Instead, he closes his eyes, takes a breath, opens his eyes and cups his hands gently around Hannah's, slowly releasing himself from her grip. Hannah tries to follow him, can't accept that he won't try again, that he won't even get back in the car. Zoe goes to her, tries to comfort her, but Hannah pushes her away, falling to her knees, a howl escaping, the noise spreading through them all. Martha stands with Finn, as if they are witnessing something on the news, feeling vulnerable but unable to assist, while Rick and Barb remain in the Land Cruiser, helpless in the face of their situation. Martha takes the nearly finished cigarette from Finn, drags on it and stubs it out, before lifting her backpack up on to her shoulders, making once again for the Salt Centre.

36

Finn sits on one of the salt-carved seats in the circular room. On his knee there is a cushion and he's stroking the fur-like fabric, running his fingers through it, tugging on a knot. He's tried to charge his phone, now that it has been returned to him, but it's of little use, the plug sockets too weak. Beside him, Hannah is rocking her upper body backwards and forwards and now that he's noticed the rocking, he can't take it any more.

'You need to stop that,' he says.

'What?'

'The rocking.'

Rick and Barb are perched on one of the uncomfortable sofas, stuck in position like statues. Finn is aware that Barb is turning an unhealthy shade of grey, wants to ignore it. He's sure that he wasn't present for whatever happened to her ankle, is confident that he would remember even if in a salt-brew fog. Bones have always kind of amazed him, so easily broken but also so keen to grow, to fuse back together, like two halves calling to one another. He thinks of that film from his childhood with Meryl Streep and Goldie Hawn. *Death Becomes Her*. He smiles; he always loved that film. The concept, of realising that immortality wasn't something to perhaps aspire to.

'We should eat something,' Rick finally says to the void in the room. 'Once we've eaten, we'll be able to think more clearly. Come up with a plan.'

Instinctively, pleading eyes fall on Ofelia.

Rick brings his hand up to his mouth and mimics eating. 'Food,' he says, loudly, eyes wide and receptive to her.

Ofelia looks from him to Elbert and then around the group. Finn has found another knot in the fur cushion and is tearing at it. Slowly, Ofelia gets to her feet and makes her way into the kitchen. Elbert is quick behind her and from the other side of the door their words of Spanish can be heard, their voices raised and clipped. And Finn can feel the dynamics of the group changing before him – a tone and energy previously dictated by Oscar no longer exists and there is a vacancy to be filled. He wonders if he should go into the kitchen and offer to help prepare the food. But he's a terrible cook, his meals having always been made for him, and he wouldn't even be able to take instruction. He grips the cushion's fake fur, curls the strands of fabric around his finger until they're tight, until they could cut off the circulation. He looks at Barb again, thinks about the poor circulation in Martha's fingers, the tips going grey, how she has to shake them forcefully to get them to return to their natural, blood-flowing colour.

'We need to do something about Oscar,' Hannah says. 'We can't leave him lying there in the sweat lodge. He'll begin to rot.'

'Surely that's for Elbert and Ofelia to decide,' Rick says, rubbing at his face. 'That's not something for us to deal with.'

'Do you think?' Martha says.

Rick nods his head, with an air of disgust about the conversation. 'We've not paid all this money to deal with that. We are in their care still,' he says, nodding towards the kitchen door.

'I don't know if that's how they see it any more,' Finn says.

For what feels to Finn like the millionth time, Rick takes out his mobile phone, now returned to a holder on his belt, waving it in the air as if this will help him find a signal.

'Some of us could take a walk,' Martha says. 'Maybe head back towards the lagoon, see if we can pick up a signal there . . . '

'It'll be dark soon,' Finn says.

'Tomorrow,' Martha says. 'At first light.'

The kitchen door swings open, and Ofelia comes through, balancing several plates between her hands and arms, Elbert behind her carrying a jug of water. Everyone who is able-bodied migrates to the large dining table, only realising afterwards that little thought has been given to Rick and Barb. Finn loops back, standing in front of Rick, offering help, gripping his arms and attempting to straighten him up on to his feet. Rick manages to hobble over towards the table, sitting down beside everyone, and Finn makes his way back over to Barb but she refuses to move, isn't sure she's got it in her to make it to the table.

'I'll bring you a plate,' he says.

'Thank you,' she manages.

When he returns, Ofelia and Elbert are already eating, forcing food into their mouths, heaped spoons of quinoa salad, pitta bread, brown rice, all leftovers from the day before, refusing to wait for anyone. Finn gathers a plate for Barb and sets it down on the arm of the chair in which she sits. He returns and pulls up a seat next to Rick, taking an empty plate, spooning a little of everything on to it, acknowledging that no smoothie has been made for him. He swallows experimentally; there is little pain now in his throat, and he's starving – can't remember a time when he wasn't starving – but he's still too hesitant, hasn't finished his medicine yet. He can see Martha watching him, cutting into a fried egg whose yolk is completely dried out. It occurs to him that this is probably all the food that is left. And he's hardly consumed any of it.

Everyone finishes within a matter of minutes, yet no one rises from their seats. Finn can feel a tension building across the table, Ofelia and Elbert in one corner, sitting close, and the rest of them bunched together, an unspoken division permeating everything they do. Something is being weighed, a reluctance to move, because to move means to accept a change in the rules. The strain is almost too much for him to bear. Should he rise from his seat? Would that defuse the situation? Normally, Ofelia has everything whipped away and back in the kitchen before they've had the opportunity to acknowledge that their plates are indeed empty. Zoe's fork clatters off her plate and a surreal awkwardness sits in the air. He can sense they are on the cusp of change, that one false move will start a chain reaction that he has no desire to see.

Ofelia forces her chair back, nearly tipping it over into the salt. She exhales, before gathering the plates in front of her, moving around the table, dropping knives and forks in her wake. Finn rises from his seat, hesitates for a minute, almost looking for reassurance from others around the table, from Martha, but it does not come.

He enters the kitchen. Ofelia looks from the plates to him, standing by the sink, turning on the tap, yellow-tinged, spluttering water coming out of its corroded mouth. She hands Finn a tea towel and they wait; it takes a long time for the basin to fill up with enough water, the hydraulic pump appearing to fail them. Finally, Ofelia plunges the first plate into the water. She begins to scrub at it, with an unnecessary level of force, before handing it to Finn, and he takes it, wrapping it in the tea towel, which feels as though it is ingrained with salt. As he attempts to dry the dish, fearful of dropping it in his grip, he can see now that Ofelia is crying. It's silent and perfectly controlled, yet he still sees it.

He stacks the plate in the rack sitting by the sink and waits for the next one, but Ofelia is still scrubbing. Instinctively he reaches out and touches her shoulder, but she shrugs it away. Finally, she hands him the plate and they carry on in this quiet, repetitive and oddly peaceful manner.

37

Martha lies awake in her single bed of salt. She is acutely aware of her breath, of how loud it is. She turns on to her side, the duvet shifting with her. She knows there will be no sleep. How many nights can you go without properly sleeping? When she first moved into university halls it was a shared room and she couldn't sleep for what felt like a week – walked around like a zombie, revived only by consuming huge amounts of alcohol.

She can't see Finn in the darkness, but she can hear his breathing, is convinced that he is already asleep. How can even the best of sleepers settle under these conditions? Any noise causes her heart to quicken, fight or flight, readying herself for the possibility of an intruder, and for the briefest of moments she allows her mind to think that Oscar might try knocking. They went to bed as mourners, having lost someone of significance to suicide, yet their fear and uncertainty lingers on. As they tucked themselves into their duvets and kissed their loved ones goodnight, there was still the unspoken assumption that a threat existed; but did that threat come from within the room, or from the other side of their unlocked door? Without discussion, and as if by accident rather than with intent, some backpacks have been left by the door, the salt helping to wedge them in place against it, a ballast against whatever direction the threat is likely to come from.

Martha realises that she's given very little thought to the existential environmental crisis facing the world in the past few days, finding it easier perhaps to focus on more contained matters. But still, there is a change in her, a sense of allowing former worries to wash over her, refusing to let things pierce her in a way that would previously have stabbed. She wonders what Elbert and Ofelia are thinking, wonders what their sleeping arrangements are, having never ventured into their private quarters. She worries about tomorrow, about what another day might bring, with little food, knows Finn too is concerned by the prospect of rain.

She realises then that she needs a pee. She'll never be able to sleep now, but nor can she get up easily and go to the bathroom. She wills herself not to need the toilet. None of it makes sense – she's dehydrated, has been so cautious with her water intake, a collective understanding with regard to their limited supply. Is irrationally irritated that her body requires such a mundane need when everything that is happening is so extreme.

She turns again, noisy in her actions.

From across the room someone is awake, shifting under their duvet.

Martha realises she can't wait, is going to piss herself if she doesn't move. She sits up and pushes her covers back, feeling for her shoes in the dark. She forces a socked foot into her right shoe, salt stabbing at her toes. She tips both shoes upside down in her hands and shakes them to ensure the salt particles fall out, attempts again to put on her shoes.

Someone switches on a torch.

'What's wrong . . . ?' Zoe whispers.

But Martha ignores her. At the door, and by the glow of Zoe's torch, she bends to move one backpack and then another, dragging them by their straps, the salt crunching under her feet.

'Martha . . . '

She's aware of the others now awake, sitting up.

Desperation takes hold; she can't get a good purchase on the remaining backpacks. She pulls at the door, panic rising in her throat – she's going to piss herself and she stops, crosses her legs, but her body is disobeying her. The shame of it. And she can't stop it, the warm sensation, her bladder refusing to constrict. And she thinks, *let it flow, relieve yourself of the discomfort. What is left to be judged?*

She's aware of the silence. The warmth against her skin is already turning cold. She takes one sharp intake of breath, and it catches in her mouth. She is crippled by the moment and sensation. This has happened, she thinks; accept it. She is on the brink, her throat sore from holding in this pressure, of all the staring eyes. And Finn is there, standing directly in front of her, shielding her from the others, and she's crying, her sobs loud and mortifying, but there's no point in holding anything in. She might as well let it all come out in one go and be done with it.

Finn has his towel, the travel one with its velvety texture, and he's wrapping it around her waist, telling her that it's okay. And he's bending, forcing the backpacks away from their wedged position, salt under his fingernails, and she grips the towel he has gifted her, grateful, so very grateful.

With a torch guiding them, he gets her to the toilet. She doesn't know what to do except stand there in her own piss. He perches the torch on the sink and pulls the towel away from her, peeling her trousers and pants down, shuffling her backwards on to the toilet, and she wants to tell him that there is no need, that there is nothing left. But she sits there, her upper body convulsing as she tries to regulate her breathing, while Finn continues to pull her wet clothes from around her legs, struggling at the ankles.

He crouches in front of her, places his hands on the tops of her thighs where urine has moments before been seeping through the fabric of her trousers. He grips her tighter and looks into her eyes, forces her to look back at him.

'It's okay,' he whispers. 'Martha, it's okay.'

She nods, but still she can't seem to catch her breath.

He reaches forward and places a kiss on her cheek.

'I'm sorry,' she whispers, sobbing.

'You've nothing to be sorry for.'

'I'm so scared,' she says.

He nods. 'Me too.'

She waits alone in the dark while he goes to retrieve some dry clothes from her backpack. She can do nothing, hears the others ask Finn if she's okay, imagines him diplomatically nodding. He returns with a pair of her running leggings, a ridiculous multi-coloured pattern plastered up the seams. They feel wrong for their environment, a joke, something to ridicule under the circumstances. Finn hands her a pair of pants which aren't clean, but she doesn't bother to tell him; what does it matter at this point? She struggles with the leggings, which are uncomfortable against her not-quite-dry skin. She smells of piss, strong in her nostrils. Finally, she stands straight, waits to be surveyed by Finn and he nods, offering her a smile and a thumbs-up.

Monday

38

The sun is blinding, the dorm distorted, and Finn visualises the room catching alight, shards of salt, then flames. Except, of course, salt cannot burn. For the briefest of moments it is easy to forget about Oscar, before the reality of it all comes flooding back. He shifts in his single bed. There is little room, Martha having climbed in beside him during the night. Martha smells strongly of piss, and perhaps he does now too, but he doesn't mind. He thinks about being able to smell other people's smells, their washing. It infuriated him as a child that he was never able to smell the scent of his own family, could only hope the smell of his washing was as nice as that of his friends. He remembers when it occurred to him that he and Martha no longer smelt as though they came from different households, that this was the marker of a serious, permanent relationship – everything entwined – and he's grateful for the enlightenment he's received, despite everything. There probably wouldn't be much left of him if he had gone about hacking their relationship to pieces as previously planned. He can still feel the fear of losing her, the salt ceremony, the sensation of thinking that she no longer existed.

He sits up, does his best not to wake Martha, is relieved if anything that finally she is asleep. He swivels, places his socked feet on the salt, the grains no longer bothering him underfoot. His last medicine bottle is in sight, a strange, yellowish residue around the rim. There's hardly any left – enough for today and then he's done. As he takes a swig he marvels at his commitment; everything that has happened, and still it has not deterred him from taking his medicine, exactly as the doctor prescribed. He wonders what meaning there is to be found in this. Is he still hopeful of a return to normal life? Is there a normal life to be had? Or does he just like following instructions, compartmentalising?

Finn makes for the door, grabbing the same travel towel he'd wrapped Martha in the night before, glancing behind to see a few faces awake, some still asleep. In the bathroom he attempts a shower, standing under the shower head, but there is only a trickle of cold, murky water. He sticks his tongue out and catches a droplet. It tastes of salt. Everything, he accepts, tastes of salt. How much has he consumed?

The pressure of the water weakens to practically nothing and he turns off the tap, shaking the dribbles of salty water out of his hair. He grabs his towel and, wrapping it around his waist, is repulsed by the velvety, sticky texture, which leaves him with a lingering sensation of dampness. He steps out of the shower cubicle on to a bath mat, but a sharp grain of salt cuts into his heel and he jumps, dropping his towel. As he bends to retrieve it, he has a sudden sense that someone is watching him, through the keyhole. He secures his towel and brings his eye to the level of the keyhole, but he can't see anyone. He places his hand on the door, can feel something unfamiliar, a prickling, his skin goosebumping but not from the cold. He straightens, runs his hands through his hair – it feels brittle, and he has no idea how his hair looks, how he looks; everything is based on memory and touch. He stares down at his sunken torso, his stomach almost concave in shape. He's painfully thin, and he's relieved now that he can't see himself fully, suspects it will only remind him of his cancer.

Dressed, he walks into the circular room to find it empty. He opens the patio doors, and stands outside for a long time, staring at the vast expanse of salt. All these days and no vehicles have passed by, not even in the distance. Nothing. Is it the threat of rain that keeps them away? He looks up at the sky, clear and blue. How long before someone at home realises that something is wrong? No one is looking for them and they didn't leave an itinerary, liked the freedom of being accountable to no one. His family knew they were taking a three-week trip to South America, but he hadn't told them they were coming here; he'd been embarrassed, he supposed, hadn't wanted to be ridiculed for partaking in something he didn't quite believe in himself. Mostly, he didn't want them talking about Martha – his nearest and dearest dissecting their marriage behind closed doors, pensive expressions, wide eyes. They had never quite bought into the relationship from the start.

Hannah arrives, standing beside him. 'I'm going to see if I can cobble something together for breakfast,' she says. 'Can I get you anything?'

He shakes his head.

'Are you sure?'

'There isn't much food left.'

They look at each other, something unspoken, a gauging of intention.

'I'll wait,' she says. 'I'll wait for the others.'

She's taken the small ring out from her septum. The skin around her nostrils is red and irritated.

'Will anyone be looking for you?' he asks.

She shakes her head, defeated. 'We're not due to check in with anyone for a couple of weeks.'

A sad smile settles on his face, and he begins to count the days they've been here on his fingers. 'Six days . . . ' he says. 'Is that right?'

'Do you think we'll get away from here?' she asks.

'I don't know any more—'

She holds her hand up, needing him to stop. 'I am thankful,' she says, her voice fragile. 'Oddly, now, Zoe's the best she's been in a long time. She's all I have. All I need.'

Finn begins to walk across the broken slabs, turning the corner. He sees the llama and goes to it, offering it his hand, which it begins to lick. The sweat lodge is in his sight, the flaps of the entrance blowing slightly in the breeze. He takes a step closer, stares at the bloodstained ground, visualises Oscar lying on the other side, can almost feel him. He reaches out, his fingers brushing up against the material. He's so close. He goes to lift the fabric, imagines peering in to find him gone. Like a miracle, Oscar will have risen from the dead and walked away, lost to them in the salt. It really is as if it never happened; Finn can convince himself of it.

'Finn . . . ' Martha says, standing behind him. 'What are you doing?'

He stops, turns to look at her. 'I . . . I wanted to check that he was okay,' he says.

She extends her hand out towards him. 'Come back,' she says. 'Come back with me.'

He stares at her. 'No one is coming for us,' he says.

She is quiet for a moment, hugging her arms to her body, and he thinks again of her in the night, of her shame, of having to peel her wet clothes off her. 'Elbert and Ofelia . . . ' she says. 'They have families, don't they? A husband and wife, children . . . They have people waiting for them, even if we don't.'

He nods. 'I suppose they do. We never thought to ask.'

She extends her hand out towards him again. 'Please, don't stay out here with him. Stay with me.'

39

They decide to have a meeting, gathering in the circular room. Martha asks Finn to help her retrieve Barb, hates the idea of Barb being left alone in the dorm room, as though already considered irrelevant. They lift her, under the armpits, shuffling her along, nearly tripping in the salt, a stench travelling, while Barb appears to hallucinate between them. Hannah rolls out one of the mattresses and when they have her settled they crouch before her, can see she's struggling, a fever beginning to take hold, a red, angry and inflamed colour tracking down her foot, bulging from the bottom of her bandage. The pain seems unbearable, Barb barely able to string words together, a near constant state of drowsiness. Martha doesn't really know what to do. She has an image then of Ofelia removing cactus needles from Barb's skin, of the mottled bruises on her body, the break of bone, the ruined tango shoes. Martha's presence.

Rick's mobility has improved slightly, yet he cannot hide his pain as he attempts to crouch down beside his wife. He places his hand on her clammy forehead, bites down on his cheek. 'She really needs to see a doctor,' he says. 'My lovely Joni.'

'Who's Joni?' Hannah says.

Rick stares at her. 'My wife.'

'But that's Barb,' she replies.

Rick looks around the room, momentarily confused.

'It's okay,' Martha says, patting Rick's arm. 'He knows it's Barb.'

Outside, Ofelia and Elbert stand in the patio area, debating something as they survey the salt, their backs turned to the circular room.

Zoe sits down in one of the salt-carved armchairs, Martha joining her, Finn and Hannah following, occupying the seating area, all of them looking out towards Elbert and Ofelia.

'After today there won't be any food left,' Zoe says.

'And once the rain comes, we won't be able to leave,' Finn adds, chiming in.

Martha rubs at her temples. 'We need to focus on things we can control right now,' she says. 'Like walking out, back towards the lagoon . . . To try and get a signal or see another vehicle.'

There is collective nodding.

'Will someone come with me?' she says.

'I'll go,' Zoe replies.

Hannah is shaking her head. 'No, Zoe . . . '

'I'm not going to do anything,' Zoe says, focusing on Hannah. 'I'm fine.'

Martha gets to her feet, looking out through the patio doors, past Elbert and Ofelia to the bright, clear day. 'Everyone give us your phones,' she says. 'Between six of us, surely we'll be able to get some sort of signal out there.'

Zoe stands too, placing a kiss on Hannah's lips. 'We'll need the balaclavas.'

'Take some water with you too,' Finn says.

Martha nods.

When they are ready, they depart down the steep slope from the patio area, and Martha can hear Finn attempting to explain to Elbert and Ofelia where they are going and what they're doing. Martha feels unsteady as they begin to walk on the flat, as though she has stepped off a boat and is struggling to find her footing on solid ground. Zoe is beside her, head tilted downwards, and it occurs to Martha now that they've barely ever been left alone together, have only exchanged words within the context of the group. If Martha's being honest there is something about Zoe that intimidates her. She is a young woman who has suffered unfairly, without choice, arriving with trauma that was real and tangible, in a way that Martha's was not.

'Do we actually know our way to the lagoon?' Zoe asks.

Martha brings her hand up to her eyes as though to survey the land. 'I'm pretty sure this is the direction we went the last time.'

They continue to walk in silence, the Salt Centre remaining in view, when they turn to look, anchoring them still to the people they've left behind.

'I was reading this short story collection,' Zoe says. 'And there's this one story where a woman is held up at gunpoint by a child, of nine or ten, in a back street of Rio de Janeiro.' She pauses. 'I don't know why I'm telling you, except that I can't stop thinking about it.'

'Did you bring it with you, to the Salt Centre?' Martha asks.

Zoe nods. 'It's beautiful and unsettling . . . Like, in the right set of circumstances anyone is capable of anything, even a young kid.'

'I suppose so,' Martha replies.

When Martha glances round again, the Salt Centre is no longer in view.

'Has being here worked for you?' Zoe asks. 'Minus Oscar dying, obviously . . . '

Martha stops, rubs at her face under the balaclava. 'Yes, I think so. In that I'd pretty much wanted to stop living . . . ' She hesitates. 'But I don't feel like that now.'

'I'm glad,' Zoe says.

'I think before, if you'd told me we'd get stuck out here, I wouldn't have put up a fight.' Martha pauses. 'What about you?'

'The person who raped me still works at the dance company where I was an apprentice,' Zoe says. 'And I keep thinking about how he must be going about his day. How nothing has changed for him, and I'm here . . . But I feel oddly calm, is that weird?'

'Did you report it?' Martha asks.

'You know there's no point in doing that. It would come to nothing. I'm not the first person to experience something like that and I won't be the last.' She pauses. 'Oscar didn't hurt me, but his face was projected in my hallucination, and now I feel as though I can deal with it all better because he's gone . . . as if, somehow, Oscar has taken the harm with him that this other person caused. Like, I'm ready to finally move on.' She exhales, almost laughs. 'I don't think any of that makes sense, does it?'

'I think I get it,' Martha replies. 'He sacrificed himself, in a way, for all of us.'

'Yeah,' Zoe says, nodding.

There is the ping of a message, it echoing through the open landscape. They look at each other, a disbelief. Martha's hands are moving frantically, searching her pockets, pulling out all the devices in her possession. She presses buttons, bringing the screens to life, sees nothing.

'Whose phone is this?' Zoe says, holding it up.

'I think it's Rick's . . . '

It pings again in Zoe's hand, and she nearly drops it in her excitement.

'What is it?' Martha says, peering forward to read the screen. 'What does it say?'

They can't open the phone properly, hadn't thought to get Rick's passcode. But they can see the notifications on the screen – two messages from a telecommunications network welcoming Rick to Bolivia, warning him about roaming charges.

In the corner of the screen there is nothing: no bars of telephone signal, no internet. Zoe lifts the phone above her head, waving it in the air, as though this will help. She shakes the phone vigorously but still there is nothing. Martha crouches down on to the salt, laying all the other phones out, illuminating their screens, desperate for something to come through, but still there is nothing.

'Did we move?' Martha asks. 'From when that first beep came through, did we step forward?'

Zoe takes two steps backwards. 'Was it about here?' she says, still holding the phone above her head.

Finally, she stops, her arm tiring, Rick's phone turning itself off.

Martha looks over her shoulder, the Salt Centre still out of sight. 'Zoe . . . ' she says. 'That's the direction in which we came, yeah?'

Zoe stops, looks around. 'I think so . . . '

For a moment Martha is convinced that they are lost. That they will die out here. And she can't believe how foolish they were to come this far without leaving a trail of sorts. She remembers reading an article online about a woman who, alone in a remote cabin, had accidentally locked herself inside an empty airing cupboard. She'd tried to force her way out, days spent attempting to break the door, dig with her fingernails through the wood, but it wasn't enough, and she was eventually found dead. And Martha remembers thinking that it was all so senseless. What a pointless and wasted death. If that woman had caught the latch of the door before it closed behind her, she wouldn't have given the situation's potential danger another thought. She would have carried on with her life, moved on to the next routine task of her day. Martha thinks the news programme said that the woman had been mere millimetres from breaking through the wood and being able to open the door. And she wishes they hadn't provided that last detail – what good did it do? This idea of the world knowing that a woman nearly, nearly made it out alive but didn't. Couldn't that be said about so many deaths? Everything in life seeming like chance, with so many near-misses, the obliviousness to it all almost the most beautiful part.

'We need to go back,' Martha says, scooping up the phones from off the salt. 'We're never going to find the lagoon without help.'

Zoe catches up with her. 'Briefly, there must have been signal,' she says. 'So that's got to be positive, no?'

But Martha can't bring herself to speak. Something has changed in her; something defeatist from her old world has surfaced, maybe because she's out of suggestions now for what they should do, or maybe because she'd thought coming out here to look for a signal would work – had read on an old online forum when doing her salt flat research that years ago a vehicle had got stuck in sludge during the rainy season and a woman from New Zealand had managed to phone her mother all the way back in Queenstown, seeking rescue when all other means of communication had failed.

They keep walking, and when the Salt Centre comes into view Martha is almost surprised, having accepted her fate. But there is no elation or joy; to be back to exactly where they started, with zero progress made, is punishment in itself.

As they get closer, they can see Hannah, waiting for them on the patio. She must see them because she begins to wave frantically, hopeful, as though in their absence progress has been made. Perhaps Elbert has managed to fix the Land Cruiser and they are waiting for them to leave.

They reach the top, Martha ahead of Zoe, and Hannah embraces each of them.

'Come,' she says, an almost singsong tone to her voice. 'They've slaughtered the llama.'

'What?' Martha says.

'Ofelia slit its throat and Elbert is butchering it.'

'Why?' Martha asks.

Hannah stares at her as if she is stupid. 'For food, of course.'

They follow, turning the corner, the sweat lodge once again in Martha's view, and standing before them are Ofelia, Elbert and Finn. Ofelia's hands are relatively clean, which surprises Martha, while Elbert works his way along the animal with a knife, perhaps the same knife used to slit Oscar's throat. The pink ribbons in the llama's ears are still visible, bright and electrifying. Martha watches on, a sorrow filling her insides, nauseous from the smell of so much blood and iron. There are two buckets, familiar also from the salt ceremonies. She peers into them, flinching; one is filled almost to the brim with the llama's blood and the other contains its heart. The heart looks as if it could belong to anyone, that it could still work, this beautiful muscular organ.

Finn turns to Martha. 'It didn't suffer,' he says. 'It was quick. Painless.'

Martha nods, a tear running down her cheek, her skin dry and desperate for hydration. 'It sacrificed itself for us,' she says.

'And we are grateful,' Finn says. 'So grateful.'

40

Finn can see skin being pulled from muscles and tendons, Elbert exerting himself over the task. He wonders how long it takes to skin and dismantle an entire llama. Does Elbert need to work quickly to stop flies from infiltrating it, laying their larvae? Are there even flies out here? He can't recall ever seeing one, the noise of their buzz absent. Perhaps the salt really does preserve everything.

He watches as Ofelia lifts the bucket of the llama's blood, struggling to keep the contents steady. She clicks her fingers to get Hannah's attention, motions for her to come, clicks her fingers again at the rest of them too.

They make their way round to the patio area and watch as Ofelia struggles down the hill, the bucket still in her hand, gesturing for them to continue to follow. Finn worries that Ofelia will fall, that the bucket of blood will be tipped across the hillside, across the rubble and on to the ancient cacti. But Ofelia is sure-footed, never faltering as she eases herself down the land, finally stopping at the edge of the salt flats, standing on a huge slab, its crust thick. She remains stationary, looking upwards to the clear blue sky, before finally tipping the contents of the bucket out across the salt.

Finn comes closer, feels compelled to see how the blood behaves. It sits there, mesmerising, isn't sure what it should do – he could swirl it around with his shoe, paint a picture. He thinks about a documentary he watched about men searching for Tutankhamun's tomb, the discovery only happening because a young servant boy spilled a can of water and instead of spreading across the dry land, the liquid seeped downwards, suggesting there was an empty cavity below. But Finn knows the salt is solid under their feet, compacted, up to ten metres in depth, the world's largest lithium deposit, sitting undisturbed for thousands of years. And he thinks now about the giant conglomerate working with the Bolivian government, the constant excavation, the Salt Centre, it all disappearing, inch by inch, encroached upon, forever being dug for treasure. Elbert's son employed by the company, and Elbert perhaps now wishing that he were there too. Oscar was right: all the money, and yet the poverty is evident, only getting worse – the water contamination, the disregard for anything sacred, people like Finn lapping it all up, believing in it. And he doesn't know what the answer is, feels as though he's exploiting the world regardless, whichever way he turns. Maybe he should stay here, let nature take its course.

He bends, careful of the cacti, and picks up a rock, but is it a rock or is it a piece of ancient coral? He looks out from the spreading of blood, across the horizon. Nothing but salt and sky. Ofelia is muttering something, perhaps a prayer, and he lowers his head in respect. The air feels heavy, and he begins to think that the rain is close by, that it will arrive and wash the llama's blood away. But he knows that blood doesn't really wash away, not truly. Somewhere in his mind sit Bible readings from his childhood, God telling them that blood will remain, that the land will expose it, that its mark will not be hidden. There will always be a trace of everyone through blood – all the blood that was used to keep him alive, all the blood that didn't belong to him, sacrificed by others, all of it still within him.

Afterwards, there is nothing for them to do but follow Ofelia back up the path, wanting to stick close, tight and solid and a member of her pack. At the top, Elbert is waiting, having finished his butchering. He's asking Finn to do something, shouting *vamos, vamos*, one of the few words that Finn does understand. They return to the site of the llama except it no longer looks like a llama. The carcass and skin have been discarded to one side, while pieces of meat are stacked in piles, different parts, perhaps all with different tastes. It could be any type of meat, pink and fleshy on the inside. He stares at the scene, contemplates how uncompromised Elbert appears, a man who knows how to survive.

Elbert instructs Finn, forthright in his words, acting out the action of lifting the meat with his hands, and Finn doesn't think he's ever seen him talk as much as he is talking now, words tumbling out of his mouth, spittle on his chin. Finn grabs at the meat, lets his fingers sink into an animal that still feels warm. What would it be like to take a bite? Overpowering? He's eaten raw fish, likes his steaks rare, so maybe this wouldn't be so bad.

Elbert loads more meat into his hands and arms, in this feral way that feels normal now. Finn presses the contents against his chest, feels the juice of blood soak into his T-shirt, drip down his skin. Elbert too is taking his share, leading the way in through the back door of the kitchen, where he tips the meat in his hands on to the counter and Finn copies him. There is relief at not having the meat pressing into him any more, yet he can still feel it, a phantom sensation, his T-shirt sticking to his skin. He does not dare look down at himself, except to see that his shoes are stained red too.

Elbert waves him out of the kitchen then and he accepts that he is in control of nothing – isn't sure how to articulate it. Perhaps to articulate it is to confess that he was happy with the imbalance of power before, when it tipped in his favour, when Elbert and Ofelia were there to serve and be instructed.

Afterwards, Martha leads Finn past the sweat lodge, and they descend to the makeshift steps of the thermal pool. They do not speak but begin to peel their clothes off, until they are completely naked and making their way into the cloudy water. It is too hot, uncomfortable. But there is a sense that it must be endured, another experience to be grateful for. They wade through the water, the terrain underfoot nothing more than rubble. Martha brings her hands to Finn's head and begins to pat down his hair, pushing it back behind his ears, washing the blood away, turning him around, lapping the water over his shoulders. Finn begins to do the same, a tender exchange that requires no words.

When Finn looks over, Ofelia and Elbert are there. They too begin to strip off, Ofelia finally unpinning her hat from the top of her head, and Finn realises that it's one of her hairpins he's been carrying in his pocket. Together, they enter the water, settling into their natural pairings: Finn and Martha on one side, Ofelia and Elbert on the other, an intentional distance being kept.

Finn feels nothing, only the overbearing heat enveloping his body, his chin dipping under the water.

'What are you thinking?' Martha whispers.

'I'm thinking about sacrificial anodes . . . ' he says.

Martha stares at him. 'And what are they?'

He turns to look at her, meeting her eye. 'The platforms we work on are predominantly made from steel, but the seawater will corrode the structure over time if we don't do something.' He pauses. 'Seawater acts as an electrolyte, pulling ions from the steel through oxidisation . . . '

'Okay . . . ' Martha says.

'To protect the steel from this process we coat it, but we also use zinc or aluminium anodes; their metals are more positive . . .

We attach them to the steel and, since they oxidise more easily, they turn the steel platform itself into a cathode.'

'What's a cathode?'

'It just means you turn the steel from positive to negative . . . '

'I don't understand,' Martha says.

'These anodes, they sacrifice themselves to protect the steel.' He takes a breath, his body adjusting now to the heat of the water. 'So much sacrificing . . . And so little acknowledgement. From everyone. The whole world.'

Martha dips her head back, hair submerged, and she closes her eyes. 'I'd sacrifice myself for you,' she says.

'Even now?' he replies. 'After everything?'

She nods.

'Well, I don't want you to.'

'But if you had to, would you eat me?'

'Martha . . . '

'Only if you *had* to . . . '

'Please . . . ' he says.

She shrugs. 'I wouldn't mind, honestly. If it meant you got to live.'

Finn is quiet for a moment. 'I'd eat others before I had to eat you,' he says.

'I'd eat you, if I *had to*,' she replies.

Finn nods, believes that she would.

41

Martha checks on Barb. Beads of sweat trickle from her forehead and down on to the mattress, while Rick sits uncomfortably, worry etched across his face. Martha's never been good at offering the right facial expression during times of worry. Or words. She cringes then, thinks about the last funeral she attended, the father of one of her schoolfriends – how when she'd arrived her friend was crying and Martha had leant in for a hug, smiling, and whispered *It's lovely to see you.*

Ofelia comes and offers Rick a hot water bottle filled with water from the thermal pool, and he forces it down his back, grateful, thanking her in Spanish. Her expression is one of comfort, and she retreats, her head bowed. Shame surfaces once again, Martha's cheeks red with it – the accusations and assumptions from the day before too close to be ignored.

'I don't deserve Barb,' Rick says.

'She loves you,' Martha replies.

He nods, his eyes welling with tears that he tries to rub away. 'I'm going to make it up to her,' he says. 'I'm not the man you saw . . . during the salt ceremony. Not any more.'

'None of us is perfect,' Martha says.

Ofelia returns, bringing a cup of herbal tea to Barb's bed, nodding encouragingly. But Martha doesn't think Barb is able to drink it unaided. 'Thank you,' Rick says, while Martha crouches behind Barb's head, attempting to prop her up, taking the cup from Ofelia. The tea is the colour of peppermint but smells completely different.

'Barb, we need you to try and drink this,' Martha says.

'What's in it?' Zoe asks, approaching.

'Some sort of herbal medicine,' Martha says, shrugging, bringing the liquid to Barb's lips, Barb doing her best to lap at it like a kitten. 'There must be an infection . . . She's so warm.'

'What should we do?' Rick asks.

Martha looks at the grubby bandage, shakes her head.

Ofelia raises her hands, offering them as a gesture of peace, before reaching forward and touching the knot on Barb's bandage. Slowly, she begins to untie it, and Barb suddenly screams out against her movements.

'What's she doing?' Rick shouts.

Martha hesitates. 'I think she's trying to help.'

Ofelia begins to unravel the bandage slowly, Martha peering over. There is fabric wadding pressed on to the side of Barb's ankle, which is swollen and thick with blood. Ofelia tries to peel it back, but it is stuck to Barb's skin, and as she tugs on it Barb lets out another elongated howl of pain.

Martha looks down at Barb. 'We'll pull it quickly, like a plaster, okay? I think that's the easiest way to do it . . . '

Barb is at risk of passing out.

'My love, we need to check the damage . . . ' Rick says. 'We need to do all we can until we can get you to a hospital.'

Martha shifts from behind Barb and waves Ofelia out of the way. Taking a breath, she pulls firmly on the wadding, the corner of the fabric tight in her grip. It comes away, leaving strands of thread sticking to the skin. Martha can see bone now; it's disgusting, and she wants to retch. It reminds her of oxtails in a butcher shop window. Bone should never be seen, she thinks, but she still cannot take her eyes off it.

'Do you know how it happened?' Zoe says.

'I—' Martha stops, a faint memory surfacing. 'I think it was . . . an accident.'

Ofelia departs, everyone else looking around, confused, but she returns almost immediately, her hands dripping wet with water. She comes and crouches down again in front of the wound and signals to Martha as if seeking permission to continue.

Martha nods.

Ofelia begins to gather handfuls of salt off the floor, inspecting it in her cupped hands, before forcing it on to the wound. Barb comes to life again, screaming, high-pitched and piercing, but Ofelia does not stop; if anything this encourages her. She keeps going, fistfuls of salt, forcing it in around the exposed bone.

'What is she doing?' Rick cries.

'She must think it will help,' Martha replies, nodding, already convinced by Ofelia's actions. 'I read in my salt book that salt draws bacteria-causing moisture away. Reduces the risk of infection . . . Or maybe slows an infection down.'

Martha watches on, tries to block out the noise of Barb screaming as Ofelia forces more salt into the wound, gathering what she can in her hands, scavenging. Martha thinks about bath salts, the tub at home, the taps in the middle, the chrome plughole that she presses up and down with her toes. She misses her house in Aberdeen now, would do anything to be back there.

When Ofelia has pushed in as much salt as she can, and Barb is at risk of passing out once again, she stops, returning the same bandage as before, wrapping it tighter, a barrier between the salt wound and the rest of the world. There is no thought for contamination, no suggestion of finding a fresh bandage. Maybe there isn't one, and Martha reasons that there's no point seeking out further disappointment. The bandage is secured neatly, a tight short bow at the top; for some reason Ofelia's handiwork reminds Martha of a strapped-up ballet shoe. She's never done ballet; imagines the shoes to be unbearably painful – bleeding feet, toenails coming away.

Ofelia stands, stares down at Barb, and nods.

'I think that was a success,' Martha says.

42

The sun is dipping in the distance and Finn is helping Elbert cook some of the llama meat outside on a makeshift barbecue – a metal barrel, cut lengthways, in half, stabilised by large rocks, with a rusting grill and charcoal. It feels out of place and Finn is wondering why they even need a barbecue when their diet is meant to be meat-free.

Elbert has a pair of tongs in his hand and he's flipping the chunks of llama over, unevenly cut, unevenly shaped. Finn swallows, realises that tonight is his last dose of medicine, that it's time to properly reintroduce solid food, but as he continues to watch Elbert turn the meat, juice dripping down into the charcoal, he feels anxious. The end of one thing and the beginning of another. Elbert's cheek, as per usual, is full of coca leaves, and Finn wonders how much of his supply is left – has he started rationing yet?

Elbert clicks his fingers, needing a large plate, and Finn brings it to him, holding it carefully in his hands while Elbert places each piece of cooked meat on it, stacking the slabs like pancakes. Finn looks at Elbert, attempts to offer him a smile that suggests they are in this together, that they are a team, but it doesn't land, feels insincere.

Finn takes the platter to the dining table, and everyone is already sitting, waiting. Rick has joined them, but Barb remains where she is, lying out on a mattress on the floor, Ofelia's tea from earlier appearing to have knocked both her and her pain out.

There is little else left for them to consume, but no one is greedy, waiting first for Elbert and Ofelia to take their turn, a demonstration of gratitude for how this meal was provided. Finn catches a look being exchanged between Elbert and Ofelia, an understanding, and he suspects that they really are a couple. He likes the idea of it, wants to build the fantasy of their lives up in his head. They must miss their son, worry terribly. How easy it is to create a narrative for another person. All of them strangers.

Finn takes one of the thinnest pieces of meat and begins to cut it into small chunks. A mix of colour between pork and lamb. He's feeling guilty for eating it, for personally knowing the animal, for breaking his promise to it. It was a smart creature – as all animals are, he concedes. And he's reluctant, doesn't want to commit to eating solid food, not here – to commit is to accept their eventual fate.

Rick is putting as much of the meat as he can into his mouth, speaking as he swallows, telling them about this ludicrous restaurant he ate in once where you could try any meat you wanted – shark, kangaroo, alligator. Apparently it all just tasted like chicken.

Finn forks a sliver of meat into his mouth. It is dry. He summons as much saliva as he can gather and attempts to swallow. There is no pain, nothing at all, and it amazes him despite the doctor telling him this was exactly what was going to happen. He visualises the clinic in Uyuni, the rubber tubing going down his throat. It feels like a lifetime ago.

When he glances up, he realises that he is the only one without water in his cup and he reaches for the jug almost in panic, fears that if he doesn't immediately take his share it will be gone, stolen by someone else. He swallows another tiny piece of llama, and another, nothing but fragments until his plate is empty.

As soon as everyone is finished, Finn gets to his feet, gathering plates, Hannah too. Then Martha. Suddenly, all the able-bodied guests are more than capable of helping, while Elbert and Ofelia remain in their seats. Finn reaches over and takes Rick's empty plate, stacking it under his own. He collects the other plates and walks into the cramped kitchen, placing the dishes down on the counter, plugging the sink, rolling up his sleeves.

Martha comes in behind him, standing, taking stock, and he hands her a tea towel. They work in silence, methodical, a well-oiled machine, and Finn thinks about their dishwasher at home, about the orange-tinged slime that coats the blades and the salt cap, and how he can't understand where it's coming from. He's run salts and cleaning fluids through the machine several times and still it will not disappear. He's manually removed parts, scrubbed each of them by hand, yet after a few uses the orange-tinged coating returns, despite the dishwasher being only two years old. And he has an irrational fear now that he will never know what has been causing it: something elusive, teasing him. Sometimes he'd wonder if it was Martha, if she was doing it intentionally. He's never asked her, and he doubts he ever will.

When they emerge from the kitchen everyone is still sitting around the table, a silence spreading through the space, and Oscar's absence suddenly feels so palpable, each of them carrying it.

'What do we do?' Zoe says, looking at Finn, pleading, as though he has the answer.

He shakes his head.

Elbert gets to his feet, departing, and everyone gazes after him. He returns, moments later, carrying a bottle of rum, half-full, and places it down on the table, then retrieving nine glass tumblers, the same cups that they drank from in their salt ceremonies. Ofelia begins to pour a healthy measure into each tumbler, sliding them across to everyone in turn. The generosity of both Elbert and Ofelia, after everything they have endured, is startling to Finn, crushing, and he doesn't know how to repay them.

Elbert raises his glass, and everyone follows suit. '*Salud*,' he says.

Two tumblers remain unclaimed, one for Barb and one for Oscar.

Finn takes a large gulp, bracing himself for the burn, and it stings as anticipated. His glass has flecks of grime on the outside and like a reflex his fingernail scrapes at it. He looks over at Barb lying out on the mattress, thinks about her on their salt trek, running off into the distance and Elbert having to drag her back. And now it seems inevitable, that she was destined to become more distant from the rest of them. He wishes he knew what had really brought her here, has a lingering idea, but nothing concrete, nothing he can cling to.

Already, he feels light-headed.

'We should toast to Finn's medicine too,' Martha says. She has his last medicine bottle in her hand, the dregs of a dose, a crust around the rim of the bottle.

'Can I smell it?' Zoe asks.

He nods, amused by this request.

Each of them in turn sniff at the bottle, Elbert and Ofelia too.

Ofelia begins to pour more shots of rum and they wait, watching as Finn finally swallows his last dose, everyone toasting him as he does so. And for a moment Finn has this overwhelming sense that he's never been closer to a group of people in his entire life. If they are to die, he thinks, stuck out here, at least they will die together. At least they will be with Oscar.

Tuesday

43

By first light Finn is hungover and starving. It's a hunger different from his longing over the past week, a sense that he is denying himself, a form of self-sabotage, of wondering how much longer he can continue in this manner. Seven days, a full week of enduring nothing but liquid and the smallest scraps of solid food. When he pulls on his trousers they won't stay up, the latest belt hole too loose. He sits back down on his bed, trying not to disturb Martha as she sleeps under the covers, and removes the belt from around his jeans, cutting another hole into the leather with his Leatherman pocket tool. How much more room is there to go? It is as if he is only now coming to terms with what he has physically lost, feels that he's made of little else but bone and skin, is fearful that he will continue to fade into nothing. He runs a hand over his face, the jagged stubble, a grittiness in everything from his hair to his toes that cannot be removed.

Martha stirs. 'You need to eat,' she whispers, as if capable of reading his mind.

'Eat what?' he says.

She rises, grabbing her shoes. 'No one is going to begrudge you a piece of fruit, an apple even, not when you've barely been able to eat anything all week.'

He nods, craving her care, loving the bones of her.

They make their way to the circular room, the table cluttered still with their tumblers stained with rum, the empty bottle, the rest of the room as dishevelled as they left it. They stop for a moment, standing over Barb as she sleeps, her breathing heavy and laboured, hair matted to her face with sweat. Finn looks at Martha, sees the worry on her face.

He begins to gather the cups from the table, feeling a sudden desire to have them tided away before Ofelia surfaces, while Martha retreats to the kitchen in search of an apple. He reaches forward and accidentally knocks a tumbler over, a clattering noise ringing through the space, reverberating painfully in his head. He's quick to grip it, his posture tight, already apologetic for the disturbance he's created. Martha appears with a bruised apple in her hand, handing it to him and he takes a bite, is fearful that his teeth are not up to the challenge, mulches it for a while, sucking the juice from it.

'Where are Elbert and Ofelia?' Martha asks.

He looks around the room again, taking a full sweep of it as if he has missed them the first time around. And it all feels off now. Something is wrong. He's not sure what compels him to do so, but he walks with purpose towards the entrance, apple in hand, and he can sense it, the knowledge he's about to acquire but not yet willing to accept.

He fixes his gaze on the handle of the door, wraps his fingers around it, this heavy metal thing that feels wrong, not in keeping with the rest of the structure, too grand. He wonders if the metal reacts to the salt, each corroding the other. How many times has this structure been built and rebuilt? How quickly does it dissolve into nothing?

He presses down on the handle, pulling the door back with effort, Martha now standing behind him. And he's aware that she must be able to feel the change in his body, his shoulders falling, his head tilting downwards in defeat, chin practically resting on his chest.

Martha pivots her body around him, peering out into the early morning light.

Before them, there is nothing but salt. The red Toyota Land Cruiser is gone.

If Finn focuses hard, really squints his eyes against the sun, he can make out the outline of the tyre tracks, stretching into what he imagines is forever. Yet still he stands, not reacting, the absence of the Land Cruiser something he can't quite understand. He remembers a famous American magician from his childhood, with dark, floppy hair, who dated supermodels. Finn had stayed up late one evening to watch live on television this man's greatest illusion, the disappearance of the Statue of Liberty in front of a live audience. And to everyone's astonishment the illusionist did indeed appear to achieve the impossible. Despite this impressive feat, Finn hadn't dwelt on the *how*; instead, he maintained an air of uninterested scepticism when it came to this and other magic tricks – he knew they were false but had no drive to discover their design.

And now, this same feeling is sweeping through him. Panic has not yet set in. He is looking from left to right, his eyes taking in as much expanse of salt as he can manage, waiting for the Land Cruiser to reappear as if by magic. Perhaps Elbert and Ofelia have tucked the vehicle away somewhere; but of course that makes no sense; there is nowhere to hide it.

He bolts out of the door and moves as quickly as he can down the makeshift path until he is on the flat. He begins to run across the salt, which is hard and uncomfortable underfoot. He keeps going, circling the outcrop of land that the Salt Centre sits on, a blur of cacti, passing the thermal pool at the back, waiting to find the Land Cruiser. But it is not there, and he needs to understand now how this particular illusion was achieved.

He circles a full lap and climbs back up to the Centre and in through the front door. Everyone is waiting for him, even Rick and Barb. He's sweating, his T-shirt clinging damp and cold to his torso.

'It's not there,' he says. 'The Land Cruiser. It's gone.'

'No,' Martha says, shaking her head. 'That can't be true.'

Finn won't settle, feels the need to keep moving, keep circling. He makes for a room that until now has been off-limits – Oscar, Elbert and Ofelia's sleeping quarters. He thrusts the door open, storming in, ready to impose his presence, but the space is empty. It's a smaller room than the dorm, four single salt-carved bed blocks with mattresses and stripped-down duvets. Nothing has been left behind, everything bare, no possessions to offer clues. It is as if they were never there in the first place.

Finn returns to the circular room, where everyone is waiting for him to provide them with information. He shakes his head. 'They're definitely gone.'

But Martha can't seem to accept what he's saying. 'Why would they leave us? Why would they do that?'

'Maybe they've gone to get help . . . ' Hannah says. 'Proper help, and they'll be back to rescue us.'

Zoe sits in one of the salt-carved armchairs, an expression of defeat. 'Do you think . . . ' She shrugs. 'Has it occurred to anyone else that this might just be the way of things? That we're not as special as we think? Why should we be rescued?'

'But no one deserves this,' Martha says. 'To be abandoned like this.'

'Well, maybe Elbert and Ofelia believe it *is* what we deserve . . . ' Zoe counters.

Rick whacks his hand down against the salt. 'No!' he shouts, on the verge of tears. 'Barb doesn't deserve this. Do not ever imply that she deserves this. Think whatever you want of me, but not her . . . ' he adds, tears swelling, rubbing at his eyes, and it's startling to Finn, even now, to see someone like Rick express his emotions so publicly. 'They could have at least taken Barb with them,' he whispers. 'Surely that's not too much to ask . . . To take a sick woman to a doctor or a hospital.'

'Thousands if not millions of people are placed into horrific situations every day that they don't deserve,' Zoe says. 'That's the reality, isn't it?'

'We are not bad people,' Rick says. 'What is the use in trying to make us feel guilty for just being who we are in life.'

Zoe shrugs again. 'We didn't treat *them* like real people, not really, not until we realised how much we fucking needed them.'

'That's not true,' Rick shouts. 'That isn't true. We were always respectful.'

But no one responds, and Finn knows it's because there is truth in everything Zoe is saying.

'They've killed us . . . ' Rick says, almost to himself. 'By abandoning us, they've left us to die.' He pauses. 'Maybe it was them after all; maybe they did kill Oscar.'

It's too much for Finn. He walks away, making for the kitchen, pressing his head to one of the cupboard doors. He can't breathe properly. He tries to inhale through his nose, exhale through his mouth. His heart is racing, his body running on an adrenaline that he doesn't want. Is this grief? There is only disbelief, a refusal to accept that any of this is happening to him, and he longs for the elusive feeling of acceptance. He wonders how long it took Elbert to fix the Land Cruiser, questions if it was truly ever broken in the first place, has no idea what is real any more.

He straightens, looks around the space, tries to focus on the mundane. The dishes dried the night before are still sitting in the rack, the counters as clean as he remembers them being left. He focuses on the fridge, and sees a Post-it stuck to the door that he's sure wasn't there last night. *Lo siento*, it says. Sorry. He stands, reluctant to open the fridge, fearful that it will be empty, but then he remembers that Martha brought him an apple and she hadn't been alarmed, so there must be some food.

When he opens the fridge, its motor deafening, he sees that Ofelia has left all the remaining food, mostly pieces of cling filmed llama meat, some cooked potatoes, browning avocado slices, a bowl with sweetcorn in it, a few bottles of water and some overripe fruit. He stares at the fruit, two brown bananas, and he accepts that he'll never see a yellow banana again. At the back of the fringe, tucked behind the plates and bowls, he sees then the familiar glass jug, the last of the murky brown salt brew contained within it. He peers closer, feels the need to really take it in. He tries to remember everything – the lightness, the profoundness of the universe. But also, his own flaws and weaknesses, his cruelties. Simply looking at the salt brew, feelings of guilt are once again pitted in his stomach, swamp-like in their consistency.

'You need to close the door,' Martha says.

He looks up, startled.

'The fridge,' she says. 'You're letting all the cold out.'

He shuts the door, more forcefully than he means to.

She comes closer. 'I don't know what we're meant to do now,' she says. 'How we're meant to make things right.' She stares at him, really takes him in, and he feels scrutinised by her gaze. It feels as though she can see inside him, knows exactly what he's thinking.

Finally, she says, 'I want to give Elbert and Ofelia the benefit of the doubt, because I didn't before. And I'm ashamed about that.'

He nods.

'Maybe they were worried they'd break down again with the weight of us all in that shit heap . . . ' she adds, her eyes pleading with him, begging for some reassurance. 'They might still send someone for us.'

'Maybe . . . '

She grips him and he can feel her heart beating in her chest. 'It was stupid of me to have drunk the rum,' she says, 'Maybe, if I hadn't, I would have been awake, I would have heard them . . . I could have begged them to take us too.'

And he wants to say something, of comfort, but he can't find the words that she wants to hear, realises in that instant that she's been looking for his reassurance for so long, about everything – about the climate emergency – and all he had to say was *everything will be okay*, even if he wasn't sure, because that was love. But he hadn't done, and now they are here. If he'd tried a little harder, if he'd been able to offer her even a little of the hope she craved, perhaps she wouldn't have felt the need to seek out a solution so extreme in nature. And he nods to himself, racking his brain now to find a way to make things better for her.

'I want to live,' she whispers. 'I so desperately want to live this life I've been given.'

Something solidifies within him. He has already endured more than most, yet he's not fighting their fate – there is a sense of acceptance that he understands, that he's faced before. He wants to spend the remainder of his time in peace, feeling euphoric and grateful.

'They left us the last of the salt brew . . . ' he says.

And, now that he's said it, he's sure this is exactly what they should do. There is nothing left to fear. Like an addiction, he's desperate to experience all of it again. A means of numbing their reality, a gentle ease into the abyss.

44

Martha is the one to collect the six glasses. The others have gathered themselves around the mattresses on the floor, Barb beside them coming in and out of consciousness, Zoe retrieving buckets and toilet roll, placing them at the bottom of each bed, as before. Finn pours the brew into the first cup; Martha passes it along to Rick. As she continues to distribute the cups, she realises that there is no one left who has any specific knowledge about what they are consuming, or how they should conduct themselves. They should all be accustomed to this blend, capable of tolerating its potency, and therefore nothing drastic or dramatic is likely to happen, but what if it becomes more potent with time, rather than less? What if they're all doomed? But then what does it matter? she thinks. Maybe this should be their glorious end.

When she looks up, everyone has a cup in front of them, and they're waiting.

'Who will lead?' Hannah asks. 'The ceremony . . . '

Martha casts her eyes around the group. Everyone else is doing the same.

Rick brings his cup to his lips. 'Let's just promise to look after each other, okay?'

They nod in unison, raising their glasses in something of a toast before drinking.

The concoction is thicker than Martha remembers, something having settled and somewhat solidified within it. There is a residue in her mouth, a coating she imagines to be bark or mud. She watches then as Rick instructs Hannah to lift Barb's cup to her lips.

'Are you sure?' Hannah says, trying to part Barb's lips with the rim of the glass, some of the liquid dribbling down her chin.

'She has to do it with us,' Rick says, insistent. 'She can't be left out.'

Hannah tucks her hand in behind Barb's head and is doing her best to align the glass with her mouth, struggling, but refusing to stop. Martha feels the need to help, so she crouches down to part Barb's lips with her fingers, to help get her into a sitting position, as Hannah forces more of the thick mixture down her throat.

Afterwards, Martha looks around and is aware that, unlike before, people seem reluctant to spread out from one another. Hannah lies on a mattress next to Barb, looking up at the salty ceiling, while Zoe sits on the edge of the same mattress, hands cupping her chin, fixing her sight on the ground, kicking salt gently with the toe of her shoe. Martha has a sudden pang of affection for all of them, loves them each, individually. She goes over and kisses Hannah on the cheek. It takes Hannah by surprise, but she embraces it, putting her arms around Martha and hugging her. Martha then goes to Zoe and does the same, Zoe returning a kiss to Martha's left cheek.

She makes her way to Rick, who is lying down on a mattress to the other side of Barb. She bends and offers him a kiss on the cheek, and he takes it, is grateful, squeezing her hand, blowing her a kiss as she stands and straightens. She comes to Barb, crouches close again, and places a kiss on her forehead. It tastes of salt, but Martha doesn't mind; everything tastes of salt. She is overflowing with love, doesn't know what she would do without them, these people now her family. Finally, she comes to

Finn and cups her hands around his beautiful face, smiling at him, kissing him on the lips before pulling away. She can see the love he has for her in his eyes; she could bask in it, thinks about how lucky she is to have someone who loves her this much. She curls up next to him on his mattress, pressing her body close to his, needing to stay like this. If they are to die, she wants to die pressed up next to him, two skeletons, embracing until the end. She marvels at his mere existence – the fact that a team of doctors and a strategy of treatment allowed him to live, that so many people worked tirelessly to keep him alive when often she feared they might stop. To have his thoughts and feelings continue to be distributed out into the world when so many others don't. He is a miracle to her, and she helped create it by caring for him.

They all lie on their mattresses, not speaking, seeing the world as they want to. The sun is streaming in through the windows and patio doors, and Martha is oblivious of time, the digits on her watch redundant. When did they last move from their mattresses? Was it hours? A day? Has the sun set and risen again?

'I wish there was music,' Zoe says. 'I think that's what I miss the most . . .'

'You can still dance without music,' Hannah replies.

Zoe sits up, takes in the room. 'No, I don't think so . . .'

'Barb's tango shoes . . . the pink ones . . .' Rick says. 'I bought her them as a gift in Buenos Aires. She's always loved to dance.' He pauses. 'You should wear them. I think that would please her.'

'Thank you, but that's not the type of dancing I do,' Zoe says, her tone gentle. 'It's nice that she wore them, though . . . managed to enjoy them.'

'You could still dance for us,' Hannah says.

Zoe hesitates, a hint of a smile surfacing.

Rick sits up, his back still causing him pain. 'I'd love to see you dance,' he says.

Zoe is quiet for a moment. 'Okay,' she finally says. 'I will, if you'd like to see it.'

'I would,' he says. 'I'd like that very much.'

Hannah, excitedly, begins to usher everyone up on to their feet and out on to the patio. Rick, unable to contemplate the thought of Barb missing this, asks Martha and Finn to lift her between them, while Rick hobbles behind, kicking the weight of his left side forward, dragging his right.

Outside, they stand together, and as Martha and Finn come to a stop with Barb between them Barb seems to come to life, her eyes bright and expressive, the momentary presence of someone who is in no pain or distress. This ease elates Martha, and she kisses Barb on the cheek once again. She looks back out across the expanse of salt, watches as Zoe makes her way down the rocky and cactus-laced path. There is salt in the air, there is salt everywhere, and Martha sticks her tongue out, feeling its harshness. Perhaps out here you can never really die, she thinks, instead being preserved by the salt, becoming part of the landscape; and, oddly, this offers her comfort.

Zoe has made it to the flat, everyone else above watching her as she steps past one salt crust and over on to another, positioning herself perfectly in the middle of one beautifully formed slab of salt, while not so far away there is the blood of the llama, less bright now, a browning in the sun, a seeping into the land, a thing to now be ignored.

They watch Zoe kick off her worn trainers and stand stationary in her socks, bending her body down gracefully. She is completely still, feet close together. She lifts her head up, tilts her chin to the sky, arms stretched back, like a bird waiting to take flight. Martha is desperate to get closer, toes creeping over the edge towards the rubble. It is as though the group have taken a collective breath – the anticipation for what is about to come feels overwhelming.

And Zoe begins. She kicks one leg and begins to move through the air as if held by an unseen force. Her body wheels and contorts, and they can hear the silent music, understand the rhythm she moves to. It is majestic and awe-inspiring to Martha, perhaps the most graceful thing she has ever encountered. As Zoe continues to move across the salt, never faltering or hesitating, tears begin to form in Martha's eyes. There is a sense of privilege, that not everyone gets to experience this sight; that Zoe has allowed, chosen, *them* to witness this. And Martha can't imagine what it must be like to harness such talent. The discipline. She has never stuck at anything in her life. But instead of feeling sad about her own choices she is elated, claiming part of this for herself, special by association. She never wants it to stop; she could watch Zoe move until the end of time.

Finally, Zoe takes a controlled kick, her body bending, lowering herself close to the salt. She dips her head, remains poised for a moment, before finally straightening and bending to take a bow.

The group erupts in applause and Hannah wolf-whistles. It is glorious, Hannah scrambling down the rocky terrain until she is embracing Zoe, the greatest gesture of love. Martha watches as they return up the slope together, clawing at the dirt, one heave and step up after another, huge beaming smiles plastered across each of their faces.

'That was my best,' Zoe says, arriving at the top. 'The greatest dance of my life. Nothing will beat that.'

Martha nods, breathless with the life she is experiencing.

Barb is beginning to feel heavy in Martha's arms. Whatever consciousness that was stirring inside her seems to be dwindling, and Martha manoeuvres, attempts to turn. Finn understands. They return Barb to her sweat-soaked mattress, placing her down as gently as they can. As they pull the blanket back over her, Martha sneaks in a glance at Barb's ankle: the obscene swelling of the salt, the redness tracking, the grubbiness of the bandage. But she chooses not to dwell, chooses to believe that the salt brew will be able to work its magic on Barb, as it will on everyone else.

Finn is staring at her, and she leads him away from the others to Oscar, Elbert and Ofelia's room, closing the door behind them. She picks a bed, imagining it to be Oscar's, and climbs in. She's pulling her clothes off and beckons to Finn to do the same, and then he's on top of her and she adores him, as she has never adored him before, and she's so sorry for everything she's ever done to hurt him. There are a hundred things she wants to tell him, but her mind is moving too quickly; her body feels electric, that she could spark, that she could combust from all his love, from their love for each other. The sadness and despair that had enveloped her, that clung to her like fur, feels so foreign now. And she can see that Finn feels and thinks the same, that they are one again – she can see his world, his thoughts, his mind. She is him and he is her. If this is eternity she doesn't mind. She has the whole world here.

45

Finn lies in the bed beside Martha, a hand reaching out towards the salt on the ground, his fingers making contact. It is as though he is expecting his fingers to morph from five, to less, to more. He thinks about his thumbs and how valuable they are. People don't give their thumbs enough credit, he decides. Most people's day-to-day existences rely heavily on thumbs, and he cups his then, protecting them from the world and its hazards. He's melancholy. The elation from before has faded and he doesn't know why – the emotion dangling in front of him, teased and pulled away just when he thinks it is within his grasp. This slow, thudding sensation fills his chest, the inevitability that he will always be here now.

He sits up, naked, and closes his eyes, watching colours pass across his eyelids. He takes a breath. When he opens his eyes, he feels a little more anchored, reaching for his clothes, picking up each item and shaking off the salt. He stumbles up and out of the room, famished, can think of nothing but food, doesn't care about the pact he made with himself about not eating solid food here; he'll eat whatever he can get his hands on.

In the kitchen, he opens the fridge and stares at the plate of llama meat, its cling film hanging loose and open from the plate, not how he remembers it. He peers at the meat, is sure that some cuts are missing. He looks around the kitchen space, sees nothing to suggest anyone has been cooking. He glances in at the fridge again, checks behind him, and pulls a slab of pink meat out from under the cling film. He holds it up, his thumb and index finger acting as tongs as he carries it, making for the back door, droplets of blood landing on the floor. The carcass of the llama remains but he does not allow his eyes to linger, doesn't want to know if insects are enjoying it. He makes a mental note to find something that can cover the animal, offer it dignity. He refuses to acknowledge the sweat lodge too, circling round, making for the hammock that is sitting stationary in the static air. He attempts to climb in but struggles with only one free hand. Without hesitating, he places the piece of meat between his teeth, biting down for grip, and climbs into the hammock. His mouth fills with blood, oozing out past his lips. He swallows, takes no issue with it; if anything it is soothing. It's cold and rich and feels like something that will be nourishing. He lies there, relaxed, and continues to gnaw at it, only really wanting the juice, his mouth so overwhelmingly dry.

Hannah peers into the hammock, watching him chew at the raw meat, a strange expression on her face. Suddenly he is filled with a deep sense of shame, and needs to be rid of the meat. He throws it away, hearing it smack against a slab. He struggles to get out of the hammock, falling to the ground, his elbows hitting the hard surface, a sensation that feels distant travelling through his body, his pain receptors off-kilter and confused.

Hannah looks from him to the piece of raw, chewed-up meat on the ground. She bends to retrieve it, but he shakes his head, needing to distance himself from it now.

He walks back inside, passing Rick and Barb on their mattresses, feeling a desire to drink more salt brew, but the jug is empty. He can hear Rick apologising to Barb, asking her to stay with him, but it's frantic, as if he is unsatisfied by his own words.

Finn sees Zoe then, positioned in a kneeling stance, face hidden, the heels of her feet exposed, her hands pressing up against a wall of salt. He reaches her, crouching down on his own hands and knees to see what is holding her attention. She's licking a section of the wall, again and again, working her tongue around one of the plug sockets, the four sharp edges, the intensity of it. His reactions are muted but he can still tell that this is dangerous. He tries to pull her away, but she pushes him off.

'No,' he says, the words sounding strange in his mouth.

He keeps pulling at her but somehow she always manages to release herself from his grip. She takes another lick around the four corners of the antiquated plug socket. She stops then, pulls back to look at him.

'I've been to see him . . . ' she says.

'Who?' he asks, but he knows who she's talking about. He feels as though he can predict the words that she's going to say, even before she knows.

She bites down on her lip.

'He spoke to me,' she says, nodding as if she needs it confirmed for herself. 'He accepted my apology.'

Confused, he looks at the plug socket where she has been licking and there is a transparency to the edges that he doesn't think was there before.

'It was me who did that to him,' she says.

Finn shakes his head. Didn't she dance on the salt only minutes ago, and wasn't it the most incredible thing any of them had ever seen?

Zoe reaches for him, grips him. 'Have you gone to him?' she asks. 'Did he speak to you too?'

Rick is standing behind them, doubled over, a forty-five-degree angle, and Finn imagines him tipping over. He points outside, the words in his mouth stuck, a strange foaming noise emerging instead. Finn stares at him, a sense of dread creeping in – he's not sure how it came to pass but he believes, is sure, that

Rick no longer possesses a tongue. Finn suddenly springs up on to his feet and begins to clamp his hands around Rick's jaw. Rick is resistant, despite his body barely being able to shift from the position in which he finds himself. The noise is still echoing out of his mouth and Finn works harder, digging his fingers into Rick's skin, piercing it, desperate to open his mouth wide and inspect this missing tongue. Rick bares his teeth, clamped together, and Finn is furious, is working hard to force Rick to open his mouth wide, is conscious of the fact that he might be bitten, but not willing to stop. Finally, Rick swallows, parting his teeth slightly, enough for Finn to see his tongue, pink and muscular and completely intact.

Finn lets go and tries to apologise but can't find the words.

Rick is still pointing to the patio area and Finn feels compelled, shamed, into seeing what holds his attention. He walks, Zoe now following, but the patio is deserted. He glances around, Zoe clasping her hand to his as they turn the corner and see the remains of the llama. He remembers then, something that felt important before, something he needs to do. He drops Zoe's hand and returns to the circular room, looking around him. His feet are on a cowskin rug, its edges gritty with chunks of salt. He leaps off it and begins to roll it up, salt coming in with it. He attempts to up-end it, but it is thin and floppy, and he cradles it in his arms instead, another animal worthy of respect.

He carries the rug outside and begins to unroll it at Zoe's feet. Zoe stares at him and then the rug. He nods down at it, wordlessly telling her to lift it with him, and slowly she bends and retrieves its edges. Together, they lift the tanned skin as far as their arms will allow and thrust it down, it landing almost like a parachute. It sits beautifully over the llama, all blood and carcass gone from view. All that remains are the front feet, and a trail of pink ribbon. He begins to look for rocks, positioning them on the periphery of the cowskin so that it is pinned into place and not at risk of moving. He feels encouraged, as if finally, he has done something right. He runs a hand over the cowskin, in line with the grain. To him, he is stroking the llama, hoping that it is enough, seeking acceptance and forgiveness. His fingers hover over a foot, before tapping it affectionately, this hard substance like brittle toenails.

When he looks up, he sees the flap of the sweat lodge open, the fabric rolled up and pinned back. He and Zoe crouch to get inside, on to their hands and knees, and when he sees Oscar again he gasps involuntarily, as if he were seeing the body for the first time – the slit of the throat, protruding around the edges of his neck, the blood-soaked beard hiding everything else. He looks down at his own hands in the dimness, visualises the knife in his grip. He cannot speak; the grief and guilt will not allow it. He feels capable of having caused this harm. He knows it; can sense it in every part of his body. 'It was me,' he says, turning to Zoe, his voice nothing more than a croak. 'It wasn't you, it was me.'

46

In the sweat lodge, Martha is oblivious to Finn and Zoe. She is busy, Hannah too, scooping salt from a bucket with their hands, packing it into the ground, trying not to look directly at the body, only flickers and sideways glances. Her hands feel raw and blistered but she doesn't care. She's working on Oscar's left foot, Hannah on his right, and they're padding him now with salt, pressing down on him to compact it. She worries they won't have enough salt to complete the job but then she laughs, erratic and maddening, because she's nearly forgotten where they are, that there is probably nowhere else in the world that has more salt than here.

She leans back, her knees pressing into the salt, and looks up. The light seems different now, lesser. Finally, she sees Finn and Zoe crouched near the entrance. She opens her mouth to shout but there is nothing, a muted silence. She thumps her hands on the ground, some animalistic gesture, a creature of dominance asserting itself. Finn and Zoe don't need to be told what to do; they too begin clawing at the salt, gathering it from another bucket, their palms cupped together, tipping what they can on to Oscar. Martha nods, satisfied by their actions; believes it is the least they can all do.

They work quickly as a team, Finn and Zoe coming and going from the main building, returning with buckets of salt gathered from the floor, while Martha and Hannah continue to pack the salt around Oscar's body. She has no idea how long they spend working in this way but gradually Oscar is disappearing before them. She smiles. A shrine of salt, a place that will keep him safe, where he'll still be himself.

Until now, his face has been completely off-limits, but she can no longer avoid it. She breathes in and out, taking deep gulps of stale, damp air. Crouching at the back of his head, she hovers, finally looking at what she believes she has inflicted on him, the image of this sacrifice before her. There is no clear memory of her actions, only the knowledge, a sense that she is capable of taking life away from another. She gathers salt from the bucket Finn has placed beside her and begins to pack the wound around his neck, pinning his beard hair to one side, gentle with her fingers as she presses down. She scoops up more salt and forces it around his neck and shoulders, mounting it up on each side until it begins to spill on to his cheeks, her hands moving to his face. She thinks of Irish relatives who have open caskets at their funerals, her mother swearing that it helps with closure, lends itself to the grieving process, to be able to physically see the person no longer breathing, to touch them.

Another bucket is brought to her and she scoops again, as much as she can, filling in his eyes, both nostrils. She is making a statue out of salt, carving and shaping him into something that will be beautiful. She attempts to open his mouth, but his teeth are clamped shut. Instead, she pulls at the gums and lines his teeth with as much salt as she can. Somewhere in her mind she knows this is the greatest gift she can give him – to be immortalised, cured, mummified within the salt, the substance that is everything to him. When she leans back, his mouth looks odd, all packed out and protruding from the rest of his face, but it feels vital. She carries on, suddenly alone now in her actions, as she continues to heap salt over him until she can no longer make out the details, only his outline. Running a hand over the length of him, she worries that she hasn't done enough; fears that he will continue to rot, his organs and other openings letting him down.

Finally, she departs, the sun setting in the distance. There is a cowskin rug covering the remains of the llama and she has no idea what this all means. She swallows. There is salt on everything: on her tongue, in her hair, under her fingernails. She can taste it, is bearing down on her back molars, painfully. There will most likely be blood when she swallows again. She looks up at the sky, feels so insignificant. There could be thousands of versions of her across the universe, all acting out different versions of the same day. But she is here; this is her now.

Hannah comes to her and rests her head in the crook of her neck. Martha leans into her too, closes her eyes for a moment.

'I'm sorry for what I've done,' Hannah whispers, her voice husky and sore-sounding, as if she's only just learned to talk for the first time. 'I didn't mean for it to go this far . . . I didn't mean to hurt him.'

Martha shakes her head. 'No,' she says, insistent. 'It wasn't you.'

Hannah straightens, looks at her. 'It wasn't something I wanted to do.' She pauses. 'I have this vision of blood, of dipping my finger into a little pool of it. It's on loop in my mind, but it doesn't feel like something that happened here, it's as if it happened somewhere else – that I was in two places, simultaneously. Does that even make sense?'

'Yes,' Martha says, placing her hand on Hannah's head, stroking it. 'Maybe it was all of us,' she adds, her words slow, things growing hazy.

She makes for the circular room, unsteady on her feet, and stumbles in through the patio door. The space is darkening but Martha can see that Rick is lying beside Barb on her mattress. She goes to Barb and crouches down, watches her breathe, her eyelids fluttering, perhaps from a dream. There is a sickly texture to her skin and Martha tries to visualise the infection that has taken hold, remembers Finn's PICC site, the discoloured adhesive tape, the Sharpie pens the doctors used to track the spread of infection, the pumping of more drugs into his body. But Barb has had none of these things. That was a different world, a different life – intravenous antibiotics and doctors don't exist any more.

She turns on one of the torches, forcing its base into the salt so that the light projects up on to the ceiling. She believes nothing bad will happen to Barb while there is light in the room; only in darkness does she believe there is risk.

She settles on the closest free mattress, gripping at a cover, needing to envelop herself within it. The circular formation of the room continues to unsettle her – a space where you are forced to look at one another, no sharp lines or edges to avert your gaze, constantly drawn back to the centre. She turns over again, the mattress so thin under her, salt pressing into her hipbone, and she wonders if the salt is beginning to poison her – a fine line between the same thing having a positive or detrimental effect. From where she lies she can see the others coming in, copying her, settling on different mattresses, Finn sliding in behind her, so they are once again pressed together, their natural way of sleeping now.

'Did we hurt him?' Finn whispers as though he's asking a perfectly rational question. 'Did we kill him?'

'What happened here can't be changed,' she says. 'It was probably always going to be this way . . . '

Martha can't feel Finn's emotions any more, is already missing the intimacy. But she can still feel the energy of the salt, of their collective effort to preserve Oscar. She is free of all burden and at peace, wishes she could have lived her whole life like this. They say that as death approaches people often look peaceful; that maybe whatever awaits them on the other side isn't something to fear. Is it easier to see everything nostalgically, through rose-tinted glasses, when you know it will all disappear? Is it only at the end that people learn to appreciate the beauty before them? Martha smiles, a warmth spreading through her. Despite everything they have done to strip the Earth of its resources, it will continue to spin, with or without them, perhaps for billions of years, as long as the sun continues to burn. But briefly, very briefly, Martha got to exist within it.

Wednesday

47

Finn wakes to the sound of vomiting. He lies on the thin mattress he's sharing with Martha and stares at the torch that is still on, shining upwards, despite the early morning sunlight. He's trying to remember the details of the day before, everything hazy, and then it comes to him with a jolt: Elbert and Ofelia left.

He attempts the breathing exercises Oscar taught him, in and out, to clear his mind and focus on a happy memory – camping with Martha, him slicing open bananas and her forcing eighty-per-cent dark chocolate into the slits. They are on a beach, rain falling. He has been in a terrible mood, thinking that the trip was a mistake, like so much of their relationship, but briefly the rain stops, and they barbecue the bananas, turning their insides into a delicious gooey mess that he scoops with a spoon, chocolate all over his face, and Martha is laughing, coming over to lick his mouth in the most unattractive manner. And, in that memory, he loves her in a way he didn't think possible. He can't think of a better way to imagine love now.

The noise of retching from somewhere close by is persistent. He sits up, socked feet sinking into the salt, shaking Martha awake. The vomiting is coming from Barb, Zoe helping her, trying to direct her mouth into a bucket, while Hannah hovers, worried.

'Is she okay?' Finn asks.

Hannah's eyes widen. 'How did you not hear her through the night? She was hallucinating . . . she's convinced she killed Oscar.'

Finn can see Rick lying on his side, curled up behind his wife, his hand rubbing her back, a comforting gesture.

Finally Barb's vomiting begins to subside, and Zoe wipes her mouth with toilet paper. She places her hand on Barb's damp cheek and looks up at the rest of them, shaking her head.

'We need to get some water down her,' Finn says.

'There's hardly any left . . . ' Zoe replies.

Finn gets to his feet, the stench of vomit strong. 'I thought there was a bottle of water in Oscar's office . . . '

He moves, unsteady on his feet, needing to be away from the circular room. Oscar's office is as he remembers it, cluttered, more so for their having rifled through his possessions. He stands, looking around, not seeing any bottle of water, wondering now if he ever saw one in here in the first place. He makes for Oscar's office chair, sits down in it, swivels a little from side to side. There is a carving under the desk, and he runs his fingers over it, imagining for a moment that he is Oscar.

Martha is standing over the threshold of the door, watching him.

She comes and sits opposite, ready to have their very own one-to-one, and Finn understands, prepares to probe and question.

'What do you remember from the salt brew?' he says.

She hesitates, her eyes darting around the room. 'We all thought we'd killed him.'

Finn's heart sinks at the knowledge, the confirmation. 'And do you think that's true?'

'We've covered this already,' she says, her voice shaking. 'We're not capable. None of us.'

He falters, the memory of gathering salt, the image of Oscar's body, of Martha's attempts to preserve him, to keep him bound to this world with them.

'What's going to happen?' he asks.

'Barb is going to die without help . . . '

Finn places his hands on the surface of the desk, before clasping them in a gesture of prayer, actively mirroring his perception of Oscar.

'And after that?'

'We're going to starve . . . Or go mad. Probably both. It's happening already.'

'And what do you want?' he asks.

'I'm mourning but I'm ready to move on . . . I want to put the darkest stage of this behind me.' She straightens in her seat. 'I won't die here, Finn. I want to find a way back. And I want to take the good with me.'

He shakes his head. 'It's too late for that,' he says. 'We belong here now.'

'No,' she says, standing, coming to him, crouching down and placing her hands on his knees. 'We should go. Surely that's a better alternative to staying here?'

He looks at her, is ready to accept their fate. 'Why would you want to return to the world we left behind?' he says. 'I doubt it has changed.'

'But I've changed. And you've changed. We have Oscar to thank for that.'

'But . . . ' A tear runs down his face, his jaw clenching. 'What if . . . ?'

Martha holds his face in her hands. 'We could just leave. Right now. We don't even need to tell anyone . . . Please, Finn, I'm begging you. Let us at least try.'

They return to the circular room, eyes falling on them. 'Did you find the water?' Zoe asks.

Finn shakes his head. 'There was no bottle. I don't know why I thought there was.'

Rick attempts to sit up, his hands gripping the edge of the mattress. 'You need to save as much water as possible for your journey.'

Finn stares at him, confused, wonders if Rick can now read their minds.

'What are you talking about?' Hannah says.

Rick nods his head, as if he is agreeing with something he has already said. 'You're going to leave today.'

'What are you talking about?' Zoe says.

Rick places a hand on Barb. 'Don't tell me you've not considered it?'

'We're not leaving . . . ' Hannah says.

Rick smiles. 'But of course you are.'

'Someone might still come for us . . . ' Hannah counters.

'No one is coming,' Rick replies.

'In a few days your back will be better,' Hannah says. 'If your back is better, then we can all leave together, carry Barb between us. We'll figure out a way . . . Each of us can take it in turns to help. We can make a crutch out of something.'

Rick shakes his head. 'Be practical. Be realistic. You don't have a few days. It'll be too late for everyone by then. There is not enough food and once the rain comes there will be no way to leave. And anyway, Barb and I have grown quite accustomed to this place.'

'No,' Hannah says. 'No. We're not having this conversation.' She turns, addressing Zoe, needing her support. 'Tell them . . . Tell them we're not leaving.'

But Zoe doesn't reply.

'When you find help, as I'm sure you will, then, if you think it's appropriate you can send someone for us. But,' Rick says, pressing all the strength of his voice into the word, 'we're *not expecting anything*, do you understand? We have resigned ourselves to being here. Perhaps we were always destined for this, to stay here with Oscar.'

Finn takes all of this in, Rick's words moving around them, traces of the salt brew perhaps still taking effect.

'I'm sorry, I just think . . . ' Hannah says. 'It's reckless trying to walk. Martha and Zoe already attempted it. What, realistically, are our chances of surviving out there under the sun? What if we find no one? What if we get lost?'

Rick nods at Zoe, a look of genuine affection. 'Yes, I suppose you might get lost,' he says. 'Or you might not.' He stops. 'But you must try, no? If this trip has taught us anything, it's that you at least try . . . '

'What if some of us go and a few of us stay with you?' Hannah says.

'No,' Rick replies, shaking his head. 'It only works if the four of you go together. We stay in our couples. That's what we do.'

'Maybe I don't want to go,' Hannah says. 'It feels like you're forcing us to leave.'

'That's exactly what I'm doing,' he says, as if attempting to end the debate. 'I am forcing you to go. There is nothing left for you here.'

Everyone else continues to remain silent.

'Rick . . . It doesn't have to be like this,' Hannah says.

'You'll take whatever food remains, too,' he says, nodding, as if to reassure himself. 'And it's probably best that you don't waste too much time. You don't want the hours of daylight to run away from you.'

It is as though Rick has always known what they were going to do, long before the rest of them; as if it is all inevitable. And Finn won't fight it – he's grateful; grateful that Rick took the burden of that decision, fatigued by the idea of having to make any more decisions. He will take the food, pack his bag, place a balaclava over his head and walk. He'll do as he's told.

Afterwards, Finn helps bring the remaining food and water out on to the dining table, where collectively they can see that there is little left. Zoe takes a banana and begins to peel it, removing the skin entirely. She breaks the banana in half and then does something Finn has never seen before – she presses her thumb down on the torn end, splitting the banana apart into three perfectly separated segments. She does the same with the other half and now there are six pieces of banana, one for each of them. Finn takes the piece that is offered to him, and it feels symbolic, a final supper. He begins to mulch his piece in his mouth, drawing as much saliva as he can, still sceptical of his healed oesophagus.

'We should cook the llama meat,' Martha says.

There is the image of him chewing on a raw slab of meat; of its juice, metallic in taste swirling around his mouth. He thinks he's conjured it from his mind like so many other thoughts and hallucinations since arriving here. He finds himself moving towards the patio doors, pushing them open and staring at the hammock as it sits limp in the morning light. He goes over to the fabric, hesitates before opening the folds. And there it is: the dried-in streaks of blood that confirm to him that some things, if not all things, that he sees in his mind are true. He tries to rub the marks away but they will not budge – a physical reminder of something he would rather forget. He walks around the corner, casts his eyes over a cowskin rug, another memory surfacing. The sweat lodge is in his sight, but he does not dare go near it.

He enters the back door of the kitchen, finding Martha inside, can hear the hiss of the oil and the sizzle of the meat against the pan. Its smell is strong, and he wants none of it.

'Leave Rick and Barb their share of the meat,' he says.

'But they don't want it . . . '

'We need to at least give them a chance.' He clings to her, inhaling her, but she's unfamiliar, smelling only of iron and salt. 'I don't know about this . . . What if it doesn't work?'

'Is it because you don't think you'll manage?' she whispers, placing a kiss on his neck, salt on his skin.

'I'll hold you back . . . '

'You won't,' she says.

48

Martha sorts through her possessions as she packs her bag, trying to discard anything she won't need. She wants to be prepared for the heat and force of the sun by day, but also the freezing cold of night. Can she discard the travel towel she doesn't like? The silk sleeping bag liner that she bought because she'd worried about bedbugs in Bolivia and was told they couldn't bite through silk? She grips a set of pyjamas in her hand, stares at them, reluctant. In truth, she has no desire to leave any physical object of hers that will tie her to this place. She's attempting to protect herself, and Finn, from any repercussions, continuing to build a narrative and version of events she can make peace with, that doesn't make her stomach churn. Everything precarious. The pyjamas stay in the backpack, and so does everything else.

She's tried to charge her phone too, be as prepared as she can be, but still there is only fourteen per cent battery, the power supply practically non-existent. She hauls her backpack on to her shoulders and glances around the dorm room one last time, kicking at some salt before departing, thankful to be leaving a space where she doubts she's ever really managed to sleep. She moves through the corridor, her balance feeling unsteady between the uneven floor and the weight of the bag on her shoulders. When she arrives in the circular room everyone is waiting. Already she knows there is too much in her bag, that she'll struggle to walk any distance, everything seeming heavier than it was before.

They stand ready, reluctant to say goodbye – to do so confirms what they all know to be true – that they're not going to see Rick and Barb again. There is such a finality to Martha's thinking that it shocks her how ordinary the moment feels. They are compartmentalising the severity of their situation for the sake of social norms. But Martha wants to pause, wants to study this encounter, wants to marvel at the strangeness of human nature. She peers over at Barb lying on her mattress, seeming to float in and out of consciousness. Martha wants to believe that Barb sees her and is encouraging her to go.

Rick leans against a curve of wall, his back clearly on the mend. The idea of leaving him behind, able-bodied, feels wrong, as though they are committing him to the loneliest of existences. But she knows there is no point in being pragmatic, in telling him that he might as well come with them – he'll never leave Barb. He owes her too much.

Rick smiles, a large, booming, white-toothed smile, as he surveys each of them.

'If you find yourself our way in the future, we'll go out on the boat,' he says, and he speaks with such conviction that Martha begins to worry that he is deluded, has misunderstood what is about to take place. 'There's nowhere like San Diego,' he adds. 'We'd love to have you.'

Martha smiles back. It is a smile that she hopes will convey something of love, of respect, of gratitude for placing no guilt on them for leaving. Sometimes words spoken without sincerity or intention can be the most comforting. She thinks of her aunt in the hospice – of them both finding small talk the easiest form of communication – anything to avoid saying goodbye or thanking that person for being in your life. Everyone playing into the illusion that things will never end.

'We'll hold you to that invitation,' Hannah says.

Zoe nods, smiling, wiping a tear away from her eye.

Rick walks back towards Barb, peering down at her with such affection. 'I used to love hide-and-seek when I was a boy,' he says. 'So, I'll count to ten and when I open my eyes . . . I don't want to see any of you, okay?'

Martha nods. They're all nodding.

'One . . . ' he says.

Martha looks at Finn.

'Two . . . '

Martha heaves her backpack further up on to her shoulders.

'Three.'

She looks around the circular room one last time.

'Four.'

They are moving.

'Five,' he says, his voice tight.

They are silent in their actions, four people making a line for the door.

'Six,' he says, his voice booming now, desperate for it to be over.

Finn opens the door, lets Hannah and Zoe cross the threshold first.

'Seven,' Rick calls.

Martha lingers for a second, suddenly indecisive, scared, but Finn takes her hand, linking his fingers with hers.

'Eight.'

Finn slams the door closed behind them.

They stand by the entrance, looking at each other, needing reassurances. They could go back inside. That feels like the easiest thing to do in the moment. But they don't. Instead they make their way down the makeshift path, passing gravel and cacti, until the terrain under their feet is once again salt, thick and sparkling and grained with the lines of history.

'What now?' Hannah asks.

'We follow the tyre tracks,' Martha says.

They nod, shifting the weight of their backpacks on their shoulders, tightening straps. They pull balaclavas down over their faces and walk, because there is nothing else to do.

49

Finn is already struggling. His backpack was only ever half-full to begin with, so accustomed is he to not being able to carry any real weight for any length of time. Now, he's made a point of taking hardly anything, casting off the majority of his possessions and only bringing what he deemed essential or personal, yet it does not seem to help as he moves forward. He thinks about what he left behind, likes to imagine he's unique, but really he's no different from everyone else. When someone does return to the Salt Centre, as someone inevitably will, they'll pick up one of his plain T-shirts and wonder, who could this have belonged to? And the answer will be *anyone.*

They walk in silence and Finn focuses on the tyre tracks, tries to find a rhythm and pace, stops himself from looking too far ahead, from looking back too. The tracks are faint, the sweeping of something passing over, a shading that could so easily be washed away. He glances at his watch, reminding him of the date and time, but he regards it with suspicion now – a part of him doesn't know if he believes in the social construct of time. Apart from its repetition, which he agrees can be comforting, who decided that everyone had to have their lives organised by time? He can't imagine a life in Aberdeen any more. He can't visualise going back on to an offshore platform, gripping the same painted handrails, his hard-hat, the cabin-like office where he's spent years of his life looking at monitors, controlling devices, interpreting their data. And the house – the idea of that is foreign now too. He can't remember what it is like to feel grounded in possessions, to be comforted by his middle-class existence.

He glances at Martha, wonders where they should go if they do make it off the salt, if they're given the opportunity to start afresh? Their passports don't offer them the same freedoms they used to. He taps his pocket, feels the hardness of his new black passport, is reassured, despite its limitations, at having it so close to him. He thinks about all the people in the world who would still love to have this form of travel in their pocket, the doors it still has the potential to open. He finds himself glancing at his watch again, a reflex, but he doesn't want to know; he just wants to keep moving, fill his mind with random thoughts that distract him from the pain of what he's left behind, coupled with the fear of walking into nothing.

He tries to make a game out of counting how many salt crusts he crosses over, his feet careful never to step on a line, like avoiding cracks in a pavement. He can see that he's slowing the group down; regardless of how hard he tries, the lag is beginning to stretch. But he does not moan, does not ask them when they think they should stop and set up a makeshift camp for the night. He doesn't want to be seen as weak; he will endure for as long as he has too.

They stop at random, but he is relieved at the reprieve. Zoe opens the zip of her small backpack, the one she has strung over the front of her torso. She removes a green apple from her pouch, and for some reason she reminds Finn of a kangaroo. She drops the bag to the ground, then her large backpack, and they all follow suit, opening compartments, removing items of food, all except for Finn. Instead, he takes a small sip of rationed water from his bottle.

Zoe sits down on the salt beside her bags, crossing her legs with ease. Finn can't remember his body ever working in such a way. She takes the apple, the greenest apple he thinks he's ever seen in his life, and she rubs it on her T-shirt as if somehow this will cause it to shine even brighter. As she goes to take a bite, Finn shields his eyes, it glinting at him in the bright sun. He hasn't seen a green apple at the Salt Centre, all of them were red, and he realises that Zoe has had this apple since before, when they were still part of the old world. He marvels at the notion, almost wants to touch the apple, an artefact from a time that no longer exists. And it's a peculiar sight, her biting away at it, every morsel accounted for, her balaclava still in place. He thinks about the scraps of llama meat in his bag, wrapped up in cling film, sweating in the heat.

'You're not eating,' Hannah says, staring at him as she peels an orange.

He shrugs. 'I will . . . later.'

Martha lifts her balaclava, rolling it up past her face. It bunches up on her forehead. He can see the sweat that has been pouring from her, hair sticking to her head, top lip saturated. He offers her his water, but she shakes her head, applying a lip balm.

'You need to eat,' she says.

He looks back in the direction in which they've travelled and can no longer see the Salt Centre or incline of land it sits atop. It feels as though it is an optical illusion. How can they walk along a perfectly flat terrain and lose sight of something that should so clearly be seen? And, secretly, he wants to go back, is overwhelmed by the prospect of continuing, of holding them all up.

'Does anyone have any idea when the sun will set?' he asks, willing their first day of walking to end.

Hannah shrugs. 'I think we'll know when it's thinking about it.'

'We have the track,' Zoe says, pulling her big backpack on to her shoulders. 'That's the most important thing. And we have each other.'

Zoe's camaraderie reminds him of his backpacking days before he got sick – of friendships being formed almost instantly, where it feels like fate, that the universe is directing specific people to come together. Where, in reality, their only commonality is that each of them happens to be here at the exact same time. Nothing else holds them together. And he wants to be optimistic, be grateful too, but their hope is fragile, and the tracks perhaps are endless.

50

The weight of the large backpack is overwhelming Martha. She feels stupid now for having brought so much with her. Despite the sun, despite the warmth of the balaclavas, they are moving quickly, the pace dictated by Zoe and Hannah, and she continues to be impressed by this younger couple, doesn't want to be seen as a weak link in the group, is too embarrassed to ask them to stop. But her body is beginning to buckle under the prolonged weight – she worries she will pull a muscle, hurt herself and become nothing but a burden to the others as they continue to follow the tracks.

She can't take it any more. She stops, telling the others to keep going, that she'll catch up. She takes her backpack off her shoulders and nearly topples over from the freedom. She takes a few deep, freeing breaths, removes the balaclava from her face, reasons that the heat of the day is behind them now.

Despite her saying not to, they've stopped ahead of her anyway.

'Are you okay?' Finn says.

She nods, rubbing the sweat away from her forehead.

'What's wrong?' Hannah asks.

She closes her eyes for a moment, takes a breath. 'I'm sorry, my bag is hurting me.'

'We need to keep going, Martha,' Zoe says, a warning to her tone.

She nods, bending to retrieve her bag. She slips one arm into the strap, attempts to swing the weight of the bag on to the rest of her back, but she can't do it. It won't budge. She stands, wishes that they would just keep on walking. She sits the bag upright, straps protruding and eases herself down on to her knees, shuffling towards the backpack, slipping her arms into the straps. From this crouched position, she clips the strap around her waist into place, feeling the weight of it all resting on her hips. She tips herself on to all fours, like an animal getting ready to stalk. And slowly, somehow, she manages to manoeuvre herself back on to her feet, finally standing to full height. Her breathing is heavy, and she is willing herself to continue, is furious with herself for taking the backpack off in the first place; her body, briefly free from the burden, is now refusing to co-operate. And she knows this is all illogical, that she has created this situation, but it is easier to focus on small dilemmas than to face reality, so desperate is she to burden herself with the trivial.

Zoe walks back towards her, the action paining Martha, wastefully repeating steps already trodden. 'You can't do this. Do you want to leave some stuff behind?'

'I'll be fine,' Martha replies.

'No, you won't be.'

Martha takes one step and then another, but her back is breaking from the weight. She wants to cry – how dare she be made to feel that some things are not essential, be forced under these circumstances to part with possessions that make her unique? She's already given up so much.

She unclips the buckle from around her waist again, lets a groan escape from somewhere down inside her and drops the bag to the ground. 'I'll drag it.'

'Martha . . . ' Zoe says, anger surfacing.

'I won't keep anyone back, I promise,' she says, gripping some of the long straps used for tightening the backpack. She tugs on it, the backpack catching on the rough texture of the salt. The others are watching but she is determined and stubborn, and she continues to drag it, the expensive fabric scraping across the salt.

'No,' Zoe says. 'We're not doing this.'

She realises that it would, at this stage, be easier for Hannah and Zoe to take their equipment and continue on their own, leaving Finn and Martha to fend for themselves. Yet this suggestion has never been put forward, their sense of togetherness overwhelming, almost to a fault.

'Remove some of your things from your bag and leave them here,' Zoe says.

Martha looks at her backpack, hesitant. Logically, she knows that it is foolish to continue as she is, but she does not feel ready.

'Now,' Zoe presses. 'Throw your things away now.'

Martha swallows. Feels she's at risk of crying. 'Okay,' she says, crouching down to her backpack and unzipping it. She can't think clearly. Why is this so painful for her?

Everyone is watching. Overwhelmed, she balls a T-shirt with her fists and attempts to throw it as far as she can. It lands a couple of metres away, ungraceful. She was expecting to feel a release, but it only heightens her anger – she's angry that she is here when she should now be somewhere else, angry that she has no control over this situation, angry at how tired she is, at the sheer exhaustion, angry at Oscar for dying and putting them in this position, angry because she so desperately wants to live and fears that she will not. She grabs a pair of jeans and thrusts them away from her, a grunt escaping. She keeps going, more items of clothing being cast across the salt, catching on the jagged crust formations, a silky pyjama top, another T-shirt fluttering in the wind, teasing her with the idea of taking off like a kite. She's grabbing everything now, flinging it all, one item after another, the backpack practically empty.

Finn is beside her, telling her to stop but she won't listen. He runs across the salt, bending to retrieve what he can, gripping each item to his chest, bringing everything back, while she turns her face, frantically rubbing at her tears, the skin itchy to the touch.

He returns to her, clutching her things to his chest. 'I'll help you,' he says, bending now to the ground. 'We'll do it together and it'll be okay.'

She nods, grateful, needing him more than ever.

'We need to keep going,' Zoe says, an anxiousness to her tone.

'This will only take a couple of minutes,' Finn replies.

They begin to sift through Martha's possessions, Finn being the one to decide what goes back into the backpack and what is left behind. Afterwards, there are two piles, stacked in heaps, one anchored down by a spare pair of shoes, the other by a half-read book.

As Martha begins to walk again, the backpack significantly lighter on her shoulders, she looks back at her stack of possessions and they remind her of standing stones, of structures made for others to see. If someone does stop and look at them, she hopes they will be sufficiently interesting and that she isn't considered boring, because isn't that what most people strive for in life: to be seen as an individual, to be intriguing?

They continue, hours passing, and Martha knows that she and Finn are holding Zoe and Hannah back, can feel the tension of it starting to build, questions where it will end.

51

With the sun setting in the distance and however many miles behind them, Hannah suggests that they set up camp and Finn wants to weep with relief. He and Martha watch as Hannah and Zoe unpack their compact orange tent, the fabric thin and breathable. And within minutes an odd-shaped triangular structure has been erected, high at one end, the gradient falling steeply to the other. Finn does not know how they will manage to fit four of them inside, but he is grateful for the assumption that they can make it work.

A wind arrives just as the last of the sun dips in the sky, but the tent pegs have no real means of being forced into the salt and Zoe is quick to unzip the tent and sit inside, anchoring herself to the ground and to the tent. Finn thinks of their garden at home, of the parasol slotted into a hole in the middle of their glass garden table – of the wind coming along and lifting the parasol clean out of its holder, of it landing next to one of the apple trees. What force would be needed to lift them all up in the tent?

'I think the rule should be that at least one of us has to be inside the tent at any time,' Zoe says.

They nod.

Next, Hannah removes a small rolled-up mat that Zoe proceeds to blow air into, offering a thin layer of insulation from the ground, before they repeat the process with a second mat. They then pull their two sleeping bags out from their pouches, laying them down on top of the mats, everything compact and innovative.

'Do you have sleeping bags?' Zoe asks.

Finn shakes his head. 'We have sleeping bag liners.'

'That's not going to keep you warm,' Hannah says.

'We can put on lots of layers . . .' Martha says.

'Hannah and I will share her sleeping bag and you guys can take mine,' Zoe says.

'No,' Martha replies. 'Honestly, we'll be fine. We're not taking your sleeping bag . . .'

Zoe shakes her head. 'It'll be too cold otherwise.'

'Thank you,' Finn says, somewhat feebly.

'Did anyone pack a torch?' Hannah asks.

They look around one another, a pulsing pain in Finn's chest at the error made.

'Fuck,' Zoe says.

'What about your fancy pocket-knife?' Hannah presses, addressing Finn. 'Surely it has a little torch.'

He shakes his head. 'There's a torch on my phone but I don't have much battery.'

'Shit,' Zoe says. 'How could we be so fucking stupid.'

'We need to get into the tent before the sun fully sets, before it's pitch black,' Hannah says. 'And we don't want to be wasting our phone batteries on a torch.'

They work quickly then and as a team, layering up, forcing small chunks of food into their mouths. They agree to sit in the tent and take it in turns to go for a piss. There has been no discussion of what they'll do if they need more than that. No sign of shelter anywhere.

As the last of the sun slips away from them, they zip themselves into the small, compact tent. Finn and Martha are positioned at the bottom, where the structure tapers down, and Finn can feel the fabric of the tent flapping mere inches from his face. He and Martha are tight together, lying on one of the mats, layers on to keep warm because they can't zip the cocoon-shaped sleeping bag up fully when both are inside it. They're positioned back-to-back, reasoning that it will be more comfortable for sleeping, their sides pressing into the ground. Outside, their bags remain in a heap, and he finds this unsettling, as if someone in the night will come along and take everything they have.

In the darkness Hannah asks, 'Do you think they're okay?'

No one speaks for a moment.

'They have each other,' Martha says. 'And Oscar too.' She pauses. 'They've had years of life,' she adds, sounding somewhat detached. 'They'll be grateful for that.'

'Their lives are not worth any less than ours,' Hannah says, her words sharp, and Finn is grateful for the darkness, is relieved not to be able to see their faces.

'That's not what I'm saying,' Martha replies. 'I just mean . . . I guess I'm jealous of people who have lived for longer, who have enjoyed the world more.'

'We're going back for them,' Hannah says. 'We'll find help . . . '

Again, no one speaks.

'If we do get found,' Finn finally says, 'will we even be able to direct a rescue team back here? We don't really know where we are . . . '

'We'll get the police,' Hannah says, her voice growing frantic. 'There will be a record of the place . . . '

Finn pauses. 'I doubt the Bolivian police will take much interest in any of this.'

'No,' Hannah insists. 'We'll get the media involved, international press and police. We'll find Elbert and Ofelia too.'

'And Oscar?' Finn asks.

'What about him?' Hannah says.

'What do you tell the international press and media about him?'

Silence.

Finn is conscious of his breath; thinks it is especially loud. He wishes he could turn over. He shifts his hand slightly, attempts to reach for Martha's but he can't find it. He stops, closes his eyes and opens them again but still he can't see anything.

He's not sure how long they lie like this in silence. Despite Martha's nature, he's pretty sure she has fallen asleep, and he likes to think that his body has helped her, that his heart beating continuously next to hers has lulled her into a relaxed enough state. He wonders if Hannah and Zoe are asleep too, hearing nothing from them.

The balaclava he's wearing for warmth is irritating his skin. He's so acutely aware of the cold, was not prepared for how cold it is. He thinks about mountaineers stuck in snowstorms, huddling to make snow caves and shelters on the mountainside. He imagines these spaces to be cosy but knows it would be freezing, unbearable. He thinks about people taking their clothes off, torsos and limbs pressed together for nothing more than warmth.

He exhales and can feel his breath fogging out of him, the dampness in the air. It's blistering. He tries to estimate how far they've travelled on foot, could track the distance on his watch if he wanted, but something stops him from doing so. Every muscle feels as if it is on fire, every joint aching. He tries not to think too much about tomorrow and what that will bring. He closes his eyes again, focuses on his breath, in and out, nothing but the breath, but his mind is wandering, he can't help it. He remembers Martha telling him that most fatalities on the salt flats are because of Land Cruisers. And he feels vulnerable, begins to imagine a vehicle speeding through the flats, oblivious to them until it is too late. He feels like an ant, ready to be trodden on.

Every part of him wants to sit up, climb out of the sleeping bag and stand to his full height, be seen, be ready to jump out of the way.

He attempts to soothe himself, decides that the odds of someone driving through the night will be non-existent, too dangerous. But he *wants* to see a car. That's the aim, isn't it? To find someone else out here. To seek help for himself, for everyone. He lets his mind go to Rick and Barb, can visualise them before injury, creates an image of them in San Diego, of their wealth and ease of life. This is the image he wants to stick with.

He tells himself to go to sleep, wills himself to let his mind settle. But now there's a noise, a husking sound, breathing that doesn't carry a regular rhythm. His ears begin to echo with the concentration it takes to listen, to be sure the noise is not his imagination. He's convinced that whatever is making the noise is coming from outside. He's remembering the time he and Martha took a trip to Australia for a friend's wedding, when they were sitting at a table outside in rural Victoria and a wombat walked into their midst: the grunt, a sudden smell, the hoglike animal scrounging for scraps of food. He thinks about their backpacks outside again, the traces of food that animals will be able to smell. But what animals can be here? He's seen nothing but flamingos and llamas since coming out on to the salt, but why couldn't an animal walk on the salt, migrate across the land, especially with the changing climate. The noise is getting louder; he can feel his heart in his chest. They were foolish to leave the Centre, he decides; at least there, there were doors. Things could be kept outside. The tent bends and flexes in the wind, an animal's breath on the other side. It circles them, takes its time. Finn waits for the rip in the tent's fabric, for teeth to sink into him.

Nothing happens. But he's sure a creature is out there, can smell something that is different, that doesn't belong here, yet it's familiar. He knows then, in an instant, that it is Oscar. The odour he carries, of sweat and leather, of incense – it's his smell and it is here now, with them. Finn swallows, doesn't understand it but believes it regardless. He clamps his eyes shut. 'I'm sorry,' he whispers. 'Please . . . Don't follow us. Stay on the salt. I'm begging you.'

Then it's gone. The smell has disappeared. All he can smell is himself and the scent of the sleeping bag that does not belong to him. And he can't decide if he's imagined it all, if this is what it will be like forever – his thoughts constantly sitting between the fault-line of reality and fantasy. He thinks about the brews they have consumed, the lack of solid food in his body. What if all this salt consumption has done something irreversible to him?

There are too many bodies crammed inside this space, the orange fabric of the tent rippling only inches from his face. He can hear Hannah then, he thinks, shifting in the sleeping bag she shares with Zoe. He feels beached, like a creature washed up on the shore, wanting to live but unable to push himself back into the sea. He prepares to speak, wants to know if she heard Oscar, smelt him, but he loses his momentum. To say something aloud is to acknowledge Oscar. He takes a breath. Decides that it was nothing. They are completely alone, and, in a way, this terrifies him more.

Thursday

52

It is 5.42 a.m. and the sun is shining through the tent. Despite the freezing temperatures of the night the space is now unbearably warm, sickening, and Martha is attempting to peel herself out of the sleeping bag. Her tongue is like fur, and she can't remember the last time she didn't feel dehydrated. Hannah unzips the door of the tent and Martha crawls out on to the salt, relieved to see that their backpacks are exactly where they left them, untouched, their walking shoes too, all tucked in between the bags. No one makes any reference to their having survived the night, or to their conversation in the darkness.

Martha opens her small bag and inspects her food supplies: one apple, one pear, a few pieces of cooked llama meat in cling film, and some crushed crackers in a packet, nothing but crumbs to grip at. In the belly of the bag, as she reaches down further into a hidden space, she finds a chocolate bar she's had since before La Paz, completely forgotten about. She marvels at it, can't believe it, before suddenly growing scared, superstitious, worried now that it will be the last chocolate she ever eats. So she takes the pear instead, slightly dented on one side, even though the chocolate is the only thing she actually desires.

Finn is out of the tent, sitting down on the salt, munching on a little satsuma. She doesn't let her eyes hover over him for too long, is too concerned by his thinness. She bites into the pear. It hurts her teeth, and there is a trace of blood on the pear when she looks down. The salt, she thinks – it must be eroding her teeth. She runs her tongue over them, finding nothing unfamiliar, yet she is sure that they have changed.

She watches as the tent is disassembled in record time, marvels even at this small feat of engineering, at how efficient it all is. Hannah and Zoe are a safe pair of hands, and she feels reassured in their company, but foolish too, because it shouldn't be the younger couple's responsibility to offer her security.

They keep their backs to one another while they each squat for the toilet. Despite everything, Martha is still incredibly self-conscious, the nerves nearly stopping her from relieving her bladder. She's grateful that she doesn't need a shit, that she's never been that regular; the idea of defecating on the salt flats, of it sitting there with nowhere to go, with nowhere to hide, feels particularly humiliating and demoralising.

They continue to follow the track left by Elbert's Land Cruiser, but there is a faintness, even from yesterday, the wind scrubbing away at the tyre markings. Martha is careful to never step directly on the tracks, concerned that she'll somehow rub them further away, their thinnest, most fragile map. She thinks about the red Land Cruiser, of the seats and the back bench, of the broken seat-belts, the stacks of supplies and backpacks fastened to the roof. What effect would the salt have on a vehicle's undercarriage after so long? Why weren't the salt flats a cemetery of old, broken-down Land Cruisers, just like the trains they'd seen on their first day? She imagines Elbert and Ofelia stuck, stranded in the Land Cruiser, and Martha stumbling across them, having followed their trail. What would she say to them? What would she do? To think her biggest fear had been the idea of colliding with another vehicle when they first made their way here. She looks around. How is it possible that there is no one here? Is it the threat of rain that keeps people away? She's thinking about the rain now, inevitably arriving, dry and cracked earth suddenly sodden. She had a dream last night, or perhaps she simply imagined it in her half-wakened state – they were in the tent and rain began to fall but it was so heavy, and like quicksand, she had imagined the tent and them within it, sinking into the ground. The sky before her shows no signs of rain but she doesn't trust it, visualises the compacted, cracked salt flats turning into a slimy, flooded surface, the scenario playing out in her mind, anticipating the disaster properly before it happens. Always two steps ahead in her doom.

She has no idea of their geographical location in relation to the salt and the world around them. They might only be a few kilometres from the edge of the salt flats, but they have no way of knowing. How stupid, how trusting, to get into someone's vehicle and let them take you somewhere without having any sense of where exactly you'll end up. She wishes she'd done orienteering at school, the Duke of Edinburgh Award Scheme, or something similar. She remembers going to join, the pack they gave you, the tasks you were expected to complete, and her walking away, the effort seeming too great, the reward negligible. She focuses on the tyre tracks again, thinks about Elbert and Ofelia, tries to visualise the lives they were leading when not on the salt. She had seen glimpses of them through the salt brews, but still she struggles to paint a picture, as though they only exist when she is there to see them, their lives background to her own. In another universe, there is the version where Elbert and Ofelia do come back to the Salt Centre, bring help, Barb already on her way to a hospital, a search party looking for the rest of them. The version where Elbert and Ofelia don't leave them in the first place. And there is also the version where Oscar does not die. Too many versions to choose from.

53

Finn is struggling – despite the lightness of his backpack, he doesn't know how much longer he'll be able to carry on. It's not necessarily the physical aspect, although his body is incredibly weak; it's more the idea of spending another day walking further into oblivion. Who is to say that they are even going in the right direction? Their whole strategy was to follow these tracks, but the other side of the Salt Centre might have brought them closer to the edge. He's lost all sense of logic. And he misses the Salt Centre, a longing as though for home. Maybe it's dehydration – the little water he's consumed, the salt overwhelming his body, his organs, his mind. His balaclava is sticking to his skin, perspiration seeping through the fabric. He wonders about taking his chances in the sun without it, but the thought of his face blistering is enough to deter him. He thinks about his parents, his friends, carrying on with their domestic lives. What must they be watching on their televisions? What are they eating? He begins to fantasise about food – would give anything for scallops, bubbling in garlic and butter. He's surprised by his choice, would never have assumed that if he could wish for any meal it would be scallops. He shakes his head, tries to adjust his balaclava, feels as though he's suffocating from within. Oscar appears then, always lingering, packed with salt, breath heaving, and Finn averts his gaze.

Zoe and Hannah are ahead, the distance increasing between the couples. He focuses on them, can see them talking to one another, their balaclavas constantly turning to face each other. He questions what they make of him and Martha, if their opinions have changed from the beginning of the week to now. He doesn't know why he cares so much about what they think, but he does. He can't hear what they're saying to each other, but he can see that their exchange is agitated and clipped. He's fought enough with Martha in the past to read the cues of a couple in distress.

They stop for a break, casting their bags once again to the ground. Zoe sits a few metres away, her back turned, staring out in the opposite direction, while Hannah settles close to Finn and Martha. Finn lets a sip of water swirl round his mouth as if by prolonging the swallowing he is allowing his tongue and gums to absorb what they can. As Martha applies lip balm to her chapped lips, Hannah lifts her balaclava up past her face and forces a piece of chewing gum into her mouth, her jaw working hard, anger bubbling under the surface.

Martha gets to her feet, walks further away and squats.

'Are you okay?' he asks Hannah.

'Remember how fucking euphoric it all felt?' she replies.

He nods. 'The weight of everything lifting off.'

'I'd give anything to have that back,' she says, glancing over to Zoe. 'All this was my idea . . . coming out here. We paid money through a third party and got into a vehicle with a stranger that couldn't speak to us . . . ' She laughs. 'Surely, on reflection, that was a fucking stupid thing to do, right?'

'We came because we wanted to help those we love,' he says. 'We wanted to help ourselves too.'

'Do you still feel changed?' she asks, chewing loudly, constantly. 'Because, I'm not sure that I do. Maybe it was never meant to last.'

He is quiet for a moment. 'I wanted to end my marriage and I don't feel like that any more . . . '

'And what if that feeling wears off? What if it's like every other drug?' She pauses. 'What if we die out here?'

He pauses. 'I . . . don't think it's something to fear any more. I feared death so deeply before, when I . . .'

'When you had cancer,' she replies. 'I remember.'

He nods. 'But now I think that when it comes, it'll be okay.'

'What d'you mean?'

He exhales, is struggling to articulate his thoughts. 'Maybe the salt ceremonies were something of a rehearsal. We all die, we can't pretend any more that we don't, but now we know that it won't be too bad, whenever it does come. It's inevitable.'

'And Oscar . . . You think that's what he thought too, before he died?'

But Finn doesn't reply, conscious of Zoe coming towards them, her backpack back on her shoulders. 'We need to keep moving,' she says, a coolness in her voice, and Finn senses that the source of their friction is perhaps him and Martha.

'What do you think happened to Oscar?' Hannah asks, not really directing her question at anyone.

'Why are you asking that?' Zoe snaps.

'I'm just trying to make sense of things . . . ' Hannah says.

Zoe extends her hands out as if needing to take in their surroundings, exasperated. 'I think he killed himself.'

Hannah bites down on her lip. 'So why am I confused . . . ?' she says.

'For fuck's sake, Hannah,' Zoe shouts. 'We don't have time for this shit right now. We're in the middle of fucking nowhere and we're going to die if we don't find someone or something soon . . . You get that, yeah? Like, you understand how precarious our situation is right now?'

Hannah starts to cry, her shoulders heaving up and down.

Finn reaches forward, placing his arm around Hannah, patting her back.

No one says anything for a moment.

Zoe crouches down in front of Hannah. 'Hannah, I'm sorry. I'm so sorry, okay?' she says. 'I didn't mean to . . . I'm just scared. We're not moving quickly enough.'

And Finn feels he's intruding, witnessing something that should be private.

He gets to his feet, walking to meet Martha halfway. 'Are we putting them in further danger by keeping them back?' he asks.

Martha lifts her backpack on to her shoulders. 'We should go,' is all she says.

They set off again in silence. He feels defeated, a sadness that is not his own, scooped up from Zoe and Hannah's exchange, thinks of the salt bucket they did on their first night – he didn't believe it then but now he sees it: strangers exchanging energy, negative ions, casting off old problems but acquiring new ones. He tries now to remember and harness the elation he felt during the second salt ceremony, the sensation of being in another world completely. He hopes that what he's witnessed in those moments exists, that there really is so much more to the human experience than what he's currently enduring. It's not so much the end he fears, it's the suffering beforehand. Rick and Barb enter his thoughts then, but he shakes his head, physically needing to cast them from his mind.

Hours seem to pass in continued silence, Hannah and Zoe always ahead, and he's sure at some point soon they will turn, finally cut him and Martha loose, break out into the stride they want to keep. He wouldn't blame them if they did. He almost wishes they would put him out of his misery, in the same way he remembers wanting Martha to leave him as he lay in his hospital bed all those years ago.

Hannah and Zoe come to a sudden stop, a good stretch ahead, and he's so certain this is the moment. Everyone has their limit. But they're turning and waving their hands in the air, a sense of ecstasy that doesn't seem possible. He hurries then, Martha too. And they see it, understand now.

They race towards the rock formation, dropping their bags and abandoning them on the salt as they get closer. They recognise what they are seeing, remember curving round it in the Land Cruiser on their way to the Salt Centre.

Finn can't accept the reality of seeing something that links them to their old world. Hannah is scrolling desperately through her phone, and she squeals out in delight, forcing the device in front of Finn's line of vision. And there it is: a picture, a blurring of this very rock, standing alone, completely out of place in the salt. A spindly base, top-heavy, the same wide eroded hole in the middle.

Martha is crying, but she's happy, and she hugs him, elated, so sure that things are going to be okay, that this is perhaps the miracle they've been hoping for. And in this moment it does feel as though anything is possible, that all problems are solvable. He doesn't know how, and he isn't the person to offer the answers, but this piece of rock, or coral, or whatever it is, is their totem for everything they have come to understand.

They walk around it repeatedly, touching it, Finn running his hands up and down its texture. There is a grittiness from it that sits under his fingernails, pieces of it with him.

But it's only as Finn goes to retrieve his backpack that he remembers the tyre tracks, their one guiding force that brought them here. He looks around, seeing now the many tyre tracks present in the salt. He returns to the rock, circles it again but this time with his eyes to the ground, thrusting his balaclava off, stretching on to his toes to get a better view of the sprawling salt. In every direction he looks, there are tracks. He traces his way back to his bag, until he's fixed on the markings made by Elbert's vehicle, and starts again, following it like a piece of string, bringing him closer to the rock. But he's realising that the track they've been following is now muddled, lost to the array of other tyre tracks that cover the land. And he feels his chest tightening, at this sudden realisation that he can't follow the line any more; that it is somehow gone, abruptly.

Martha is staring at him. 'What's wrong?' she says.

But Zoe has realised too, is staring down at the ground as she walks, quickening her pace with each step.

'The tracks,' he says, 'they're everywhere . . . From around the rock, they head in every direction.'

Martha shakes her head, refusing to acknowledge any sense of jeopardy. She and Hannah begin following different tracks, trying to differentiate one set from another, their panicked and confused state distorting time. Finally, they stop, struggling even to remember what tyre track they were initially following.

'What the fuck do we do now?' Martha says, more to herself than anything else. 'What direction do we take?'

Finn shakes his head. 'Can anyone remember exactly what direction we came from on our journey to the Salt Centre?'

There is silence, Finn turning himself around in a circle, trying to take it all in.

'Maybe this could be a good thing,' Hannah says. 'It shows us that vehicles come here. That this is a place that people travel past all the time . . . So, we should wait it out. Stay here, don't you think, until someone comes? There can't be many hours of sunlight left now anyway . . . '

'As in pitch the tent here?' Martha says.

'Maybe . . . ' she replies.

'But what if no one does come?' Martha asks. 'Then we've lost more walking time.'

Finn looks up at the sky, a few more clouds present than before.

'It's the only marker we've seen since leaving the centre,' Hannah says.

Finn sits down on the ground, exhausted, his face feeling hot in the sun.

'We have to sleep somewhere,' Zoe says. 'It might as well be here.'

54

Having committed to staying put for the rest of the day, they decide to pitch the tent, the rock offering a sense of comfort and familiarity. And Martha suspects that the gods of this land are taking pity on them, offering them this as a sign of hope, and that it would be unwise, ungrateful even, not to receive it as a gift.

Zoe busies herself, assessing the land, taking in the tracks again, circling the rock formation for what feels like the hundredth time. Martha watches all of this, imagines the rock to be the centre of a town, the monument that's meant to hold all the people together, but after a while she's sure that people stop looking, stop noticing, until they can't even tell you what the statue is any more, only that there is one there, that it is *something*.

Finn has taken to carving out shapes in the salt with his Leatherman, his manner solitary and a little manic, while Hannah sits in the doorway of the tent, taking shelter from the sun, flipping through pages of a stapled manuscript.

Martha, having no desire to sit alone, comes towards Hannah, settling cross-legged on the salt opposite. 'What are you reading?' she says.

Hannah looks up, appearing startled by Martha's presence. 'A film script I was sent to give notes on,' she replies, somewhat detached.

'What's it about?' Martha asks.

Hannah flicks through a few more pages, as though her hands need to be kept busy. 'It's about this man who works the night shift at a cryogenic freezing centre, you know, where people are frozen and shipped off to one of these facilities where they're preserved in liquid nitrogen with the hope that, as technology progresses, they'll be brought back to life.' She pauses. 'Basically, there is a power outage, where everything fails, even their emergency back-up generators, and the worker is in a panic because if they can't keep the liquid nitrogen at the right temperature the bodies will begin to decompose.'

Martha leans forward. 'And . . . '

Hannah smiles, melancholy. 'Basically, it doesn't matter. The bosses don't really care because nobody in the company actually believes these bodies will ever be brought back to life. They're just offering an expensive comfort service to those desperate to live on.' She pauses. 'I don't know why I've kept the script, to be honest . . . False hope, maybe.'

'Is it good?'

'It's great,' she says, handing Martha the script.

'I can read it?'

'If you'd like to.'

Martha lies out on the salt flats with a jumper behind her head as a pillow and begins to read. It's well written and engaging and in different circumstances she'd digest each page carefully but today she's more fascinated by Hannah's notes: her intuition, her thought process and reflection. Her care. These are notes that are intended to be seen and Martha marvels at the notion that somewhere in the world there is a writer waiting, wondering with anticipation as to what Hannah's thoughts will be on their work.

Martha lies there for hours, flicking backwards and forwards between the pages, finally closing her eyes, the evening sun covering her face, dancing across her eyelids. She could so easily fall asleep, feels oddly at peace now. The others are already snoozing, having migrated to the tent to shelter from the sun. But something is filtering through, a noise she initially wants to ignore as though it is a hindrance, a plane flying across the sky. It is persistent, gnawing at her.

She sits up then, realises with a jolt that she can hear what is perhaps a car. She stands, turns herself around in a circle, is convinced that what she is hearing is the noise of a vehicle. She begins to run, the surface of the salt harsh under her socked feet. And in the distance she sees it, is sure of it – a car is driving across a stretch of salt. She has no real perception of the distance because of the flatness of the land, but there is a car moving at speed, heading left, away from them. She begins to shout, waving her arms frantically in the air. The others are scrambling out of the tent, surrounding her. She screams at the top of her lungs, as loud as her body will allow her. She's desperate, cannot comprehend the possibility of this vehicle not seeing her. They're all waving their hands now, shouting over one another, indecipherable. But the vehicle is getting smaller, a dot that she can just about keep her gaze fixed on. Finally, it is gone.

Martha sits down on the salt and screams up towards the sky. It is a howling, painful noise but she can't keep it inside her any more. She balls her hands into fists and begins to pound them into the salt, again and again. It is a noise of despair and she's not sure there is much left in her to give. Everything she has gained from the salt feels as though it could trickle out and return to the ground, allowing space for old habits and thoughts to seep in. She thinks of Oscar. Of what happened to him, her memory hazy but distressed. And she remembers covering him in salt, curing him, forcing it into his cavities, her fists still hammering into the salt flats, knuckles bleeding, the llama's blood, everything mixed into one single moment and that car passing them by in the distance, most likely carrying tourists back to civilisation. She wishes simply being a tourist could have been enough; she wishes she'd never felt the need to push for something more. When she looks down, traces of her blood are smeared across the salt.

Finn comes to her, attempts to place his hands on her shoulders but she pushes them off. 'Martha,' he says. 'It was too far away. It was always going to be too far away.'

She's shaking her head, bereft.

'At least we know that vehicles are still driving across,' Hannah says. 'That's something . . . '

Zoe unzips a small first-aid kit, removing plasters and an antiseptic wipe. Martha continues to sit on the salt, vacant, while Zoe tends to each knuckle, the sting of the wipes causing her to wince. The tightness of the fabric plasters against her skin is soothing. She looks at Zoe and thanks her. Zoe shrugs.

'If I had just moved a bit quicker,' Martha says. 'I shouldn't have been napping . . . It's my fault.'

Zoe shakes her head. 'It's not your fault.'

'We need to follow it,' Martha says. 'The car . . . '

Zoe stares at her. 'Martha, it'll be dark soon. Even if we did trek out in that direction, we might not even find a track once we make it to where you think you saw it.'

But Martha is suddenly so sure that that is what they need to do. They've been following signs and markings this whole time and now they've seen a vehicle drive with purpose, headed for somewhere, and it feels illogical to let that go.

'It was going the wrong way,' Zoe says. 'We're heading right, the way we came from Uyuni.'

'How can you be so sure we came from the right?' Martha says.

Zoe shrugs. 'I just remember . . . Don't you? It's the opposite direction from where you think you saw the car.'

'Where I *think* I saw a car?'

'No, I mean . . . '

'I saw a fucking car, Zoe. We all saw it. I'm not delusional.'

'No . . . I didn't . . . I just . . . I don't want to waste energy on something that leads us to a dead end.'

'We all saw a car,' Martha says. 'A few miles straight ahead of us, travelling leftwards. I don't have a compass, and I don't know how you tell direction from the sun, except that it sets in the west, yes?'

'Yes, we saw it, okay? I'm sorry. We saw it.' Zoe takes a breath. 'I just think we need to stick to the plan of going the way we've come.'

'What do you think?' Martha asks, turning to Finn.

Finn runs his hands up and down his cheeks. 'Honestly, I kind of thought we'd come at the rock from straight ahead . . . '

'I'm going up and left,' Martha says with certainty. 'I'm following the only vehicle we've seen since leaving the Centre.'

Zoe shakes her head. 'I think you're wrong Martha, I'm sorry, but I really think we need to go right and trace our way back from there. There are enough track marks in that direction to follow.'

Martha can feel her anger rising, is ready to lash out, everything hinging on this one decision.

'We don't need to make any decisions now,' Hannah says. 'Please, let's just have this night, okay? We don't need to force anything yet. It's getting dark, let's get some sleep, okay?'

Slowly, Martha nods. 'Okay, yes, we can decide tomorrow.'

There is little else for them to do but zip themselves into the tent, settling in their practised positions, until eventually they are surrounded by complete darkness, Martha listening to Finn's breathing, unsure as to whether he's sleeping or not.

There is movement within Zoe and Hannah's sleeping bag – murmurs, soft whispers, an attempt to be as silent as possible, but Martha understands. She listens intently to the sound of discreet love, of something feeling forbidden and desperate. Their breath becomes ragged, a willingness for something to never end. A quickness, a relenting and giving in. It is a thing to celebrate; it is uncomplicated, passionate love that is present, still present, in the face of all else.

Her thoughts shift to the script Hannah gave her earlier, the writer sitting, waiting, the idea of cryogenic freezing centres even existing. She thinks about Finn's frozen sperm, how it waits in limbo, and she feels sorry for it, this potential baby, tries to imagine herself growing another human, her worries and anxieties being projected on to them. She attempts to draw from her memories of the salt ceremonies, anything that might offer her wisdom, solace, but there is nothing. Oscar eclipses it all.

Friday

55

Finn tugs at the zipper of the tent but it's stuck, the fabric caught in its teeth. Panicked, he does his best to free himself, clawing and pulling, at risk of ripping apart their only shelter. Finally there is enough of a gap, and he wriggles out on his hands and knees, into the fresh morning air. The tent flutters in the breeze, bending and flexing, and no one else appears to be in any immediate rush to get up. He sits on the salt, taking a few sips of his remaining water. The air feels different, he decides, heavier, yet the sky still shows no signs of rain. He takes his phone out of his bag, turns it on. Nine per cent. Still no signal.

He's so hungry and weak, doesn't know if he has another day of walking in him. He opens his bag. A piece of banana, split from its skin, has mushed itself into the front pouch. He tries to wipe it away, scrape at the mush with his fingers, and it all goes under his fingernails. He sucks on what he can scoop, lets the taste of banana circle around his mouth, attempts to quench his thirst with it. He would always choose a banana milkshake over all the other flavours. He keeps swallowing, testing his throat and oesophagus, but it all feels fine. He wonders what food Martha has left, and opens her small backpack, rifling through her possessions. At the bottom, almost hidden away, he sees a chocolate bar. He stares at it, assumes she's forgotten all about it, is tempted to open it, let a piece of it melt in his mouth. He shifts his posture, really thinks about it. Then he hears movement from within the tent, someone trying to fix the zipper, and he closes Martha's bag over, leaving the chocolate bar untouched.

Martha emerges, yawning in front of him. Silently, she places a kiss on the top of his head, and he watches her walk away, barefoot, across the salt, stopping about the length of a football pitch away, to pull her trousers down and squat. He continues to watch, more because there is nothing else to look at. She comes back, looks at him inquisitively before sitting down beside him, opening her bag and retrieving a half-eaten packet of broken crackers. It is as though all worry has left her, completely detached from where they find themselves.

'What?' she says.

He shrugs, gazes out at the rock that yesterday they were so elated to see, but today it has lost its shine. He can feel the weight of uncertainty, of choices, of grappling with the strong possibility that today might be his last day on Earth, amazed that his body has managed to endure so much.

Eventually, Hannah and Zoe stir, tipping themselves out of the tent, practically rolling across the cracked slabs of salt, the warmth of the tent almost too much. After relieving themselves, they come and sit close to Finn and Martha, eating the last of their llama meat, forcing bits into their mouths, a silent acknowledgment that after today everyone will be out of food and water. And Finn almost wants to marvel at how quickly everything can unravel, that there is no such thing as a sure footing in this world.

Zoe runs her fingers around an Australian flag patch stitched on to her bag. She takes a breath, has been building up to what she is about to say.

'Hannah and I are going to walk back towards Uyuni,' she says. 'It's what makes sense to us and it's what we know. We think that to follow the car from yesterday is to walk into further uncertainty, and we're not going to take any extra unnecessary risk.'

Martha nods, casting her gaze from left to right, shielding her eyes from the sun.

'But we'd like you to come with us,' Hannah says, the words rushing out of her.

'Okay,' Martha says.

'Okay?' Hannah replies.

'I totally understand that,' Martha says. 'If you want to go right, then I think you should. But I need to go left.'

'Martha, please,' Hannah says. 'We need to stick together. We can't separate, not now.'

'I've been thinking . . . ' Martha says. 'Maybe separating isn't such a bad idea.' She presses her palms into the salt. 'If we go our separate ways, then we double our chances of finding help. And this way, we get to go at our own pace, so we won't hold you back any more.'

There is silence and Finn can feel the blood pulsing through his body, his heart beating. He thinks about the llama's heart in a bucket, that every heart must constantly beat in order for its host to live, never taking a break. He can't think of anything else that works as hard as a heart, and instinctively he places his hand on his chest, as if needing to feel its burden.

'We don't care about that,' Hannah says. 'Do we, Zoe?'

Slowly, Zoe, almost hesitantly shakes her head.

'And we have all the camping stuff . . . ' Hannah presses.

'It's okay,' Martha says, with certainty, completely convinced. 'We'll be okay.'

'Martha . . . ' Finn says, confused. There was no conferring on the matter, and he feels robbed, the decision taken for him, from him. He doesn't understand her sureness – it's as though there is something primal inside her, begging her to listen to her instincts.

Martha stares at him. 'You don't need to come with me if you don't want to,' she says. 'I'll understand. But every fibre of my body is telling me that I need to follow that car. And I'm going to do it, regardless of this debate.'

He can't believe what she's saying to him. After everything. And a new fear works its way through him, something he hadn't anticipated – that Martha might no longer want him. His long-standing assumption that it would be he who decided the fate of their relationship is shifting, everything now completely unhinged.

'You don't need to look so horrified,' Martha says.

'How could you ever even suggest that I wouldn't come with you?' he says. 'I'd never let you go alone. Never.'

'I just don't want to force you . . . '

'We're not having this conversation.'

'Okay,' Martha replies. 'I'm sorry.'

Everyone sits for a moment, glancing at one another.

'So, it sounds like we've made our decisions, then,' Zoe says.

With nothing left to do, Hannah and Zoe begin to roll up their mats and force their sleeping bags back into their pouches. Next, they take down their tent, synchronised in their movements, bending and folding, coming to meet one another. They have the orange canvas packed away in minutes, pressed into its compact holder, everything strapped up on to their backpacks, ready for another day, no trace left.

They stand in their pairs.

'Are we sure about this?' Hannah says.

'It's going to be okay,' Martha replies. 'We'll see each other again.'

'Uyuni?' Zoe asks.

'We'll get a pizza,' Finn says. 'At the American place.'

'Yes,' Hannah says. 'The Hot One. It's a date.'

'And a PJ Tips tea and a homemade brownie for dessert,' Martha says.

'It'll be the best meal we've ever had,' Zoe says.

There is silence, a pause. Finn isn't sure he's physically capable of turning away from them, the act of walking in completely opposite directions too great a task.

'You have to hug us,' Hannah says, trying to not cry. 'You can't not hug us.'

And they begin to embrace each other, Finn taking Zoe in his arms; there are traces of her pain that he can still feel. Next, Hannah rests her head against his shoulder, gripping his shrivelled torso. She's really crying now, she can't seem to help it, and he can feel his own throat tightening, a sting in his eyes, but he can't cry here. Not here.

'I love you guys,' Hannah says, wiping her eyes, kissing Martha on the cheek.

'We love you too,' Martha says.

Finn lifts his backpack, grips the straps.

'Wait,' Zoe says. 'We don't have your phone numbers . . . For when we get a signal . . . '

Martha pulls hers from her pocket. 'Give me your number,' she says.

Zoe recites the digits to Martha, and Martha recites them back. 'Got it,' she says.

'Put your number in my phone too,' Zoe says, handing the phone to Martha, waiting as she taps her digits in.

'Okay,' Martha says, handing it back.

They step into their natural pairings, looking at one another, pulling down their balaclavas over their faces.

Finally, they turn and start walking in opposite directions.

Finn doesn't look back, not initially anyway, not until there is enough distance to ensure they don't change their minds. And, when he does turn, he can only make out a blur of orange from the tent and two tiny dots of people he used to know and doubts, realistically, he'll ever see again.

He keeps moving, reluctant to stop for anything, it feeling easier to just continue in spite of his weakness, the churn in his stomach at the possibility that they've made a grave mistake, that they won't find the tyre tracks Martha is so sure about. And he understands Rick staying with Barb, the love it takes to sacrifice, to accept a fate. But there is also the fear of being rescued, of perhaps having to face the reality of what has happened to them. How do they explain any of this? His throat constricts, his stomach muscles tighten, at the mere thought of Elbert and Ofelia, of Oscar. He looks down at his hands, filthy and smeared with sweat and banana, and worries still about what they are truly capable of.

He can feel himself slowing, Martha a few steps ahead. He glances at his watch, estimates it's been about three hours since they parted ways with Hannah and Zoe. He pulls on the straps of his bag, tightens the support around his waist. He looks from left to right, seeing nothing whatsoever. He misses the rock with the hole in the middle already, misses the familiarity of it.

'Are you okay?' Martha asks. 'Do you want some of my water?'

He shakes his head.

'Do you regret it?' she says.

'What?'

'Leaving them . . . '

'We didn't leave them, we went our separate ways,' he replies, struggling with the energy it takes to talk.

'Is there a difference?'

'I think so, yes,' he pants. 'To leave implies that we left them in a fixed location, that they still remain there. We left Barb and Rick, and Oscar . . . But Hannah and Zoe are walking in the opposite direction.'

Martha nods, seems encouraged. 'With every step we are sweeping more of the territory.'

'Three hours our way, three hours their way,' he says.

'But you don't think we made the wrong decision?' she asks.

He stops suddenly, faces her, balaclavas in place. 'Well, it's a bit late to be questioning it now, isn't it?'

'But if you had thought I was wrong you'd have stopped me, wouldn't you?'

He doesn't say anything for a moment. 'Honestly, Martha . . . I don't know. I mean, if I'd had a gut instinct that you were wrong and they were right then yeah, maybe I would have spoken up, but . . . '

'But what?'

'But I didn't, and you did.' He pauses. 'At this point, it feels like a fifty-fifty toss-up and there is no real way of knowing.'

He looks up at the sky again, the clouds circling in, the sun feeling less harsh. Change is in the air, and he can feel it; he just wishes he weren't still on the salt for its coming. He pulls his phone from his pocket. Dead.

And that's when Martha starts shouting, elated.

There are tyre tracks. Faint, but there.

56

The tracks are something to focus on, energising Martha, compounding her belief that their decision to split up from Hannah and Zoe was correct. She allows herself a moment of celebration, but it does not abate her anxiety – she thinks they were too slow to take any decisive action, wishes they had continued walking yesterday, or set off earlier today. Far in the distance she can see the outline of mountains, the Andes, but she knows there is no possibility of walking to the range's base from here. Its proximity is an illusion, like looking up at a plane in the sky, like astronauts being able to see the Great Wall of China. It is all out of reach.

She can see change in the sky, in the sickly air that is desperate for rain. Everything feels thick, her body wading, gravity fighting against her. When she looks back at Finn, she fears he is at risk of collapsing. She allows doubt to slip in – for all anyone knows, they could be travelling further into the heart of the salt. She shakes her head, physically needing to rebuff that thought – they are following a track, potentially the track of the only vehicle they've seen since setting off. There is urgency in each step she takes now, unlike anything before – a sense of needing to find shelter before the sky opens, the rainy season soon to be upon them. She goes over the things that they could have done differently: they could have spent less time waiting to see if Elbert and Ofelia were going to come back; they could have suggested, when they first discovered that the Land Cruiser wasn't going to work, that they start walking as one big group, the contents of the Salt Centre already packed up. But so many small moments and decisions factor into anyone's fate. Would they still have found themselves here regardless of whether Oscar had lived or died? She stares at her knuckles wrapped in plasters, at the hands that worked so hard to preserve him.

The drops of rain start then, lightly, almost nothing, easy to miss, especially with her balaclava on. But slowly she can feel the weight of the fabric turning damp against her face. She pulls the balaclava off, lets the drops of rain land on her skin. It is drizzle and she does not panic immediately, thinks they can continue in drizzle, that this rain is not capable of turning the baked salt into slush yet.

She looks to Finn. 'I love you,' she says, but she's not sure he can hear her over the rain.

They continue, the rain getting heavier, large drops of water falling with a thud, their waterproofs appearing to offer little protection. If Martha were under a shelter she would take comfort from the noise of it all hitting a roof, find it soothing and calming. But, out in it, it is painful and relentless. The salt is so dry that the water bounces off the surface, little appearing to be absorbed. She knows what to expect – first, a watery sheen covering everything, acting as a mirror that reflects the sky, but then the rain will continue, without reprieve, the natural rhythm of nature having broken down – a delicate ecological balance finally in freefall. And she imagines the salt flats filling up again, a lake swallowing them whole, a biblical tale of people being sucked under.

They stop, their soaked backpacks too heavy, dropping them to the ground, looking at each other as if searching for answers. When Martha looks at her phone it is off, either out of battery or water-damaged.

'We have to leave our stuff,' Finn says. 'We can't carry it all.'

She nods, is accepting of this, doesn't want any of it any more.

They force some layers of clothing into their smaller bags. The compact silk sleeping bag liners too, perhaps their only form of shelter. And Martha attempts to remain logical, going through the motions, encouraging Finn to continue, but she knows it is too late, that none of this will save them now, that they won't see another sunrise.

She waits for Finn to ask her to stop. And she will, but she needs him to tell her that it's enough now. She visualises them picking their spot, sitting down, getting inside their silk bag liners, pulling the fabric up as far as it will go, and simply lying down and waiting for the inevitable. She can already feel the weight landing, her breath being removed from her, the silk pressing against her face. But Finn is still moving, and she is too.

She thinks about her family, wonders if they'll ever know what happened to them. There are so many things to be grateful for, and it's astonishing to her that she is only seeing and appreciating this now. Crying from the joy of someone making her laugh. Finn sending her Rightmove links that he finds on Reddit, simply for the banter of seeing the random and sometimes extreme ways people decorate their homes. She thinks of music. Of never understanding why when she hears 'Sunshine on Leith' it always makes her cry. Of why she likes to take naps watching *Murder, She Wrote*. That among the awfulness and fear there was still so much to love. There was still so much to live for.

Her steps are slowing. She thinks about her visions under the influence of the salt brew – a glimpse of infinity. Maybe dying really will be one of the most euphoric moments of her life, reserved for the end so she can never re-live it or describe it to others. Maybe she will be transported to those places in her hallucinations, there being no physical way to reach another universe except through the act of death. Maybe this was something Oscar was trying to show her, all of them, all along. And she tries to harness this as Finn finally turns to look at her, reaches for her hand, mouths the words she has been waiting for.

It is enough now.

They stop, looking at one another, nodding. An acceptance.

But Finn turns his head, sees something, slowly begins to point.

The lights of a vehicle are illuminating a path, cutting through the space ahead of them. It's close, much closer than the vehicle from the day before, and it's speeding through the salt, water spitting out from under the tyres. They can hear music, Lewis Capaldi of all things, his voice so familiar.

Finn starts running, but Martha stands completely still. The rain is hitting her face, falling into her mouth as she attempts to shout and tell him to stop. She is prepared to accept that it is a mirage; an optical illusion, one final trick on them before they accept their defeat.

But it is slowing. It sees them. It is real.

57

For the briefest of moments Finn believes that it's Elbert and Ofelia coming back for them. But this vehicle isn't red and it's not an old Land Cruiser. It's a modern black pick-up truck, cruising with ease through the rain. He continues to run, waving his arms up and down, his lungs ready to explode, his whole body soaked.

The vehicle comes to a stop beside him and only then, as he peers back at the young male driver, does he accept that this is real. The driver and his male passenger stare at him with suspicion, confused, and he can't imagine what he must look like. Words begin to tumble out of his mouth, an explanation that they clearly can't understand.

'English?' he asks.

They shake their heads.

He keeps speaking, knows he's not making any sense, has no words in Spanish to explain any of this. He points to Martha. '*Esposa*,' he says, bringing his hands together, begging. 'My wife.'

The driver, with his eyes narrowed, points to the open bed at the back of the truck, nodding. And finally, Finn waves Martha over, willing her to hurry, terrified that these men will change their minds and drive off without them.

He climbs into the empty uncovered truck bed and reaches for Martha's hand, tugging her up with everything he has; she lands beached on the ridged metal surface. The vehicle is already moving before they are settled and he panics at the idea of falling, of landing on the salt once again and being forgotten about – the stories from Martha about collisions, people dying, propelled from vehicles on to the salt. He presses himself up against the back of the cabin, his hand gripping the side. Martha settles in beside him, her hand frantically reaching for his, their fingers locking together, the rain coming down forcefully, battering against them as they move at speed through the salt.

The pick-up truck continues to travel at pace while the rain falls in sheets, relentless. Finn tilts his chin down into his chest, seeks to protect himself against its force, while he grips Martha's hand. 'I love you,' he whispers, but he knows she can't hear him, the rain and the vibration of the vehicle all-consuming. He has no idea where they are going, accepts that he is at the mercy of his rescuers: these two men, perhaps in their early twenties. But wherever they are headed, he feels certain it is off the salt, and for this he is grateful.

They drive for hours, the rain never stopping, darkness creeping in. Finn looks at his hands – the skin is pruned beyond recognition, the colour so pale it could almost be described as blue. Everything is distorted, the noise of the vehicle and the rain blocking out any coherent thought.

The truck is now slowing, the terrain underfoot feeling less bumpy. Finn turns his head, attempts to look past the front cabin, and now he understands where they are going. He nudges Martha, points, mouths the word *look.* In the far distance, directly ahead of the truck are giant pools of water, hundreds of football-pitch-sized excavations, the liquid inside the brine pools varying wildly in colour, each one a different shade, like a metallic rainbow. There are buildings too, solid structures created from concrete and steel, towering over the pools, an enormous network of mining infrastructure. Huge pipes. They are approaching Bolivia's largest lithium extraction plant, the conglomerate's white and red logo visible. And, despite having seen pictures of it, Finn finds its scale hard to comprehend.

He takes it all in. This company pride themselves, won the tender contract even, on the basis of using new technology, *direct lithium extraction*, meant to pull lithium straight from brine, not requiring solar evaporation or anywhere near as much water, in this already water-scarce land. But that's not what he's seeing here. Everything before him shows the old, laborious and natural-resource-draining method of lithium extraction. This site is their saviour, but it's also a disappointment.

Martha stares at him, her hair matted to her face, a quizzical expression, and he shakes his head, can't explain what troubles him, knows there is no point in explaining.

The truck finally slows at a checkpoint barrier, and two guards talk to the driver before coming to inspect Finn and Martha. One of the guards attempts to speak to them in Spanish, but Finn shakes his head. '*No español*,' he says, shame creeping across his face.

'*Inglés?*' the guard asks.

Finn nods. '*Escosia*. Scotland.'

The guard returns to the driver's window, more words are exchanged, and Finn has this sinking feeling that they're going to be denied entry, that they'll be forced to get out, be stranded outside this huge lithium plant. But the barrier rises, and the truck is moving forward, down a long stretch of road, flanked on either side by giant water pipes, travelling the length of the plant, pulling resources from wherever they can, drinking everything up. And he can't help but be inquisitive, finds himself wanting to know how everything works, can understand the draw a place like this has for workers. Feels it himself in the affinity he has with his own job. He thinks of Elbert's son then, perhaps working right now, somewhere close by. He could be one of the young men in the pick-up. And he has this desire to confess then, to tell these young men that he's sorry for everything – for the way he's treated the land, for Elbert and Ofelia, for Oscar, for those who came to the Salt Centre with him. But there is no one to speak to, so he says nothing, and continues to gaze out, taking in as much as he can, expecting at any moment to meet Elbert's son, naively assuming that he'll be able to pick him out in a crowd.

The truck comes to another stop outside a building with the letter 'C' on the front. The driver and passenger get out and come around, waving Finn and Martha down from the back. They gesture for them to follow, opening a door to the building and ushering them inside. There is a pristine-looking reception area with bright lighting and air-conditioning. A few chairs are set out and a woman sits behind a clutter-free desk. The driver motions once again to Finn and Martha to sit while he speaks to the receptionist. The woman nods at what he is saying before lifting a phone to her ear and dialling a number.

They sit, filthy and soaking wet, a squelch with each movement against fake leather.

In the middle of the waiting area there is a coffee table made of wood, industry-focused magazines sitting on top. An artificial plant. From somewhere out of site, there is the smell of freshly brewed coffee.

And, in the corner, a water dispenser.

Finn gets to his feet, Martha following him, and they begin to fill one plastic cup after another, gulping water, again and again, oblivious to the eyes that stare at them in this clean and clinical space.

58

A man with the blondest hair that Martha has perhaps ever seen comes out of a side door and approaches them. He is wearing a shirt with the same logo that is plastered all over the walls and on the front of the receptionist's desk.

'English?' he says.

They nod.

'I must ask how you found yourself here?' he says. His accent is hard to place, but he's European, Swedish maybe.

'We have been walking . . . ' Martha says, her voice breaking, completely overwhelmed.

Finn reaches for her. 'We thought we were going to die out there,' he says.

The man is shaking his head, his confusion growing. 'Why were you out on the salt?'

'We got stranded,' Finn says, his words tumbling, breathless. 'We were on this . . . '

But Martha tugs him, needing him to stop speaking. Under these lights, in this pristine and clinical space, everything feels unreal, and she is ill-equipped, her thoughts and words unreliable. What is their story? Is now the right time to explain everything? It is hard to describe the course of events that led them here, that even the smallest detail is important to gain a true understanding and perspective. It suddenly feels as though everything is at risk and she is terrified, so desperate to live – desperate to return to their old world.

'We're cyclists,' she says. Finn turns to look at her, and she herself is confused by her words but she can't stop. 'We had been cycling and camping on the salt flats, but we underestimated the season, had issues with the bikes and then the rain started.'

The man stares at them. 'Are you mad?' he says. 'The rainy season is much more unpredictable than it used to be. No domestic vehicles should be travelling across the salt from late November.' His words are short and clipped, no room for pleasantries. 'You could have died.'

She nods, tears falling, willing herself to tell this man the truth. 'We miscalculated . . . ' she whispers.

Finn looks from her, eyes wide, to the man and back again.

'Are you alone?' the man asks.

'Yes,' she replies. 'It's just us.'

And her thoughts are moving quickly, desperate to rationalise the words that she is saying. This man does not want to be burdened by them. Would anyone even be willing to go back out into that terrain, now that the rain has arrived? But really, she knows that it is fear that stops her from speaking, that to say it all aloud will make it true, and she doesn't know if she can admit to that, not when they're so close to making it back to civilisation. Perhaps she can convince herself that everything was an illusion. She thinks of the centre's health questionaries, of her and Finn not receiving theirs beforehand, imagining now that they were never really there.

'Do you have passports?' the man asks.

She nods. Finn is nodding too. He's not correcting her narrative; he appears on board with rejecting their trauma.

'Where were you trying to get to?' the man says.

'Tupiza . . . ' she says. 'Then eventually Argentina.'

'From here?'

'Well, gradually . . . ' She's committed now; it's too late to change tack.

'And money? You have some?'

'We have money,' Finn replies.

The man takes them in, before nodding again, curt. 'Someone will drive you to the bus station.'

'Okay,' Martha whispers, trying to compose herself. 'Thank you.'

'Tupiza is nice,' the man says. 'For Bolivia, I mean. You can ride a horse if you like. From there, another bus will take you to the border with Argentina.'

'Thank you,' Martha says. 'Really, thank you.'

'Now I suggest you go on your way,' he says, turning to nod at the woman sitting behind the desk.

The woman leads them back outside where a car is already waiting, its engine idling. Inside, another man is sitting in the driver's seat. Martha slips in the back and Finn sits up front in the passenger seat. It is quickly established that this driver also doesn't speak English and Martha is relieved, has no desire to talk any more. Everything is moving quickly, decisions made for them, at the will of others.

They depart the same way they came, driving down a beautifully tarmacked road, pipes and pools of colour on either side. The barrier opens and they return to the familiar bumpy terrain of rough road, but thankfully, almost in disbelief, they do not return to the salt but continue on an unmade road, the man driving fast through the rain, no markings to define any lanes. The driver presses his foot down on the pedal, overtaking another vehicle, the engine roaring, a bend up ahead, visibility non-existent as they propel forward. If they are to die now it would be a tragedy, Martha thinks, to have made it off the salt yet still perish.

But the journey is short. The bus station is nothing more than a kiosk with a small shelter. The driver of their vehicle pulls the car up next to it and lets them out. Finn thanks him and climbs out, waits for Martha to close her door, and then the man turns the vehicle around harshly and returns in the direction in which he came. They stand for a moment watching him retreat, their limited possessions in their hands.

'Finn . . . ' she says. 'They would be too far away . . . '

'Not now,' he replies.

There is a timetable pinned to the wall of the bus shelter and Finn inspects it while a local woman and young boy wait, regarding them with suspicion.

'I think there will be a bus in an hour,' Finn says.

'Okay,' she replies. 'How long is it meant to take?'

'Four, five hours . . . '

And Martha stands, oddly calm. She's struck by how ordinary their exchange is, normal sentences about logistics in a regular world. They are just people, waiting for a bus, like everyone else.

The bus arrives exactly as the timetable said it would, and Finn forces bolivianos into the driver's hand, offering him more than is required.

The bus is busy with passengers, having come from Uyuni town, they realise, and Martha looks at the faces as they walk up the aisle, really takes them in, half-expecting to see Hannah and Zoe. As she settles into a seat towards the back, Finn claiming the window seat, she begins to imagine, really buys into believing that Hannah and Zoe have been found too, that they are being dropped at the border to Chile where they had planned to go next. She looks at Finn, whose eyes are fixed on the seat in front. Lurching forward, the bus finally leaves.

Numb, Martha reaches for her small backpack, brings it up on to her knee. She unzips it and there is the chocolate bar. She stares at it, before taking it and tearing open the wrapper. She breaks some off and offers it to Finn, but he shakes his head. She bites into the chocolate, closes her eyes, chews, lets the taste circulate. She forces the rest into her mouth as quickly as she can. She could easily choke. Finally, she tries to turn on her phone, but it refuses to come to life. Another decision taken out of her hands. And she's grateful.

Saturday

59

It is after midnight when they arrive in Tupiza. Having not spoken to anyone for the entire journey, Finn finds it overwhelming now to step off the bus and be met with numerous touts vying to shepherd him to different hostels and guesthouses – all these faces, too many people in his personal space. He stands on the pavement, damp and uncomfortable. The thought of a clean bed, of dry sheets, is so tempting, but they can't stop now. They weave through the crowd, and queue to ask about the next bus to the border town of Villazón. From Finn's limited understanding of what the man behind the counter is saying, there should be another bus shortly, *veinte*, twenty minutes or so.

They wait, his chest tight, his heart beating fast. There is a boy selling packets of American-branded crisps and Martha buys some and two large bottles of water, spending too much on the items. She offers Finn the packet, but he shakes his head, nauseous.

'Please, Finn . . . You need to eat.'

'I will,' he says. 'But not here.'

He listens to the noise of the crisps in her mouth, everything too loud and overstimulating. He's desperate to be moving again, for them to be further away from the narrative they've created – there's no going back now. His mind briefly flits to the dorm room, to the circular living space, to the mattresses laid out on the floor. There is the smell of the sweat lodge, the trekking to the lagoon. It could so easily all be an illusion.

Finally, they board another battered old bus, the seats worn. Most of the people on the bus appear to be locals, carrying huge suitcases and crates. At the back of the bus, next to their seats, is an out-of-service toilet, and the sign is almost too much for Finn to bear, as if everything is about to finally unravel, and he can take no more. It makes no sense because logically he knows that he is safe, that they are moving in a direction of travel he understands. But he's not convinced he deserves any of this.

He sits down, crosses his legs, shifts in the aisle seat next to Martha. She turns to look at him, taking a sip of water from the bottle she bought earlier, condensation dripping down the plastic. 'You okay?' she mouths.

He shakes his head, begins to crumble, tears running down his face. She reaches for him, but he only wants to hide away, is embarrassed at the idea of others watching him on the bus. He tucks his chin into his chest, placing his hands on the top of his head, sheltering himself. Huge, silent gulps of emotion and sadness, his body rocking forward as he tries to contain them. Martha's hand is on his back, rubbing it, the way she used to when he was sick and vomiting after his chemo. There is so much guilt and he doesn't know what to do with it, or where to put it. And he knows that they should have said something when they arrived at the lithium plant, when they finally had someone in front of them who could speak English. Why didn't he tell the man about Hannah and Zoe? Or about Rick and Barb? Why didn't he tell them everything, about Oscar, Elbert and Ofelia?

But he knows the answer, knows why he didn't contradict Martha's story. It was fear, the genuine, crippling fear of the fallout, fear of being taken back to the Salt Centre, of being blamed.

And so, he sits, having said nothing, and isn't sure how to make it right. Realises it is already too late.

Martha's cheek presses against his back, her arms stretching around him. They'll never leave each other now. And he's grateful.

She shifts, kisses his back. 'It'll be okay,' she says. 'Once we get over the border, everything will feel better.'

He nods, into his chest, wipes at his eyes, attempts to compose himself. People must live with guilt every day; they must endure it, swallow it, convince themselves that it shrinks away with time. They must lock it away, train their brains to never go near it. Compartmentalise. Settle on a version of the truth, one that they can live with. When you don't know you're lying, life must be more bearable.

'I love you,' she says.

'I love you too.'

60

They are herded off the bus in Villazón and follow others across a concrete walkway to the Argentinian border, flanked with make-shift currency exchanges, all open, despite it being the middle of the night. 'We should change some pesos,' Martha says, eyeing up the kiosks. 'I doubt we'll get a decent rate, but . . . '

Afterwards, they continue to walk to the immigration building, a Bolivian flag on their side, an Argentinian one on the other. Beside them, an elderly man with a bad back is struggling to carry his suitcase and Martha stops to offer help, thinking of Rick. The man seems hesitant at first but then agrees; she lifts the suitcase, keeping in step with him so that he doesn't worry that she'll run off with his possessions. She is a good person, a decent person. She needs to remind herself of that. When they reach the checkpoint, she hands the suitcase to the man and he bows his head, clasps his hands together and says *muchas gracias* several times. *It's nothing*, she wants to say, but instead she smiles, and nods in return.

They join the long queue. Martha looks down at herself – she is made of nothing but salt and dirt, it consuming every part of her. They shuffle forward, so many people, all pressed up together, night lights illumining them all in this harsh orange glow. She takes in the faces of the people who pass her, wonders what brought them all to this point, imagines where they are going with all their bags and suitcases.

At the Bolivian border, the officer barely looks at them, not really caring if their passport photos match the people standing in front of him, quick with the exit stamp. They are then ushered down another concrete path, a section of no-man's-land, where they are adrift, claimed by no one. When they make it to the front of the Argentinian immigration booth they slide their passports through to the officer and this time he looks at each of them, holding their passports up to their faces, studying the images. But he does not ask them any questions; does not want to know what their intention is in coming to Argentina or how long they intend to stay. He stamps their passports and passes them back, pointing them onwards to another queue.

Here, they are divided into men and women, their bags to be searched. Martha stands in line, anxious at being separated from Finn. No one is speaking any English but above the checking station there is a sign about bringing goods in, illustrations of prohibited items. And she thinks of Elbert, wherever he is, and his coca leaves, his constant consumption, protruding from his cheek.

A Bolivian woman in the queue in front of Martha is waved forward, the Argentinian officer shouting orders at her to unzip her bags. He rifles through her things aggressively, with little respect. In the other queue, the Bolivian man whose suitcase Martha helped carry is at the front and another Argentinian officer is throwing some of his possessions on to the ground, barking words at him, as the man struggles to bend and retrieve his things. Martha watches all of this, uncomfortable at the hostility, at the assertion of power by the officials, their contempt, those with Bolivian passports clearly being discriminated against. But she does and says nothing – it's not her place.

Martha is beckoned forward, and the officer holds his hand out for her passport. He opens it, looks at the stamp and then her picture, before handing it back to her. She places her small backpack on the counter, and he opens the zip only a fraction of the way, half-heartedly peering in through the gap before handing the bag back to her.

'Welcome,' he says, in English.

They board another coach, but this one is new and luxurious, with reclining leather seats, and she is overwhelmed by the decadence. There are even televisions positioned up the aisles, and an American film is playing, staring George Clooney, dubbed comically in Spanish. And it is easy for her to watch the film, her mind occupied by the task of reading the subtitles. Finn returns from the working toilet, settling next to her. She can barely keep her eyes open, the lull of the television soothing. As a child she used to find comfort in the television being on. At university, she had a TV in her room, setting a timer on it so that she'd fall asleep to its background noise. But when she and Finn had moved in together he'd refused to have a television in their bedroom, saw it as a bad habit, and she's not sure she's ever really slept well since. She looks at him, wonders if she'll be quite so happy to go along with his preferences from now on, knowing they are bound together, forever. She's thinking too about maybe having a baby because she has love to give, and she could give it to a baby. Her eyes are heavy and there's no point in fighting it. There is still so much to be worried about: those she left behind out on the salt, the climate emergency, the excessive greed and consumerism, war, populism, fascism, the list goes on and on. The change needed feels insurmountable, but she feels less burdened by its weight. Sleep is pulling at her now, and she's submitting to it, not fighting it any more. Her eyes close; she'll miss the end of the film, will have no idea what happens.

61

They pull into a large bus station in Salta. It's morning, and there is a hotel that isn't too far away, so they walk, the sun shining beautifully over this colonial-looking city. The person at reception takes pity on them and gives them an early check-in. The room is clean and bright, and Finn makes for the bathroom, stripping off his clothes and turning on the shower. He steps in, lets the water fall over his head, closes his eyes and leans against the tiled wall. When he opens his eyes, he looks at the discoloured water by his feet, making its way down the plughole. He rubs his foot into the grime below him, a grainy texture he knows is salt. He turns off the tap and wraps a towel around himself. He goes to open the door and Martha is standing there.

'It's warm,' he says. 'The water.'

She nods, passes him, turns the shower back on and he leaves her, returns to the bedroom and sits on the bed, looking around the room, staring out of the window, listening to the buzz of life out on the streets. The salt ceremonies are on his mind, and he stretches his arm out as if to grip something of the experience, to capture it and keep it close, but it is fleeting and out of reach. Beside him, Martha's phone sits on charge. He presses it, the screen coming to life. He hesitates for a moment, listening to her in the shower, before typing in her passcode. He clicks on her pictures and sees then the many photographs he took of everyone on the salt, the optical illusions of dinosaurs, and each of them being cupped in the palm of the other. He deletes them all, can't stand the sight of them, knows that at some point people will come to the Salt Centre and find those left behind, begin to piece everything together and follow the trail. And he accepts all of it, so much out of his control. It is all inevitable. He bends and retrieves a clean T-shirt and a pair of boxers from his small backpack. They are all the clothes he has left apart from what lies discarded and filthy on the floor. There is the noise of someone honking their horn loudly on the street below and he flinches, reluctant now to enter this world.

62

They make their way to a beautiful square, lined with cafés, sitting at a table outside, a waiter wearing a white apron offering them a menu. Other people are ordering and eating the same thing – plates of delicious-looking little savoury pastries – and when the waiter returns to take their order Martha points to the table next to them.

'*Empanada?*' he says. '*Sí?*'

'*Sí*,' she replies.

'*Carne?*'

She nods again.

'*Tres, seis, doce?*'

'*Doce*,' Finn replies. '*Gracias*.'

They wait for their order, looking around, rarely at each other. People are walking past with placards, headed for a protest, someone shouting something in Spanish from a megaphone, and it serves as a reminder to Martha that the old world is as she left it.

As though reading her mind, Finn asks, 'Do you worry that everything you couldn't bear about this world will wear you down again?'

She pauses before shaking her head. 'Do you think you'll stop loving me again?'

He shakes his head.

There is a bottle of fizzy water on the table, and she pours some into their glasses, taking a sip. Finn gets to his feet, making for the toilets, and Martha sits alone, watching everyone around her make a success of living. She removes her phone from her bag, presses Zoe's number and brings the phone to her ear, but it goes straight to voicemail, an automated voice telling her that this number is currently unavailable and would she like to leave a message? She ends the call and places the phone back in her bag. And she decides then, on what she believes to be true, her narrative as good as any, watching and smiling as Finn makes his way back to her.

The waiter places twelve *empanadas* down in a basket with two small plates and a tomato salsa dip on the side, before departing.

They stare at the food.

Martha takes one *empanada* and puts it on her plate. She tries to take a bite; it is too hot, scalding her mouth. But Finn doesn't wait. He bites into one and it's clearly burning his tongue, but he doesn't care. He dips his half-eaten *empanada* into the salsa and takes another bite, gorging on it, him mouth stuffed. Martha pushes the basket further towards him, watching as he takes another, chewing, swallowing, everything as it should be. And she thinks, nodding to herself, that after this they'll phone the police and raise the alarm. They will tell them everything they know to be true about the Salt Centre, about Elbert and Ofelia, about Rick and Barb, about Hannah and Zoe. About Oscar. But after this. After Finn eats. After. There is always after.

Acknowledgments

Thank you to Tallulah Lyons and Sorcha Rose for your editorial insight and belief in this book; to Alainna Hadjigeorgiou and Charlea Charlton for publicity and marketing; and to the whole team at Hodder & Stoughton for continuing to champion me and my writing.

To my literary agent Cathryn Summerhayes, as well as Jess Molloy, Annabel White and everyone at Curtis Brown. Thank you.

To the Scottish Book Trust and Creative Scotland for their continued support, and to Moniack Mhor for providing such a nurturing space in which to write.

Thank you to my generous writing peers and friends, in particular to Heather Parry for her invaluable thoughts and notes, as well as Kirstin Innes and Cailean Steed for their support in the earliest days of writing this novel.

To my parents, family and friends, thank you again for your endless enthusiasm and encouragement. To Fraser and Phoebe – it's not easy having a writer for a mum. Thank you. And finally, as always, to Angus, for everything.